A Dream to Share

Allison & Busby Limited
12 Fitzroy Mews
London W1T 6DW
www.allisonandbusby.com

Hardcover published in Great Britain in 2005.
This paperback edition published in 2006.

A CIP catalogue record for this book is available from
the British Library.

10 9 8 7 6 5

ISBN 978-0-7490-8249-9

The paper used for this Allison & Busby publication
has been produced from trees that have been legally sourced
from well-managed and credibly certified forests.

Printed and bound by
CPI Group (UK) Ltd, Croydon, CR0 4YY

A Dream to Share

JUNE FRANCIS

Chapter One

May, 1907

Emma Griffiths shovelled the last of the ash and cinders into the bucket and was about to get up from her knees when a hand landed on her bottom. She fell forward, scraping her wrist on the edge of the brass fender, and swore beneath her breath. She had not expected Doctor Stone to be up to his tricks this early in the day and had forgotten to close the drawing-room door. The sound of its opening should have given her fair warning that someone had entered, but considering his bulk, it was amazing how light he was on his feet. He made a circular movement with his hand, humming beneath his breath as he did so. The anger that still burned in her chest since the death of her eldest sister, Aggie, erupted and Emma hit out at him with the shovel.

Dr Stone wrenched it out of her grasp and caught her on the ear with the handle. 'My, my! You're getting saucy. We'll have none of that. Now you get up and let me have a fondle and a nice kiss...there's my girl.'

The blow to her ear had brought tears to Emma's eyes and, scrambling to her feet, she cried, 'I'm not your girl!' Placing both hands to his fat belly she pushed hard. He staggered backwards, lost his balance and fell heavily on the shabby Axminster carpet.

'What's going on here?' The voice was icy.

'You work it out for yerself, missus,' said Emma, struggling to unfasten her sacking apron.

Mrs Stone, who was as slender as her husband was rotund, fixed him with a rigid stare. 'You really are a fool, William. Get up off the floor!'

His florid face wore a sulky expression. 'The girl's gone completely mad. Just a bit of slap and tickle, Josie, dearest.

She's never complained before.'

Emma finally got the knot undone and wrenched off the sacking apron. 'Well, I'm complaining now and I'm reporting yer to the Servants' Registry Office.' She threw the apron at him and would have stormed out of the drawing room, if Mrs Stone had not caught her by the arm.

'Don't be silly, Emma! You think they'll care? They'll put you down as difficult and you'll have trouble getting another position. Stay, and I'll see this doesn't happen again.'

Emma's mouth set in a stubborn line and she shook her head. Mrs Stone was all right but she was never going to be able to keep wandering-hands Willie in order. Cook had told Emma that he'd got the last all-purpose maid pregnant and the missus had sent her away to some place for unmarried mothers on the Wirral. Well, that wasn't going to happen to her. Men! You could stick the lot of them. Well, that is except for her brother Chris, who was with the army in India.

'I'm sorry for you, Mrs Stone, but yer've had it. I'm off!' Emma wrenched herself free and marched out of the room. She felt a familiar aching frustration that girls like her should always come off the worst in such a situation.

The brown velveteen skirts of Josephine Stone's gown whispered as they brushed the floor. 'Please, Emma, stay! It's getting more difficult every time to find decent help like yourself. I'll give you three pence extra a week. You know I've got a meeting in Birkenhead today and I need you here.'

Emma's step faltered. The offer was tempting. Mrs Stone knew how she was placed, giving most of her small earnings to her mother to help clothe and feed her younger siblings. Not only that, she had taken on work as a live-in domestic so as to move out of her parents' overcrowded house in Cornwall Street, up near the railway wagon and carriage works in Newtown.

'Emma, answer me! You know I've got to go down to the surgery and get everything ready. Please change your mind?' pleaded Josephine.

Emma's hand strayed to a strand of russet hair that had come loose from her mop cap. Her father would call her a bloody fool for walking out of what he considered a good situation and as for her mother, she would blow her top and demand to know how she was going to make ends meet.

Slowly Emma turned and, resting a hand on the newel post at the bottom of the stairs, was about to accept Mrs Stone's offer when she caught sight of the doctor hovering in the doorway behind his wife. His slack mouth hung open and his protuberant eyes were fixed on Emma's rapidly rising and falling bosom.

'Sorry, missus,' said Emma regretfully. 'Pity *you* weren't the doctor. His patients would fare a lot better if yer were.' She did not linger to see or hear their reaction to her words but ran upstairs.

Emma knew from Cook that Mrs Stone had wanted to be a doctor. Unfortunately there had been three brothers in need of an education, so there had been no chance of her fulfilling that dream. Instead the young Josephine Beeston had done what she thought was the next best thing and married a doctor.

Emma reached her bedroom on the top floor of the three-storeyed terraced house and hurried inside. She locked the door before pouring water into the bowl on the washstand. She lathered her hands with carbolic soap, then rinsed and dried them on a rough towel, before unfastening the buttons on the front of her grey frock and removing it.

There was a rap of knuckles on the door. 'Four pence, Emma. That's my last offer. You do realise if you leave without notice I will not pay you for this week's work and neither shall I give you a reference.'

Her employer's words were a blow to Emma, although

she knew it was what most employers would do if a servant quit without giving notice. Yet somehow she'd expected Mrs Stone to pay her the money she had earned. Her mistake! 'Sorry, missus,' she called through the door, 'but I don't trust the doctor. If you had any sense yer'd leave him, too.'

Josephine gasped. 'You really do have a nerve for a girl in your position, Emma. No doubt you'll live to regret acting so recklessly.'

As Emma listened to her retreating footsteps, her knees seemed to turn to jelly and she sagged against the bed. What had made her say that? For better or for worse Mrs Stone was trapped in her marriage – and without what some would see as the consolation of children.

Emma straightened and stood shivering in drawers, chemise, flannelette petticoat and black stockings. She caught a glimpse of her reflection in the small mirror on the chest of drawers. Anxious brown eyes gazed back at her from a small heart-shaped face. Why was she worrying about Mrs Stone? There was no way she was going to be any worse off for Emma's leaving. No doubt she would be able to hire a maid prepared to put up with the master's advances. She should be worrying about herself.

Emma sighed and drew back the chintz curtain that concealed the alcove next to the fireplace and took out her Sunday-best clothes. As she dressed in a plain brown skirt, a cream blouse buttoned to beneath her chin and a snugly fitting brown jacket, a sound at the window caused her to look up.

She stared in dismay as hailstones pelted the glass making a noise like rapid gunfire. It was a good twenty minutes' walk to the Servants' Registry Office on Brook Street and she would get soaked if the weather carried on like this. It was hard to believe yesterday had been Empire Day and there was blossom on the trees.

With a moue of irritation, she reached for the hat that

Cook had given her after Emma had put a finger through a green felt one that had once belonged to her dead sister. Despite its age, Emma had been reluctant to dispose of Aggie's hat because she was reminded of her every time she wore it. In her mind's eye she had been able to picture her sister with the hat tilted to one side and her eyes sparkling beneath its narrow rim. She had been so pretty and full of vim that Emma still found it difficult to believe her sister had killed herself. Aggie had been gutsy, not one to give up even when the worst kind of trouble befell her. How Emma would love to get her hands on the bloke who had made her sister pregnant. She dreamed of seeing him get his comeuppance.

Emma's eyes were bleak as she placed a brown hat sporting a cock pheasant's tail feather on her small head and tucked a wayward tendril of hair behind a dainty ear. It had been good of Cook to give her this hat and she was going to miss her.

Collecting the rest of her belongings, she unlocked the door and hurried downstairs. Raised voices could be heard coming from the surgery on the ground floor. Emma's footsteps faltered but then she squared her shoulders and made her way to the kitchen.

The hailstones had stopped and the sun was shining through the sash window, reflecting off the copper pans hanging on a bilious green painted wall. Bacon sizzled in a heavy cast-iron frying pan on the gas stove and the smell of it made Emma feel hungry all over again.

'You going then?' said Cook, sounding vexed. She was plump and motherly looking and answered to the name of Mrs Pomfret despite never having married.

'You heard the row,' said Emma, trying to sound cheerful.

Cook scowled. 'I thought *you* might have stuck it out.'

'It – It's not you who he takes advantage of, Mrs Pomfret. Surely yer can't b – blame me for not wanting to end up like the last all-purpose maid?'

'No, Emmie.' Cook heaved her enormous weight up from a chair and waddled over to the stove. 'It's just that I've got fond of you and I know Mrs Stone likes having you around. You remind her of her own dear sister; she had russet hair and brown eyes just like yours.'

Emma wrinkled her tip-tilted nose. 'You've never mentioned a sister to me before.'

'That's because she died. The old man wouldn't give his permission for her to marry an American archaeologist, who came over here to look at the Roman artefacts. It broke her heart and she just wasted away.'

'Fathers!' exclaimed Emma in disgust. Hers had been stiff with condemnation when his wife had told him of Aggie's condition. Within the hour, he had chucked her out onto the street and told her never to darken his door again. When his eldest daughter's body had been found floating in the canal, instead of being filled with remorse, he'd put his head in his hands and vowed he'd never forgive her for bringing shame to his name. The way he'd gone on about *his* name, anyone would think he was the Duke of Westminster living at Eaton Hall rather than a porter at Chester General Station.

'Mine was all right,' said Cook, her eyes softening with reminiscence. 'What with Mother dying when I was born and him never marrying again, I was his own little ewe lamb until he passed over.'

Emma's lips twitched as she stared at Cook, trying to imagine her as a little ewe lamb. 'I'd best be getting along to the Servants' Registry Office right away, make me complaint and enter me name on their books as available for work.'

Cook placed a hand on the girl's arm. 'Well, good luck. I'll pray for you, Emmie. Don't forget us now. Come round and see me when you get the chance, let me know how you're getting on.'

Emma was touched. 'Thanks, Mrs Pomfret.' She leaned forward and, with tears in her eyes, kissed the woman's rosy cheek before making a hasty departure.

She left the house and headed for Northgate Street. Crossing the road to the cathedral, she went through an archway to the side of the building that led to the cobbled Abbey Square. Making for an opening in the city wall, believed to have been a short cut used by monks in medieval times when they needed to attend their vegetable gardens, she was soon crossing the Shropshire Union Canal, it was then the sky darkened again. Marble-sized hailstones rained down and she ran, hoping the onslaught would be of short duration. It wasn't and she sought shelter in the cocoa house on Brook Street.

An overpowering smell of damp clothes, cigarette smoke, toast, baking scones and milky chocolate greeted her. The last thing the shivering Emma wanted to do was to spend money but, recklessly, she decided a mug of cocoa would warm her up nicely. Spotting a place at a table in a far corner of the crowded room, she made her way towards it. Two of the seats were occupied, one by a woman Emma estimated to be in her mid-twenties, and the other by a younger, auburn-haired woman. The elder wore a fashionably large hat, trimmed with ostrich feathers and pale mauve silk flowers, and was obviously well-to-do.

What was she doing in a common cocoa house and so early in the morning? wondered Emma, and hesitated before asking whether they minded if she sat at their table.

Dark eyes looked up from beneath the ostrich plumes and regarded her slowly. 'Certainly,' said the elder woman with a smile, removing a large crocodile handbag from the empty chair before resuming her conversation with her companion.

'So Hannah is worried, Alice?'

'Yes, Miss Victoria.'

Emma seated herself, shooting a glance at the redhead,

Alice, who delved into a drawstring bag on her knee and produced an envelope. She was obviously of the servant class, although dressed with some style in a close-fitting dark green costume and a narrow brimmed straw hat trimmed with daisies and green ribbon. She handed the envelope to her mistress.

'Before Bert disappeared, he popped this under her bedroom door,' murmured Alice. 'Kenny says she should ignore it and that Bert only did it to try and spoil the wedding. But it's not herself or me she's frightened for – well, that's not exactly true – it's Tilly. She's not yet four, and he threatens to snatch her on Hannah and Kenny's wedding day in a couple of weeks' time.'

'Shush, Alice. Let me read it for myself.' Victoria bowed her head.

'So what can I get you, miss?' The waitress's sharp voice startled Emma, who had been listening unashamedly to the exchange between the two women.

She glanced up. 'Cocoa, please.'

'Anything to eat?' The waitress's pencil hovered over a notepad.

Emma shook her head.

The waitress moved off and there was silence at the table.

'She really should take it to the police,' Victoria's cultured voice continued.

'Hannah won't have that. She said they might call at the house and upset her mother, who's in a state as it is over Bert's disappearance,' said Alice, her knuckles gleaming white as she clutched her bag tightly. 'If only we knew where he's gone. Mrs Kirk has told the neighbours that our wedding was cancelled because Bert suddenly got the opportunity of a better job in Liverpool and I refused to go. All lies, of course,' she added indignantly. 'She just can't bear for the neighbours to know the truth about her precious son.'

'I do see your problem but he could just be making empty threats. It's not as if he knows where you're living – and as it's unlikely Tilly will be left alone now he's made known his intentions, I would stop worrying.'

'But you don't know him, Miss Victoria!' she burst out. 'He's crafty…and his threat to spoil Kenny and Hannah's wedding makes me feel sick with worry. He's caused them enough unhappiness as it is.'

It was at that point the waitress arrived with Emma's cocoa and so she missed what was said next. Swiftly she glanced at the bill and paid what she owed, wanting to get rid of the waitress so she could hear more of the conversation. As she spooned two sugars into the steaming liquid, she wondered what else was in the letter. He sounded a bit of a swine this bloke, Bert. Warming her hands on the mug as she sipped the hot beverage, she cocked her ears.

'I think you should take note of what your half-brother says.'

Alice sighed. 'I just wish Seb and Mr Waters hadn't been involved in that shipping accident off the coast of America. I'd feel safer with a couple of men in the house.'

Victoria nodded. 'I would feel happier if they were both home too. For Papa to break a hip at his age is a serious matter. I really wish I could be with him – but what with my heart condition and Grandmamma getting more forgetful by the minute – it was out of the question. We just have to be patient.' Victoria crumbled the remains of a scone on her plate with restless fingers. 'I've written to Sebastian ordering him to hire a nurse. He can't deal with Papa's business affairs and look after him now he's out of hospital.'

'You still haven't told Seb that I'm working for you and living at the house, Miss Victoria?'

Her employer smiled. 'Certainly not, Alice! It would distract him from his work. Besides it'll be a lovely surprise for him when he eventually arrives home to find you waiting for him.'

'I hope so,' said Alice, her expression uncertain. 'If only I hadn'tbeen so scared of Father in the past and trusted Seb more. If I'd been less impatient and intolerant. If I'd listened to Hannah and not got myself engaged to Bert.' She sighed. 'I just hope Seb's mother hasn't written to him about me.'

Victoria said firmly, 'Gabrielle might sometimes behave as if she rules the household but I've told her she's not to. If she disobeys me then I'll be very cross with her.'

'She still doesn't approve of me,' said Alice gloomily.

'That's not surprising. You hurt her son and you're not of her faith.' Victoria glanced towards the window where a shaft of sunlight pierced the condensation and her face brightened. 'It looks like the hailstones have stopped. We'd best make a move or we'll miss the train and be late for the meeting.'

'What time have we got to be there?' asked Alice, getting to her feet.

'We must be in Birkenhead by ten o'clock. I've not visited Mrs Abraham's house before and I'm hoping that a good number of the Ladies' Liberal Party will be attending. We really need more of them involved in the Movement.' Victoria placed a penny under her saucer, picked up her large, crocodile-skin handbag and stood up.

'I hope you enjoy your meeting,' said Emma boldly.

Victoria smiled and hurried towards the exit.

Alice looked at Emma and winked. 'It'll be all talk and little action,' she whispered. 'They're all so ladylike, you see. Bye!' She followed her mistress out.

Emma knew what she meant. She had attended a couple of meetings in support of the Women's Suffrage Movement with Mrs Stone. Thinking of her previous employer caused her spirits to plummet. Soon she would have to leave the warmth of the cocoa house, not only to face Mrs Roberts at the Servants' Registry Office, but also her mother. She could expect a scolding from both of them about the foolishness of leaving a job without a reference. It meant that she couldn't pick and choose. Emma's first job when her schooling had finished five years ago had been with a childless widow. The situation had suited her down to the ground. Unfortunately the job had ended with her employer's sudden death and no one to provide a reference. The only piece of paper Emma possessed was the character reference written by her teacher, stating that she was honest, hardworking and would benefit from training, as she had an excellent memory.

Emma rubbed the tip of her nose absently, thinking of the household that she had just left. To run through several all-purpose maids so swiftly must surely mean Difficult was written in large black letters in the margin against the Stones' name. Emma's eyes darkened and her mouth set determinedly. What she wanted was another position with a childless widow or a nice rich spinster. It wasn't beyond the bounds of possibility that she might walk into such a job right away. She drained her cup and left.

Melting hailstones crunched beneath Emma's feet as she passed the Glynne Arms on the corner of Francis Street. Within minutes she arrived at a red-brick building with small paned windows, displaying a board with the words Servants' Registry Office painted on it. There was another such office nearer the river Dee, but this one was only a short walk from her parents' house.

Emma wiped her feet on the mat in the vestibule, opened the door and entered Mrs Roberts' sanctum. To her surprise, a flaxen-haired giant of a man stood the other side of the counter, resting a shoulder against a shelf and reading the *Chester Chronicle*. He wore working overalls over a shirt and looked out of place in the office. 'Take a seat. She'll be back shortly,' he said, without looking up.

'Does that mean five minutes or half-an-hour?'

He glanced up and Emma watched with a fascinated eye, as a tide of colour ran up from the open neck of his grey flannelette shirt to the roots of his hair. He cleared his throat and answered in a deep baritone voice with more than a hint of a Welsh accent. 'She didn't say. She just had news that a friend's husband has died and felt she had to go and see her.'

'She could be some time then?'

'You think so?' He sounded dismayed and glanced at the clock on the wall. 'She did say she'd be back in a jiffy.'

Emma placed her bag on the counter and said mildly, 'Are you a client or are yer related to her?'

He folded his newspaper and smiled faintly. 'My mother was a cousin twice removed. Now there's only Dad and me. We moved to Chester just a year ago. Is there anything *I* can do for you?' He rested his elbows on the counter and brought his head down so that his face was now on a level with hers.

The expression in his grey eyes was slightly unnerving but her voice was steady enough when she spoke. 'Well, unless *you* can give me a job, then all yer can do is write a message from me to Mrs Roberts. There's a pen and inkstand right next to yer elbow.'

He hesitated but then straightened up and reached for the pen. She dictated to him what kind of employment she wanted. Despite the largeness of his hand, he wrote in a neat copperplate style. She was impressed. Her handwriting was terrible because she could never get the words down quickly enough. They ended up looking like she'd dipped a spider in ink and used that for a nib.

He blotted the sentences before lifting his head. His cheeks dimpled in a smile. 'It's a pity you stipulate not wanting to work where there's a man in the house. My dad and I could do with a live-in housekeeper. We've been muddling through on our own since we've been here.'

She shook her head. 'Sorry. But my experience of male

employers is the reason for me dictating to yer that I don't want to work where there's men. I'm sure, though, Mrs Roberts will find yer somebody, Mr...?'

'Davies. David Davies.' His dimples came and went. 'I can assure you, Miss Griffiths, my father and I are perfectly respectable.'

She raised her eyebrows. 'You'd think a doctor would be respectable, wouldn't you? I tell you, he wasn't.' She twiddled her fingers at the Welshman and left.

Emma crossed Brook Street, avoiding a coal cart pulled by a tired-looking horse. Eventually she came to a street of Victorian terraced houses and, reaching in through the letterbox, she pulled out a key on a string. She opened the door onto a narrow lobby at the end of which was a flight of stairs that led up to two bedrooms and a box room. She went through a door on her left into a small front room, furnished with a shabby sofa and a couple of armchairs. A rag rug covered the torn linoleum in front of the fireplace but there was no fire in the grate and wouldn't be until her father arrived home from work.

She went through into the kitchen and could hear her mother Olive's voice, and found her in the tiny washhouse to the rear. The iron set-pot stood on bricks over a fire, sending out billows of steam. The grimy whitewashed walls were dripping with condensation. Emma groaned. Where was her mother's commonsense? Surely when she had seen the weather that morning she should have known to put off the task of washing blankets until another day. Just because *her* mother had always washed blankets in May, Olive felt she had to do the same.

'Hello, Mam.'

Olive had not heard her daughter enter the house and whirled round with her youngest on her hip and a wooden spoon in her right hand. 'What the hell are you doing here at this time of day?'

With her heart hammering and a defiant tilt to her chin,

Emma said, 'I've quit!'

'What! How the hell d'you think I'm going to manage?' With its patches of scurvy and dried blood, Olive's hollow-cheeked face was ugly in her fury.

It took all of Emma's nerve to defend herself. 'I couldn't stand him p-pawing me any longer. Dirty old man!'

'And who made you so fussy?' snapped Olive, placing a lid on top of the steaming pot and dropping the wooden spoon on top of it. 'If you had my life, yer'd have something to complain about.'

'I thought yer'd want me to have a better life than yours,' countered Emma defiantly. She was swamped with guilt, noticing how bony the wrists were that showed beneath the shrunken mutton sleeves of her mother's blouse and the thinness of her chest. A navy blue skirt clung to Olive's skinny legs and her feet were shod in a pair of boots, which she had found in the entry, with the soles coming away. She had boiled them before having one of the twins tack the soles back into place.

Olive thrust her youngest son at her daughter. 'Yer a dreamer just like our Aggie! Beggars can't be choosers. Yer should have put up with things just like I have to.'

'I'll get another job,' said Emma.

'Too right yer will.'

Emma held her little brother tightly as he wrapped scrawny arms about her neck and rested his head on her shoulder. He wore no nappy and his nightgown smelt of wee, his feet were bare and stone cold. She clasped them in one of her hands in an attempt to warm them. 'I will. I'll take anything if it makes you feel happier.'

Olive's expression hardened. 'If you'd played your cards right yer could have got money out of him or little gifts we could have pawned.'

Emma flinched. 'You can't mean that, Mam.'

'I do!' she retorted fiercely. 'Yer don't appreciate your good fortune in escaping this house. God, I wish I was your age again. I'd be off to Liverpool. Plenty of sailors there with money to spend. I was good looking once and could have raked it in. With your looks yer could make a fair amount, I bet.'

Emma could scarcely believe her ears. 'What's up with yer, Mam, talking like this? I could get the pox!'

'Yer know about such things then,' said Olive sharply, dragging her blouse more tightly about her thin body and hugging herself.

Emma blurted out, 'I've flicked through some of the doctor's medical books. Yer'd be surprised how many diseases there are in the world and the kind of thing you can catch from doing what yer oughtn't. You're talking stupid, Mam.'

Olive looked shamefaced. 'OK, Em, keep your hair on. Perhaps I should have thought twice before saying that but I get desperate at times. I need the money *you* earn, duck.'

'I know, Mam, I know.' Emma hesitated before adding, 'I've a couple of shillings saved. I'll give them to yer.'

Immediately Olive's expression changed and she said angrily, 'I never knew yer had any savings. Wait'll your dad hears that yer've been keeping money from us while living in the lap of luxury.'

Emma gasped. 'Living in luxury! I worked bloody hard for every penny I earned, cleaning out grates, scrubbing floors, fetching and carrying coal and water up flights of stairs from dawn to dusk. What's stopping *you* from making some cash? You could take in washing. It's something yer good at after all.'

Olive exploded, swearing and calling her daughter all the names she could think of, adding that she already worked her socks off. Emma was almost blown over by the force of her words. Then her mother stopped and into that well of silence fell the patter of wee on the stone floor as little Johnny lost control of his bladder. Emma thrust him away from her skirt, already damp, and into her mother's arms. 'I'll go back to the registry office right now and I won't return until I've another job.'

She walked out of the house, wishing life wasn't so hard, not only for herself but her mother and so many working-class women like them. She thought of Mrs Stone and that Miss Victoria in the cocoa room with the time to attend meetings and felt even angrier than ever. She pushed open the door of the Servants' Registry Office and only then did she remember the fair giant of a man with the deep musical voice, who wanted a housekeeper. Would he be there still?

No. A vague disappointment made itself felt, surprising her. She hadn't wanted the job, so what was wrong with her? Taking a deep breath and crossing her fingers, she pinned a woebegone expression on her face as she approached the woman behind the counter. 'You remember me, Mrs Roberts? Emma Griffiths. I left you a message.'

The grey-haired woman in the black dress fixed her with a stare. 'I hope you have references with you this time, Miss Griffiths.'

Emma's bottom lip quivered and, in a trembling voice, she explained her lack of them. The woman sighed. 'I'm afraid there are no women on my books at the moment that would take you into their homes without references. I suggest you give up the idea of living in and seek daily cleaning work. I know of one such job if you are interested. I will write a note putting in a good word for you with the employer.'

Emma's heart sank but as her mother had said *Beggars can't be choosers.* She asked where the job was and was told it was in a furniture shop. That didn't sound too bad, she thought, waiting while Mrs Roberts scribbled a quick note.

Emma left the Servants' Registry Office telling herself that things could be much worse. At least she no longer had to put up with being pawed by Dr Stone. She thought of Aggie, remembering how her father had laid all the blame for her condition on her sister's shoulders. He hadn't even asked the name of the swine who had got her into trouble. He was the kind of man who always blamed the victims of suffering and hardship, saying that they had brought it on themselves. For the umpteenth time she wondered about the identity of the man responsible for her sister's pregnancy. Oh, why hadn't Aggie confided in her? All she had ever said was that she'd found herself a smashing fella, but, otherwise, she had been very secretive about him.

After the first flush of grief had passed, Emma had tried to discover the man's name by visiting Bannister's Bakery where her sister had worked. She remembered Aggie mentioning a workmate called Annie. But when Emma had called at the shop to ask for her, she had been told that she had left. When asked where Annie lived, the crabby ol' spinster in charge had shown her the door, reminding Emma that Agnes had been sacked for stealing.

Emma sighed, remembering how her sister had taken buns for their younger brothers and sisters. Sooner or later she would have to make another attempt to track down the swine and see that he paid for what he had done. But she was damned if she could work out how to trace him without finding Annie first.

Chapter Two

June, 1907

Hannah Kirk hoisted her damson-coloured, imitation silk gown and starched cotton underskirts above her ankles and headed for the front door. It was a beautiful summer day and her wedding was due to take place in an hour but already things were going wrong. Alice had not yet arrived and...

'Hanny, where are you going?' Joy, her younger sister, swivelled her dark head in her direction.

'To find Freddie and Tilly,' replied Hannah. 'I don't know how they managed to sneak out without us seeing them but they have. If they've mucked themselves up they're for it.'

'Should you be going out dressed like that?' Joy had spent hours helping to tidy up and prepare the wedding breakfast. She was still in the throes of getting herself ready for the big occasion; otherwise she would have gone in search of her younger brother and Tilly herself.

Hannah shrugged slender shoulders. 'As long as Kenny doesn't see me what does it matter? The neighbours should be used to our comings and goings by now. You know what Bert threatened in May, so I can't take any chances. Although, I think Freddie would have been back here by now if Bert'd turned up.'

Joy agreed. 'It wouldn't surprise me if that's what Mother's hoping for.'

With a sigh, Hannah paused with a hand on the front door. 'I still think Mother believes I led him on.'

'Surely she can't,' said Joy in disbelief.

'He's always been her blue-eye,' said Hannah grimly. 'You'd think after what she knows about him now, she'd realise he's no angel. She just doesn't want to believe him capable of ungentlemanly behaviour...despite walking in on him beating up Alice, too.'

'Alice isn't here yet.'

'I have noticed. It could be that Miss Victoria needed her for something at the last minute and that's made her late.'

'I'd make a better job of being chief bridesmaid, you know,' stated Joy, buttoning up her bridesmaid gown that was blush pink cotton. 'Honestly, the kids'll do what I tell them. Alice has no idea how to handle them for all she says she wants lots of children one day.'

Hannah, a warm smile in her blue eyes as she gazed at this well-loved sister, said, 'I know, but she is my best friend, as well as being Kenny's half-sister. Now I'd best scram in case Mother comes down and delays me even further. I have to go.' She managed at last to leave the kitchen and get out of the house.

Already the neighbours were gathering. They wanted a good view of the bride, and not only because she was a popular young woman but also because the shock waves from the last minute cancellation of the wedding of the Kirks' eldest son Bert to Alice Moran had not died down. Even the most persistent gossipmongers believed handsome and charming Bert Kirk was a real catch, with a good job in engineering. Most thought Alice crazy not to want to move with him to a better paid job in Liverpool. A few weeks later had come the surprise announcement of Hannah's engagement to Kenny Moran, who hadn't been on the scene for ages. A mute, as long as they had known him, he had suddenly re-appeared from Scotland of all places able to talk. It had been rumoured that his dumbness had been *all in the mind*. All this after his father, Malcolm Moran, had been arrested for beating up a policeman and had ended up being committed to the lunatic asylum.

Hannah had no trouble gleaning from the neighbours that Freddie, clad in kilt, frilled white shirt and black velvet doublet for his role of page boy, was playing in Chesham Street, a cul-de-sac, a few minutes' walk away.

'Tilly?' she asked, trying not to sound too anxious.

'Was with him last time we saw her, skipping along as merry as a sand-boy, Hanny dear,' said one woman, smiling. 'Will Bert be at the wedding?'

Hannah shook her head and lied smoothly, 'He's much too busy.'

The neighbour looked at her disbelievingly but was silent.

'You'd best be careful not to spoil that lovely dress,' called another woman.

Hannah thanked them with a smile and went on her way. She found Freddie playing marbles with several boys, and was reminded of a peacock amongst a huddle of sparrows. He was kneeling in the dust, the handle of a small dirk jutting out of the top of his right stocking. The outfit had been sent from Scotland by Kenny's maternal grandmother, who, unfortunately, couldn't attend the wedding. Hannah tapped Freddie on the shoulder and he glanced up at her. 'Where's Tilly?' she asked.

'Isn't she here?' Absentmindedly, he attempted to put his marbles in a pocket that was not there and so resorted to the sporran.

'I wouldn't be asking if she was,' said Hannah, shaking her head at him in exasperation. A twist of fear was forming in her tummy. 'I told you to keep your eye on her. The wedding's in less than an hour.'

Freddie pulled a face. 'She was supposed to stay put, but you know what she's like for wandering off.'

'If you knew that then you should have kept a better eye on her,' said Hannah severely, dragging him to his feet and dusting him down. She smoothed his tousled black curls and gazed into his eyes. 'Now, straight home or you're in trouble.' She was thinking that perhaps Tilly had gone to Granny Popo's, the old woman who had helped take care of the little girl from the day she was born.

Hannah parted from her younger brother on the corner of the street and hurried in the direction of the Shropshire Union canal, intent on reaching the house as quickly as possible. Granny Popo had helped bring Tilly into the world and her granddaughter, Dolly, had been the girl's wet nurse after her mother had died in childbirth.

Halfway across the bridge at the bottom of Egerton Street, Hannah caught sight of Tilly outside Granny's house on the other side of the canal and she was talking to a man. For a moment Hannah's heart seemed to stop beating and then he turned his head and she realised he was Dolly's soldier husband, newly returned from abroad.

Hannah hastened towards them and coming up behind Tilly, grabbed her by the shoulders. 'Gotcha! What did I tell you about wandering off?' she chided.

'She's only just got here…said she came to show Granny her frock,' said the fair haired man, his teeth flashing white in his sunburnt face.

The girl tilted her head and beamed up at Hannah. 'I wasn't going to be long.'

'You should have told Freddie where you were going. Now we've got to get back home double-quick.'

'But Granny hasn't seen my frock yet,' said Tilly.

Hannah was just about to say that Granny could see it later when she heard her name being called. She whirled round and saw Alice coming towards her. 'Thank God! Where've you been? I was getting worried,' she cried.

'Don't ask me to begin to explain now,' gasped Alice, whose face was flushed and damp with perspiration. She placed a hand to her side. 'I've got a stitch with running.'

'Well, just slow down. The wedding can't happen without me being there,' said Hannah, gazing anxiously at Alice as they began to make their way towards the canal. 'Was it you-know-who?' she added in a whisper.

Alice glanced down at Tilly, who was a picture in the

pink cheesecloth frock trimmed with rosebuds that Alice had made, and placed a trembling hand on her younger sister's shoulder. 'I wasn't exactly sure it was him but decided to make a run for it just in case. I was late as it was because Miss Victoria had one of her turns so we sent for the doctor.'

'Is she all right now?'

'Resting.' Alice took one of her sister's hands and Hannah took the other and they hurried her along, swinging her off her feet every now and then.

'If it was Bert...where did you think you saw him?' asked Hannah.

'Near the river! I was on Queen's Park footbridge and I could have sworn...' Alice's voice trailed off but then she took a deep breath. 'It was stupid of me to run but I get this tight feeling in my chest where Bert's concerned and I just have to get away. It's as if my brain's telling me that if I don't escape, something terrible is going to happen.'

Hannah understood her fear. Both of them had suffered at Bert's hands. 'That's how he wants you to feel,' she said fiercely. 'He's determined to spoil mine and Kenny's wedding, but I *won't* let him do it.'

'That's the ticket,' said Alice. 'But what about Tilly?'

At the mention of her name, four-year-old Tilly turned her pretty face up to her sister. 'What about me?' she asked.

Hannah exchanged a warning glance with Alice because she did not want the little girl frightened. 'We don't want you wandering off again, Tilly. So you mustn't go anywhere without our permission.'

'Why?' asked Tilly.

Alice placed a finger against her sister's rosebud mouth. 'No more questions, just do as you're told.'

Tilly sighed and was silent.

When they arrived back at the house, Hannah's father,

Jock, Freddie and Joy were waiting for them. 'Good, you've arrived,' said the latter, looking relieved. 'Time was going on and we were getting concerned.' She handed posies to Alice and Tilly and a bouquet to Hannah.

'Where's Mother?' asked Hannah of her father.

'Gone ahead with cousin Joan,' said Jock; a tall, rangy figure of a man with a craggy face and salt and pepper hair. 'I think we'd best make a move, lass.'

Hannah nodded. 'Is she OK?'

'Don't be worrying about her, lass. Joan will look after her,' he assured his eldest daughter, squeezing her shoulder.

Hannah placed her arm through her father's and swept out of the kitchen with him. Alice followed, leaving Joy to bring up the rear with Freddie and Tilly. Joy took them by the hand, threatening them with no strawberries and blancmange if they didn't do exactly what they were told.

Susannah Kirk was managing to keep her tears in check. The hot toddy of rum, brown sugar and warm water made by her elderly cousin, Joan, had definitely helped, but she could not get Bert, her blond, blue-eyed son, out of her mind. She was still having trouble coming to terms with what he had done to Hannah and Alice. It just didn't match up with how generous and attentive he had always behaved towards herself. Maybe Hannah had led him on? But if she was to believe that, then that meant her eldest daughter was wantonly wicked. She had to stop thinking about her. Easier to believe that Bert had just cause to lose his temper where Alice was concerned. She had hurt him deeply when she had cancelled their wedding two days before it was to take place – after Bert had spent weeks doing up a house for the pair of them. Of course, he shouldn't have hit her the way he did. She had been shocked by the sight of Alice's bruised face...but Susannah had been even more shocked when Bert had come to her the evening of the following day with his face bruised and battered after Kenny had given him a beating.

Her fingers tightened on her handbag and her mouth quivered as she remembered that day. Seeing what Kenny had done had been like discovering a rabbit had turned into a wolf. She thought of her eldest son pleading with her to forgive him. He'd said he deeply regretted losing control and hitting Alice, but that he'd loved her and having that love thrown back in his face had made him see red. There had been tears in his eyes when he had said those words. Susannah had been too much in shock at the time to listen to him and had told him to go away. Said she never wanted to see him again. So he had left and she still did not know where he had gone. To save face she had lied to the neighbours about his reason for leaving and his whereabouts.

When she had repeated his words to Hannah, her daughter's response had been harsh. 'His so-called love almost ruined my life!' She had held a clenched fist to her breast. 'He raped me! A strange kind of love, Mother. Not only that but he got Agnes from Bannister's pregnant and she threw herself in the canal. No wonder Alice changed her mind about marrying him. You knew how violent her father was, so you should be able to imagine how Alice felt. So don't talk to me about Bert's love.'

'If you were a mother, you would understand how I'm suffering.' Susannah had flung the words at her, tears rolling down her face. She still could not help but believe that if the girls had acted differently, then Bert wouldn't have behaved the way he had. Her despair and grief over not knowing the whereabouts of her son was driving her crazy, so that she was unable to give her daughter the sympathy and comfort she needed. Susannah would need to cut Bert out of her heart and she could not do that.

The organ burst into Mendelssohn's 'Wedding March', startling her. The music was the signal for the congregation to stand, which they did with a rustling sound reminiscent of autumn leaves beneath one's feet. The bride and groom came up the aisle towards her. Hannah gave her mother a radiant smile as she passed on the arm of her new husband. Susannah's answering smile was of a short duration as her gaze fell on Kenny and then on Alice. If it weren't for them, she wouldn't have had to send Bert away.

Jock tapped his wife on the shoulder as the best man and bridesmaids swept past. 'Come on, Sue! Our turn now.' He took her hand and drew it through his arm and they followed the bridal procession out into the sunshine.

Emma was on her way home when she spotted the wedding party outside St Bartholomew's church. Conflicting emotions warred inside her as she paused on the corner of the street to watch. She could not help but envy the love that shone on the faces of the happy couple, but still she pitied them. How long would that love survive the realities of married life?

Her eyes glinted as she remembered her father's blustering excuses as to why he could not give her mother more money. Even now she could hear Olive's whining voice in her head; going on about being unable to feed and clothe her family properly. He had accused Olive of being a lousy manager. After he had left the house, Emma had got an earful from her mother about *her* eating them out of house and home, as well as asking when was she going to take another live-in job. This despite Emma having taken on an extra cleaning job in a solicitor's office and handing over every penny she earned in the past fortnight. If Emma was to have any peace at all, then she was going to have to move out of the family home again. She decided to put her name on the books of the other Chester Servants' Registry Office, determined to be out of the house by the time her twin brothers left school next month. They already had jobs to go to; Alf on the railways and Pete as a stable boy on Canal Side.

Emma's gaze shifted to the three bridesmaids and an involuntary sigh escaped her. How she wished she could afford to buy such dresses for her younger sisters and herself; although pink was out of the question because it showed the dirt too easily. Suddenly, she realised that the eldest bridesmaid was the young woman she had seen in the cocoa house last month – the day she had left the Stones' household – and at the same time she became aware of someone standing behind her. They were so close that she could feel their breath in her hair and smell peppermint. She was just about to turn round and see who it was, when the person moved away. For a moment she stayed where she was, gazing at the girl, whose name she remembered was Alice, and it was then she recalled the conversation she had overheard. Perhaps the worries voiced then had been unfounded. At least it appeared that the wedding had gone off without a hitch.

Alice was twitchy, longing to get back to the Waters' house where she would feel less conspicuous, less guilty and definitely cooler. The parlour was hot and stuffy and she could not help but be aware of Mrs Kirk's dark eyes fastening on her every now and again.

In the past Alice had admired Hannah's mother for her brisk efficiency. She had also been grateful for the older woman's help and support to her own mother. But now all Alice could feel was guilt, knowing she had helped destroy Mrs Kirk's illusions about her beloved son. Alice was reminded of a malevolent bird of prey as she glanced at her. Mrs Kirk was dressed in the same black costume that she had worn for her youngest daughter, Grace's funeral. The only concession she had made to today being Hannah's wedding day was the pink frilled blouse worn under the costume, as well as a pink ribbon round the brim of a black hat decorated with a bird's wing. It was as if she was still in mourning; perhaps not so much for Grace but for the missing Bert.

At least he had not spoiled Kenny and Hannah's wedding day. Within a few hours they would be leaving to catch a train to Scotland for a week's honeymoon. On their return, they would be living in a terraced house, not far from the railway goods yard. Tilly would live with them until Alice was in a position to help care for her.

Reminded of her sister, Alice got up and went into the kitchen and looked out of the window into the backyard. She sighed with relief. Tilly was still sitting on the back step, nursing the cat, and watching Freddie take pot shots at an empty tin can with a catapult. No need to worry after all. She was safe.

Alice made up her mind it was time to go. Kenny was right and Bert's threat had been just a bluff. She felt a tap on her shoulder and whirled round to find Kenny standing there, looking concerned.

'You're all on your own. Are you all right?' he asked.

Immediately she seized her opportunity. 'I've got a terrible headache. It's probably the heat. If you don't mind I'll go back to the Waters' now. I'm a bit concerned about Miss Victoria. She had one of her turns this morning.'

He nodded. 'Are you sure you don't want me to walk as far as the bridge with you? I've got a little time to spare and I'm sure Hanny won't mind.' He glanced about the room for his new wife but she was not there. 'I'll go and find her.'

'No!' Alice placed her hand on his arm. 'Don't disturb her. Just give her my love and I hope you have a lovely time in Scotland.' She kissed her brother's cheek. 'I'll look in on Tilly while you're away. Although, I'm sure Joy will take good care of her.' Kenny agreed and hugged her before seeing her out.

The flounced hem of Alice's pink skirts fluttered about

her ankles as she walked swiftly down Francis Street, into Egerton Street and past the Hydraulic Engineering factory where Jock Kirk worked and Bert had served his apprenticeship. She wondered for the umpteenth time where he was working and living now. For all they knew he could have moved to Liverpool.

She paused on the canal bridge and watched a barge go by before her gaze wandered to the circular tower on the north side of the canal. The tower was unusual in that it was one of a few in Britain where molten lead could be dropped inside and, as it fell, it hardened into lead shot. Her own father had worked there and Kenny had told her that working with lead could have affected their father's sanity. Perhaps the doctors at the asylum would have checked for signs of it by now? Apparently lead poisoning showed up in a telltale blue line in the gums at the base of the teeth. But Kenny was also of the opinion that their father's madness was due to his paternal grandmother's influence – her possessive, violent and bigoted nature destroying the man he might have been.

Alice shook herself, not wanting to think of her father any more than necessary. He was out of her life and for that she was grateful. She left the bridge and headed across town towards Queen's Park footbridge. The Waters lived on the other side of the river in the Queen's Park area of Chester, built for those of the Victorian middle classes wanting to escape the narrow streets of the ancient city.

Alice paused this time on the bridge over the Dee, her eyes searching the tree-lined riverside Groves with its cafés, landing stages and bandstand. She remembered listening to a military band playing 'We're Soldiers of the Queen, my Lads!' She had been in Bert's company and Tilly had been up on his shoulders. At the time Alice had believed him to be all things wonderful, but now, just thinking of how close she had been to marrying him, caused a familiar fear to threaten her breathing.

She forced her mind away from that evening he had hit her and looked at the scene below. Young men were showing off their rowing prowess to girls in brightly coloured summer clothes and now she was reminded of Seb Bennett. In happier days, they had walked hand in hand along the river bank, dreaming of a future together. For a moment she lost herself in a daydream, only to be brought out of her reverie by someone calling her name. She turned her head and saw Freddie, his face scarlet with exertion, running towards her.

Her heart began to thud. 'What is it? What's wrong?' she cried, hurrying to meet him.

'It's Tilly,' he gasped, leaning against the side of the bridge to catch his breath. 'She's gone missing! Kenny sent me to tell you.'

A steely hand seemed to squeeze Alice's heart and, for a moment, she could not move. Then she pulled herself together and without waiting for Freddie, lifted her skirts and raced back to the Kirks' house. She was out of breath by the time she got there. The front door was open, so she went right in, followed by Freddie.

She found Bert's mother sitting alone in an upright chair gazing into space. Alice stood with her hand against the doorjamb, gasping for breath. Slowly Susannah's head turned and, just for a moment, Alice thought she glimpsed hate in her eyes and then it was gone. Hannah came through from the scullery wearing her going away costume.

'Have you found her yet?' gasped Alice.

'The men are all out searching,' said Hannah, her face pale and drawn. She put her arm round Alice and ushered her to a chair. 'If they don't find her soon we won't be going to Scotland. I was told to stay here with Mother, just in case Tilly came home under her own steam.'

'You think she'll do that?' whispered Alice, clinging to Hannah's hand.

'Don't let's think the worst,' she said in a low voice.

Both visibly jumped when Susannah declared, 'She's in the canal. That's where she'll be – in the canal.'

'No, Mother,' said Hannah patiently. 'Even if Tilly had gone down to the canal there are plenty of people down there to notice if she fell in.'

'Besides it would have caused a commotion and I would have noticed when I crossed the canal,' said Alice.

Susannah glared at her and gripped her wrinkled hands together. 'If you'd have married my Bert, he would have been here to watch over her. But you hurt him and now he's gone and so has she. Perhaps she won't come back,' she muttered.

'Mother, don't!' cried Hannah in distress.

Alice's face had blanched and now she scrambled to her feet. 'I can't cope with this. I'm getting a bobby.' She hurried out of the house.

Immediately Hannah went after her. 'What are you going to tell him?' she demanded.

'About Tilly being missing and Bert's threat to abduct her. You go back to your mother.' Alice hurried away up Brook Street, heading for the city centre. She asked every person she passed if they had seen a little girl dressed in a pink frock with rosebuds in her hair. Several said that they'd already been asked that question but one replied that he had seen a girl answering Tilly's description in the cathedral with a man wearing a striped blazer. It took all of Alice's willpower to thank him in a sensible voice.

She was about to head for the cathedral when she heard Tilly call her name. Alice could barely believe her eyes when she saw her sister coming towards her from the direction of the Friends' Meeting House in Frodsham Street. She was sucking a lollypop and had dribbled down her chin and onto the bodice of her dress. Alice hurried towards her.

'You're not going to smack me, are you?' asked Tilly,

attempting to wipe away the mess on her dress with her free hand.

'No, but...' Alice allowed her pent up emotions some release by seizing the lollypop and throwing it away, 'what did I tell you about not going anywhere without permission? Everyone's out looking for you. We've been worried sick!'

The girl looked puzzled. 'But I was with Uncle Bert. He came out of the lav when Freddie went into the house.'

Alice went down on her knees, so her face was on a level with Tilly's. 'What did he do to you?' she asked hoarsely.

'Nothing!'

'What did he say to you then?'

'He – he said I was his best girl. He bought me the lollipop...an – and you threw it away! That was naughty.' Her bottom lip quivered.

'I'll buy you another if you promise that you'll be a good girl and never go off with Bert again.'

Tilly looked upset. 'Why?'

'Because he isn't always nice. He hit me and I don't want you getting hurt. Now promise me.'

Tilly sighed and squeezed her hand. 'I promise.'

'That's a good girl,' said Alice, wondering why Bert had let Tilly go. What was he trying to say to them by doing such a thing? That he wasn't as black as they'd painted him? Or perhaps that he could take her anytime he wanted? Whatever it was, she didn't have the time to worry about it now. She had to get to the Kirks' house as fast as she could, so Kenny and Hannah could catch the train to Scotland that evening with peace of mind.

As they walked up Brook Street, Alice noticed a girl staring at them. She looked vaguely familiar and, for a moment, Alice thought that she was going to speak to her, but then she appeared to change her mind and with a smile at Tilly and a nod of the head to Alice, she walked on in the direction of the Servants' Registry Office.

Chapter Three

September, 1907

It was four months since Emma had left the Stones' employment. There were aspects of the cleaning job in the furniture shop which she enjoyed, finding a certain amount of satisfaction in polishing the Welsh dressers, chests, tables and chairs to a gleaming shine. Her other situation she hated because she was treated like the lowest of the low by the typist in the solicitor's office. As Emma took a short cut past Christ Church and into St Anne's Street, she told herself yet again that there had to be something more she could do to help herself into a live-in position. She was fed up with her parents' quarrelling and the lack of privacy at home. Despite her fondness for her brothers and sisters, she felt a servant's tiny bedroom under the eaves was preferable to what she had to put up with at the moment. She passed the stationer's on the corner and walked up Cornwall Street and let herself into the house, only to be greeted by a sight that caused her to draw her breath in with a hiss.

'How long since Mam left?' asked Emma, staring at her younger siblings cuddled up on the sofa beneath a couple of blankets with their bare shoulders exposed. The three older children should have been in their classes by now.

'A quarter of an hour,' chimed Patsy, the eldest. 'The same ol' story, she needs money and Dad's keeping her short. When we don't turn up at school he'll get into trouble.'

'Right!' cried Emma. 'I've had enough!'

She turned on her heel and walked back out of the house again. She guessed what this was about – at the centre of all her parents' arguing lately had been the matter of her father having joined one of the railwaymen's unions – but instead of paying his subs from his own pocket he was deducting it from her mother's housekeeping. Emma had been surprised at him joining as he wasn't one to care about the majority. But, apparently, there had been talk of the railways being nationalised and if that happened, the owners of the different companies had warned there would be job losses. Only by the railway unions standing together could they protect their jobs and have a greater say in how the railways should be run.

According to Wilf, Olive should be able to manage on a drop in his money because she was getting money from Emma, and the twins now they were working, as well as a monthly money order from Chris in the army. When his wife had screamed back at him that the kids were growing and would need winter coats and new boots, he had accused her again of being a lousy manager. At that point Emma had said that the twins only earned buttons and why couldn't he cut down on his baccy. She had received a mouthful of abuse for daring to interfere.

She ran in the direction of Trafford Street where one of the few pawnbrokers in Chester was situated. She was in luck. Her mother was coming out of the door as she approached Mr Pope's premises. 'Mam!' she called.

Olive's head swivelled on her scrawny neck but, instead of coming towards her daughter, she scuttled in the opposite direction. Emma went after her and grabbed her sleeve. 'You can't start this, Mam,' she said in a reasonable voice. 'It's not fair on the kids, not only missing out on their schooling but leaving them without a stitch on. It's not decent.'

'It's none of your business,' said Olive, struggling to free herself. 'You get yerself another job if yer care so much.'

That remark infuriated Emma and, with her free hand, she delved into her mother's coat pocket. As luck would have it, she hit on the right one and drew the pawn tickets out along with a handful of coins.

Olive dragged herself free and lunged for the money, managing to seize a few pennies. 'Why do you bloody have to interfere? It's going to cost you to redeem them. A penny in the shilling interest you'll have to pay. Have you got that, girl?' She glared at Emma before stalking off.

Reluctantly Emma unpinned the brooch on her lapel, a present from Chris for her thirteenth birthday. He had told her that it was real silver and the gems were agate. She did not want to part with it but, hopefully, she would be able to redeem it one day.

With the money the pawnbroker gave her, and what she had taken from her mother's pocket, she was able to get the children's clothes and boots out of hock. She hurried home to find them still alone in the house. 'Hasn't Mam been back?' she asked.

They shook their heads and reached across the blankets for their clothing and boots. Soon they were dressed but Emma knew the older ones would not be able to get into school until lunchtime because the gates would be locked. 'I'll get Dad to write you notes when he comes in for his meal,' she said, knowing she was going to have to conjure something up for them all to eat. She went out again and bought vegetables, barley and a shin bone to make soup.

Her mother was still absent when the stocky figure of her father appeared in the doorway, wanting his midday meal. Emma told him what had happened as she cut bread to have with the broth. She could not help adding, 'Surely you get some tips from the passengers? Couldn't you give her a few extra pennies?'

'Like hell I will.' He rubbed his fat button of a nose. 'How many times do I have to tell you, girl, keep your trap shut. I work bloody hard for my money. Fifteen and a half hours a day and conditions are worse than they were ten years ago. I'm entitled to some pleasure. I need those tips for me baccy and the odd drink with me workmates.'

Emma felt like saying he'd had enough pleasure giving his wife eight children, but knew he'd accuse her of filthy talk. She decided the only way to help her mother was for her to move out. In the meantime, she produced paper and a pencil and wrote notes for the kids to take to school, saying their mother had been sick and so they'd overslept, and got her father to sign them. She hoped the excuse would satisfy the teachers.

Once everyone but herself and Johnny had left the house, Emma changed into her Sunday best, planning on going out as soon as her mother arrived home. She had been saying for ages she would visit the other Servants' Registry Office in Grosvenor Place but never had. This afternoon she was determined to get her name on their books.

Olive entered the house half an hour later. Before her mother could open her mouth, Emma said, 'I don't want to hear it, Mam. I'm off.' And she hurried out.

As she passed the cocoa house Emma recalled that glimpse of the wedding party dressed in their finery. She thought of her brothers and sisters and her mother pawning their clothes and boots and could not suppress a stab of envy. What wouldn't she give to have a job similar to that of that young woman, Alice.

'Have you managed it?' called Victoria, from her place in the driving seat.

'Yes, Miss Victoria!' Alice wiped her grimy hands on a rag and held her head to one side, listening to the note of the engine. Satisfied, she placed the starting handle and the rag behind the front passenger seat and climbed in next to her mistress. She closed the door and retied the bow in the long chiffon scarf anchoring her straw hat firmly onto her auburn curls.

'Ready?' said her employer, slanting a smiling glance. Alice nodded. 'Then let's be on our way. I just can't wait to get there,' said Victoria.

Before they could set off a woman's voice said pleasantly, 'Good morning, Miss Waters. Not a very nice day – but I do believe Mr Waters and his dogsbody will be home today.'

Victoria's mouth fell open and she stared at her neighbour for several seconds before demanding, 'How did you know that, Mrs Black? I only knew myself a couple of hours ago.'

Eudora Black's mud-coloured eyes gleamed with a wicked amusement. 'Do remember me to Thomas when you see him. I do hope he's not in too much pain.' She saluted Victoria with her umbrella and strolled towards the footbridge.

Victoria shook her head. 'She's got a nerve referring to Papa by his Christian name. As far as I'm aware they've never met.'

'She's got plenty of nerve. Probably she wants us to believe a spiritual messenger told her that Mr Waters' ship was docking in Liverpool today, when it's probably just servants' gossip,' said Alice in a seething voice.

'No doubt you're right but one has to admit that Hamlet had something when he said, "*There are more things in heaven and earth, Horatio, than are dreamt of in your philosophy*,"' said Victoria.

Alice looked baffled. 'Who's Hamlet?'

Victoria smiled. 'Of course, you won't have read Shakespeare. He might have been a mere man but he was definitely England's greatest playwright. In more than one of his plays a ghost appears with messages for the living.' Victoria set the car in motion and they headed along Victoria Crescent in the direction of the old Dee Bridge.

Alice's brow knitted. 'You don't really believe that people can get in touch with the dead, do you, Miss Victoria?'

'Depends if you believe everything that's written in the

Bible. The witch of Endor supposedly summoned up the ghost of the prophet Samuel for King Saul.'

'I know, but the Bible says it's wrong, so Mrs Black shouldn't be doing it,' asserted Alice.

'That's true. But I have heard that, as a healer, she's helped quite a number of people. She does seem to have trouble keeping maids – which, I suppose, isn't surprising in the circumstances,' mused Victoria. 'I have to admit that Hamlet seeing his father's ghost didn't do him a bit of good. By setting out to avenge his father's death, he and most of the main characters end up dead.'

'Not my idea of an evening's entertainment,' muttered Alice, thinking of Bert and how he was out for revenge. Only a couple of days ago Hannah had received an anonymous letter but from reading its contents, it could only be from Bert. There had been no postmark so she supposed Bert had either slipped it through Hannah's letterbox himself, or got someone else to do it for him. She shivered as she remembered what he had written in the letter.

Dear Hannah,

Did you think I'd forgotten you because I haven't been in touch for a while? As if I would! I proved I can get to Tilly so now it's your turn. You hurt me by telling Kenny what I did and Mother finding out. I know where you live and I'll keep my eye on you. You'll never know when I'm watching and ready to pounce. One day I'll take you somewhere, so the two of us can be alone, and then I'll show you just how forgiving I am.

He had written something obscene after that and added three *x*'s. He was sick, that's what he was – sick!

For the umpteenth time, she tried to convince herself

that he wouldn't find it so easy to abduct Hannah; she wasn't a child that could be persuaded to go with him.

'You're very quiet, Alice,' said Victoria as they crossed the bridge over the Dee. 'Nervous about seeing Sebastian after all this time?'

Roused from her reverie, Alice forced a smile. 'Yes! You're certain his mother hasn't mentioned me in her letters to him, Miss Victoria?'

Victoria shook her head ruefully. 'How many times have I told you that I gave Gabrielle strict instructions not to say a word if she were to write to him?'

Alice flushed. 'Sorry. It's just that she still behaves like she despises me, so I can't see her wanting Seb to take up with me again. Sometimes I imagine her sticking pins in a wax figure, hoping I'll take bad and that'll be the end of me.'

Victoria gasped. 'Alice, what a thing to say! Gabrielle is a good Catholic. You hurt her only son. She has such a proud and fiery nature, which means she can't forgive easily. You're just going to have to try harder to show her that you're worthy of Sebastian. Of course you're not a Catholic, so she'll expect you to change your religion and marry in her church.'

Alice's green eyes flashed. 'That I won't do. Mam would turn over in her grave if I did that. It's not Gabrielle I want to marry, so she'll just have to accept things if Seb decides *he* can forgive me and will give me a second chance. Then it's up to us where we get married.'

'Oh dear! You do feel strongly about it. Perhaps we'd best change the subject. I do believe it looks like rain.' Victoria glanced up at the sky. 'We might have to put up the hood soon.'

By the time she had navigated the bustling Upper Bridge Street and Foregate Street on a market day, it had begun to rain. So she stopped the car outside the Cathedral and both of them climbed out. As they struggled with the hood, Alice looked at her anxiously. 'You shouldn't be doing this, Miss Victoria, with your dicky heart. What we need is a man.' The words were scarcely out of her mouth when one swam into their vision.

'Want a hand?' asked the blond giant.

'That's very kind of you,' gasped Victoria, stepping aside and placing a hand to her breast. 'There are definitely some jobs that a man can do better than a woman, Mr...?'

'Davies. David Davies.' He pushed his cap to the back of his head and took her place, smiling across at Alice. Within minutes the metal rods clicked into position – but before he could go to Alice's aid, a young woman got alongside her and helped snap the other side of the hood into place.

'Just like a giant pram's hood, isn't it?' said Emma.

Alice stared at her. 'Have we met before?'

'Yes! In Brook Street cocoa house. It was the day after Empire Day and it was throwing it down. Name's Emma Griffiths.' She held out her hand.

Alice shook it. 'Thanks for your help, Emma. I'm Alice. Alice Moran.'

'We really must be on our way, Alice,' said Victoria, accepting David's help to climb into the driving seat. 'Thank you for your help, Mr...' Victoria's voice faltered. 'Sorry, I've forgotten your name.'

'Davies.' He stepped away from the car.

'Of course,' said Victoria. 'Sorry, but we must dash. Apparently the Channel Fleet is anchored in the Mersey for Liverpool's seventh centenary celebrations and there could be a long queue for the luggage boat at Birkenhead. We're meeting my father from one of the liners.'

Emma stepped back as the vehicle began to move. Alice waved. 'Perhaps we'll bump into each other again,' she called.

'Now which one of us was that meant for, d'yer think?' asked Emma, glancing at David.

'I didn't think she really noticed me,' he murmured,

gazing after the car. Then he looked down at Emma and she saw the sudden flash of recognition in his grey eyes. 'We've met before, too. Now there's a coincidence!'

'I can give you another coincidence,' said Emma, holding on to her hat. 'I saw Alice for the first time, the same day as I did you.'

'Now fancy that,' he said, dragging his cap forward to shield his eyes from the rain. 'I can go even further with the coincidences if you're related to Wilf Griffiths, porter at the General Station.'

'Guilty as charged,' said Emma, craning her neck to read his expression. 'He's my dad. I hope yer not going to say yer can see a family resemblance.'

He smiled faintly and bent his head, dislodging several raindrops from the brim of his cap onto her upturned face. 'Not at all, lovey. You're much prettier.'

'Flattery won't get yer anywhere...I'm sworn off men.' She wiped her face with a hand.

'Has that anything to do with what you had me write down in the Servants' Registry Office?' His expression was suddenly serious.

Before she could answer, a strong gust of wind whipped the hat from Emma's head. He reached out a long arm and managed to prevent it from being blown away. 'Thanks! It's the only hat I've got.' She smiled at him. 'Yer second good deed for the day.'

'So us men do have our uses,' he said, grinning.

'I wouldn't deny it,' said Emma. 'But now I'd best be on my way.'

'If you're going home, perhaps I can walk with you.'

She shrugged and pulled on her hat. 'It's a free country, so yer can do what yer want.' She began to make her way up the side of the soot-begrimed sandstone cathedral. He fell into step beside her and, for a while, neither of them spoke. They were crossing Abbey Square when she asked him how he knew her dad.

David hunched his shoulders against the rain. 'I belong to one of the railwaymen's unions and your father asked a mate of mine to drop some literature off at his house. I happened to mention I was going that way and offered to do it for him.'

'Yer live near our street?' she asked, hanging on to her hat.

'No, but it's close enough to the Servants' Registry Office and I want to pop in there. Our last housekeeper has quit – but my aunt's sent a message saying she's got us someone else,' he added.

Emma stopped looking where she was going to look up at him and slipped on the cobbles. She would have fallen if he hadn't grabbed her and jerked her up against him. She was very conscious of the strength in those arms and her pulse raced. Reminding herself that it wouldn't be sensible to allow herself to be attracted to him, she quickly freed herself. 'I'm glad to hear it. Now how about you giving the stuff for Dad to me. If you go knocking on our door and my mam answers, she'll put it straight in the bin. He's been turning over less money since he joined the union and she's finding it difficult to make ends meet. Your other option is to go to the General Station and give it to him, yourself.'

He shook his head. 'If I was seen, I could be accused of inciting trouble. I could lose my job.'

'And what is your job, Mr Davies?'

'I'm an engine driver.'

Emma thought of her brother, Alf, whose ambition it was to drive a train, and smiled. 'At least yer better paid than me dad...but then yer do have more responsibility.'

A sharp laugh escaped him. 'You're right there, lovey. And the job's more dangerous due to the long hours we work...and safety regulations aren't all they're cracked up to be. That's why the union is such a good organisation to belong to. If we work together then we can make a difference and get the owners to shift their stance on lots of things.'

Emma knew he was right about the workers pulling together to change things. It was the same with the women's movement. If they were to improve a woman's lot in life, then they had to help each other. She held out a hand. 'Give it to me then.'

He smiled and took from an inside pocket a pamphlet and handed it to her. 'Thanks, lovey.'

'Anything to help the working classes.' She shoved the pamphlet inside her jacket. 'One thing – I'd tell yer mate not to count too much on Dad being a shining light for your cause.'

'Not many are but numbers are important.'

She agreed.

They both fell silent, thinking their own thoughts. They parted half way up Brook Street. 'Bye, Mr Davies. It was nice meeting you again,' she said politely.

'Good day to you, Miss Griffiths. Perhaps we'll bump into each other again sometime.' He raised his cap and walked away, shoulders hunched against the rain.

Emma arrived home to find her mother sitting on the sofa with her eyes closed. Johnny sat on the floor a few feet away, banging a couple of blocks of wood together. On Olive's lap was an envelope bearing a foreign stamp. Emma's face brightened and, forgetting the pamphlet inside her jacket, she reached for the letter. Droplets of rain fell on her mother's face.

'What the hell...' Olive's hand folded over the envelope and her eyes opened. At the same time the union literature slid down the inside of Emma's jacket and fell to the floor. Hastily she bent to pick it up.

'What's that yer've dropped?' asked Olive, getting to her feet.

'Nothing important.'

'Then leave it. I've been waiting for you to read this to

me.' She wafted the letter beneath her daughter's nose.

'Hang on, Mam! Let me get my things off.' Emma placed her sopping hat on the hearth to dry and hung her coat on the back of the door.

Olive had wandered across the room and was peering out of a rain splattered windowpane. 'The kids'll come in soaking wet. Hope you haven't been spending or it'll be bread and jam for tea. Put whatever you've got down and read our Chris's letter to me.'

Emma looked for somewhere to put the pamphlet but while she dithered her mother snatched it from her, placed it on the mantelpiece and thrust the letter in her hand.

Emma slit open the envelope with a finger, praying that it would say Chris was coming home. She loved her brother's letters because they were always full of colour and interest. This one told of bustling city life where fakirs walked on hot coals and boys disappeared up ropes, of hot, dusty plains and poisonous snakes that reared their heads to frighten men and horses. It was the kind of information her younger brothers and sisters loved hearing – but there was no mention of the unrest in India that she had read about in the newspapers. Probably, Chris didn't want to worry them. He asked after the family and ended with the news that he had been promoted to sergeant and there was talk of the regiment going to the Holy Land. She was disappointed that he wasn't coming home but at least Palestine was nearer than India.

'I don't know why you always have to read it all quiet to yerself first,' grumbled Olive. 'It makes me wonder if yer do that because there's something in it you don't want me to know about.'

'Yer know there's only two things you want to hear, Mam, and they're – is he coming home or is he due for a rise. Well, I can tell you that he's not coming home but he has been promoted to sergeant.'

Olive looked gleeful. 'Which means more money and

knowing my big son, he'll see that I get a share of it in my next money order.'

Emma sighed. 'I knew that's all yer cared about…knew you wouldn't want to hear about the snakes or the fakirs.'

'There, you've told me it all.' Olive sniffed. 'Now where did yer go when yer left here in a temper?'

'To check if there were any live-in jobs at the other Servants' Registry Office, but there wasn't anything suitable.' She picked up the pamphlet and managed to escape upstairs before her mother could ask any more questions. Tomorrow and tomorrow and tomorrow she would badger both registry offices for that elusive perfect job. She thought of Alice riding around in a motorcar with her employer: what she wouldn't give to be in her place.

Alice chewed on her lower lip and clenched her hands; her nerves were as taut as stretched drawer elastic. She rested her back against the car parked on the deck of the luggage boat, gazing across the surface of the river to where battleships were anchored as far as the eye could see. Despite the wet weather there were plenty of smaller boats, loaded with sightseers, threading their way between the naval giants because, in a day or so, the Channel Fleet would leave the Mersey.

Restlessly, she changed her position and looked towards the Liverpool waterfront with its famous docks. The last time she had been there had been with her father, terrified of what he might do to her after she had witnessed him pushing Mrs Kirk down the stairs. Leaving Hannah's mother unconscious, the crazed Mal had forced Alice to go on the run with him.

Suddenly Victoria, who was sitting in the driving seat, cried, 'Look, Alice, the *Baltic*. What a beautiful ship. I wish I could have sailed on her.'

Alice stared at the liner of the White Star Line and realised that the decks were almost deserted. 'It looks like most of the passengers have already left the ship,' she said.

Victoria nodded. 'You'd best get in the car. The ferry will be docking soon.'

Alice complied swiftly.

In no time at all a ramp was lowered and the car chugged onto the George's landing stage. Crowds of people were milling about, getting pestered by scruffy urchins wanting to carry their bags, whilst recommending a respectable hotel or boarding house. A short distance away vehicles were queuing up for the floating bridge that led to the dock road. Seagulls wheeled overhead and pigeons cooed on the roofs of the customs and baggage sheds on Princes Parade. It was there that Victoria headed, parking a few yards from the entrance.

Alice scrambled out of the front passenger seat and hurried to assist her employer from the motorcar. As they approached the doors, a handsome, middle-aged man, wearing a Homburg hat and a raincoat, emerged, walking stiffly, his gait uneven. He was supported by a dark curly-haired young man. Alice heard the hiss of Victoria's indrawn breath and then she was running, her hands outstretched.

'Papa!' she cried, flinging her arms round him.

Greedily, Alice stared at the dark-haired young man, remembering their first meeting four years ago. His attractive face had matured and his wiry frame had filled out so that his shoulders appeared broad in the navy blue suit he was wearing. He had not noticed her yet because his attention was focused on his employer and Victoria. Now the moment had come, Alice shied away from pushing herself forward to greet him. What if Seb rejected her? After all, she had rejected him.

Alice watched him speak to two youths lugging a couple of suitcases and a Gladstone bag. Suddenly she realised that her employer was beckoning her. She hurried forward, not taking her eyes from Seb's face. She knew when he recognised her by the widening of his eyes and the slight flaring of his nostrils. When he spoke his voice sounded flat, devoid of emotion. 'Alice, what are you doing here?'

Victoria looked disappointed. 'Is that all you've got to say, Sebastian? Alice has been working for me for ages but we kept it quiet so as to surprise you.'

'You've certainly done that, Miss Victoria.' His voice shook and there was no mistaking his anger.

Victoria reddened and glanced at Alice, who was doing her best to appear indifferent to his reaction but inside she was howling like an animal in pain.

'Who is this young woman?' demanded Mr Waters, staring at Alice.

Victoria heaved a sigh. 'Alice Moran, Papa. She works for me. I don't know how I'd have managed without her with you and Sebastian being away so long.'

'Then she's welcome,' said Mr Waters and smiled at Alice.

Sebastian's dark eyes regarded the woman in front of him. 'Well, I have a surprise for you both.'

Mr Waters' smile deepened. 'You tell them, Sebastian.'

'Tell us what?' asked Victoria, her eyes going from one man's face to the other.

Before Sebastian could speak, Mr Waters said, 'An engagement could be imminent. Sebastian met a lovely young woman whilst we were staying in New York. A volunteer at the hospital – her family's respectable and comfortably off – and they've taken quite a shine to this young man.' He patted Sebastian's arm. 'There was talk of her visiting England in the not too distant future. Isn't that correct, Sebastian?'

He nodded curtly.

Alice stared at him, her spirits sinking further. She wanted to weep. Muttering an 'Excuse me,' and with her head held high, she blundered over to the car and picked up the starting handle. She stood there, clutching it to her breast as if her life depended on it. She felt so miserable that she wanted to curl up and die.

When the others came over, she avoided looking at Sebastian as he helped Mr Waters into the front passenger seat and Victoria into the rear seat, paid off the youths and strapped the luggage onto the back of the car. Alice inserted the starting handle in its socket, thinking this could be for the last time. There was no way she could stay on working for Miss Victoria now Sebastian had fallen for someone else. Why couldn't he have written, hinting that he had met another woman and an engagement was on the cards?

'What the hell are you doing?' demanded Seb, startling Alice so much that she fell forward onto her knees.

She averted her eyes. 'What does it look like I'm doing? I'm going to crank the engine as I do every time Miss Victoria uses the car. I presume you'll be doing the driving, so hadn't you better get in the driving seat? I'm not down here for the good of my health, you know.' She was proud that she had managed to get all those words out without stuttering or breaking down.

'It's no job for a woman.' He lowered himself onto his haunches and reached for the handle but she kept a firm hold on it.

'Typical remark from a man,' she muttered. 'I've managed all these months while you've been away, so you do your job and I'll do mine.'

'You're not here to give me orders,' he said through gritted teeth. 'And what on earth *are* you doing here? You were as jealous as hell of Miss Victoria last time we met. You wanted me to leave Mr Waters' employment and walked out of my life when I refused.'

Before Alice could respond, Thomas Waters bellowed, 'Sebastian, is there something wrong? Are you driving this motorcar or not?'

Alice gazed into Sebastian's furious face. *This isn't*

finished, he mouthed silently before saying loudly, 'Yes, sir. Coming.'

As soon as the engine sounded sweet in her ears, Alice drew out the starting handle and climbed into the back seat alongside Victoria. She caught her employer's arm with her elbow and apologised.

'Forget it, Alice. I guess you're in a bit of a state,' she whispered sympathetically. 'I'm so sorry...as well as surprised that Papa seems so delighted with the idea of Seb marrying an American. I wonder what she's like. I guess we'll get to see.'

Her words dismayed Alice. Had Seb told his future fiancée about how close they had been in the past? She felt mortified and knew for definite that she would have to seek new employment. It would be too painful to stay and watch Seb with his new love, knowing that she only had herself to blame.

Chapter Four

September, 1907

Alice was tense as a violin string as she pushed open the door of the Servants' Registry Office on Brook Street a week later. She expected to see Mrs Roberts behind the counter but instead there were two people in the room, whom to her amazement she recognised. They appeared deep in conversation and seemed unaware of her existence. She sat on a bench and soon realised they were talking about the troubles on the railways. The blond giant, Mr Davies, was an engine driver, apparently, and firmly believed he should receive danger money on top of his wages; whilst Miss Griffiths was talking about her father only earning eighteen shillings a week as a porter at the General Station. Believing the conversation might continue for some time, Alice decided to interrupt them.

'Excuse me! Is Mrs Roberts around?' she asked tentatively.

David glanced in her direction. 'In the back, Miss. I'll get her for you, shall I?' Then he stared at her. 'Haven't we met before?'

'Yes, as it happens.' Alice smiled sadly. 'A week ago you helped put the hood up on Miss Victoria's car, and so did Miss Griffiths.'

'It's Alice Moran,' said Emma, her eyes filled with a lively curiosity. 'What are you doing here? I hope you haven't lost your job. Your mistress didn't seem a bad sort.'

'Oh, she's OK!' said Alice. 'Only it's...erm... circumstances are forcing me out.'

Emma glanced at David and said firmly, 'Well, go and tell Mrs Roberts there's someone to see her.' He hesitated but she nudged his arm and reluctantly he went into the back premises. Emma turned back to Alice. 'Randy ol' man in the house, is there? I know the sort. Can't keep his hands to himself.'

'No! It's nothing like that,' said Alice, shocked.

Emma nodded. 'If yer say so…but if it's not that then why are yer leaving?'

Alice hesitated and then burst out, 'You're right in thinking there's a man involved. He's an old flame, who works for Miss Victoria's father, who's been in America but is now home. The house just isn't big enough for the two of us now Seb's found himself someone else.'

Emma said eagerly, 'Nice bloke Miss Victoria's father, is he?'

'I don't know him that well. The house is his mother's and she's going senile.'

'And he's never laid a finger on yer since he's been home?'

Alice shook her head and smiled faintly. 'He'd have a job catching me. He had an accident in the Spring and damaged his hip; he still has trouble walking.'

Emma's face lit up. 'Well, if it's like that – why don't yer give me their address? I'll be there like a shot because I'm looking for a live-in position.'

Alice was taken aback. 'I don't know if you'd suit. I'm not just a maid, you know! I'm Miss Victoria's dogsbody.'

Emma wrinkled her nose. 'What's that involve?'

'I fetch and carry, take messages – write letters if she's not up to it. I do all sorts of other things, as well – like, I make her hats. I've had some training as a milliner.'

Emma was thoughtful, 'The hats might be a problem but I'm prepared to have a go at the rest. By the way, if yer've come here looking for the same kind of job then yer in the wrong place. Mrs Roberts handles domestics, pure and simple.'

Alice's face fell. 'In that case, maybe I should think again.'

No sooner had she said those words than David reappeared. 'She won't be a minute.' He smiled at Alice. 'It's nice to see you again. How are you doing?'

'How am I doing?' Her face quivered. 'I think I've made a mistake. Bye!' On those words she walked out the office.

David looked crestfallen. 'What did I say?'

Emma shrugged. 'I don't think it's anything we said. There goes a troubled woman. Time I was going.' She lifted her bag from the counter. 'Be seeing yer. I hope your new housekeeper is better than the last one.' She left as Mrs Roberts bustled in from the back.

As Emma walked slowly home, she thought about David and how well they got on. She also thought about Alice and her mention of an old flame. Emma remembered the expression on David's face when Alice had left. Perhaps he fancied her. The thought irritated her. Then she shrugged. Why should she care if he did fancy her? She wasn't on the hunt for a husband. She'd seen enough of married life to make her think twice about tying the knot. As for falling in love, no thanks! Look what love had done for Aggie. She sighed. What had happened to her determination to trace that swine? As soon as she got herself another live-in job she would definitely do something about finding Annie and making a start on her enquiries. Right now she was ready for a nice cup of tea and a thick slice of toast.

Hannah placed the hotpot in the oven of the black-leaded range and then straightened up. She glanced in the direction of the table where Tilly was chalking on a slate that Kenny had bought her. This time next year the girl would be at school and Hannah was determined she would know her letters and be able to count to ten by then. Once she wanted to be a teacher but her mother had told her it was out of the question.

Reminded of her mother, Hannah sighed and wished she would stop calling round every day. She knew she was fond of Tilly but Susannah had started to ask questions about why Hannah hadn't started a baby yet. She wondered how her mother could be so thoughtless, knowing what she did. She had almost been tempted to tell her about Bert's threatening letters.

Yesterday, Hannah had received another one. Its reference to the past had filled her with such anguish that, instead of showing it to Kenny, she had burnt it, poking the charred remains until they had completely disintegrated. Whilst up in Scotland on honeymoon, Hannah had been able to put Bert out of her mind and her marriage had been consummated but since returning home and the arrival of more letters from Bert, she was finding it more and more difficult to relax and allow Kenny to be intimate with her. As soon as he lifted her nightgown and she felt his bare flesh against hers, panic rose inside her and she went rigid. Last night he had soothed her, holding her in his arms and kissing her tear-stained face, telling her it didn't matter. But of course it did. As well as trying to ruin her life, Bert was now threatening to find Alice and make her pay for jilting him.

'Look!' Tilly held up the slate. Relieved at being distracted from her thoughts, Hannah went over to the girl and sat at the table. As she took the slate from her, she thought how attractive Tilly looked in the powder blue frock, covered by a white starched pinafore, frilled at the hem and over the shoulders. 'You're not saying anything,' said Tilly, pulling on her arm.

Hannah gazed down at the drawing of the cat and smiled. It was cross-eyed and its head was much too big for its body. Even so Tilly had caught its likeness near enough. 'Clever, Tilly! You must take after Kenny. He's good at getting a likeness too.' Kenny was a bookkeeper for Mr Bushell, the coal merchant, and any spare time he had was spent writing articles and drawing cartoons, which he sent off to the *Chester Chronicle* and the Liverpool's

Daily Post. 'Now let's write the word CAT underneath your drawing – and in the corner your name.'

Carefully Hannah wrote c-a-t and then M-a-r-t-h-a M-a-t-i-l-d-a M-o-r-a-n, saying each letter aloud as she did so. Hannah was ambitious for the girl, dreaming of *her* becoming a teacher one day. Hannah had attended meetings of the Women's Suffrage Movement where some women advocated better education and opportunities for girls like Tilly, so she was making certain that if the opportunity should arise then the girl would be prepared.

Tilly climbed onto her knee and snuggled up against her, demanding a story. Hannah was happy to sit and tell her fairy stories, it helped her to forget her problems for a while. She gazed into the blazing fire, grateful that Kenny's working for Mr Bushell meant they were never short of coal. Tilly relaxed in her arms, Hannah's own eyelids began to droop.

'*Little pig, little pig, let me in*!'

She started and struggled to open her eyes. Sleepily she looked in the direction of the window and her heart seemed to jerk inside her breast. Carefully, as if in a dream, she got up and placed Tilly on the sofa before walking slowly over to the window. A sheet of paper appeared to be stuck to the outside. Bump, bump, bump went her heart. She did not want to believe that Bert had climbed over the backyard wall and shouted the words from the nursery rhyme, which he had once shouted outside her bedroom door. She reached out a hand. The paper vanished and a grinning face flattened itself against the window. Hannah had time only to recognise Bert before she slid to the floor, unconscious.

Kenny put his key in the lock and the mouth-watering smell of hotpot welcomed him in. 'I'm home, Hanny,' he shouted.

He removed his shoes and padded into the back room in

his stockinged feet, only to freeze at the sight of his wife on the floor. For a moment Kenny felt as if his heart stopped beating and then he took a deep breath. Crossing the room he slipped his arms beneath her and lifted her up. He was about to place her on the sofa when he saw Tilly curled up fast asleep, so he looked about him for somewhere else to put Hannah. It was then that she stirred in his arms, her eyelids fluttered open, and she gazed anxiously up into his face before smiling at him. His relief was intense. 'Thank God! I found you on the floor. What happened?'

She did not answer him immediately but frowned and, twisting in his arms, gazed towards the window. Bert had been outside! She looked round for Tilly and saw her asleep on the sofa. She sighed with relief, glad the back door had been locked and she had removed the key on a string from the front door. Kenny had insisted on her taking no chances when she was alone in the house since the first letter had arrived.

'Hanny, are you OK?' said Kenny, giving her a little shake.

She decided he had to know the truth. 'I was telling stories to Tilly and I dozed off. Then I heard a voice saying '*Little pig, little pig, let me in*!' I looked towards the window.' She moistened her lips. 'Bert was there grinning at me through the glass. I was so terrified I must have fainted.'

'I'm going to report this to the police.' Kenny's expression was grim as he felt her head. 'There's a bump here. You're sure you're OK?'

'I'm fine. You can put me down now.'

'If you're sure?'

'Of course, I'm sure.' She kissed his cheek. 'I'll see to supper while you get washed.'

'No! Supper can wait. I'll get washed and changed then I'm going to report this to the police.' Kenny set Hannah on her feet and then ran water in the sink.

Hannah watched him removed his outer clothes and hang them on a hook on the inside of the door. 'If you think it'll do some good. Will you tell them about the letter?'

Kenny nodded. He loved his wife and, although it was frustrating and a grief to him that Bert was still managing to come between them, he was determined to do something about it and not let it get him down. The worst thing in life he could imagine was losing Hanny and he worried constantly that, somehow, Bert would get to her. He washed his hands, neck and face at the sink, drying them on a rough towel.

Hannah smiled at him and then kissed him. 'I love you,' she said.

At that moment Tilly woke and rolling over, gazed at them for several minutes. Then she laughed and slid off the sofa and skipped over to Kenny. 'I want a love too,' she said, holding up her arms to him.

Kenny lifted his half sister onto his knee and hugged her to him. He was so grateful that he had the two of them to love and was loved in return – and who was to say that he mightn't get his hands on Bert one day and choke the life out of him. He went upstairs and got changed and left the house.

But Kenny was to get little satisfaction from the police. The sergeant on the desk said that as Bert had made no attempt to break into the house and attack Hannah, no charge could be brought again him. Regarding the threatening letter, without it to show as evidence, there was no proof of his having sent it. The only comfort Kenny could draw on from his visit was that if Bert were to send any more letters then he could take them straight along to the police station. Also, the bobby on the beat would be alerted to keep a watch out for a man answering to Bert's description in the vicinity of Hannah's and Kenny's home.

* * *

Bert hummed beneath his breath as he took off his overcoat and hung it on a hook in the tiny lobby. A black and white cat stropped his trouser leg and he pushed it away with the side of his foot.

'Is that you, Mr Temple?' called a woman's voice.

Bert had decided that having a pseudonym was not only fun but sensible. 'Unless you've got yourself another lodger, Mrs Evans,' he responded in jocular tones.

'You will have your joke,' she said with a chuckle, popping her grey head round the kitchen door. 'Your supper's ready.'

'And excellent suppers you make, Mrs Evans. The sun was really shining on me when I was led to your door.' Bert smiled as he removed his cap and smoothed his flaxen hair. 'I'll just have a quick wash and change. I had to go on an errand for the boss to Chester – and what with all the smuts from the engine, I feel filthy.'

As he went upstairs, Bert thought back to the day he had arrived here. He had been taken on by a shipping engineering works in Ellesmere Port – where the Shropshire Union Canal joined the Manchester Ship Canal – and whilst strolling round the town had seen a card in a shop window advertising a room to rent and that's how he had found Mrs Evans. His landlady was a widow; her children had married and moved away so she was lonely.

She looked after him well, although, of course, she could never take the place of his mother. His blue eyes were bleak as he remembered Susannah sending him away, despite his knowing she was hurting as much as he was at the time. Over six months had passed since then and he was hoping that she would be ready to see him now.

As he removed his jacket and shirt, his mind was composing a letter to his mother. Its tone would be very different to the ones he had sent to Hannah. He laughed suddenly, remembering her terrified face through the window earlier that day. Yet, he had no intention of hurting her physically. No! He just wanted to make sure that she would never forget what had happened between them. As for Alice – his eyes darkened and his mouth set in an ugly line – he had every intention of making her pay dearly for jilting him and playing her part in making his mother so distressed she had felt that she had to send him away.

Alice sat in the back of the motor car, eavesdropping on Victoria's conversation with Seb in the front. They had been shopping and were now on their way home. She was asking him whether the letter he had received that morning from America had given any hint to when they could expect a visit from his lady friend. He muttered something indistinct about Juliana having to fulfil other commitments before she could arrange to come to England. Alice found some comfort in hearing those words. It was difficult enough living in close proximity with Seb, without having to cope with seeing him with the new woman in his life. She wondered, not for the first time, just what Seb had told his future wife about her. Was he in love with the American as much as he had been with her? If he was then perhaps they would get married before the year was out.

She gazed at the back of his head where his dark hair curled into the nape of his neck. He seemed so much more confident and refined since his return. Perhaps it was Juliana and her family thinking so much of him that had boosted his morale. Her heart ached. The memory of their kisses made her doubly realise what a fool she had been to give him up. If she had been sensible they could have been married by now and there would have been no need for her to have ever got involved with Bert. Thank God, he had no idea where to find her. How different it was for poor Hanny. Could his mother have possibly told him where her eldest daughter and Kenny lived or had it been one of the neighbours, who believed he could do no wrong?

To Alice's surprise, as the car neared the house, she caught sight of Hannah leaning against Mrs Black's garden wall. Alice waved and called her name. Hannah looked up and, lifting her skirts, ran after the car. By the time she caught up with the vehicle, it had parked and Alice was holding open the garden gate for Victoria to pass through. Seb, who was unloading the shopping, glanced her way. 'Hanny!' he exclaimed in astonishment.

Hannah's face lit up. 'Seb, how are you? It's lovely to see you.'

He smiled. 'Nice of you to say so.'

'I presume Alice has told you that Kenny and I were married in June,' she said.

Without looking at Alice, Seb shook his head. 'We haven't really had a chance to talk.' He bent his head and dropped a kiss on Hannah's cheek. 'Congratulations. I wish you and Kenny all the best.'

Jealousy welled up inside Alice and, for an instant, she wanted to scratch her friend's eyes out but, instead, she demanded to know what Hannah was doing there.

'I had another letter yesterday,' she whispered, 'and also a visit from him.'

Alice stared at her, not wanting to believe her. 'What did he do?' she breathed.

'He just grinned at me through the window.' Hannah shuddered. 'It was horrible! Kenny doesn't know about the letter because I burnt it...but I thought you should know that *he* threatened to find *you*.'

Alice's nervous fingers released the gate and it banged shut. 'You're serious,' she said in a trembling voice.

Hannah nodded. 'Kenny went to the police but they said they couldn't do anything as he didn't break in,' she whispered.

'What about the letters?'

'I should have kept them as proof. I will the next one.'

Alice's bottom lip quivered and she had to clear her throat before asking, 'You weren't followed?'

'Only by our Joy watching my back. No sign of him so far.'

Sebastian's frowning gaze went from Alice to Hannah. 'Who are you talking about? Is it Alice's dad she's scared of?'

'No,' said Alice shortly, thinking now was hardly the time to start explaining to him about her involvement with Bert. Besides, what right had she to expect any help from him even if he was prepared to give it? She took the astonished Hannah's arm. 'Let's go somewhere we can talk in private,' she whispered, hurrying her away.

Hannah glanced over her shoulder at Sebastian, a question in her eyes. He shrugged and walked up the garden path, carrying the shopping. Hannah withdrew her arm from Alice's grasp and stared at her. 'When did Seb come home? Why haven't you sorted things out with him?'

Alice swallowed. 'It's too late for that.'

Hannah stared at her in dismay. 'What d'you mean *too late*? And hadn't you better check with Miss Victoria first that it's OK for you to come with me?'

Alice brushed her eyes with the back of her hand. 'I should have told you. He met someone at the hospital in New York. There's talk of an engagement and her coming over here. When she does I'll have to find another job and somewhere else to live. I did have one go at it but backed out when I realised I'd be just a domestic.'

Hannah's face fell. 'Oh lord!'

Alice rushed into further speech. 'You don't have to look like that. I'm not going to dump myself on you and Kenny. I'm going to get out of Chester and live somewhere else. I'll take Tilly with me. It's time I took responsibility for her.'

'Now stop right there,' said Hannah, scowling.'How

will you manage to support the pair of you? You'll end up in the workhouse in no time at all.'

Alice sniffed back tears. 'Most probably. Perhaps I'll go and live somewhere else on my own then. A place where I won't have to see Seb everyday and Bert can't find me…Manchester maybe.'

Hannah put her hands on her hips and cried, 'That's stupid! Even if you got a live-in job you wouldn't be able to afford the rail fare to visit us very often. You'd hardly see Tilly at all. Besides, you'd be lonely. You can't go running away,' she added firmly.

Alice felt like saying *It's easy for you to say that because you've got a husband now* but she knew Hannah's words made sense. 'OK. I won't run away but I must look for another position when Juliana comes.'

'Is that her name?'

Alice nodded, wiping her face with the back of her hand as they walked slowly side by side.

Hannah said, 'They can't have known each other long. It could be a flash in the pan. I wouldn't give up on him yet.'

'He hates me!' Alice reached for the handkerchief up her sleeve and blew her nose violently.

'Has he said he hates you?'

'If you could have seen the way he looked at me in Liverpool. He's hardly spoken to me since he's been back.'

'Well, you did throw him over.'

Alice stopped in the middle of the bridge and rested her arms on the rail, gazing down at the water. 'I don't want to talk about him anymore. What are we going to do about Bert? He'll probably have realised by now that Kenny'll have told the police. If only we knew where he was living.'

Before Hannah could agree, they were joined by Joy. She had been keeping a lookout at the other end of the bridge. 'No sign of him,' she said, leaning on the rail next to her sister. 'You do realise you're conspicuous standing here.'

Instantly Alice fled back the way she had come.

The sisters stared after her in astonishment. 'Should I go after her?' asked Joy.

A wan-faced Hannah shook her head.

Alice pushed open the Waters' gate and rushed up the path, blinded by tears. She went round to the back of the house and opened the door, hoping the kitchen was empty, only to find Seb's mother, Gabrielle, in the act of removing a steaming kettle from the gas ring. Their eyes met and the girl was surprised to see that the hauteur and suppressed anger, usually present when the woman looked at her, was missing.

'You hungry? I could make you a ham sandwich if you wish?' said Gabrielle, her dark eyes searching Alice's flushed face.

'Th – Thank you!' Alice wondered to what did she owe this change of attitude. Supposedly not a drop of English blood ran in Gabrielle's veins – and it was true that despite the navy blue dress, white apron, and frilled cap on her silver streaked black hair, there was something exotic about her. Victoria had once waxed lyrical about Seb's mother being like a tropical flower that had somehow managed to adapt to cooler climes without losing any of its beauty. Yet since Alice had come to live under the same roof as Seb's mother, there had been times when Gabrielle's accent had slipped, causing her to wonder just how foreign she was. The tale she had heard had been that old Mrs Waters had found Gabrielle singing outside a theatre in America. She had been dressed in rags and half-starved, so Victoria's grandmother had taken pity on her and brought her back to England.

'A cup of tea – or a mocha chocolate if you would prefer it?' said Gabrielle, pulling out a chair from the table and indicating that Alice sit down.

Alice blinked her astonishment. 'The latter, p – please.' Victoria had once said that the cook's mocha chocolate was out of this world but Gabrielle had never offered to make Alice a drink before. She sat on the chair and watched her percolate the coffee and melt chocolate in a bowl over a pan of hot water. Alice was bemused, but grateful for this lessening of the tension between them. She found her mind drifting, thinking about Bert and Seb, but was startled from her reverie by Gabrielle's voice.

'So what is your opinion of my son having found himself an American woman?'

Alice watched as she placed the steaming beverage on the well-scrubbed table. Then she lifted her eyes to the woman's handsome face. 'I hate her without having seen her and pray that she never comes here.'

Gabrielle smiled and placed a hand on her shoulder. 'An honest answer, that is good.' She pushed the plate of dainty ham sandwiches she had made across the table and sat opposite her. 'She is not in love with my son. I, his mother, can tell.' She pressed a clenched fist against her left breast. 'I feel it here. If she loved him then she would not have let him return home without her.'

Alice only just stopped herself from smiling. Seb's mother definitely liked to turn on the dramatics. 'What about him? Do you think he loves her?'

Gabrielle's expression changed and she reached for her own steaming mug. 'He tells me he is mad about her but he left her to her own devices in America. That is like a trumpet blast to me.' She took a deep draught of the mocha coffee. 'I ask myself is it possible she has an eye to Mr Waters.'

Alice almost dropped her sandwich. 'I can't see why. No one who could have Seb would look at Mr Waters.'

Gabrielle lowered her mug, revealing a creamy moustache above her upper lip. Her liquid brown eyes glinted. 'Pah! You are so young. It is true that my son is a handsome boy but Mr Waters is a man with his own business.'

Alice said bluntly, 'Well, if she wanted Mr Waters then

she's gone a funny way about it making up to Seb.'

Gabrielle closed her lips and swallowed and several moments passed before she said solemnly, 'It is possible that her parents thought Mr Waters too old for her and she decided to settle for my son for the moment. Maybe she will insist on his going to live in America if she and Sebastian marry. I wouldn't like that. You made mistakes in the past and there are little difficulties we would need to sort out if you were to marry my son, but you will not want to take him away from England.'

'Seb might refuse to go and live in America.'

'America is a beautiful country and a go-ahead young man could make his fortune there, so he could be tempted.' Gabrielle's eyes narrowed. 'There are a lots of rich Americans. I wonder how her family made its money.' She added with relish, 'I think a little detective work, that would not put to shame Mr Sherlock Holmes himself, is needed. We will prove she is unworthy of him and then there will be a chance of my son turning to you.'

The woman was crackers, thought Alice. But she was not going to argue with Seb's mother in this mood. Whilst Gabrielle could not match her own father for cruelty and bullying, she knew she was just as determined to control her. As for her suggestion that she cast herself in the role of Sherlock Holmes to discover more about Juliana's family, that had to be a joke. She couldn't even find out where Bert was, never mind trying to delve into the past of a family that lived in America.

Maybe she should simply seek alternative employment. Emma's stories had been enough to put her off the idea of working as a domestic but there was always shop work or sewing, although that would mean finding another place to live and she could not afford to pay for lodgings with the kind of wages she would get. Again Alice thought of Emma, who had also been looking for a live-in position and wondered if she had had any luck with her search.

Chapter Five

October, 1907

Emma entered the Servants' Registry Office in Grosvenor Place just in time to see a woman, dressed strikingly in an outfit of red and black, at the counter.

'The last girl really was no use to me at all, Mr Jones,' she said in a voice that carried. 'I need someone with vision, plenty of common sense, and who is utterly loyal and discreet.'

'You're asking too much. You didn't tell me what went on in your house, Mrs Black,' he said, shaking his head. 'Some of these girls come fresh from the country and find what you do frightening. I have to confess that I don't approve either.'

The woman laughed. 'I don't seek your approval, Mr Jones. I don't need it. I will pay you a handsome fee if you find me the right girl.'

He flushed. 'I'll do my best but I can't promise anything. Good day to you.'

'Good day to you, too. Such a pity you feel the way you do, I could have helped you with your problem.' Mrs Black smiled as his jaw dropped, and made for the exit, wielding her umbrella like a wand.

Emma watched her departure with interest before taking her place at the counter. Mr Jones was opening and closing the ledger, and muttering, 'Now where is my pen? I know I had it here. What did she mean problem? I have no problem. I'm perfectly well.'

'So what about a live-in job? Preferably no men in the household?' said Emma, resting her elbows on the counter and gazing at him hopefully.

The man lifted his eyes and sighed. 'Not you again! No, Miss Griffiths, I have nothing for you.'

'What about that woman who's just gone out?' Emma jerked her head in the direction of the outer door. 'She sounded needy.'

Mr Jones's manner thawed slightly. 'Well, she certainly meets your criteria and you've enough nerve for anything.' He found his pen and, dipping it in the inkpot, wrote down a name and address. 'She lives the other side of the river in one of those big houses not far from Queen's Park Bridge…Victoria Crescent. Tell her I sent you.'

Emma thanked him, and was glad she had put on her Sunday best.

'There is just one other thing, Miss Griffiths. You'd best be prepared.' He fidgeted with the blotter. 'Mrs Black is a self-professed healer and medium. According to the last two girls, very strange things happen in her home.'

His words came as a surprise but Emma was determined not to be put off. She'd rather put up with ghosts than continue to live at home or risk becoming the object of an old man's lust again.

As Emma sauntered across the footbridge over the Dee, a young woman brushed past her on the way into town. She murmured an apology and hurried on. Gazing after her, she felt certain it was Alice Moran. It was at least a month since she had last seen her. Was it possible that she worked over this side of the river? Emma hoped she did, pleased at the thought of having someone she knew nearby – always assuming she got the job with the medium.

Emma pushed open the gate into a garden that was bright with the last of the chrysanthemums. The house was much bigger than that of the Stones'. It had large bay windows on the ground floor and a shiny black front door. I reckon I could enjoy living in here, as long as it wasn't too scary, thought Emma, as she pulled on the bell.

The door opened almost immediately and the woman she had seen in the Servants' Registry Office stood in the doorway. She had removed her hat and coat and was clad in a plain black skirt, a red blouse and a braided black velvet waistcoat. She gazed down at Emma in silence, and the girl was unnerved by that unblinking stare.

'You're here about the job. Do come in.' Mrs Black smiled and stood to one side and, with a sweep of a large capable looking hand, waved Emma inside.

Emma took a deep breath, crossed her fingers and stepped over the threshold into a large hall. Her eyes widened as she gazed on walls papered with golden dragons on a red flock background, she was entranced.

'Upstairs,' said Mrs Black, slipping past her and leading the way.

Emma followed her, sparing a glance to the doors up the lobby on the ground floor. She wondered what was down there. No doubt she would find out. She was led into a room on the first floor.

Mrs Black went over to a french window, opened it, and stepped outside. 'I like to sit out here and watch people enjoying themselves,' she called over her shoulder. 'I have lodgers renting three of the rooms downstairs. Their view isn't half as good as this. Do come and look.'

Emma hurried over but hesitated to step outside onto the wrought iron balcony that overlooked the river. There didn't appear to be much room for two people and she was scared of heights. Then she reminded herself that she needed this job and, not wanting Mrs Black to consider her a coward, took a deep breath and stepped outside. She stuck close to the wall of the house, resting a hand lightly against the brickwork but even from where she stood, she could hear people's voices and see the river. Although, at this time of year there were few enjoying the pleasures of boating.

'Are you interested in people, Miss...?'

'Griffiths. Emma Griffiths. Mr Jones told me about yer ghosts.' As soon as the words were out Emma could have kicked herself. Discretion; that's what this woman wanted in a servant. Perhaps she wouldn't employ her now. 'Sorry! I shouldn't have said that,' she said, grimacing.

'Ghosts?' Mrs Black shook her head sadly. 'Those who have passed over are living souls, Emma. You must try and think of them as being just like you and me, needing to communicate with those they loved and who love them.'

'I wish I could,' said Emma bluntly. 'Our poor Aggie…' She stopped.

'Go on,' urged Mrs Black, her mud coloured eyes intent on the girl's face. Emma had not intended mentioning her sister and was unsure whether she wanted to talk about her to this woman. 'Is Aggie your sister? Has she passed over?' Emma almost asked how did she know that, but then decided it wasn't so clever of Mrs Black as she'd only picked up on her saying *Our poor Aggie*. Unexpectedly there was a twinkle in the older woman's eyes. 'I know what you're thinking and you're right. Come back inside and I'll show you around. But you mustn't close your mind, dear, to the possibility of finding some comfort in believing the spirit lives on. Your sister could be happy in the other world.'

'Yes, Mrs Black,' said Emma politely. How could she believe Aggie was happy? She must have been deeply unhappy in her condition. Perhaps her spirit wasn't at rest, and if this woman was right, then maybe she might try and get in touch with her.

'An open mind and a closed mouth, as well as the usual chores that you would expect to do – and can you cook?' Mrs Black's voice brought Emma out of her reverie.

'Nothing fancy, missus. I'm good at soups, scones and can do a roast.'

'Bacon and eggs?'

Emma smiled. 'Sunday breakfast for me father – whereas us kids only ever saw a bit of bacon rind, if we were lucky.'

'I see.' Mrs Black paused a moment and then said, 'I shall

pay you two pounds a month and you'll live in, of course.'

Emma just managed to prevent her jaw from dropping. Junior male clerks on the railway were only paid five shillings a week and she'd have her board as well. What would this woman expect from her for all that? 'It – it's a lot of money,' she stammered.

Mrs Black smiled. 'I'll expect you to work hard for it. Now come this way.'

Emma was shown a bathroom, Mrs Black's bedroom, a room that she called the healing room and another where she did her sittings. Emma gazed about her, trying to sense if there was anybody there, aware that Mrs Black was watching her with a tiny smile playing about her mouth. Then she crooked a finger and Emma followed her up to the attics. She was shown to a bedroom in which the window was in the eaves and the ceiling slanted to a wall five feet from the floor on one side. The furniture consisted of a single bed, an armchair, a narrow wardrobe and a chest of drawers – on which stood a shaded oil lamp.

Mrs Black opened the wardrobe door and indicated two plain gowns, one grey, one dark blue, as well as two white aprons, pinned to which were two frilled mop caps. 'You might have to take up the hems. The last girl was a bit taller than you. There's bed linen in the chest of drawers.'

'Thank yer, missus.'

Mrs Black sighed. 'You will call me madam or Mrs Black…and try and say *you* not *yer*.'

'Yeah, madam. I mean… Yes, madam.' It was not the first time someone had tried to improve Emma's speech, so she took no offence. Her gaze shifted to the wall behind the bed where a framed text hung and read *How great are His signs, how mighty His wonders*.

Mrs Black's gaze followed hers. 'There was a different one when I first took over the house. It read *God's eyes are always upon you*. I presume it was to frighten the maid into making sure she did her job properly.'

Emma nodded, remembering the text in her room at the Stones', which had read *Thou shalt not steal*.

Mrs Black led the way out of the bedroom and downstairs to the ground floor. She showed Emma the kitchen. It was fitted out with a gas cooker, as well as an old black range and there were shelves with plenty of pots, pans and dishes, and a walk-in larder. Under the stairs was a cupboard in which were stored the ironing board, mops, buckets, brushes and one of those new-fangled vacuum cleaners. She had noticed electric switches in the main rooms upstairs and guessed there must be plug sockets, as well, for the vacuum cleaner. She had never used a vacuum cleaner before and felt a mixture of nervousness and excitement.

Scarcely able to believe her good fortune, Emma was delighted when Mrs Black told her to go home and ask her parents for their permission to enter her employment. If they agreed, then Emma was to hand in her notice with her present employers and move into Mrs Black's house as soon as possible.

'Oh, they'll agree,' said Emma with a chuckle, thinking not half they would when they knew how much she was to be paid – although perhaps she wouldn't tell them the exact amount, so she could start saving for a rainy day.

Later, as Emma crossed the river, she was reminded of that glimpse of Alice earlier in the day. She hoped they'd meet again so she could tell her that at last she had found the situation she wanted.

Alice was late. Having been sent by Miss Victoria to order some leaflets to be printed, she had made a diversion afterwards and called on Hannah so she could see Tilly and discover if there was any more news about Bert. She had stayed too long, enjoying her small sister's company, and discussing Bert. Kenny had walked with her as far as the bridge and then left her. She hurried on up the road to the crescent, wondering if Seb would be home. More often than not he was in Liverpool, dealing with Mr Waters' business matters. Victoria's father was still enduring pain and difficulty walking. This made him grumpy and he attempted to drown his sorrows by drinking too much, which, according to Gabrielle, was adding to his health problems.

Alice reached the front gate, breathless with having rushed across town. She paused for a moment to get her breath back and found herself remembering the first time she had seen Seb in this very garden.

As if the thought had conjured him up, he suddenly appeared from behind the motorcar, wiping his hands on an oily rag. She almost jumped out of her skin, and her mouth felt dry, and she was conscious of her dishevelled appearance as they gazed at each other without speaking.

'You've been ages.' His voice was brusque.

'I'm surprised you noticed.' She pushed open the gate and would have walked through if he had not seized her arm. 'Miss Victoria has had one of her turns and was asking for you.'

Immediately, Alice was all concern. 'Has the doctor been sent for?'

He nodded. 'Fortunately I was able to stay with her until the medicine did its job.'

'Good for you,' said Alice tartly, attempting to free herself but his grip tightened.

'There's no need to take that tone.' He frowned. 'Why did you have to take a job here?'

There was no way Alice was going to answer that honestly. 'I became interested in the emancipation of women and I needed a place to live when Dolly's husband came home from India because there was no room for me at Granny Popo's. Satisfied?'

'No! Why here? And what happened to your father?'

Alice raised her eyebrows in surprise. 'I thought Miss

Victoria might have told you by now – he's in a lunatic asylum.'

'No!' He looked taken aback. 'How did that happen?'

Alice hesitated. 'It's a long story and I've got no time to go into it now. Miss Victoria will be wondering where I am, so will you please let me go?'

He looked about to say something more but she wrenched her arm out of his grasp and ran up the path and round the side of the house. Immediately, she was aware of raised voices and thought she heard Mrs Black, as well as Miss Victoria, mentioned. Opening the kitchen door, Alice instantly found herself the focus of three pairs of eyes.

'I know you! Do you work here?' asked Mrs Waters, an upright, tightly corseted figure in a lilac twilled-cotton gown, who was sitting at the kitchen table with her son. The woman was definitely losing her marbles, thought Alice, wondering what she and her son were doing there.

Gabrielle scowled at her. 'Surely it did not take you all this time to order some leaflets from the printers?' she snapped.

Alice decided to ignore her question and instead turned to Mr Waters. 'Sebastian told me that Miss Victoria's had one of her turns. Is she all right now, sir?' she asked in a soft anxious voice.

He looked worried. 'She says she's fine but I'm not so sure. She's bothering her head about some meeting or other. You're her assistant so you're going to have to do something.' He reached for a glass at his elbow and gulped a mouthful of what looked and smelt like navy rum.

His remark caused Alice's heart to sink. Miss Victoria had a knack for making people feel they could do a lot more than they believed they could and Alice enjoyed attending the meetings where all she had to do was to hand round cups of tea and cakes – but to get up onto a platform or a soapbox and challenge those not committed to make a stand for women's rights was just not in her nature.

Mrs Waters sniffed. 'You can't expect...' There was a long pause and they all looked at her as she struggled to remember what she had been going to say next. This was happening more and more lately. At last she said with a wave of her hand in Alice's direction, 'This girl should be able...to do what – what...Victoria does. The girl's task is simple. She will cancel everything my...is involved in with these...' She paused and looked bewildered. 'What are they called? I can't remember.'

'Suffragists.' Gabrielle, who was pouring custard over a dish of stewed plums, added sharply, 'And you're wasting your time. You should know by now the Cause is what she lives for.'

Alice would not have dared to speak to Mrs Waters like that, but Gabrielle seemed to be able to get away with it.

Mr Waters downed the rum before saying gruffly, 'It's time she was married. Not that I want to be rid of her, you understand, but having a husband would give her no time to interest herself in such things. I thought you might have invited some young men here while I was away, Mother.'

Mrs Waters looked blank. 'I think I...'

'Miss Victoria shows no interest in young men at all,' said Gabrielle, handing the dessert to Alice. 'You can take this up to her.'

Alice knew she was being deliberately dismissed. She wanted to know what Gabrielle was going to say about her mistress's lack of interest in young men.

'Upstairs with you, Alice. Don't stand there as if you've taken root,' ordered Gabrielle, shooing her out of the room with both hands.

Alice went, wondering how Mr Waters and his mother put up with Gabrielle's bossiness. She supposed it was because she had been with them so long. Alice hated the way she spoke to her at times, and she spoke to Mary, the all-purpose maid, like she was muck. Here was another reason for her to leave Miss Victoria's employment – and yet Alice had to admit that she did love this house. She had a biggish bedroom overlooking the crescent, nicely furnished and with plenty of space. If only Seb had come home unattached, she thought glumly for the umpteenth time.

She knocked on the door of a bedroom on the first floor. 'It's Alice, Miss Victoria.'

'Come in!'

Alice turned the crystal doorknob and entered the bedroom. Victoria was alone and resting against a couple of lace-edged pillows. She was writing by the light of a gas lamp on the wall behind her. 'Should you be doing that, Miss Victoria? Shouldn't you be resting?' asked Alice, going over to the bedside table and placing the bowl on it.

Her employer smiled wearily, closed the writing pad and screwed the top on a bottle of ink. 'I'm much better now. But I need you to take a message. I'm afraid we'll have to cancel the rally again,' she said with a grimace. 'But don't think I'm giving up. Sebastian made me see the sense of delegating more. Even so I've told him I won't be mollycoddled. Would you believe Juliana is involved with the Cause in America? What do you think of that?'

'It's not important what I think,' said Alice stiffly. Although, she was relieved to discover that she was only expected to take a message.

Victoria reached out a hand to her. 'Of course your opinion is important. You've been so brave and controlled where Sebastian and Juliana are concerned. I'm proud of you, Alice.'

Alice was silent.

Victoria sighed. 'What is it, Alice? Are you finding it so difficult here that you want to leave? Please don't. The Cause is greater than any problems either of us have. If

Juliana comes here Sebastian won't mind if we involve her. He used to take a great deal of interest in my work.'

Alice tried to steer the conversation away from Seb and Juliana. 'I think Mr Waters wants you to give up the Cause and get married.'

Victoria frowned and wrapped her arms round her hunched up knees. 'That's not exactly news to me...but even if I wanted to marry, I wouldn't foist myself on any man with my heart condition. He'd want to have babies and all the labour involved in producing offspring would most likely kill me. I know it's hard on Papa as I'm his only child, but I'm sure he'll want what's best for me. As for giving up the Cause...I'll be damned if I'll do that.' Her eyes smouldered. 'I want to leave my mark on the world before I die.'

'I wish you wouldn't talk about dying,' burst out Alice.

Victoria shrugged and reached for the dish of plums and custard. 'You mustn't worry about me, I've every intention of living quite a few more years yet.'

Alice hoped that was so but, suddenly, she was wavering again about staying here or looking for another job. If only she knew what Seb and Juliana planned to do. No point in leaving Miss Victoria's employment if they married and decided to return to America. Her nerves were in shreds as she considered every possible situation. Sometimes Alice wished that she could foretell the future as she imagined Mrs Black doing.

'Another chair,' said Mrs Black, stepping back from the mahogany tripod table. The top of the column fitted into a kind of birdcage, which allowed the table to revolve and tilt unless secured with an extra wedge. Not that she needed to use chicanery to convince her clients that she was able to receive messages from their dear ones.

Emma went out onto the landing and brought in a shield-back chair, which had ebonised floral motifs worked into the back. She moved the four mahogany dining chairs with their serpentine shaped tops to make room for the extra chair. Mrs Black really did have some lovely furniture. The table and chairs were centuries old and polished up beautifully. She just hoped it all stayed in place and there was no jiggery pokery that afternoon.

A month had passed since her arrival and she remembered how during the first séance, a picture – a nice scenic one of mountains and trees and highland cattle – had come crashing to the floor for no apparent reason. It had startled the life out of those gathered for the sitting. One of the men, a friend of Mrs Black, had got up and checked to see if the cord had snapped but it was all in one piece. He had said in a deeply serious voice that there was too much energy being produced and perhaps it would be best if Mrs Black rested. Emma remembered how the hairs on the back of her neck had stood up. She had wondered what this energy was and whether it really did have anything to do with ghosts. Perhaps Aggie was trying to get in touch with her? It had been a really weird feeling but, after a couple of days when nothing else untoward happened, she had calmed down. Besides, hadn't her employer told her that there was nothing to fear from the dead and that it was only the living who could harm you?

Emma was kept busy not only with housework and cooking but with people, only that morning two women had called for private sittings. She had not expected there to be so many wanting to get in touch with the dead; although some came just for healing.

The healing room had pale blue walls painted with scenes of flower-filled meadows. In a corner next to the net draped window was a harp, which was occasionally played by a middle-aged Welsh woman from the spiritual church. Her music reminded Emma of trickling streams. There was also a marble-topped table, an armchair and a chaise-longue, covered in a blue and gold damask material.

Most of the clients seemed to leave looking better than when they came; although there were some who said it was a whole lot of nonsense and stormed out. Emma did not know what to believe. Only the other day when she was wielding the "Rapid Dust Extractor", which was an awkward thing to push and pull about, the candles in the holders attached to two gilt edged mirrors had fallen out.

Emma watched her employer as she put a taper to the candles in the silver candelabra on the sideboard. Despite having electricity, she seemed to prefer candlelight for sittings. She recalled Mrs Black saying that she had been given her gift from God. Emma wondered how she knew that God had given her a gift when what she did was forbidden in the Bible. Mrs Black had no need to work, her husband had left her comfortably off. She had inherited a number of properties which she rented out in Liverpool. Yet despite having money, she could still be bothered with all this healing and getting in touch with live souls, which often left her exhausted. Emma considered it a pretty miserable way of spending time when her mistress could have been out spending money in the shops, having meals out, attending the music hall, or travelling to interesting places.

'Will you need anything else?' asked Emma.

'No! But I'll want you to bring in tea and angel cake at half past three. I'll be going out later and won't be back until tomorrow. If you want to stay at your parents' house that'll be fine by me, but I'll need a fire in the sitting room and some of your lovely lentil and ham soup for lunch when I arrive home.' With that she shooed Emma out of the room.

Emma went, thanking her lucky stars that she had gone to Mr Jones' Employment Agency when she had. Later that day, she planned on writing to her brother in India, knowing Chris would enjoy reading all that she had to tell him about her new job.

On the way to visit her family, as well as to redeem her brooch from the pawnbroker's, Emma bumped into David Davies on Cow Lane Bridge. He asked her how she was getting on in her new job.

'How did you know I've a new job?'

'Your brother Alf told me,' David's eyes danced. 'He imagines all sorts of ghostly things happening but says you don't say much.'

'I'm paid to be discreet,' said Emma, smiling. 'But I'll tell you one thing – during a sitting, a picture came crashing down from a wall.'

'As if pushed by an invisible hand!' teased David.

Her lips quivered but she controlled the giggle in her throat, saying severely, 'Don't be flippant! I have it on good authority that it's caused by too much energy emanating from Mrs Black…and don't repeat any of this because I'd hate it to get back to her and lose my job. She definitely has a gift and I don't want her to think I'm laughing at her.'

His expression sobered. 'So you like working for her?'

Emma nodded. 'It's just what I wanted.'

'That's marvellous. Remember that young woman coming into the Servants' Registry Office?' His brow creased. 'What was her name?'

'Alice Moran.'

'Have you seen any more of her?'

'Only in passing,' she replied with a shrug. 'Her employer lives just aa couple of doors away from where I work. If you're interested in her, I think you'd be wasting your time.

'I didn't say I fancied her. I asked only because I remembered you saying she was a troubled woman.' He smiled down at Emma. 'See you around, lovey.'

Emma watched him walk into town, wishing she'd kept her mouth shut. Why should she care if he did have feelings for Alice? Oh bother the man! Bother Alice! She hadn't spoken to her since she had come to work for Mrs Black. From the upstairs window, she had seen her with Miss Waters in the motor car driven by the handsome, dark-haired Sebastian Bennett, who worked for Mr Waters. Mrs Black had told her that he was an old flame of Alice's. Emma's brow puckered as she recalled eavesdropping on Alice's and Miss Waters' conversation in the cocoa house. Alice had spoken of being engaged to another bloke. What was his name? Bert! If she remembered rightly he wasn't nice at all and wondered what had happened to him.

Chapter Six

December, 1907

Bert smiled at his mother across the table covered with a snowy white tablecloth, enjoying the rapt expression on her plump face as she darted surreptitious glances at the middle classes, partaking of afternoon tea. His gaze followed hers to a neighbouring table where four women were talking loudly and animatedly.

'But, Miss Waters, surely you've heard the new liberal leader's comments?'

'You mean what he said about women's suffrage doing more harm than good?' replied a woman in her mid-twenties, wearing an outrageously large hat with ostrich plumes.

'Exactly. Do you believe we can change his mind?'

Bert did not catch Miss Water's reply because she lowered her voice, so he turned his attention back to his mother. It was the week before Christmas and this was the first time he had been able to meet his mother since his disappearance. The fact that she had been willing meant Hannah had not mentioned the letters to her; he had thought she wouldn't want anyone else seeing them. Having decided a special treat was in order he had splashed out and brought her to the Grosvenor Hotel for afternoon tea. It would be worth every penny if she could provide him with the information he needed. 'Enjoying yourself, Mother?'

Susannah started and turned her head and smiled at him. 'Your dah could never afford to bring me here. You've made my day, son.'

Bert's chest swelled with pride and he picked up the silver-plated cake stand from the middle of the table and held it out to her. 'Only the best is good enough for my mother.'

She flushed and thanked him and took a fresh cream slice. 'What about yourself?' she asked, before biting into the confectionery, causing jam and cream to ooze out.

He took a chocolate éclair and returned the cake stand to its position in the middle of the table. 'What about another cup of tea?'

'I'll pour,' she said, hastily placing the cake on her bone china plate and reaching for the teapot.

He watched her, considering how they'd already discussed his lodgings and his new job. He had lied to her about where he lived, saying that his digs were in Liverpool and had made no mention of his sisters and younger brother, leaving it to her to tell him how they were doing. He rejoiced at the news that there was still no sign of a baby yet for Hannah. Now he was wondering how he could turn the conversation round to Alice. He desperately wanted to know where she lived. He no longer found satisfaction in just slipping a threat to her in the monthly letters he sent to Hannah. He decided he would have to bring her into the conversation himself.

He waited until the tea was poured and his mother had eaten her cream slice. 'And how is Alice, Mother?' His tone was casual.

Susannah's mouth fell open and then she closed it, swallowed and said, 'I'm surprised you're interested after what she did.'

He adopted a soulful expression. 'It's true she hurt me, Mother, but time heals and we're told in the Good Book, we have to forgive.'

'If only your sisters and Jock felt like that,' she said passionately. 'But they're so hard.'

He sighed. 'Perhaps one day, Mother.'

Susannah seemed to go off into a trance and Bert waited impatiently for a few moments before clearing his throat loudly. 'Alice! How is she? Met another man yet?'

Susannah stirred and blinked at him. 'I've no idea. I see

hardly anything of her. She works for some woman the other side of the Dee. Tilly told me Alice is going with the family to the country for Christmas through into the New Year.'

Bert hid his annoyance but did not bother asking the address, doubting that Tilly would know. At least, he had his first clue to Alice's whereabouts and he had every intention of following it up in the New Year.

Alice hung on to her hat as she hurried past the Grosvenor Hotel, heading in the direction of Bridge Street. It was the long way round to get to the Waters' house but she'd rather that than go through the park. Christmas had come and gone but it had not been a white one, the north had had to wait until Spring arrived for a fall of snow, and the streets were almost deserted. Hannah had told her of the latest letter from Bert and now Alice felt nervous and kept glancing over her shoulder.

The river came into view and soon she was walking along the tree-lined Groves. She scrutinised the faces of those braving the weather to walk their dogs, remembering a pale and tense Hannah telling her that she just couldn't pass it on to the police. What Bert had written was so crude and personal that she could not bear for anyone else to read it. Hannah had told Alice that she must always be on her guard. 'He's playing cat and mouse with us. If I'm alone in the house with Tilly, I make sure all the doors are locked and I have the poker handy. If I go out, I make sure I have a pepper pot in my pocket. You must do the same.'

Alice thought if anyone had told her two years ago that she would one day be this scared of Bert, she would have called them a liar. His smile, his warm caring manner, his churchgoing and protectiveness towards her and Tilly, had convinced her that he was good, honest and kind through and through. Yet even then Hannah had warned her there was another side to him. Alice had refused to listen to her friend, convinced it was jealousy that caused her to talk of her brother in such a way. Alice went hot and cold when she thought of how close she had been to tying herself to him for life.

She quickened her pace, her plain green serge skirt swirling about her button-booted ankles. She found herself praying for the household she had just left. Then she began to pray for herself and the Waters' household. At the beginning of January, two thousand textile workers had gone on strike in Oldham and she had overheard Seb and Mr Waters discussing how it might affect the cotton market. It was cotton that had taken the two men to America and there had been talk of Seb going again once the weather improved. Alice hated the thought of him crossing the Atlantic, picturing him with Juliana. The latest news from her had been that her mother was ill so she had had to put off her visit to England. How Alice wished Mr Waters had never had his accident. Seb would never have met Juliana and would have been here when she had finished with Bert. She could have explained what happened to her father and how that led to her getting engaged to Bert. As it was, they both avoided each other as much as they could. She sighed, thinking *If only*!

Deep in thought, Alice was halfway across the bridge when she was seized from behind and a familiar voice whispered against her ear. 'Hello, Alice, fancy meeting you here.'

She stiffened with fright, realising that she had done what Hannah had warned her against and let her guard down. 'Let me go,' she gasped.

'Not until you give me a kiss. I've missed your kisses, Alice. The feel of your body pressed against mine,' murmured Bert.

She felt the blood rush to her face as he rubbed up against her bottom. For a moment she couldn't breathe, and then she managed to stammer, 'You – you're mad! Let me go – go.'

His breath stirred an auburn curl beneath the tiny rim of her felt hat. 'It's not me that's crazy, sweetheart. It's your family that's tainted with madness. You would have had a jailbird for a father if they hadn't locked him up in the loony bin. I reckon I had a lucky escape when you ditched me...even so you're going to pay for the trouble you caused me.'

She struggled wildly, lashing out at him. He caught her arms and clamped them to her sides, forcing her round to face him. To her amazement, he was wearing a balaclava, so she could only see his eyes and mouth. She saw the flash of his teeth in one of those smiles that had once had the power to charm her. 'Do I frighten you, Alice? I've thought of joining Haldane's volunteers and being taught to kill. Just think of that: A bayonet in the guts or a bullet in the head, which would you fancy?' He put a hand to her throat and she felt sick with terror and tried to scream. 'Don't be silly. I'm not going to hurt you. I'd rather do other things.' He whispered obscenely in her ear.

She shuddered. 'That's disgusting. Let me go!' He didn't release her but instead rammed her against the side of the bridge. His hand slipped from her mouth and she managed to let out a scream.

Then to her relief she heard a voice yell, 'Hey, deaf lugs! You heard what she said...let her go!'

Bert spun Alice round in the direction of the voice. 'Well, are you going to let her go?' demanded the young woman, silhouetted against the darkening sky, swinging a shopping bag. He did not move and she took several quick steps towards them.

Bert released Alice so abruptly that she jarred her elbow on the bridge and pain shot down her arm to her fingertips. Astonished, she looked at him. He appeared to be frozen in his tracks. Then he made a noise in his throat before suddenly turning and running. Alice could scarcely believe he had been routed so easily and watched as he reached the end of the bridge and then disappeared beneath the trees along the Groves.

'Blooming heck!' exclaimed Emma. 'I didn't know I was so scary.'

Alice began to laugh hysterically, and it was several moments before she managed to splutter, 'You certainly frightened him the way you swung that bag. What have you got in it? A brick?'

Emma shook her head. 'You OK?'

Gingerly Alice felt her elbow. 'I hurt my funny bone but I can cope with that...but if you hadn't come along I don't know what I'd have done. Thanks!'

Emma smiled. 'Want me to walk with you?'

'I'd appreciate that. Who's to say that he mightn't double back.' Fear rose in her throat and she felt as if about to choke. She swallowed hard. 'Bert's one of those men who can't take no for an answer.' Alice took a deep breath because she was feeling shaky. 'I was engaged to him once but I broke it off just before the wedding because I found out things about him that...that...well, they were bad. Now he's out for revenge.' She shuddered.

'So that's Bert,' said Emma. 'I knew about the engagement. I eavesdropped on your conversation in the cocoa house in Brook Street the first time I saw you.'

'I see!' Alice rubbed her arms. 'Shall we make a move? It's going to be dark soon and I'd like to get away from here.' She began to walk towards Queen's Park.

Emma fell into step beside her. 'Have you thought of going to the bobbies?'

'My brother's told them about him. Bert's been sending threatening, obscene letters to my sister-in-law. But we don't know where he's living so it makes it difficult to trace him.'

'Would your sister-in-law be the bride you mentioned in

the cocoa house last year,' said Emma, hastening to keep up with her.

Alice stopped and stared at her. 'You have got a good memory. Yes! Hannah is my sister-in-law. She married my half-brother Kenny. My little sister Tilly lives with them in a house near the railway works.'

Emma smiled. 'Now there's a coincidence. I come from Cornwall Street a few streets away. At the moment I'm living in Victoria Crescent a few doors away from the Waters' house where you work. There's another coincidence. I managed to get a well-paid, living-in job.'

Alice's brow puckered. 'I've probably heard about you – and even seen you – but my head's been in the clouds lately so I haven't realised it was you. How long have you been there?'

They had reached the other side of the river. 'I came a few weeks before October. Pity we didn't have the snow then, hey? The kids would have loved it.'

Alice held a hand out as if to feel the snow falling and, as she did so, it suddenly stopped. 'I doubt it's going to last now for them to have any fun.'

It was true, there was only the thinnest of covering on the ground, even so it was slippery underfoot and they were silent, watching where they stepped as they made their way up to Victoria Crescent.

'He was wearing a balaclava,' said Emma out of the blue. 'Seems a bit daft when you recognised him anyway.'

'Perhaps it was so other people wouldn't recognise him,' said Alice, glancing nervously behind her. 'He said something about joining Haldane's volunteers so he could be trained to kill…but perhaps that was only one of his sick jokes.'

'Definitely doesn't sound a nice bloke.' Then she hesitated before adding, 'How do you feel now? If you want to calm down a bit more before you go in, why don't you come and have a cup of tea with me? Mrs Black is out at a meeting.'

Alice was silent. She had once sworn she would never set foot in Mrs Black's house. She knew that without the medium's help, Kenny would never had been reunited with his Scottish relatives, but she could not forget her father's association with the woman and how he had handed over money in his search for healing and forgiveness that should have been spent on his family.

Emma peered into Alice's downcast face. 'You don't like what she does, do you?' she said dryly.

'How d'you find working for her?' asked Alice, lifting her head.

Emma cocked an eyebrow. 'I don't get my bum pinched and I'm not going to get into the worst kind of trouble. I know people think what she does is wrong but she genuinely wants to help. I wasn't sure at first, myself, but now I'm getting to know her I can see it's true.'

'I don't want to know her,' interrupted Alice sharply. 'You need to watch what you eat and drink in her company. She gave my friend something and she almost died...and I know for a fact she killed someone.'

Emma leapt to her employer's defence. 'That's slander that is! I know Mrs Black mixes herbal potions for some of her clients. She also lays hands on them and prays with them...but I've yet to hear anyone come back and accuse her of murder. But I suppose it's early days and there might be a whole string of them out there.'

Alice's eyes glinted. 'Very funny. But this victim lived a long way from here.'

'What about your friend...does she live nearby? Has she accused Mrs Black to her face of trying to poison her?' demanded Emma.''Cos I tell yer now I don't believe you. Mrs Black doesn't have to do what she does but believes God had given her a gift and she must use it to help others.'

'God! How can that woman bring God into what she

does?' said Alice scathingly. 'Trying to get in touch with the dead is the devil's work and that's all there is to it.' On those words she walked away.

Emma groaned as she watched Alice turn into the Waters' gate, then made her way to Mrs Black's house. Having believed she had found a friend, she was terribly disappointed.

During the weeks that followed, Emma worried off and on about Alice's accusations against her employer. She did not want to believe there was any truth in them and was concerned that if Alice were to repeat them, then not only would Mrs Black's business reputation be damaged, but more seriously the accusation of murder would be reported to the police...and where would that leave her? She'd be out of a job.

Eventually she decided to tell her employer about the incident. Mrs Black was about to set out for a meeting where the Rev. S Barnett was to talk about how he had made the leap from Methodism to Spiritualist lecturer. When Emma started speaking, Mrs Black stiffened in the act of easing on a tan coloured kid glove. 'Alice Moran said all that? Did you believe her?'

'I told her she had to watch what she said and that it was slander.'

'And so it is, my dear.' Mrs Black smiled sadly. 'The trouble with Alice is that she's always resented the part I played in her father's life. He was and still is a very sick man. One of my failures, I'm afraid. The family suffered at his hands and she's never forgiven him or me. He's an inmate in Upton Asylum. I know one of the doctors there and he keeps me in touch about Malcolm's condition. As for what she said about her friend...' She paused and took her handbag from the back of a chair. 'Dear Hanny! I helped her at a difficult time in her life and I assure you that she was glad I did so. Does that satisfy you?'

Emma nodded, relieved. 'I thought there must be a

reasonable answer. But d'you think you should warn Alice Moran against repeating what she said about you?'

Mrs Black looked thoughtful. 'A solicitor's letter perhaps. I'll think about it. In the meantime, if you bump into her again, tell her that if she doesn't want to become like her paternal grandmother, then she must change her ways. Perhaps she should take her half-brother's Christian faith as an example of how to behave towards people. He might not agree with the work I do but he believes that *God is love* as it says in St John's gospel and that he should try and love all people. I believe it was Alice's mother who instilled those principles in him.'

After her employer had left, Emma had much to think about as she settled down to hem a dress she had bought from a second-hand stall in the market. She had just tacked up the hem when the doorbell rang. She put down her sewing, hoping it wasn't a desperate client.

To her amazement Alice stood on the doorstep. She had no coat on and was wearing a brown skirt and cream blouse; her auburn hair was loose about her shoulders and she looked lovely but tense. 'I know I'm more than a bit late in doing this but I've come to say sorry,' she blurted. 'You rescued me from Bert and I should have been more grateful.'

Emma thought how strange that she should turn up on the step just after she and Mrs Black had been talking about her. 'Thanks for the apology. Better late then never but don't yer think you ought to take back what yer said about my mistress?'

Alice's brow clouded. 'I'd like us to be friends...but that doesn't mean that I'm not entitled to my opinion about Mrs Black.'

'I wouldn't argue with that,' said Emma promptly, folding her arms and resting her shoulder against the doorjamb. 'But you can't go around calling people murderesses without getting yourself into trouble. It doesn't do to judge people without really knowing them.'

Alice pursed her lips and Emma thought she was going to continue with her accusations but then she said in desperate tones, 'Kenny and Hannah have taken Tilly out for the day so I can't unburden myself on them. I really need someone to talk to. We could go for a walk?'

Emma did not feel like going for a walk. She had been on the go most of the day and her feet were aching. 'No thanks, I'm tired. Why don't you come in? Mrs Black's gone to a meeting, so she's not going to turn you into a toad or anything,' she said with the hint of a smile.

Alice hesitated, then shook her head. 'No, I won't if you don't mind. You might think it's a joke my feeling the way I do but I can't take what she does so lightly.'

Emma sighed. 'I'm sorry. I do understand. I know that your dad used to come here in search of healing and wasn't cured.'

Alice's hands curled into fists. 'Is that what she calls what she did to him? Healing! I have another name for the kind of service she provides. She and my father together destroyed my mam.'

Exasperated, Emma's eyebrows snapped together, meeting above her nose. 'I thought you said you were sorry? But if you're going on about her again you might as well take back your apology and wait for the solicitor's letter.' She made to close the door.

Alice wedged it open with her foot. 'What d'you mean by that?'

'I mean that you can't slander people without proof and get away with it. Now shift yourself!' Emma attempted to push her away.

Alice swayed but grabbed the door and held her ground. 'Why can't you just stop sticking up for her? I want us to be friends. I need to talk about Bert. You know what he did.'

'Do you realise you can be heard halfway down the

road?' interrupted a terse male voice.

Alice released her hold on the door and, turning, saw Seb. He pushed open the gate and strode up the path with an easy grace. Emma looked at him with interest. He was definitely worth a second look. 'Mr Bennett, isn't it?' she said.

'That's right. Sebastian Bennett! And you're Emma Griffiths if I'm not mistaken. I've heard one of the maids mention your name.' He held out a hand.

'Nice to meet you,' she said, shaking it.

'So what were you and Alice arguing about?'

'That's none of your business,' said Alice, flushing.

'Your shouting makes it my business.' His dark eyes took in her appearance in a quick head to toe appraisal.

'I don't think I've got anything to say to you,' said Alice, tilting her chin.

'I suppose not,' rasped Sebastian, the muscle of his jaw clenching. 'You said it all when we parted.'

'You mean the time you told me that you'd always love me?' she said, her voice shaking.

He whitened. 'You didn't want my love! It was you who walked away.'

'What was the point of my staying? There were people who were more important to you,' she cried.

'That wasn't true! You were jealous of anyone else who needed my attention. You didn't trust me and refused to see my point of view.'

'I was terrified of my father but you just couldn't see how badly I felt.' Her voice rose another octave.

'There was no need for you to feel like that. I would have looked after you...but you never gave me the chance,' he said heavily.

Alice looked as if she had been slapped in the face.

Emma decided this was the right time to intervene, having noticed they were collecting an audience. 'Er – hem! I think the whole neighbourhood is starting to take an interest in your business,' she said in a low voice. 'How about coming inside and having a cuppa? You could try and sort this out.'

'Sort it out! It's too late for that,' said Alice, her voice quivering. 'He can't wait to waltz off to America and see his ladylove. At least when he does I'll have some peace again.' She brushed past Sebastian and marched down the path, skirts swaying and her head held high.

Emma glanced at Sebastian's angry face. Both winced as Alice slammed the gate shut. 'You're not going after her?' asked Emma tentatively.

At first she thought he hadn't heard her and then he laughed mirthlessly. 'After that parting shot? No! Lead me to the teapot.'

She sighed. '*You* don't mind entering this *house of sin* then?'

'Can't wait to see what goes on inside, luv.' She caught the hint of a Liverpool accent. 'My Ma doesn't have a good word to say about Mrs Black but, as far as I know, she's never done her any wrong.'

'Come in then.' Emma smiled and held the door wide.

Seb stepped over the threshold, wiped his feet on the mat and followed her to the kitchen. Her mind was buzzing. She wouldn't have been human if she wasn't dying to know more about his and Alice's past but guessed it was going to be nigh on impossible to broach the subject. She clicked on the electric light and Sebastian's gaze wandered round the tidy and up-to-date kitchen. 'Not what I pictured,' he murmured.

Emma chuckled. 'What did yer expect? A cauldron over an open fire.' She put on the kettle. 'We have an electric vacuum cleaner. I tell you, there's no flies on us.'

'Mrs Black's not short of money,' observed Sebastian, pulling out a chair and sitting down. He was silent a moment, his brow knitted in thought, and then he sniffed. 'Something smells good.'

'I've been making scones. I'll get to take some home to the kids. Mrs Black's no skinflint,' said Emma, taking crockery from a shelf. 'She pays me well…something my mam's glad about, I can tell you. I've five brothers and sisters that need feeding and clothing. I've another brother in the army. Our Chris. He's abroad, hasn't lived at home for years. Dad and he were always arguing, so he left home as soon as he finished school and went to Liverpool. We didn't hear much from him for a while but now he writes regular. Dad's a porter up at the General Station and doesn't earn much.'

'You're the eldest girl?'

Emma poured milk into two cups with an unsteady hand. 'I had a big sister…she…drowned,' she said with difficulty. 'Mrs Black's offered to try and make contact with her but I said no thanks. It's something I baulk at despite having seen and heard things since working here that convinces me she has some sort of gift. You can tell that to Alice,' she added absently, picking up a tin. Taking off the lid, she took out a scone and buttered it and gave it to him.

He took it and said in a bitter voice, 'It won't make any difference, you heard her. Her feelings towards Mrs Black are all tied up with her father and what happened to Hanny Kirk.'

'Hanny Kirk!' exclaimed Emma, fixing him with a stare and remembering that Mrs Black had referred to a Hanny. 'Do you mean Alice's sister-in-law, Hannah?' He nodded and she added, 'Mrs Black said she helped her when she was in trouble.'

'I wouldn't know about that but we believed she used hypnotism to get information out of her. I don't know what happened after that because I lost touch with Hanny and Kenny.'

'I see. Would you like to talk about Alice?'

'No,' he said shortly.

Emma changed the subject. 'D'you have any family other than your mother?'

'No.' He brushed crumbs from his mouth. 'I never knew my dad. Ma told me he was a musician but I don't remember him at all. She chose not to remarry.'

'She's a very striking woman.'

He nodded and finished the scone. 'That was good.'

'Have another. I hear your mam's a good cook.'

He smiled faintly. 'Her speciality is the macaroon. Sometimes she dips them in chocolate. Maybe next time Ma makes them, I'll bring some round.' He ate the scone but then his next words caused her to start. 'This Bert? What's the trouble Alice is having with him?' His tone was almost too casual.

Emma hesitated, unsure whether Alice would like her talking about Bert but then she decided the other girl needed all the help she could get. After clearing her throat Emma said, 'He's a nasty piece of work in my opinion but if you want to know more, ask Alice.'

'That's not an easy thing to do. You heard the pair of us. You must have met Bert to know he's no-good,' he said, a stern expression on his attractive face.

'Can't say we actually met,' said Emma dryly. 'He had her squashed against the side of the footbridge with his hand about her throat when I first saw him. He beat a hasty retreat. I didn't know little ol' me could be so frightening, unless it's that I've caught a bit of the aura that hangs about upstairs and he thought I was a ghost.'

Sebastian smiled faintly. 'That's all you know?'

'I know that Alice has found someone else to be terrified of now her father's in the asylum. You ask her if you want to know anymore.'

Sebastian looked thoughtful as she poured out the tea and handed him a cup. 'Perhaps I will when I get things sorted out with Juliana.' Then he said abruptly, 'Actually, I'm here for another reason: Mr Waters was in an accident while we were in America and apparently he knows Mrs Black from way back...'

Light dawned and Emma smiled. 'Healing not going so well? He's thinking of paying a call on my employer?'

Sebastian nodded. 'Apparently he consulted her as a medium years ago...before I was born. His wife died after they'd had some kind of falling out; it played on his mind, so he wanted to try and get in touch with her.'

Emma said gravely, 'Unfinished business. Mrs Black probably passes on more messages of forgiveness than any other kind.'

'Mr Waters said he definitely felt better afterwards,' he said good humouredly.

Emma nodded. 'I've heard her say that's what it's all about...as well as to open people's minds to the idea of communication with the spirit world.'

'You won't get Alice agreeing with that.'

'I wouldn't argue with you.' Emma smiled and offered him another scone.

He refused it. 'You like Mrs Black, don't you?'

Emma's small face was thoughtful. 'I respect her and she's good to me. But just because I work for her, that doesn't say I know all there is to know about her. Alice said that her father and Mrs Black destroyed her mam. I asked her about that and she told me she'd tried to heal him but he was one of her failures. A doctor at Upton Asylum keeps her in touch with how he's getting on. She doesn't like failure.' Emma picked up the teapot. 'More tea?'

He shook his head and drained his cup before getting to his feet. 'I'd best be going. Thanks for everything. I've enjoyed our chat.'

'Me, too. I'll tell Mrs Black about Mr Waters wanting to see her but he might have to wait a while as she's pretty busy right now.'

Sebastian nodded and Emma saw him out, watching him

stroll in the direction of the Waters' house, thinking that it was a pity he wasn't in touch with Hanny or she would have asked him to find out whether she had worked at Bannister's Bakery and had known Agnes Griffiths, thinking that *Hanny without the H sounded a bit like Annie* but she supposed it was a bit of a long shot, thinking they could be the same person. Perhaps if she got the chance to talk to Alice again she might ask her. Sebastian's relationship with Alice puzzled her. How much did he care for this woman in America? The way he and Alice had gone for each other on the front step spoke of a heck of a lot of suppressed emotion. Marriage could be hell as it was but married to someone while loving someone else must be even worse.

Chapter Seven

June, 1908

The setting sun cast a shifting light upon the walnut chest of drawers and wardrobe through a gap in the curtains. Hannah sat on the bed, brushing her hair, waiting for Kenny to come up. She was glad it was summer because despite it being months since Bert had attacked Alice, she felt cold inside; the memory of his attack was causing both of them nightmares still. Kenny was icily angry about it, suspecting Mrs Kirk of giving Alice's address to Bert – despite Hannah's assurances that she had never told her mother where Alice lived. He would have reported the attack to the police if he believed they could catch him but he had little faith in them doing so. Bert was such a crafty sod.

Hannah gazed at her husband's nightshirt draped over a chair. Suddenly she heard footfalls on the stairs and her heart seemed to leap into her throat. She threw the hairbrush onto the chest of drawers and dived beneath the bedcovers and lay still. Her eyes were wide open in the gloom and her heart was pounding, remembering how Bert had crawled beneath the blankets, covering them and her sisters completely, so the evil he did to her was done in darkness. She felt as if she was about to suffocate and swiftly pushed herself up with a thrust of her feet so that her head was out in the open and chided herself for behaving so stupidly.

Recently she had been in such a state of anxiety that she had begun to think that despite his words of love, Kenny would soon start getting fed up with her moods and reluctance to make love. She tormented herself with the thought that her husband would soon start looking elsewhere for sex; after all that's what her dah had done when her mother had been out of her mind and wouldn't let him near her.

Kenny entered the bedroom and smiled at her as he began to undress. She watched the fading light wash over his muscular chest and arms as he stood in his drawers and her heart beat rapidly. She thought how he had matured since his father had gone from their lives. Sometimes she found it hard to recall the times her husband had been a puny boy, terrified of his father's shadow.

Kenny dragged the nightshirt over his head and crossed the room. He lifted the bedcovers and slid in beside her. She knew he left his drawers on to reassure her and wished there was no need for him to feel like that. She inhaled the smell of him, carbolic soap overlaid the slightest hint of sweat and coal dust. He reached for her and she allowed him to draw her against him and her mouth opened beneath his as he kissed her. Despite the layers of her flower sprigged cotton nightgown and his nightshirt she could feel the heat coming from him.

A voice inside her head said, *He'll get hotter and hotter when he forces himself into me and the heat will destroy me! Just like Bert almost destroyed me.* She fought against such thoughts as his hands explored her body beneath the nightgown; she must relax. There was no need to be frightened of her husband. Yet still she found herself turning rigid in an attempt to control the panic that seemed to threaten to stop her breathing. She clamped her thighs together and her fingers curled into her palms.

Kenny's hands stilled and his mouth lifted from hers. 'Stop it, Hanny! There's no need to go as stiff as a scrubbing board. I'll go no further.' He drew away from her.

She felt terrible and placed a hand on his bare arm. 'You have rights.'

He covered her hand with his. 'I vowed to cherish you and I meant it.'

A surge of love filled Hannah and she slipped her arm around his shoulders and drew him down to her. Yet even as she brought him closer, she was angry with herself for allowing her fear of Bert to have such control over her. At least that girl Emma seemed to have scared him off as there had been no further attacks, but that wasn't to say he wouldn't strike again. But Alice would be safe for the next few weeks as she was in London with Miss Victoria.

'Do you know what the writer, Lytton Strachey, said about our Prime Minister, Alice?' asked Victoria, straightening her sash in the WSPU colours of white, green and purple, as they prepared to leave the hotel bedroom.

'No, Miss Victoria, you tell me,' said Alice politely, still scarcely able to believe that she was in London. Although, it would have been nicer if they were here simply to see the sights. Instead they were here for a rally, having travelled down from Liverpool on a hired train in the company of thousands of other supporters of the Cause, including Mrs Stone.

'He said that Mr Asquith is a fleshy, wine-bibbing, gluttonous, lecherous and cynical old fellow,' she reported with relish. 'Everyone knows that he hates suffragist puritans.'

'Then what's the point of the mass demonstration in Hyde Park?' asked Alice, forcing herself to show interest.

Victoria frowned. 'I wish you would listen, Alice. I told you it's because Mr Asquith promised before he became Prime Minister that if it could be proved that most women wanted the vote – and it would benefit society – then he would abandon his opposition. So we have to give a peaceful demonstration a chance.'

'And if it doesn't work?' asked Alice, opening the door.

'Then we'll have to do something else that will make him change his mind,' said Victoria firmly, her skirts sweeping the floor as she hurried along the carpeted corridor towards the stairs. Alice locked the door and followed her, hoping all the excitement would not bring on one of Victoria's turns.

They were to be part of the Liverpool procession, one of seven columns marching on Hyde Park with banners flying. It would set out from Central Street in the commercial heart of the city and then head towards the Embankment, past Trafalgar Square and along Piccadilly past the Wellington Monument, where they would turn into Park Road and enter Hyde Park. It would have been much more sensible for them to join the rally in Hyde Park but Victoria was determined to be seen marching with the procession. At least she had consented to join the march at Trafalgar Square instead of walking all the way. Outside the sky was overcast, so Victoria asked the doorman to hail them a cab and soon they were on their way.

Alice gazed longingly at the passing scene, thinking how she would have preferred to be going shopping than joining the rally. As they drew closer to Trafalgar Square she noticed that the area was thronged with people. Victoria told the driver to stop and they descended from the cab. Alice took a deep breath of the warm air and noticed that it tasted gritty against her teeth. She gazed with wonder at the towering edifice that was Nelson's Column.

'Come on, Alice! Let's not delay!' cried Victoria, leading the way.

Alice hurried after her to where the leaders of the procession could clearly be seen. She could hear singing but could not make out the words until they drew closer and realised the women and their male supporters were singing the hymn 'Fight the Good Fight'. She had been told that there were many who believed that God was on their side in the fight for women's equality with men, taking as their motto a verse from the New Testament, *In Christ all art equal; men and women, slave and free.* Others regarded the church as no friend of the Cause because they considered women either as daughters of Eve, responsible for men sinning, or purely as wives and mothers, whose work lay mainly in the home.

She looked up at one of the leading banners, inscribed with the words LIVERPOOL'S NATIONAL WOMEN'S SOCIAL AND POLITICAL UNION, whilst others said VOTES FOR WOMEN and WHERE WOMEN WILL, THERE'S A WAY. Then she noticed a woman waving to them and realised it was Mrs Stone, whom she'd seen at meetings in Chester and on the Wirral.

Alice touched Victoria's arm. 'There's Mrs Stone!'

They hurried over to her and fell into step a few rows behind the leaders. The woman on the other side of Mrs Stone broke off from singing and smiled a welcome before continuing to bellow out a slightly changed version of the final verse of 'Fight the Good Fight'.

> *'Faint not nor fear, his arms are near;*
> *He changeth not and thou art dear;*
> *Only believe and thou shalt see*
> *That our Cause is all in all to Him.'*

Victoria was soon in conversation with Mrs Stone, leaving Alice to her own thoughts. They were of Seb, who, if all had gone well with the crossing, was probably in America by now. She imagined, instead of his being thousands of miles away, his being here with her now; not marching along surrounded by supporters of the Cause but in one of the parks, lying on the grass and whispering in her ear that he still loved her, not Juliana. Alice sighed, wondering how she was going to bear it if he arrived home in company with that American woman. She supposed it was best not think about it.

She glanced at Victoria, who was still talking animatedly to Mrs Stone; albeit in a slightly breathless manner. Alice was worried that she might overdo things before the day was out, and hoped she had her pills with her. She'd had her orders from Mr Waters that she was not to let his daughter exhaust herself. Of course, he had no idea that Victoria had come to London to join the rally. They were supposed to be shopping and seeing the sights, of which they had done little yet. Alice glanced about her, wondering where they were now. At least she knew when they reached Piccadilly Circus, because Mrs Stone pointed out the statue of Eros to her.

Alice's left shoe began to rub her heel, halfway along what she believed to be Piccadilly, but she made no complaint. Instead she began to cast furtive glances at Victoria, certain she was beginning to flag for she had fallen silent and her colour was higher than usual. 'Are you all right, Miss Victoria?' she asked.

'Don't fuss, Alice,' she croaked, staring resolutely ahead.

Alice sighed inwardly, thinking she would have taken her mistress's arm and helped her along if she hadn't known the gesture would be unwelcome. She would just have to continue to keep an eye on her.

Eventually, after what seemed ages, they arrived in Park Lane, a thoroughfare flanked on one side by multi-storey large terraced housing and on the other by Hyde Park. The leaders put on a spurt. Suddenly Victoria stumbled.

Alice reached out a hand and steadied her. 'You all right, miss?'

Victoria shrugged off her hand but her breathing was laboured.

Alice said reassuringly, 'Be in the park in a few minutes, miss, and you can rest.'

Victoria did not answer but limped on.

As the procession wended its way into the park and across the grass, Alice could see what appeared to be thousands upon thousands of women and their male supporters. Banners blazoned the towns and cities they

represented: Cardiff, Leicester, Worcester, Manchester…
and there was even one saying The Men's League for
Women's Suffrage. She had never seen so many people
crammed together in one place. The noise was tremendous
and she felt a stir of emotion.

She turned to Victoria. 'What a turnout, miss. If they
don't…'

Alice's voice faltered as before her eyes Victoria swayed
and sank to the ground.

'Oh my dear!' With her skirts billowing, Mrs Stone knelt
on the grass beside her. She glanced up at Alice. 'She's a
terrible colour. Is it her heart?'

'Yes, Mrs Stone. She hates a fuss and will keep quiet
about it.' Alice picked up Victoria's handbag, opened it
and searched for her pills.

'Is she all right?' asked a woman's voice.

'Step back! She needs air,' said Mrs Stone, putting up an
arm to ward off those who gathered around. Gently she
removed Victoria's hat and fanned her with it. A few
moments later she began to stir.

Alice had found the pills and as soon as Victoria regained
consciousness, she handed them to her. Mrs Stone had a
bottle of water in her capacious bag and took it out. 'Here,
my dear, wash it down with this.'

Gradually Victoria's colour improved and she managed
to say weakly, 'How stupid of me.'

'Not stupid, my dear Miss Waters,' said Mrs Stone. 'I
doubt you'll be the only one who faints here today with
the weather so close and the air so dirty in London. Rest
here for a little while but then it's best you return to your
hotel and not stay for the whole rally.' Victoria opened her
mouth to protest but Mrs Stone shook her head. 'I can
guess how you feel, my dear. But you've shown your
colours, so now you must reserve your strength so you can
fight another day.'

'You're right, of course,' Victoria's voice was weak.

'Perhaps someone could hail a cab…and if you and Alice could lend me your arms to assist me to the road?'

'Of course,' said Mrs Stone, with a reassuring smile.

An hour later Victoria lay in bed, propped up by pillows, still looking exhausted. 'What a disappointment, Alice! I suppose I could have stayed longer resting on the grass…'

'You did the sensible thing, Miss Victoria,' said Alice, folding a towel. 'What would I have told Mr Waters if you'd ended up in hospital?'

'You're exaggerating how poorly I was,' she murmured. 'It was just the weather being so close that made me faint. How am I ever going to show my mettle for the Cause if you mollycoddle me?' Alice decided it was wiser not to respond to that comment but continued to tidy away discarded clothing. 'Well, we'll see what tomorrow brings,' added Victoria.

'We're not going home?' asked Alice, whirling round to face her.

'Not just yet,' said Victoria, closing her eyes.

Alice's heart sank, hoping her employer did not have it in mind to go to any other demonstrations of the WSPU whilst she was here.

'You're forgetting we've shopping to do…as well as sights to see…if Papa is not to suspect my real reason for coming to London.'

Fortunately, Thomas Waters had other things on his mind than his daughter's sojourn in London. His own health for instance. Mrs Black had sent a message saying that she could see him at last, so he wasted no time keeping the appointment.

Emma opened the front door to him. 'I am here to see Mrs Black,' he said in a wheezy voice, leaning heavily on an ebony topped walking stick.

She beamed at him. 'Good afternoon, Mr Waters. Won't you come in?'

Pale blue eyes smiled into hers and he patted her hand as he limped over the threshold. 'Thank you, my dear.'

Emma looked at him with concern. 'Do you think you'll be able to manage the stairs, sir?'

A voice from above said, 'Don't you be worrying about that, Emma. I will help Mr Waters.'

Thomas turned his face up towards her. 'Ah, Eudora! A lot of water has passed under the bridge since last we spoke but how well you look, my dear.'

Emma's ears pricked up. Then she realised her employer was gazing at her. 'You can go and visit your mother, Emma. Be back here by seven.'

Emma would have liked to have heard more of their conversation but knew there was no arguing with her employer. Besides, she would enjoy window shopping and as it was over a week since she had paid the family a visit, she would go and see them. So she fetched her coat and hat and left them to it.

'So, Thomas, it is indeed a long time since we last spoke to each other.' Eudora's voice was calm but inside she was seething.

'More years than I care to remember,' he said.

'Allow me to take your hat.'

He handed it to her and Eudora hung it on a hook on the coat stand before taking his arm and helping him upstairs. She settled him on the chaise longue in the healing room before seating herself and staring at him intently. 'No tricks,' he wheezed, not meeting her eyes.

She raised her eyebrows and pretended to be amused. 'Tricks, Thomas? It helps if one believes to be healed.'

His face turned puce and he spluttered, 'Who said I'm here for healing?'

'Your son.' Her tone was bitter. 'Although, I see he still has no idea of the truth.'

Thomas growled. 'He'll find out soon enough once I'm dead.'

She laughed. 'You'd rather I told him? As for the woman who calls herself Gabrielle, she's kept the truth hidden this long…if it came out we can both imagine the histrionics.'

He rumbled, 'She's a passionate woman but could be the death of me.'

'Is that why you're here?' Her eyes glinted. 'You think I can heal your hip and give you a young man's body so you can continue to have pleasure from your mistress? If that is so tell me why I should help you? You almost destroyed my life.'

He cleared his throat. 'That was never my intention.'

'No. Your intention was to have your cake and eat it,' she said sharply. 'I was young and foolish, I fell in love with you and when I started having a child you insisted I got rid of it. Despite the fact that hypocritical bitch was already carrying your child and had refused to do so.'

He looked uncomfortable. 'I'd known Gabrielle long before she introduced the pair of us after my wife died. Anyway, you'd have never have married Mr Black and become so successful if you'd kept the child. You did well out of your husband, didn't you?'

She glowered at him. 'At least you didn't marry her.'

He cleared his throat but his voice was still gruff when he muttered, 'I couldn't. She was already married to some musician who deserted her in America.'

Eudora stared at him. 'The dark horse!'

'So she never told you when the pair of you met up again at the concert hall in Liverpool?' He seemed surprised.

'No, she did not! I didn't even know she'd been to America.'

'Oh yes, she went there with him, expecting to make it big. Instead, he left her to fend for herself in New York. My mother saw her busking outside a theatre, realised she was English and had some talent and brought her back to Liverpool.' He sighed. 'She was proud of her protégée, dressed her up nice and introduced her to the right people.' He smiled ruefully. 'I doubt she ever forgave me for making Gabrielle my mistress and getting her pregnant. Even so she felt some responsibility for the situation and grew fond of the boy. Now she and I need them both, so I'm in no position to dismiss Gabrielle. I say that just in case you were thinking of asking me to do so in exchange for your silence.'

'My heart bleeds for you both.' Her tone was sarcastic. 'I see that Gabrielle is still playing a part...or shall we use her proper name, seeing as how it's just us? Gertie...Irish Liverpool slummy, who saw singing in pubs as her way out of poverty.' Eudora smiled grimly. 'She might have made it, too, if she had only used her common sense. Trouble was that she was not only a fantasist but she couldn't stay away from the men.'

His tone was irascible, 'She's been faithful to me. And I didn't order her to leave the stage. Now can't you forget those days? Have pity for God's sake! I don't expect miracles but you always had such...um...magic hands.'

'So you've come here expecting me to heal you!' She could not conceal her outrage.

'Why not?' he mumbled. 'It's what you do.'

Her eyes narrowed, considering how best she could use his need to her advantage. He had hurt her unbearably...hard to believe now that he had been so handsome and had such a magnificent body when he was younger. His chest was wheezy and he had a pot belly...could be that he had more wrong with him than a broken hip that might never heal to the extent he wished. Suddenly she smiled. 'Of course it is. Now let's see what I can do for you. Although, I don't come cheap these days, Thomas. Is this going to be the first of several visits?'

'I don't see why not.' He looked relieved.

'Then let us begin. And afterwards we'll have a nice cup of tea and some of Emma's special cake. It's a new recipe I gave her.'

'She seems a bright young thing.'

'She is. Don't you try to poach her, Thomas Waters. I'm fond of Emma and I intend to keep her. By the way, I hear your daughter and her helper have gone to London. I do hope they're having a nice time.'

'Here, girl, you'll be interested in this,' said Olive, thrusting a newspaper under her daughter's nose. 'Our Patsy was reading it to me.'

'What is it?' Emma shifted Johnny to her other knee.

'Didn't yer say that girl you helped on the bridge has gone to London with her mistress and they were involved with the suffragettes?'

Emma took the newspaper and began to read about a mass suffragette demonstration in London. She took her time reading the article. 'I hope it does their Cause some good.' She eased her brother off her knee and stood up. 'It's time I was going. Give the others me luv.'

'Will yer bring us some cake next time?' said Olive eagerly, and then added wistfully, 'That's something I miss about our Aggie…we got cakes or buns most days when she was working at the bakery.'

Emma found herself trembling. 'You know, Mam, that's the first time you've mentioned her name for…I don't know how long. Now you have it sounds like you only miss her for what you had out of her.'

'I miss her for more than that,' said Olive hoarsely, 'and I'm reminded of her every time I look at you and that's of some comfort to me.' She gazed at her second daughter from tear-filled eyes. 'You'll watch yerself, won't yer, girl? Don't want you going down the same road. Yer dad says there's an engine driver who's interested in yer. Don't you go letting him persuade yer into giving him what they're all after before yer've got a ring on yer finger, will yer?' she pleaded.

Emma was so choked she could not speak but pecked

her mother's cheek and rushed out of the house. She so wished Aggie was still alive. She could talk to her about things that she could never broach with her mother. Although, whether her sister was the right person to give her advice about men was debatable. So her dad thought David was after her, did he? She could have told him that there wasn't anything serious between them. She liked him quite a bit but she could not let anything grow between them. Especially when she had a nice place to live, a good job and was managing to save a bit of money.

She turned into Brook Street, still thinking of David and stepped into the road. A warning yell alerted her to danger. Her eyes darted to the right and she gasped. A runaway horse and cart was heading her way. Suddenly she was seized from behind and dragged out of the way. The sound of hooves slipping on the damp cobbles almost deafened her as the beast missed her by inches and the wheels of the cart rumbled past. Shocked to the core she could only lean weakly against her rescuer.

'Are you OK, lovey? You gave me quite a shock there.' She turned and looked up into David's white face.

Before she could thank him, another voice said, 'Wasn't looking where she was going, was she? Daft thing to do.'

'What the hell has it got to do with you?' rasped David.

Emma turned hastily in his arms and looked at the owner of the other voice. He was the handsomest man she had ever seen with fair hair and brilliant blue eyes. Yet, even as she stared at him, his eyes widened. Then he grinned and nodded at her, before strolling away in the direction of the General Railway Station, leaving a strong smell of peppermint in his wake.

'Good riddance,' said David, giving Emma his full attention.

'He seemed familiar...and he was right about one thing. I should have looked both ways but I was thinking of...'

'It must have been something really interesting for you

to forget to look both ways before crossing the road.'

Emma could not tell him the truth that she had been thinking of him; instead she said, 'I was thinking of Alice Moran. She's in London with Miss Waters…and there was an article in the newspaper about a huge rally of the suffragettes. I wouldn't be surprised if they were amongst them. I just hope it hasn't proved too much for Miss Waters because she has a dicky heart.'

David's eyes rested on Emma's pale heart shaped face and he smiled. 'You're a caring person, lovey.' And he brought his head down and kissed her. The pressure of his lips was brief but very pleasant.

'What was that for?' she asked, trying to sound casual.

He said solemnly, 'Reaction to shock. I just wanted to make certain that your near accident hasn't affected your reflexes.'

She smiled. 'I'll have to get back to Mrs Black's. I suppose you're on your way home?'

'Home can wait. I'll come with you. We don't want you fainting all of a sudden and my not being there to catch you.'

'I'm not the fainting kind.'

'No excuse then for me to sweep you off your feet and carry you to your destination.' His cheeks dimpled.

She raised her eyebrows. 'Why the blinking heck would you want to do that? I weigh more than I look. Thanks for saving me life, though, and for making me feel good.' She stood on tiptoe and kissed him quickly before hurrying away.

Chapter Eight

June, 1908

Bert sat on the train, thinking of the scene he had just witnessed and how he would have missed it if he hadn't been on an early shift this morning; so enabling him to come to Chester and wander down to the Dee in the hope of seeing Alice. His blue eyes glinted with satisfaction as he opened the evening newspaper. The girl who had almost been trampled on by the horse was the spitting image of Agnes Griffiths, so must be related to the dead girl. That evening on the bridge when he'd surprised Alice…it must have been her. Only when his panic had abated had he been capable of rational thought and remembered Agnes' mention of her sisters. For some reason he had got the impression they were much younger. She must work in Queen's Park. Now what the hell was her name? He felt certain if he thought about it long enough it would come to him.

He began to read the newspaper, idly glancing through an article about a big rally of the suffragettes in London. It was estimated that there were two hundred and fifty thousand supporters demonstrating peacefully. Daft bitches thinking they were equal to men, he thought, his eyes flicking over the names of two women, Miss Waters, daughter of a prominent cotton merchant, and Mrs Stone, wife of a Chester doctor. He turned over the page but his mind was not on the news but Agnes's sister. He must keep his eyes open for her when next in Chester; she just might lead him to Alice.

Victoria rustled the *Chester Chronicle* under Alice's nose as she sat alongside her in the back of the car. It was a week since the rally in London and they had only just arrived in Chester. 'It looks like the rally's got a mention in the local paper. I thought it only made the nationals the next day. We must read it and see what Chester's journalists have to say.'

Alice could not have cared less because, to her astonishment, Seb had come to meet them at the station with the car. Her nerves were in shreds, wondering how matters stood between him and Juliana but unable to ask him. She was roused from her thoughts by a gasp from Victoria.

'Goodness! I never noticed us having our picture taken whilst on the march, did you, Alice?'

'No, Miss Victoria!' Alice gazed down at the black and white picture. It was slightly blurred but, sure enough, she could just about recognise herself, Victoria and Mrs Stone.

'I just hope Papa doesn't see it,' said Victoria, pulling a face.

'Unless he knew where to look, I doubt he'd notice,' murmured Alice.

Victoria nodded. There was silence as both of them began to read the lines of print beneath. 'Oh dear! Let's hope he doesn't read this either,' said Victoria. 'It seems that whoever took the photograph recognised me and Mrs Stone. He might have been there as a supporter because this article is very positive towards us.'

'Mr Waters mightn't read it,' said Alice.

'You're right. He's not interested in the Cause.' Victoria folded the newspaper and placed it on her knee. 'At least we didn't end up in prison. Christabel Pankhurst has been imprisoned several times. I heard her speak once when I lived in Liverpool. She's so fluent and witty, as well as beautiful. She has the colouring of a briar rose.'

'I've heard her referred to as an Amazon,' said Alice, watching Victoria rest her head against the back of the seat and close her eyes. It had been an exhausting journey back from London.

'We might all need to be Amazons if our Cause is to succeed,' muttered Victoria.

Alice was silent, thinking she had no desire to be a

warrior woman. She wanted to be loved and cherished, marry and have children and be happy ever after. For the rest of the journey she was miserable, expecting Seb at any moment to break the news that he was engaged to Juliana.

When they arrived at the house, Gabrielle was standing in the front doorway. Her arms were folded across her magnificent bosom and she looked displeased. 'Mr Waters comes in and says ee's not hungry! Then Mrs Waters gobbles her food and is sick.' She fixed them with her dark stare and pointed a figure. 'You, three, I hope are hungry and will appreciate my cooking.'

'Yeah, Ma,' said Sebastian, frowning. 'Now if you'll get out of the way so I can carry these in.'

'That is not a nice way to talk to your mother after you have not seen her for a while,' she complained, before turning her attention to Victoria. 'You look exhausted. You should never have gone to London.'

Victoria raised her drooping head. 'We had a lovely time…enjoyed ourselves shopping. We've bought material for skirts.'

'Skirts?'

'I want Alice to try her hand at making me a couple of the new fashionable hobble skirts. We bought some black voile that only cost eight pence and three farthings a yard.'

Gabrielle pursed her lips. 'But it is unseemly. It is too tight to walk properly and makes a woman's bottom move in such a way that…'

'Yes, isn't it fun,' said Alice boldly. 'Fashions aren't about comfort, Mrs Bennett. Now will you get out of the way so we can all get past.'

Gabrielle gaped at her and then with a sniff, stalked in the direction of the kitchen.

'Alice, you help Sebastian with those parcels,' said Victoria, her voice breathless. 'I'll go on ahead.'

Alice glanced at him. 'I can manage,' he said firmly, giving her no time to speak.

'Pride comes before a fall,' she said, snatching the top two parcels from him and beetling ahead in the wake of her mistress up the stairs.

'Bert,' he said. She almost dropped the parcels at the mere mention of that name. 'Is he Hanny's brother? I've heard that he's a nasty piece of work.'

She had reached the first landing so turned to face him. 'Who told you that?'

'Emma.'

Alice paled, wondering what other information she had given him. 'Yes, he is. But why d'you ask?'

'Because I want to know why he attacked you?' he said grimly.

Now the opportunity had come to explain everything, Alice was frightened to admit to having been engaged to Bert. How could Seb believe that she had never stopped loving him if she had been prepared to marry someone else? She could only say, 'Emma had no right to tell you my business.'

His mouth tightened. 'Don't be stubborn, Alice. I know you think I let you down over your father but I did love you. Now it sounds to me like you need help with Bert.'

'I know you loved me but...'

'I got myself involved with Juliana,' he said grimly, 'so you think I've got no right to question you about Bert.'

'Yes, and...'

'What the hell's going on here?'

Alice spun round at the sound of Mr Waters' voice. He was standing in the doorway of his bedroom, wearing a paisley silk dressing gown. His plump face was flushed and sweaty.

Neither of them spoke.

'Right,' said Mr Waters, breathing heavily. 'Sebastian, I want you in here, straight away.'

Seb hesitated. 'I'll just place these in Miss Victoria's bedroom, sir.'

'Be quick about it.' He went inside his bedroom.

Seb stood there, frowning. 'Don't think this is finished, Alice. I've still got plenty to say to you.' He dumped the parcels in Victoria's bedroom and went out again.

Alice wondered what Seb wanted to say to her. She was on pins for the rest of the evening but did not get to see Seb. It was not until the following morning that she discovered that Seb had accompanied Mr Waters to Liverpool and there they both stayed for the next fortnight. When Mr Waters returned to Chester, Seb was not with him. Victoria informed Alice that Sebastian had been sent to America again and was likely to be away for several months. Not only was he on a fact finding mission but Juliana's mother was dying and she was in need of his support.

After being in receipt of that news Alice despaired and gave up all hope of living happily ever after. Fortunately she was kept busy, not only making those narrow hobble skirts which Gabrielle disapproved of, but, also, taking messages back and forth between Victoria and her friends in the Women's Suffrage Movement.

In August, the news that Emma had gone away with Mrs Black to Devon for a month's holiday did nothing to lift Alice's mood. How she envied Emma being able to get away. Instead she had to listen to Victoria read aloud her statements in support of the suffragettes' new strategy after the Prime Minister had simply brushed aside their peaceful demonstration in Hyde Park. Christabel Pankhurst had declared that peaceful agitation was useless and militant action was the only way forward. It was relief when Victoria told Alice that she could have Sunday afternoon off as she had arranged to meet a small select group of Liberal ladies for afternoon tea at the Grosvenor Hotel.

* * *

Bert was sitting alone at a table, hoping his mother would be able to join him for tea and cakes, when a group of ladies entered the dining room of the Grosvenor Hotel. They were shown to a table a few feet away. He watched them surreptitiously as they ordered and poured himself a cup of tea.

A string quartet begun to play but the music did little to drown out the sound of a woman's voice expressing her anger towards the National Anti-Suffrage League. Apparently *No Votes for Women* was their cry and they were as bad as the Prime Minister, believing women should interest themselves solely in domestic and social affairs.

Hear, hear, thought Bert.

Another woman spoke up, 'But they have a supporter in a Roman Catholic priest from Colorado in America, where women have already been given the vote, Miss Waters. He says that women having the vote has made no difference to the dirty games they play in American politics.'

Bert stared at them, realising he had not only seen these women here before but he felt certain he had seen Miss Waters' name in the newspaper.

'Ha! That's because men still make up the bulk of those in government, Mrs Stone,' she cried contemptuously.

Another woman hushed her. 'Dear Miss Waters, do lower your voice – there's a man staring.'

Victoria glanced at the neighbouring table and realised she had attracted the attention of one of the most handsome men she had ever seen.

Bert's eyes met hers and now he remembered he had seen her name in the newspapers; she was the daughter of a cotton merchant. 'If you'll forgive me for saying so, Miss Waters,' he said boldly, 'what you say is so true. The priest's remark is typical of a man who has forsworn women.'

Delighted to have a man agree with her, Victoria responded by saying, 'How right you are, sir! Most likely he's of that breed who believe all women sinful because of Eve in the Garden of Eden.'

'How ill-judged of him,' said Bert, enjoying himself. 'Women have so much to give to this world.'

Victoria's eyes sparkled with delight. 'I see you have some sympathy for our Cause, sir. May I ask your name?'

'Temple, Miss Waters,' he said, getting to his feet and offering her his hand. 'Arthur Temple Esquire. May I say what a pleasure it is to meet the Miss Waters who attended the rally in London.'

Victoria's colour was high as they shook hands. 'You saw my picture in the *Chester Chronicle*?'

'I did. How much I admire you.'

Victoria was flattered, thinking here was a man really sensitive to her cause. 'If you are truly interested, Mr Temple, then you might enjoy reading our magazine *Votes for Women*.'

'Just tell me where I may get a copy, Miss Waters, and I will buy it.'

'Give me your address, Mr Temple, and I will send you one.'

'That is kind of you.' He took a pencil and a notepad from an inside pocket, wrote down his address, and handed the slip of paper to her. 'Perhaps we'll meet again, Miss Waters.'

'I certainly hope so, Mr Temple, the Cause needs the support of men such as yourself,' she said, smiling.

Bert thanked her and, as his mother had not made an appearance, he left shortly afterwards. He would write to her, expressing his disappointment at not seeing her, and would leave the message for her at the local post office.

'Alice, will you send my latest copy of *Votes for Women* to the address on the piece of paper on the dressing table,' said Victoria the next day.

'Yes, Miss Victoria,' said Alice through a mouthful of

pins as she adjusted the hem of the skirt. She stepped back to judge the length. 'Did you have an interesting tea party?'

'I did indeed, Alice. I met a man who agreed with me that women have much to give to this world. He'd read about me in the *Chester Chronicle*. The magazine is for him. Just imagine, Alice, if there were more like him, then we'd soon see women in parliament. How I dream of a different Britain, ruled by women.'

Alice presumed she meant women of her class and was not convinced that a *petticoat parliament* could solve all the problems that plagued working-class women, spinsters or married. There was so much that needed to be done to improve their lot that sometimes the thought of the struggle ahead was too daunting. However good the intentions of women like Victoria were, they had no real idea how difficult it was for women like Alice to be involved. They had so little time to spare for such things because their lives were such a hard grind. How would Miss Victoria have ever survived if she'd had to go out to work or she'd had to live in a damp house without the benefit of the best food and plenty of warm clothing? If her father hadn't had the money to pay for the doctor and medicines, servants to fetch and carry she would probably have succumbed to bronchial pneumonia and be dead by now.

'Wake up, Alice! You seemed to have gone into a trance,' said Victoria, stamping her foot.

Alice shook her head. 'I'm sorry, Miss. I was just thinking about the Cause…men and women…sickness and health…and marriage.' She helped Victoria out of the skirt.

She slipped into her old one. 'I'm so sorry for you, Alice. Because whether Sebastian marries Juliana or not, Papa's talking about him lodging in Liverpool to run the business when he returns from America. I have not mentioned it before but he overheard you and Seb arguing, and for reasons of his own, he thinks it wiser to keep the pair of you apart.'

Alice was astonished. 'After all this time? He must have noticed we've ignored each other most of the time since they returned from America.'

Victoria sighed. 'I know. But perhaps it'll be easier for you to get Seb out of your heart the less you see of him. Life is unfair. Just think, if I'd been a boy instead of a girl, I would be running the business.'

Alice had heard this before and thought she was mad to want all the trouble involved. 'It's a shame but what would the movement do without you,' she said diplomatically.

'There is that of course.' Victoria fell silent. 'Of course, things might be different if I had a husband…'

A startled Alice stared at her. 'A husband, Miss Victoria? But you've always said…'

'I know what I said…' She smiled faintly.

Alice was amazed. Surely she hasn't changed her mind about marriage just because she's met a man who agrees with her over the Cause. Well, this was a turn up for the book. She couldn't wait to mention it to Hannah when next she visited her.

But Alice was to forget about Victoria and Mr Temple when Hannah opened the door to her a couple of days later. 'We've had a letter addressed to you come through the post. It's in Bert's handwriting.'

Alice's hands shook as she took the envelope. 'Perhaps I should just tear it up,' she said in a low voice.

'No,' said Hannah, placing a comforting arm about her shoulders. 'We need to know what he's up to.'

Alice took a deep breath and then slit the envelope open with a finger and withdrew two sheets of paper.

Hello Alice,

I bet you have been waiting to hear from me. Possibly you've been jealous of the letters I've sent to my dear sister. No need for you to be because you're number

*one in my book. I can't wait to get my hands on you
and when I do...bloody hell, I feel hot all over just
thinking of the fun I'm going to have. First I'll tie you
up with a nice big thick rough rope and then I'll get
out my weapon and...*

Alice gasped as she read the next few words then read no
further, scrunching up the sheet of paper and flinging it on
the fire.

Hannah could be patient no longer. 'What did it say?'

'Surely you can guess. It was disgusting.'

Hannah sighed. 'You're as bad as me. I couldn't show the
police my last one either. What about the second page?'

'I don't want to read it. If you want to...here!' Alice
thrust the page at her and walked over to the window and
looked out over the backyard.

Hannah hesitated and then glanced at the sheet of paper.
Bert had written,

*I see Tilly's growing up nicely. I'm keeping a look out
for a friend of yours who will lead me to you.*

'You should read this,' she said, and went over to Alice.

She turned and took the paper from Hannah and read it.
The words about Tilly sent a chill down her spine. Her
sister had started school and she feared Bert snatching her
from outside the gates.

'There's no need for you to worry about Tilly,' said
Hannah firmly, plucking the sheet from Alice's fingers and
placing it back in its envelope on the table. 'He'll not get
the chance of snatching her. If there's ever a time I can't
pick her up at school, then Joy will do it.'

'What about your mother?' Alice's eyes met Hannah's
across the room.

Hannah sighed. 'I know what you're thinking. Mother
would enjoy fetching Tilly from school but Kenny's

forbidden it. Although, he doesn't believe she would ever hurt Tilly intentionally, he doesn't trust her. You might think this is a daft reason for him believing Bert's got in touch with her…but she's stopped wearing black and is obviously happier than she's been for a while. Joy thinks the same but says she's never seen him or a letter anywhere near the house.'

'At least he still doesn't know where I'm staying. I wonder who this friend is he mentions? It makes my skin crawl just thinking of him creeping around after people.'

Hannah nodded. 'Do we give that page to the police?'

Alice was silent a moment before saying, 'Perhaps you should just hide it away for the moment. They don't seem to be able to do anything. If only we had a photograph of Bert to show them.'

'Joy thought of that but says they all seem to have disappeared from the house.'

Alice's brows puckered. 'How long since he sent you a letter?'

'A couple of months. I'd started to believe he'd guessed we'd got in touch with police and had taken fright. I began to dream that I could live a normal married life.'

Alice darted her a glance but only said, 'I wish I knew who he meant by a friend of mine. I'm friendly with a few girls at church and amongst the servants but I wouldn't call any of them a close friend.'

'You don't think he's seen you with Miss Victoria and thinks she's your friend?'

Alice stilled and then said with brutal candour. 'She's middle class and I'm not. Bert can surely tell the difference.'

Hannah nodded. 'You're probably right. Let's have a cup of tea. Any news from Seb?'

Alice shook her head. 'Miss Victoria told me Mr Waters wants him to live in Liverpool and help run the business from there.'

Hannah looked surprised. 'He seems to be giving Seb a lot of responsibility since his accident.'

Alice agreed and decided it was pointless saying any more. She had to put Seb out of her heart and Bert out of her mind for the moment.

Chapter Nine

October, 1908

'Good afternoon, Miss Waters! What do you make of the Pankhurst trial? I believe Miss Christabel defended herself nobly.'

Victoria whirled round from the newspaper stand in the General Station and glanced at the handsome man standing a few feet away from her. For a moment she only had a vague recollection of having met him somewhere but then he came closer and removed his hat to reveal a head of slicked down fair hair. She could smell bay rum hair lotion and peppermint and could see that his eyes were blue and he had a cleft chin.

'Arthur Temple Esquire. You were kind enough to send me a copy of *Votes for Women*,' he said.

Now she remembered speaking to him in the Grosvenor Hotel several weeks ago and how he had made her think of marriage and how, with the right man, it could be an honourable state. She smiled. 'Of course! Did you find it informative?'

'Indeed, I did.' Bert had flicked through the magazine and then burnt it. 'It made me want to find out more. The Pankhurst trial…'

'Yes,' interrupted Victoria, her eyes sparkling, 'the reports have been riveting, her defence speeches alive with her every meaning. They say she held the court captive as she questioned the Chancellor of the Exchequer and Mr Gladstone. How I wish I had been there,' she added fervently.

'Yet she and her mother have been sentenced to three months imprisonment for inciting a rush on the House of Commons,' said Bert, concealing his satisfaction. 'It's a scandal.'

She nodded vigorously. 'That is true. But they are willing martyrs to the Cause.'

He hastily changed the subject. 'You are alone, Miss Waters?'

'I'm meeting Papa from the Liverpool train.'

'Then I'll leave you. It was nice meeting you again.' He inclined his head, replaced his hat and made to walk away. She placed a hand on his sleeve. 'I will send you the latest edition of *Votes for Women* if you wish, Mr Temple. I'm sure I still have your address somewhere.'

He thanked her and bid her good day, thinking that it was a stroke of luck catching sight of her like that. She was no oil painting but she dressed well and must have a bob or two if her father was a cotton merchant. He made his way across town.

Down by the Dee the trees were almost denuded of leaves. Bert gazed across the river, thinking about Alice and Agnes' sister. If she had not turned up when she had then, he'd have taken Alice to the fields along the other side of the river and had his way with her. He imagined her fear and could almost feel her struggling against him. His tongue flicked out and moistened his lips, his heart thudded. He mustn't think about that now, he needed to keep calm. He wanted to play cat and mouse with her and her friend just a little bit longer. Imagining her reaction to the letter he had sent her, a grin split his face.

To his delight he spotted Agnes's sister crossing the footbridge. He leaned against a tree until she passed him by, and, after a few minutes, he followed her. It was the kind of game that Bert enjoyed playing. He followed her to Cornwall Street and waited for some time but she did not come out. So he left to catch the train to his digs.

On his way home a brilliant idea struck Bert. It was ambitious, but what was wrong with that? He might have been brought up in the working-class area of Newton but he reckoned he could ape the middle-classes perfectly. So why shouldn't he join them. Having listened to the vicar talking after church services and by attending Bible classes, he knew exactly how to pitch his voice. Without any doubt his looks were attractive to women and he'd have had to be blind not to notice the effect he'd had on Miss Waters. Victoria and Albert, the two names definitely went together…but he was getting ahead of himself. One step at a time. First he had to worm his way further into her good graces.

But matters did not work out as he planned. Over the next few weeks he visited the Grosvenor Hotel for afternoon tea but without catching sight of Miss Waters once. Then, to his delight, he received the latest issue of *Votes For Women;* enclosed was a short note saying that she hoped he enjoyed reading it. But most important of all, was that she had written her address at the top of the letter. He read the magazine from cover to cover, so he could talk knowledgeably to Miss Waters about its contents when next they met; which would not be too long if he had anything to do with it. Another magazine arrived and the enclosed letter informed him that she might have to miss sending him the next few magazines as she was going to Harrogate with her papa for him to take the waters, as his health was not too good. Then they would probably be going to the country for Christmas.

Frustrated, Bert decided there was nothing for it but to wait until the next copy of *Votes For Women* arrived. In the meantime, he would keep a watch out for the Griffiths girl, waiting for the moment when he could give her the fright of her life.

Emma's step faltered and she stopped beneath the Victorian memorial clock on Foregate Street and whirled round. Her eyes scanned the late Christmas shoppers but it was difficult to tell if she was being followed or not. She had been to her parents' house with presents for the family and then she had called at the tailoring department of Brown's and Co. in Eastgate Row to collect Mrs Black's new tweed costume. It was not the first time she had experienced that prickling feeling at the back of her neck. Once she had turned and begun to walk back the way she had come, catching sight of a vaguely familiar, handsome face, only for it to disappear before she could be certain of the owner's identity. Why anyone should want to follow her was a question that had plagued her for weeks. She had even mentioned it to Mrs Black in a joking way, half expecting her employer to say it was all in her mind. Instead she had taken her seriously and suggested a couple of defensive measures, one of which had brought an embarrassed flush to Emma's cheeks.

Emma walked on past the brightly lit, tinsel decorated shop windows until she reached St John Street, where she turned and hurried down towards the Dee. It could be really scary at this time of year under the trees by the river, especially when thin ribbons of freezing fog hovered over the surface of the water. Alert to any sound of danger, she slipped her right hand into her coat pocket. To her relief, she reached the other side of the bridge safely and relaxed. She began to climb the path towards the crescent, only to almost jump out of her skin when a dark clad figure, his face concealed by a balaclava, stepped out of the shadows.

'Miss Griffiths, I presume,' he said.

Instantly Emma knew the identity of the man and was not only frightened but angry. For weeks she had been fearing an attack from behind but here he was in front of her. She wished David was here but, according to her father, he was in Crewe on union business so there was no chance of him suddenly coming to her rescue. Despite her heart beating fit to burst, she knew that she had to conceal her fear and try and ease out the pepper container in her pocket without Bert realising what she was about.

'How d'you know my name?' she asked conversationally.

His teeth gleamed in the gloom. 'Wouldn't you like to know.'

'That's why I'm asking.'

'That's my secret.' His chuckle was muffled. 'I've been following you.'

'I guessed that! Now will you get out of my way.'

'No. You made me angry when you interfered.' He took a step towards her.

Her pulses jumped and she told herself to stay calm. She had to get out the pepper and aim for his eyes. It wasn't going to be easy because there was only that slit where they gleamed like a cat's when caught in a flash of light at night. He was so much taller than her, almost as tall as David. She managed to control her voice so that it did not shake. 'I don't know what you're talking about.'

He thrust his face into hers. 'Don't play games with me,' he snarled. 'It was you on the bridge.'

Emma jerked back her head, her fingers still busily trying to free the pepper container. 'That time you ran away, you mean?'

'Shut up! You have too much to say for yourself.' He made a grab for her but she backed away. Instead, he seized hold of her parcel and swung her round by it so that the string cut into her fingers.

'Ouch, that hurt! How dare you!' At last she managed to drag out the pepper pot and knowing she would only get one chance to use it, shook it vigorously upwards towards that gap in the balaclava.

He shot backwards, rubbing frantically at his eyes. 'You bitch!'

She tried to get past him but he grabbed her with one hand. She dropped the pepper pot and the parcel and, seizing hold of his crotch, she squeezed hard. The whistle of his indrawn breath told her that Mrs Black had been right about that move. He staggered back, moaning and clutching himself. She snatched up her parcel and legged it the rest of the way to Victoria Crescent.

Her breath was burning in her chest by the time she reached Mrs Black's house and hammered on the door. It was opened by one of the music teachers and Emma almost fell into the hall.

'What's up with you?' asked the woman, gazing down at her.

Emma managed to gasp, 'A man attacked me.'

'Oh dear, what's the world coming to?' She looked frightened but bent down to help Emma to her feet. 'You must tell the police.'

'I must tell Mrs Black first,' retorted Emma. And, as soon as she had her breath back, she climbed slowly upstairs.

Ten minutes later Eudora handed Emma a glass of sherry. 'I'm delighted that you kept your head and didn't forget my advice in what must have been very trying circumstances, my dear.'

'Will I have to tell the police what I did?' asked Emma, sipping the sherry.

'I see no need for you to go into details.'

'You should have heard him squeal.' Emma chuckled.

'I can imagine,' said Eudora dryly. 'A man's genitals are his weak spot in more ways than one.'

'What about Alice? Should I warn her when she comes back from the country with the Waters? I mean the police aren't going to catch him now. He'll have scarpered...but he could return and they can't keep a watch on the bridge all the time.'

'That is indeed true.' Eudora frowned. 'But in the meantime you will, of course, avoid crossing the bridge on your own...at least until he is caught.'

* * *

'Have you heard?'

'Heard what?' asked Alice, sitting at the kitchen table and staring across at Gabrielle, who was stirring a pan of stew.

'It's all over the neighbourhood and also in the newspaper.'

Victoria said, 'It might have slipped your notice, Mrs Bennett, but we've been away.'

'I know that! But now my son is home and your father wished to speak to him urgently. Me! I had no time to exchange two words with him.' She slapped her chest. 'Instead, he is closeted with your father in his study all this time.' Gabrielle clenched her teeth.

'Never mind that right now,' said Victoria, sipping her drink. 'What's all over the neighbourhood and in the newspaper?'

Alice thought Gabrielle was not going to tell them but then she relaxed her mouth. 'A hooded man with staring eyes has been haunting the bridge. He attacked *that woman's* maid and she reported it to the police.'

Alice moistened her lips. 'What woman?' she asked.

'That Mrs Black!' Gabrielle spat into the fire.

The colour drained from Alice's face. 'Was Emma hurt?'

'A bruised and cut finger! He tried to take something from her but she struggled and managed to escape.'

'Does she have any idea who it was?' asked Victoria.

'How could she? Only his eyes and mouth showed. I ask myself what is the world coming to when we can't walk the streets of Chester in safety! That reminds me I must buy extra pepper.'

'Pepper?' asked Alice.

'Apparently she had suspected she was being followed for weeks, so she had a pot with her and threw it in his eyes. I have to admire her. She showed great courage despite working for *that woman*.'

Victoria turned to Alice. 'You must speak to Emma

when you get the chance.'

Immediately she agreed.

Alice was in luck because an hour later, just as she was leaving the house on a message for Victoria, Emma was coming along the crescent with a loaded shopping basket on her arm. Alice hurried towards her. 'I need to talk to you.'

Emma's mouth twisted in a smile. 'Heard about the attack and put two and two together, have you?'

'Yes!' Her green eyes were anxious. 'Was it Bert?'

Emma nodded. 'He knew my name was Griffiths, don't ask me how.'

'Did he say anything about me?'

'No.'

Alice sighed. 'He sent me a letter saying horrible things, but also, that he was keeping a look-out for a friend of mine. I never thought…'

'That we were friends,' said Emma wryly.

'I'm sorry.'

Emma shrugged. 'That's OK.'

'How's the finger?'

'I'll survive,' she said cheerfully. 'If you've finished asking me questions perhaps I can ask you something. Hannah, your sister-in-law…did she ever work for Bannister's Bakery?'

The question took Alice completely by surprise but she answered straight away. 'Yes, she did. Why?'

Emma's shoulders sagged with relief and she closed her eyes a moment before opening then and smiling at Alice. 'I think she might have known my sister.'

It was several seconds before Alice made the connection and realised who she was talking about. 'Of course! Your sister was Agnes who threw herself into the canal because Bert got her into trouble.'

Emma grabbed her arm. 'Bert! You – you're serious?'

Alice's face hardened. 'He admitted to me that he had

been with her and that she was having a baby. He did try to make out that he wasn't the only one she went with but now I think he was lying.'

Emma was stunned and for a moment could not speak but then anger mixed with jubilation gripped her. 'I've found him at last. Glory be to God!'

'You've been looking for him?'

'Too bloody right I have! Pardon my language! Although, I haven't done much about it lately. I had so little to go on. Aggie had spoken about an *Annie* who was her friend at the bakery, and I did ask there but they wouldn't help me. Then a while back it struck me that *Hanny* without the H sounded like *Annie* but I thought it was a long shot but more recently I started thinking that *maybe*...' She sighed. 'But it seems I'm no nearer to seeing he gets what's coming to him despite knowing who he is. You don't know where to find him and if he reads the newspaper he's bound to avoid the bridge because a bobby patrols it every hour now. It could be that he'll stay away from Chester for a while.'

'Could be...but you never know with Bert.' Alice was silent a moment and then she said, 'We both have a good reason to see he gets what's coming to him, perhaps we should try and help each other find him?'

'So what next? Have you had any more letters from him since the one you just mentioned?' asked Emma eagerly.

Alice shook her head. 'Fortunately he still hasn't managed to trace me to the Waters' house.' She gripped her hands together. 'There's something I haven't told you that perhaps you should know...Bert's Hanny's brother.'

Emma was so shocked by the news, she felt quite dizzy and had to lean against a garden wall. 'You mean he's sent his own sister threatening letters?'

Alice nodded, knowing she couldn't possibly tell Emma what Bert had done to Hannah. 'She did warn your sister about him, just like she warned me...but neither of us wanted to listen,' she said bitterly. 'Bert doesn't look the least like the villain he is. He can be such a charmer when it suits him.'

'He must be to have taken in our Aggie. Are you going to tell Sebastian about this?' asked Emma.

'If the opportunity arises.' Her eyes were sombre and she placed a hand on Emma's arm. 'I have to go but next time I'm off duty I'll take you to see Hanny if you can get the time off, too.'

'I'll look forward to it,' said Emma, thrilled that she had made a breakthrough in finding the man she held responsible for her sister's death.

Alice was thoughtful as she made her way to the footbridge but her head wasn't so much in the clouds that she did not notice a bobby talking to a child at the far end. The sight of him eased her fear. Bert was bound to make himself scarce when he saw the report in the newspaper. She decided to tell Seb all about Bert, if he asked her again.

After buying the latest edition of *Votes For Women* she hurried back to the house. She entered by the kitchen door to find Gabrielle sitting with her hands in her lap, staring into space. It was so unusual to find her inactive that Alice knew something was wrong. 'Can I make you a mocha coffee, Mrs Bennett?' she asked.

Sebastian's mother did not answer but got up as if in a trance and took milk from the cooler and poured some into a pan.

'I'll do that,' said Alice, placing a hand over hers.

Gabrielle shook it off. 'I do not like other people using my kitchen.'

Alice pulled a face and sat down, watching her take coffee beans and grind them and then search a cupboard for chocolate. 'Is something wrong?' she asked.

'I do not wish to speak of it right now.'

'Is it something to do with Seb?'

Gabrielle turned her large dark eyes on her. 'My son is a

wonderful son,' she said, laying emphasis on the *wonderful* in her rich voice. 'He is to go to India and Egypt and see the cotton growing.'

Alice was stunned. There had been no talk of him going abroad at the farm. 'What about Juliana?'

'It is finished between them.'

Alice's heart lifted. 'Where is he? When's he going?' she asked.

'He has already left for Liverpool. Mr Waters thought it best. He will write to me, I'm sure. Such letters full of colour that I'll feel as if I am there.' Her eyes filled with tears and she sank into a chair and put her head in her hands.

Alice tried to comfort her but she wouldn't be comforted, ordering the younger woman to leave her alone as her heart was breaking. Alice had never seen such an extravagance of emotion and considered it strange. After all Gabrielle had not carried on like this when Seb had left for America, despite her being against his marrying Juliana. Alice was torn between staying with her and rushing to the railway station so as to reach Liverpool before Seb sailed away to those far distant lands. Her better self won and she made hot drinks and, knowing where a bottle of rum was kept, poured a generous measure into each cup. She held one steady for Gabrielle, whose hands were shaking so much that she spilt the drink. Alice wondered if there was more to Sebastian's departure than his mother had said. She was working herself up to ask again what was wrong when the kitchen door opened and Victoria entered. She, too, looked upset.

'Papa's just told me,' she said without preamble. 'I don't know what's got in to him, sending Sebastian so far away. It's likely he'll be away for at least six months.'

Alice's voice sank to a whisper. 'I was going to tell him about Bert. I'd made up my mind to trust him with the truth.'

'Papa said something about trust...and was rambling on about Sebastian not having had a gentleman's education but being capable of taking on even more responsibility in the business.' Victoria's voice rose angrily. 'Why couldn't he have taught me about the business before I caught rheumatic fever and damaged my heart? Instead he insisted on my wasting my time doing the social rounds.' She hitched up her hobble skirt and paced the floor. 'It could have been me going to India and Egypt. It's not fair!'

'What are we going to do?' asked Alice, wishing Victoria would calm down.

She appeared not to have heard the question because she reached for the bottle of rum, and taking a glass from a cupboard, poured a generous measure. Alice watched in astonishment, knowing her mistress never touched spirits. Then she remembered the copy of *Votes For Women* and, hoping it would calm her down, pushed it across the table towards her. 'There's an article in it about the Pankhursts' release from prison,' she murmured. 'It says they stood in an open landau filled with flowers pulled by four white horses. Christabel is being hailed as the maiden warrior. An Amazon, just as someone said in the past.'

'My goodness!' exclaimed Victoria, distracted. Sitting down she began to read the article.

'It's *that bloody woman's* fault!' cried Gabrielle.

Victoria ignored her.

'I say no more,' said Gabrielle, and swept out of the kitchen with her head held high.

'They've been through a terrible ordeal,' murmured Victoria, glancing at Alice. 'But their suffering will surely win sympathy for the Cause.'

Alice nodded, but now her employer had calmed down and Gabrielle had left the kitchen, she wanted an answer to a question. 'Where is Sebastian?'

For a moment Victoria stared at her as if she wasn't

seeing her, then she shook her head. 'You want to tell him about Bert and say your goodbyes?'

'You don't mind? I thought you were angry with him?'

'Not him! It's Papa I'm angry with! Sebastian is staying at the Arcadia Hotel on Mount Pleasant in Liverpool until he leaves for the East.'

Alice thanked her and hurried to the door, only to pause in the doorway. 'You'll be all right, Miss Victoria?' Her voice was concerned.

'Of course, I will! On your way.' Victoria smiled and carried on reading the article about the Pankhursts.

Alice thanked her again and left the kitchen. She hurried upstairs, planning what to take with her. She flung a nightgown and a change of clothes in a Gladstone bag and then left the house.

Chapter Ten

January, 1909

The strong wind coming up from the Mersey estuary whipped Seb's dark hair about his face. He stood on the Princes' landing stage, gazing over the river at the shipping going about its business and wondered what he was going to do. His mind was in turmoil having run the gauntlet of emotions from disbelief, through anger and denial and back to anger again as he tried to come to terms with the news that Mr Waters was his father. Was it only a few hours ago that his world had been turned upside down? He had not wanted to believe that his mother had deceived him all these years. She had made up such stories that Seb had genuinely believed his father was a different man altogether. The news that he was a bastard, when his mother was a devout Catholic who never missed Mass, had stunned him. A single indiscretion he might have found easier to accept, but Mr Waters had admitted that she had been his mistress for years and had hurried to assure him that he had made provision for her in his will, as well as for Sebastian. When he had spoken those words, it was as if he thought money made everything right, but it didn't.

Following the revelation, Sebastian had walked out of the room and stormed into the kitchen to confront his mother. Initially she had been shocked...speechless...a first in Sebastian's memory. Then it had all poured out, how she had come from the slums of Liverpool and ended up singing in pubs before going on the stage. There she had met a musician, Richie Bennett, and married him. They had left England for America, only for him to walk out on her after an unholy row. She had been destitute until Mrs Waters had discovered her singing outside a theatre in New York and taken a shine to her. They had returned to Liverpool where the Waters had been living at the time. She and Thomas had fallen for each other; the trouble was that she was still married and he had a wife and child. At that point, Sebastian could stand no more and left the kitchen. The two people whom he had respected and believed to be utterly trustworthy and moral were nothing of the kind. The only thing he could think about was getting away, so he had gone to his room and packed his bags. He needed time to think and was in no mood to face anyone.

His father had found him there and had hurried into speech, saying he understood how shocked he must feel but he had only told him the truth because he was worried about his health and wanted to make sure that Victoria and the business would be taken care of if anything was to happen to him. He suggested that if he felt he had to get away, then why not visit Egypt and India and see how the cotton business was doing there? He would give him a draft on his bank and, perhaps, whilst in the great subcontinent he could look for a bride amongst the British middle class. Thomas Waters wanted grandchildren and as his only legitimate daughter seemed unlikely to provide him with a grandson, then his son must do that for him.

Seb's fists clenched in his pockets and he ground his teeth. His father had obviously thought he should be grateful for his admitting his paternity. The way he saw it his bastard son had a job for life and would never be in want. But Sebastian had learnt plenty about the cotton business in the last few years and knew that was no certainty. The British had exported spinning and sewing machines to India to benefit from the cheap labour and cotton there. The idea was for the natives to produce goods at the lower end of the market but, by doing that, they were taking away more and more work from the Lancashire mills, who for years had manufactured those kind of goods for export.

Seb had never worked for anyone but his father. There had been a time when he could have changed jobs. Alice had suggested his leaving the Waters' household a few years back to find a job as a motor mechanic, but loyalty and gratitude to the employer who had kept him on, even when he had sacked other men because the business was in trouble, had caused him to dismiss the idea. Now Seb knew why his father had kept him on but what had he gained in the past by being loyal? He had never been paid what he was worth. He had been cheap labour. He should have listened to Alice.

Alice! He remembered the feel of her body against his and ached with the memory. They had been passionate about each other but far too young to cope with trouble when it came. Both idealistic and expecting too much of the other. She had shown real courage the first time he set eyes on her and that had made it difficult for him to grasp just how great her terror of her father was. Whilst she seemed unable to understand his unspoken fear of being homeless with a wife to support and struggling to find work in a trade he knew little about. He had wanted her to wait but she had rejected his words of explanation and love. So when he had seen her here in Liverpool on his return from America he had wanted to hurt Alice as much as she had hurt him, which showed what a selfish bastard he was. If you loved someone you didn't set out to hurt them. No wonder she did not trust him enough to tell him what had happened with Bert.

He sighed and decided he needed more time to think before buying the ticket that would to take him to the other side of the world. He turned on his heel and left the waterfront. There was more than one ship sailing for India via Egypt that week. A few more days would make little difference.

* * *

Alice gazed up at the Arcadia Hotel with its net shrouded windows and shiny black door and, taking a deep breath, went up the steps and opened the vestibule door. A woman stood behind a reception desk, writing in a ledger. Without looking up she said, 'I'll be with you in a tick.'

Suddenly Alice was in two minds as to whether she was doing the right thing. What if Seb wasn't here or didn't want to see her? Panic rose inside, threatening to choke her. She couldn't do this. What would this woman think of her coming in here alone and asking for one of her male guests?

She was just about to leave when the receptionist said, 'Can I help you, madam?'

Madam, indeed? That gave Alice an idea and, glad she was wearing gloves, she went over to the desk. 'I'm looking for my husband, Mr Bennett – Mr Sebastian Bennett,' she said boldly.

The woman stared over her pince-nez and seemed to approve of Alice's neatly dressed figure in the dark green skirt and jacket, cream blouse and straw hat with artificial daisies tucked into its brim. Her expression softened. 'Mr Bennett is out at the moment but he said he would be back for supper. He made no mention of expecting you, Mrs Bennett.'

Alice felt that panic again but forcefully suppressed it. 'I wasn't sure I could get away. The children, you see. One of the maids had to visit her sick mother and was of a mind she would be absent longer but her mother's health has improved and…so here I am.' She fixed a brilliant smile on her face. 'A nice surprise for my husband. Perhaps I could go up to his room.'

The receptionist looked slightly embarrassed. 'Forgive me, Mrs Bennett, but unless your husband vouches for you it would be wrong of me to allow that. Perhaps…if you don't mind waiting in the lounge until he returns.'

Alice blushed and gripped the Gladstone bag tightly, her

hands shaking. 'Certainly. I understand. Thank you.'

She was shown into a vacant room overlooking Mount Pleasant and sat in an easy chair near the window, where she would get a good view of anyone entering the hotel. She prayed that Seb would come soon and crossed her fingers for good measure.

A quarter of an hour later she saw him approaching the steps. He did not look the least like a man happy to be setting out to far distant lands on what some would see as an experience of a lifetime. Taking a deep breath, she rose from the chair and went to meet him.

Amazement and then pleasure glimmered in his brown eyes. He reached out both hands and gripped hers. 'Alice, what are you doing here?'

Relieved that he appeared to be glad to see her, she rushed into speech. 'I couldn't let you go without explaining about Bert and saying how much I'm going to miss you.' There was a hint of breathlessness in her voice.

He closed his eyes briefly and then drew her into his arms and hugged her so tightly she thought her ribs were going to crack. 'Thank God! It's time we were honest with each other.'

'Where can we talk?' gasped Alice.

He murmured against her ear, 'I'd suggest my room but women are out of bounds.'

'I told the receptionist I was your wife,' she said with a throaty chuckle.

'I've missed that sound.' The expression in his eyes made her feel hot all over. 'Tell me honestly…is that what you want to be?' he demanded.

'I wouldn't be here if I didn't still…still care about you,' she whispered as someone passed them and went into the hotel.

He kissed her ear and breathed into it, 'What about Bert?'

'I never loved him like I – I love you.'

Seb freed a heartfelt sigh. 'Then that's all that matters.'

'No!' Her mouth fixed determinedly. 'You need to know it all but it can wait.' As long as Seb loved her and they could be together, that was all she cared about. 'What do we do now?' she asked.

'We eat, talk and then go upstairs and talk some more.' He bent his head and kissed her and then taking her hand, led her into the hotel.

'By the way,' she whispered. 'We have two children. They're the reason I arrived here late.'

He grinned. 'You always did have a vivid imagination.'

Alice agreed that was true but, telling him the truth about Bert, did not come so easy. She stumbled over words and often fell silent for several minutes but Seb was patient with her. When she reached the part where Bert had beaten her up, he reached across the table and gripped her hand tightly. 'When I get my hands on him…' he growled.

Alice shushed him. 'People are watching,' she whispered.

'Sorry. Carry on.' She did so and told her story up to the part where she had gone in search of Seb at the Waters and found Miss Victoria. 'That was the only sensible thing I did in all of this. I was a fool.'

'No! You were young and frightened and I was too wrapped up in my work. I should never have taken your no for an answer. It should have been me saving you from your dad, not him.'

She shook her head. 'I was a selfish and jealous little madam. I didn't want to share you with anyone, especially your mother and Miss Victoria.'

He shrugged. 'Let's agree we were as bad as each other and put all this behind us.'

Alice reached for the glass of water on the table and gulped half down. 'I haven't finished yet, love. I don't know if you heard before you came here that Emma was attacked near the footbridge.'

'No!'

'Your mam knew.'

He was silent, his expression bleak, and when he finally spoke his voice was strained. 'I've seen little of Ma recently and when I did see her this morning we weren't exactly on friendly terms.'

Alice reached out and touched his hand. 'I know she's upset because of your going to India but I didn't get the impression she was angry with you. The person she seemed to have it in for most was Mrs Black.' Seb's forehead corrugated in a frown. Alice waited for him to make some comment but when he didn't, she added hesitantly, 'I know she's always had it in for that woman…a bit like me…but for the life of me I can't think what she has to do with your going to India.'

'I'm not certain I am going to India yet…and I've only the vaguest idea of where Mrs Black might fit in all this. But the reason Ma's upset and I'm angry with her is something I'll tell you upstairs later.' And on those words he picked up his spoon and dug it into his syrup sponge pudding.

Alice opened her mouth to protest but then decided if Seb thought his explanation needed to be said in private then she had to go along with it.

Later when they went upstairs Seb drew Alice into his arms and kissed her. It was a long and deep kiss and when their lips parted she would still have clung to him but he put her away from him. 'Let me get what I have to say out of the way first.'

'Is it bad?' she asked anxiously, perching on the side of the bed.

Sebastian drew the damask cotton curtains across the multi-paned window that almost reached from ceiling to floor and then sat on a chair several feet away from her. He took a deep breath. 'Mr Waters told me this morning that he's my father.' Alice hadn't known what to expect but it certainly was not this. She was dumbstruck. 'Did you hear me, Alice?' he asked anxiously.

She nodded and stared at him wide-eyed. 'I don't know what to say.'

His face darkened and his hands clenched the arms of the chair. 'I felt like I'd been hit by a ton of bricks and he rambled on about my future but I was only half taking in what he said. As soon as I could, I got out of there. I had to speak to Ma. For years she's played the part of a good Catholic woman and preached propriety but, suddenly, I'm discovering that she was never divorced from her first husband and has been to bed with Mr Waters and I'm his bastard! In a peculiar way I wouldn't have felt so bad if he'd forced himself upon her and that had been the end of it…but no, apparently they've been lovers for years.'

'What did she say?'

His eyes smouldered. 'Not a thing at first. I've never known Ma lost for words.'

'I remember her saying something about Juliana possibly having had designs on him and I pooh-poohed it, saying nobody would want him when they could have you. She was furious but I never realised this was why.'

'Ma's suspicious of everyone that threatened her comfortable life. She said that he was mad for her…that she's a passionate woman. Then she went on about him being the only man she really loved. She accepted that, even after his wife's death, they couldn't marry. She miscarried two babies and I never knew about it! I lost my temper after that and said that she was a hypocrite and no better than a common whore.'

That last word caused Alice to wince. 'What did she say to that?'

'Slapped my face and told me she wished I'd never been born. That if the ship sank on the way to India she would praise God for it,' he said grimly.

Alice shuddered. 'She can't mean it. She thinks the world of you.'

His frown deepened. 'I'm not so sure. The times I asked

about my father and she lied to me. I feel a bloody fool for never realising the truth.'

'So what are you going to do? Did you ask Mr Waters why he decided to tell you the truth?'

'He's worried about his health, the business, Miss Victoria…said that much stuff I can't remember it all. One thing I do remember is that he said I have a job for life and will make a good living.'

'What did you say to that?'

He shrugged. 'I know one thing and that's that I'm regretting I didn't do what you suggested years ago and leave.'

She got up and went and knelt in front of him, placing her head on his knee. 'It's never too late. I love that house but I'm with you if you want to leave and try something else.'

He stroked her hair. 'Don't think I'm not tempted. The trouble is that I do feel responsible for Miss Victoria.'

Alice looked up at him. 'D'you think he'll tell her the truth?'

'He said that after his death will be soon enough for her to know.'

'Poor Miss Victoria. It'll come as much of a shock to her as it has to you.'

'I know. That's why I must give myself some time to calm down and think things through.'

'Mmm. So what'll you do about India?'

Sebastian gazed down into her upturned face and his eyes softened as he stroked her cheek. 'Perhaps I'll go after all.' Alice's lips formed a silent O and her green eyes filled with dismay. Then he added, 'But not alone, Alice. Imagine all those moonlit nights on deck. Marry me!'

A great rush of love and delight filled her. 'Yes, please!'

He pulled her onto his lap and they kissed.

As soon as Alice could breathe again she said, 'When can we get married and how?'

'Special licence. I'm sure we can find a priest or a minister – I don't care which…to marry us. We'll do what you wanted us to do a few years back, not worry about what other people think, get married and go off into the blue.'

She laughed. 'But what about my ticket? And won't I need a passport?'

'As my wife you'll go on mine. You'll need a photograph and your birth certificate.'

Alice groaned. 'I haven't got one. After Mam died and we left the house everything was left behind. I bet the new tenants got rid of it.'

Seb thought swiftly. 'You can probably get a copy from Chester registry office. Most likely you'll have to pay for it but I'll give you the money.'

Her expression was dubious. 'This is going to cost a lot of money, Seb. Can you afford it? Have you savings?'

He said dryly, 'Not worth mentioning. Mr Waters, *my father*, never paid me over the odds. In fact, considering I'm his son, he's treated me pretty shabbily.' Suddenly he grinned. 'But I've just remembered he gave me a draft on his bank, which means I can draw out whatever money I need.'

Her eyes twinkled. 'I'm sure he didn't mean you to use it to get married and take your wife to India with you…but as you said before, you're his son and so surely entitled to some of his money. And it's not as if you're going to tell him we're married until it's too late for him to do anything about it. Are you?'

'Too right I'm not,' said Sebastian, his eyes glinting. Suddenly Alice remembered Victoria knew that she had come here and groaned. 'What is it?' he asked. She told him and he scowled. 'Damn! She's bound to mention it to him.'

Alice pursed her lips. 'She's annoyed with him because she thinks it should be her running the business and going to India. She just might keep quiet about it.'

Seb's expression relaxed. 'We'll write to her after the deed's done. But you do realise, Alice, we can't invite Kenny and Hanny or even have Tilly for a flower girl?'

Alice sighed. 'It would be lovely to have them there but we have so little time and we don't want it to leak out and for Mr Waters to put a stop on that banker's draft. I want us to be husband and wife...and the sooner the better. I'll write to Kenny and Hanny and pray they'll understand why we're doing it this way.' Suddenly she remembered that Emma wanted to meet with Hannah and told herself that she must mention that in the letter, too. That decided she placed her arms around Seb's neck. 'Now the decision's made and we've told each other our secrets...what are we going to do for the rest of the evening?'

He stood up with her in his arms. 'I know what I'd like to do.'

'Then let's do it,' she whispered.

Chapter Eleven

January, 1909

'You all right, luv?' Kenny's fingers slid gently down Hannah's cheek.

'Are *you* all right? I know how you must feel getting that letter from Alice and Seb.' His face was in shadow so she leaned towards him the better to see his expression and thought he looked sad. She added softly, 'It shook me up, too. Yet I had a feeling about Mr Waters because Seb's father was such a mystery figure. But them going away, it made me wish...'

'That it was us going on a liner heading towards the sun,' interrupted Kenny. 'I'd love us to see the pyramids and the ancient temples in Egypt, but there's little chance of it ever happening.' Hanny nodded. Just like him, she didn't hold out much hope of their ship ever coming in. 'Are you going to visit Mrs Black and speak to Agnes' sister?' he asked, caressing her neck.

'I've thought about it. Although, I question what difference it can make to talk about Bert and Agnes.'

'I think she needs to talk about them,' said Kenny firmly. 'He attacked her, too, and for that reason alone I think you should see her. From what Alice wrote, the girl's got guts.'

'You admire people with guts, don't you?'

'That's because I know what it takes to overcome fear and do something even if you're scared out of your wits,' he murmured.

Hannah wondered if he was getting at her but then rejected that idea. 'You're right. I'll dash off a letter in the morning and arrange to meet her.'

'That's my girl. Goodnight, luv. I'll let you get some sleep now.' He kissed her and rolled away onto his side.

She blinked sudden tears away, placed her arm around him and kissed the nape of his neck. 'God bless, love,' she said in a throaty whisper. 'Sleep tight.'

'There's a letter for you here, Emma.'

Wondering if it was from Alice or even David, whom she had not seen for a while, Emma placed the shopping bag on the table and took the envelope from Mrs Black. It was postmarked Chester...so not from Alice then. The news that she and Sebastian Bennett had married in Liverpool by special licence and left for India had come as a shock, not only to the Waters' household, but to everyone in Victoria Crescent; it was still being discussed by the servants when they met outside in the road.

There were plenty who envied the newlyweds. Who wouldn't want to desert England in January for that far flung jewel of the British Empire? Of course some had questioned the reasons behind such a rushed marriage. Perhaps Alice had caught him on the rebound and he had got her pregnant. But Emma guessed that the pair of them had come to their senses at last and had not wasted any time in tying the knot.

'Aren't you going to open it?' asked Mrs Black, unable to conceal her curiosity.

Emma gazed at the handwriting again. She definitely didn't recognise it but, whoever it was from, she would rather read what they had to say in private so she placed it in the pocket of her coat. 'I'll unpack the shopping first and put it away,' she said far more calmly than she felt.

But as soon as Emma slit open the envelope and read the signature at the bottom of the page she knew it was not from David. Suppressing a vague sense of disappointment that he had not shown any concern about her having been attacked on the bridge, a report of which had been in the local newspaper, she told herself that at least she should be pleased to receive a letter from Hannah. She sat on the bed and as she did so, heard the door knocker go below. She half-rose but then decided to let someone else answer it and began to read.

Dear Emma,

I hope you don't mind my calling you Emma? But Alice has written to me, asking that I get in touch with you. I'm Hannah Moran and am married to Alice's half-brother, Kenny. Just in case you haven't heard, she and Seb Bennett are married now and on their way to India. She told me that you have been looking for me, knowing that I worked with your sister, Agnes, at Bannister's Bakery. I do so miss her. She was so lively and full of fun. The times I've wished that Bert had not entered the shop that day and met her. He can be such a charmer and she was completely bowled over by him. I warned her about him but, sadly, she did not believe me.

How I wish she had come to me when she discovered Bert had got her into trouble. I know for a fact that he was responsible because he sneered about it. How I hated him for that. So, I do so understand your feelings towards him...even without taking into consideration his recent attack on you. I admire your bravery in defending yourself against him. I would so like to meet you. If you can get away, maybe we could meet in the cocoa house on Brook Street next Tuesday at ten thirty. If not perhaps you could write to me at the above address, suggesting another date.

Yours very sincerely,

Hanny.

Immediately Emma went downstairs with the letter to Mrs Black, hoping her employer would give her the time off but she appeared distracted. Only when Emma repeated her name loudly a couple more times did Mrs Black glance up. 'What is it, Emma?'

'Are you all right, madam?'

'No, I'm not,' she said bluntly. 'I've just received some shocking news from our next door neighbour. Mr Waters is dead.'

Emma gaped. 'Bloody hell!'

'Exactly, Emma.' Eudora moistened her lips. 'It's terrible but he was already on the downward path when he came to see me. Overweight, breathless, he smoked, and, of course, that hip of his was giving him a lot of pain. Then there was his stomach trouble. God only knows what that woman fed him on.'

'What did he die of?'

'The doctor was still there when our neighbour popped round to tell me that Gabrielle was having hysterics and making accusations against me.' Eudora shook her head as if more in sorrow than in anger. 'She's always been a jealous person. Apparently she found him dead in the lavatory first thing this morning. I really do wonder about that woman.'

'Miss Victoria's going to be upset.'

'No doubt about it. I'm upset. Look...my hands are shaking.' She held them out and Emma saw that indeed they were. 'Should I pour you some brandy?'

'Yes! Pour us both some brandy as I'm sure you're as shocked as I am. Then perhaps I will visit the Waters in an hour or so and offer my condolences and any help I can. With the grandmother going senile, and only the maids to help her, Miss Waters is going to have her work cut out coping with everything.'

Emma nodded, thinking that now was not the right time to mention having time off to meet Hannah. She wondered whether now was the time for her employer to go barging into a house where there had just been a death in the family...even if it was to offer help.

'She – she is responsible. That woman!' said Gabrielle, raising the handkerchief to her tear-stained face and blowing her nose. 'Believe me, Miss Victoria, I know what I am talking about. Ask your grandmother.'

Victoria looked at her grandmother sitting beside her on the sofa and clutched her hand. Mrs Waters looked totally bewildered, and Victoria knew it would be a waste of time asking her any questions. Oh why had Sebastian and Alice had to marry and go off to India the way they had? She needed them. The doctor had prescribed sedatives for her grandmother and herself and Victoria intended taking one and lying on her bed for an hour or so as soon as Gabrielle left them alone. 'Grandmamma is incapable of understanding what you are saying. So explain it to me, Gabrielle.'

She stared at her sullenly. 'You will not believe me, so I will tell the police. They will listen to me.'

'The police! What have they to do with this?' Victoria was losing patience with her...was too exhausted and upset to want to listen to suspicious nonsense from their housekeeper. 'The doctor had been worried about Papa's health for some time. That is why we went to Harrogate. He hasn't been cursed by the woman you regard as the local witch.'

Gabrielle sniffed. 'You might mock, Miss Victoria, but if you cared about your papa then *you* would send for the police.'

'I'll do nothing of the sort,' said Victoria enraged by her words. 'I loved Papa and I forbid you to have anything to do with the police. I don't want them coming here asking questions. I've enough on my hands with a funeral to arrange and Grandmamma to look after without having to deal with them. Now, ask Mary to put hot water bottles in both beds and then you can help Grandmamma to bed whilst I rest.'

Gabrielle looked as if ready to explode. The doorbell jangled and she rushed out of the room but Mary was already on her way to attend to the caller, so Gabrielle hurried to the kitchen. There she put on a pan to make coffee before sinking on to a chair. Her heart felt as heavy as lead and her temples throbbed. When Thomas had told her he had been consulting Eudora Black, she was enraged every time she thought of *that woman* and what she had told him to do. Gabrielle held her responsible for her son's anger and subsequent departure and marriage to Alice in a *Protestant* church. How could he have married outside his own church? No wonder he had not wanted her there. And now her lover was dead and Miss Victoria was angry with her. She could not bear it and determined to have her revenge.

'Miss Waters – I won't stay long. I just came to offer my condolences and to ask if there is anything I can do to help you at this sad time,' said Eudora in a soft voice.

'It's very kind of you, Mrs Black, we're still in a state of shock,' replied Victoria, holding herself erect. 'Tomorrow I will have to write to my uncle. Today I can't think straight.'

'I understand. But I would advise you to speak to your father's solicitor and ask to see Mr Waters' will. It's possible he has left money to your half-brother,' continued Eudora in that soft gentle voice that always relaxed her clients.

Victoria thought she had misheard her. 'I beg your pardon?'

'Oh dear. I see your father didn't tell you. Too embarrassed, no doubt.' Eudora sighed.

Victoria cleared her throat. 'What is this about?'

Eudora smoothed the fingers of her black leather gloves. 'I wouldn't tell you this if I didn't consider that, in your state of health, you need someone at your side to protect you from your enemies.'

'Please,' said Victoria, a hand fluttering to her breast. 'Can you speak plainly? What enemies?'

Eudora inclined her head graciously. 'Mr Sebastian Bennett is your half-brother. I only learnt of that recently,' she lied. 'Thomas divulged the truth to me when he came to me seeking healing.'

Clutching the arm of the sofa Victoria was unable to speak. Eudora took a hipflask from her handbag, unscrewed it and, rising from her chair, went over to Victoria and handed the flask to her. 'I'm sorry to give you such a shock but I really thought he would have told you before that young man left for India.'

Victoria gulped the brandy down and feeling a little calmer, replied, 'I had no idea Papa had consulted you.'

'Oh yes!' Eudora smiled. 'We're old friends. He came to see me years ago in my role as a medium after your mother's death. Guilt was tearing him apart and he needed to find peace.'

Victoria had difficulty believing this conversation was taking place. Why had nobody ever told her this? Her grandmother must have known if it was true. No! It was impossible! Her father wouldn't have behaved in such a way...besides surely he didn't believe in such things. He would never have tried to get in touch with her dead mother. He didn't even attend church. 'No!' she cried. 'It can't be true.'

Eudora sat beside her and placed an arm round her. 'I'm so sorry, my dear. You were only a little girl at the time. He was so laden with guilt, he needed your mother's forgiveness. Gabrielle was his mistress, you see, and became pregnant. Her faith was her reason for refusing to get rid of the child. Gabrielle isn't even her real name but was her stage name when she met your father. They kept up with the liaison until his death.'

'Grandmamma!' screamed Victoria, unable to take her eyes from Mrs Black's face.

Eudora gave the woman a swift glance. 'She won't tell you anything...but it's true, my dear.' Her voice was mournful. 'Such a passionate and jealous nature Gertie has. Although at first she did not recognise me when I moved here. Eighteen years is a long time and I was no longer the girl she knew as Edna Rowland. Even your father did not recognise me immediately when he moved here from Liverpool. As soon as Gertie realised who I was she determined to smear my good name. She tells lies, you know.'

'I feel peculiar,' whispered Victoria. 'Dizzy.'

Mrs Black rose to her feet and fixed her with a stare. 'Oh, my dear. I've shocked you. What a selfish woman I am. Burdening you with all this at such a time, but I tell you it only for your own good. Can you trust that woman now you're alone with her? Dear Thomas hasn't been feeling well for a while. Stomach trouble he told me. It makes one wonder what she's been feeding him on.'

'I think I need to lie down,' said Victoria, her eyelids drooping.

'Yes, my dear. I'll ring for the maid, shall I? But you won't forget what I've told you, will you?'

'No,' replied Victoria in a voice barely above a whisper.

Eudora pressed her lips against Victoria's cheek and then rang the bell to summon the maid. 'I'll see myself out. Do take care of yourself, my dear, and don't trust that woman. She'll do anything for that son of hers.'

Gabrielle pushed the door open with her foot and entered the bedroom, carrying a breakfast tray. Victoria's eyelids fluttered open and she gazed up at the housekeeper. 'You slept well? You ate no dinner so you must eat breakfast to keep your strength up.' Gabrielle's eyes were anxious, having learned of Mrs Black's visit from Mary.

'Take it away. I'm not hungry.' That would have been true even if Victoria had not had that conversation with Mrs Black yesterday. She was still finding it difficult to believe all that the medium had said. Yet why should she lie? The straightforward thing to do would be to tell Gabrielle about the accusations that had been levelled against her but Victoria knew she could not cope with any more histrionics and decided to let things lie until she had informed her father's solicitor of his death. Surely he could tell her if Sebastian was named as his son in his will? If he was, then that would prove Mrs Black was telling the truth.

'But – But you must eat,' stammered Gabrielle. 'I will leave the tray here on the bedside table so you can help yourself.'

'No! Take it away,' ordered Victoria angrily. 'I must get up. I've lots to do. Tell Mary to run my bath.'

'Yes, Miss Victoria.' Gabrielle's voice was subdued and her shoulders sagged as she carried the tray out of the room.

Emma closed the door behind her and wrapped a scarf about her neck as she hurried down the path to the front gate. She was about to turn in the direction of the footbridge when she heard her name being called and turned to see Victoria Waters seated in the motorcar whilst Mary struggled to crank the engine. 'Come here, Emma, if you please!' Victoria beckoned her with a black gloved hand.

Emma hesitated before slowly walking towards the motorcar. 'I'm sorry to hear about your father, Miss Waters.'

A muscle moved in Victoria's throat and her voice was husky when she said, 'Thank you, Emma. Are you going into town? If you are, perhaps you would like a lift? I'd like to talk to you.'

Servants were not generally offered lifts in motorcars, so Emma accepted with alacrity. 'Thank you, miss. It'll save my legs.'

'I'd like to talk to you about my father's visits to Mrs Black,' said Victoria.

Emma thought for a moment to as whether her employer would want her discussing Mr Waters with his daughter, but then decided since she hadn't actively forbidden it there must be no harm in doing so. 'All right, miss.'

Victoria indicated that she should sit in the seat beside her and Emma climbed into the car and placed the shopping bag on her lap. Victoria ordered Mary to step aside and they were off.

'Mrs Black told me that Papa has been visiting her in her capacity as a healer. I found that so hard to believe that I have to ask you if it is true?'

'Yes, miss. Twice weekly he came.'

'Twice a week! D'you know what kind of treatment she gave him and how much it cost?'

Emma shrugged. 'I can't really say. That information is confidential. Although, it is possible she only laid hands on him. There's lots of people believe she has the magic touch.'

Victoria said swiftly. 'Do *you* believe that?'

Emma did not need to give much thought to her answer. 'A lot of her clients leave satisfied…although she doesn't claim to be a miracle worker. And there are those who give up if there's no improvement in their condition after a couple of sessions. But Mr Waters knew Mrs Black from way back and I suppose that was one reason why he kept coming despite his hip still giving him gyp.'

Victoria stiffened. 'You know for a fact they've known each other a long time?'

'I heard Mr Waters mention it the first time he visited her.'

Victoria was silent so long that Emma asked if she was all right.

The muscles of Victoria's face relaxed. 'It came as a great shock to me that he had consulted her in her role as a medium after my mother died.'

'Unfinished business,' murmured Emma. 'A loved one has died and the two have quarrelled...or there's something they meant to say but never got round to it.'

Victoria's expression was bleak. 'She told me that my father was – was unfaithful to Mama.'

'And did you believe her, miss?'

Victoria hesitated and then drew back her shoulder. 'I'll answer that after I've seen Papa's solicitor. But tell me, Emma, how do you find Mrs Black?'

Emma said without hesitation, 'I've no complaints. She pays well and seems to care about my welfare and that of my family. She believes in what she does and helps people even if they can't pay the full fee. Whether that's because she really cares about them or because it makes her feel good, I'm not sure.'

Victoria said in a surprised tone, 'It's perceptive of you, Emma, to realise there is a difference.'

Emma almost said *I'm not stupid* but decided Victoria might unburden herself some more if she kept quiet. Disappointingly, the older woman was silent as they crossed the old Dee Bridge and the car chugged up Lower Bridge Street and past the Falcon Inn.

Victoria set Emma down on the corner of Castle Street and said that if she wanted a lift home then she must be outside the solicitor's office of Crane & Crane in an hour's time. Emma agreed to be there and hurried away, intending to buy a stamp at the post office and post her letter to Hannah before doing the shopping. An absentminded Mrs Black had agreed to Emma having the time off to meet Hannah.

Victoria parked the car further up Castle Street, but before she could even step down onto the pavement, Mr Crane's clerk was there holding the door open for her. 'I saw you ahead of me, Miss Waters, and when you stopped the car I realised you must be visiting Mr Crane.'

'I have no appointment, Mr Vernon,' she said hastily, 'but I am hoping he will see me.'

'I'm sure he'll make time for you, Miss Waters,' he said in a fulsome voice. 'How is Mr Waters?'

'He died yesterday. That is why I'm here. I need Mr Crane's advice.'

Mr Vernon looked shocked. 'Oh, my dear Miss Waters! What a catastrophe for you with Mr Bennett away and your grandmother not herself.'

'I see you are kept well informed about our affairs, Mr Vernon,' she said quietly.

A flush darkened his jowls. 'Your father was a garrulous man, Miss Waters.' He ushered her up the steps and held the front door open for her.

Her eyes were bleak, thinking of all the things her papa had not told her. 'What do you know, Mr Vernon, about Mr Bennett and my papa?' she asked.

'I'd rather not say, miss. It is Mr Crane's place to inform you of anymatters concerning that young man.' His thin lips pursed in disapproval.

That expression was enough for Victoria. Her black skirts swept the floor as she swayed ahead of him and knocked on the door of Mr Crane's office.

'Who is it?' demanded an irascible voice.

'Miss Victoria Waters! I must speak with you immediately,' she replied, and without waiting for his response, she turned the knob and pushed open the door.

The bald headed, thin figure sitting behind the desk rose slowly to his feet. 'My dear Miss Waters, what are you doing here?'

She closed the door behind her and said harshly, 'My

father is dead. I need to know what is in his will.'

Except for the elevation of his eyebrows, he made no other outward sign of being shocked by the news. 'You have my deepest sympathy. Please be seated and I will have some tea brought to us.'

'Thank you. That would be most acceptable.' The words were uttered in a slightly breathless voice.

'You mustn't get yourself upset, my dear. Where is the young woman who was often your companion?'

'If you mean Miss Moran, then I am sure you have heard from my father that she has married Mr Bennett, who I have been informed is my half-brother, and they are on their way to India.' She clasped her handbag tightly in her lap, willing her hands not to shake.

'A moment, my dear.' He walked over to the door and opened it to find his clerk hovering outside. 'Have the girl bring us some tea, Vernon, if you please.' He closed the door and returned to his chair, resting his elbows on the desk as he steepled his hands. 'I advised your father to tell you the truth about Mr Bennett and when he refused, I suggested that he write you a letter for you to read after his death. He did not give me any such letter but most likely he thought there was time enough to do so in the future.'

Victoria felt as if a rug had been pulled from beneath her feet. She had hoped until this moment that what Mrs Black had said about Sebastian was a lie but here was confirmation of her words.

'You've gone quite pale, my dear. But I assure you matters could be much worse.'

'How can you say that?' she whispered. 'Papa has betrayed all the trust I placed in him. He betrayed my mother, and Gabrielle whom I regarded with much affection might be responsible for his death. As for Sebastian…how do I know he doesn't have plans to cheat me out of what is rightfully mine.'

Mr Crane looked shocked. 'You are overwrought, my

dear. I cannot believe Mrs Bennett would kill your father. As for young Mr Bennett, he had no idea that he was your father's son until recently. Perhaps you could tell me who put such ideas in your head.'

'A woman named Mrs Black. She knew Papa from years ago.'

Mr Crane tapped his fingers against his teeth. 'I've heard of Mrs Black. She has a certain reputation…but I had no idea Mr Waters had consulted her.'

Victoria cleared her throat. 'She came to see me and said that I should ask about Papa's will. She hinted that Gabrielle and Sebastian would be mentioned in it.'

Mr Crane hesitated and then lowed his hands to the desk. 'She is not mistaken. They have been since that young man's birth.'

Victoria gasped and he asked was she all right. She nodded and took out a handkerchief and dabbed her eyes. 'So who is left what?'

'I really should not tell you without the other beneficiaries present but – as it is going to take a little while for the news of his father's death to reach young Mr Bennett – perhaps he will not mind my informing you about those matters that concern you both directly.' He paused. 'Your half-brother will inherit no sums of money from your father but a fifty per cent share in the business – and this only on the condition he continues to work for the company in the role of manager. You inherit the other half and the residue of your father's estate after the other beneficiaries have been paid out. Mr Bennett's wages are to be increased immediately in line with his new position, and if either of you decides to sell their share of the business then each would need the agreement of the other.'

'What if I were to die?' asked Victoria faintly.

'If you die a spinster, then there is a codicil that says everything will go to him.'

She wanted to weep. 'But if I were to marry and have

children...what would they inherit if I and my husband were to die?'

'I think I'd be right in saying they would inherit your half of the business.' He added gently, 'Are you planning to marry?'

She did not answer him but instead asked, 'Does Mr Bennett know what is in my father's will?'

'Not that I am aware.' At that point their conversation was interrupted by a knock on the door. 'Come!' bellowed Mr Crane.

The door opened slowly and a girl pushed her way in, carrying a tray. Mr Crane took it from her and waved her out. Whilst they drank their tea, he advised Victoria to write to her half-brother immediately so as to catch the next mail boat going to Egypt. With a bit of luck her letter would reach Mr and Mrs Bennett before their ship passed through the Suez Canal on its way to India.

Victoria thanked him for his advice but she had no intention of taking it. She was so angry that she didn't want to see Sebastian and surely there were other men in the Liverpool office who could manage her father's business affairs. She thanked Mr Crane for the tea and information and told him that she would let him know when the funeral was to take place and left.

There was no sign of Emma outside but as a full hour had not yet passed Victoria decided to wait and see if she turned up. She sat in the driving seat, glad of the opportunity to have this time to herself to consider not only the funeral arrangements but also to think more deeply of what Mrs Black had told her last evening. Both she and Gabrielle had in their own way accused the other of being responsible for her papa's death. Although neither had produced any proof. She baulked at calling in the police when she had only the women's word to go on but decided she must be rid of both of them. Of course, dismissing Gabrielle would be no trouble. However Mrs

Black was another matter. It was at that point in her musings that Emma arrived.

'I hope I haven't kept you waiting long, Miss Waters?'

Victoria glanced down at the diminutive figure in the shabby brown costume and said with a sigh, 'Would you mind cranking the engine for me, Emma?'

Emma did mind but, as a ride in the motorcar would get her back to Mrs Black's quicker, she did as she was asked. In no time at all they were heading for the Dee.

Victoria came to a decision. 'I wish you to tell Mrs Black something for me, Emma.'

'What's that, miss?'

'I'm considering calling in the police. Both she and Gabrielle have accused the other of being responsible for Papa's death.'

Emma stared at her and swore inwardly. 'Are we talking about murder here, miss?' she asked hesitatingly.

Victoria said soberly, 'Could be, Emma. Why, have you got some information for me?'

Emma remembered what Alice had said about needing to watch what one ate in Mrs Black's company but, for the life of her, could see no reason for her employer to want to get rid of Mr Waters, so she shook her head. 'I should imagine your father was paying Mrs Black good money, so I can't see her killing the goose that laid the golden eggs.'

'Indeed! But for all we know there might have been something more between them than has come to light. As for Gabrielle, she does have a passionate and jealous nature...and Papa was once a very g – good looking...' Her voice broke and it was not until the car drew up at the kerb outside the house that she had enough control of her emotions to say, 'Tell Mrs Black what we have discussed...and if you ever feel like changing situations, Emma, please, let me know. I would happily take you into my household now that Alice has married Sebastian. You can read and write, can't you?'

Emma said in a dignified voice, 'Of course, miss. My dad might have plenty of faults but he's always been keen on us kids knowing the three Rs.'

'Good! God only knows when Alice and Sebastian will return...and when they do I don't want them living with me,' she said tersely. 'Good day.'

Emma wished she knew why she didn't want the newlyweds back home but guessed it might not be well received if she asked. So she just collected the shopping from the back seat and thanked her for the ride.

After Emma had finished unpacking the shopping, she told her employer what Victoria had said. Waiting for her reaction she expected her to explode with anger. Instead Eudora spoke not a word. Even when supper was over and Emma had cleared away and washed the dishes, her employer only said that she could take tomorrow afternoon off to see her family.

Emma did so but when she returned to the apartment, it was to find it deserted and an envelope addressed to her propped up on the mantelshelf in the drawing room. Swiftly, she slit it open and took out a sheet of paper. As she unfolded it a five pound note fell out. Picking it up she placed it in her pocket and began to read the note with a heavily beating heart.

Dear Emma,

I hope this will tide you over until you find another position. I am renting out my apartment and going abroad for a while. I'm sure a touch of sun will do my aching bones nothing but good. I look forward to seeing you again one day.

My very best wishes,

Eudora Black.

Emma was filled with dismay. Did her sudden departure mean that she did have something to do with Mr Waters' death? She supposed she would never know for sure. Whatever, Emma lamented the loss of the best employer she had ever had and wondered where she was now.

'How are you feeling today, Malcolm dear?' asked Eudora, seating herself in a comfy chair the other side of the table.

Mal Moran gazed across at her from drooping eyelids but did not reply. His rust coloured hair had been cut very short and his face looked bloated. He opened his mouth as if to say something but then closed it again. Of course he was away to the woods, thought Eudora, drugged up to those soulful brown eyeballs of his, so he can't give the staff any trouble. He had once been such a fine figure of a man but with so much anger and frustration inside him. Sad! And all down to that murdering, narrow-minded mother of his, but Eudora had cooked her goose and set him free from her influence for good. Afterwards, as a medium, she had been concerned about the old Mrs Moran's spirit not resting easily, so she had been extra careful when conducting a séance not to leave herself open to possession by any evil spirits on the rampage.

Eudora leaned forward. 'I've come to say *au revoir*. I'm off to the mystic East. It's possible but unlikely I might bump into Alice. You haven't forgotten your daughter, Alice, have you?' She watched his eyes intently, wondering if that was a flicker of recognition in their depths. 'She's married now. Fortunately, she found out what a swine Hanny Kirk's brother, Bert, was before tying the knot. I'm sure you remember him, he was the one who helped put you in here. He certainly got his revenge for your pushing his mother downstairs and her never being the same since.' Eudora sighed. 'I know that she was an interfering busybody who set your wife against you...but your lack of self-control that day has affected so many lives. Bert has gone from bad to worse and it wouldn't surprise me if he ended up in prison one day. I can imagine that would result in his mother having a complete breakdown.'

There! Was that a flicker? She had hoped that he would have made some kind of recovery after more than two years in the asylum. The medication meant that he led a quiet life which enabled the brain to rest; although that was only good if it didn't make him brain dead, as well. It was such a shame that he had ended up in here. Mothers! They had such a lot to answer for.

From her capacious handbag, she took a box of chocolates and a bag of boiled sweets and placed them on the table. 'These are for you. Next time I come, I'll have lots to tell you about my travels.'

His hand reached out slowly for the confectionary and her eyebrows rose slightly. Something was getting through but just how much she could only guess at. She stood up and, bending over him, rested a hand lightly on that distinctive red hair and kissed his cheek. 'Till the next time, my dear.'

As she neared the end of the ward, she glanced over her shoulder and saw that two of his fingers were pressed against the spot where she had kissed him. She felt a frisson of pleasure, thinking that she hadn't lost her touch, and smiled before closing the ward door behind her.

Chapter Twelve

April, 1909

It was two months since Eudora Black's departure and Emma was sitting across a table from Hannah Kirk in the cocoa house in Brook Street, waiting for their cocoa to arrive. She'd had to cancel the first meeting because she had taken up Victoria Waters' offer of a job and her new employer had refused to allow her time off, saying she could not spare her so soon due to her papa's funeral and the departure of Gabrielle. Her absence had left a gap, although she had never heard Victoria admit to it. But at last Emma had managed to wangle a couple of hours off and arranged another meeting with Hannah.

Immediately they had recognised each other: Emma from having seen Hannah as a bride and she from her likeness to Agnes. Both their eyes had filled with tears when Hannah had spoken of Agnes, saying that she would never forget her. Then she had hugged Emma, adding that she hoped they could be friends. Such warmth had caused Emma to take to Hannah instantly.

'Shall we get Bert out of the way and then we can talk about Mrs Black?' suggested Hannah.

Emma was surprised by her mention of her previous employer but agreed and watched as Hannah reached into her handbag and took out a sheet of paper. She hesitated and then slid it across the table. Emma picked it up and scanned the lines of print then glanced across at Hannah's strained face. 'I know he's your brother but he must be sick in the head. Why is he like this?'

Hannah sighed. 'I wish I knew. He was brought up to consider other people's feelings but you wouldn't believe it from what he's written there. Sometimes I've wondered if some people are just born with a capacity for real evil inside them.'

'Could be,' said Emma, handing back the letter.

Hannah scrunched it up and dropped it back in her handbag. 'It would help if the wicked in the world looked cruel and horrible but Bert's a handsome swine.'

Emma said swiftly, 'I suppose you haven't got a likeness of him?'

A sharp laugh issued from Hannah's lips. 'I wouldn't give a photograph of him shelf room. I can tell you he's fair haired and blue eyed with a cleft in his chin, but I suppose that's not much help to you. There's plenty of men with those kind of looks about.'

Emma thought of David, but before she could say anymore on the subject of fair, handsome men, their cocoa and scones arrived. Once the bill had been paid and they'd both drunk some of the hot beverage and eaten half a scone, she said, 'What about your mam – does she have a photograph of Bert?'

Hannah shook her head. 'They've all disappeared. Whether that's because Dah didn't want to be reminded of him or Mother's hidden them away somewhere, I don't know.'

'Is there anyway you could find out? I'd really like to see what he looks like. Otherwise he could be right behind me and I'd never know it.'

Hannah nodded. 'I'll do my best. Now our Bert knows who you are he just might try to worm his way into your affections.'

'I'm not about to allow myself to be charmed by any fair men with clefts in their chins,' murmured Emma, absently eating the rest of her scone and thinking of David again. She had not heard anything from him and surprisingly, that really hurt. Perhaps she had read too much into a single kiss. Of course, maybe he'd been so involved with union affairs he hadn't read about the attack. She had asked her father for news of David but he'd told her that he hadn't seen him in ages.

Hannah cleared her throat noisily. 'You've gone off in a trance. I've spoken twice and you haven't heard me.'

Emma started guiltily. 'Sorry. I was thinking of someone who's fair but grey-eyed and has a dimple in his cheek.'

Hannah smiled. 'A boyfriend?'

Emma shook her head. 'No! Can't be thinking of having one of them, not when the family needs my wages. Getting back to Bert, though. I'm determined he'll pay in some way for what he did to our Aggie.'

Hannah reached across the table and squeezed her hand. 'I know what you're suffering.'

'My brother Chris, he would know what to do to him. I admit I'd like him to vanish from this earth.'

'In the meantime you mustn't drop your guard. Bert might be keeping out of sight since the man in the balaclava hit the headlines but it doesn't mean he's given up on getting his revenge on any of us.' Hannah glanced at the clock on the wall. 'I'm going to have to go in a few minutes. I know it's been short but Kenny picks up Tilly from school and they'll be in for lunch soon.'

'I'll see you again, though?'

'Of course!' Hannah smiled. 'Now we've broken the ice, you can drop in and see me the next time you visit your family. Hopefully I'll have that photograph for you.' She paused. 'By the way, Kenny has written to Alice and Seb. He thought he should when he saw Mr Waters' death in the obituaries.'

Emma hesitated. 'You said you wanted to talk about Mrs Black.'

Hannah nodded. 'I hadn't forgotten. You said in your letter that she'd gone abroad. I just wondered if you knew why?'

Emma sipped her cocoa. 'Guilty conscience perhaps. Apparently Seb's mother accused her of murdering Mr

Waters and Miss Waters threatened to get the police.'

'You're joking!'

Emma could not help smiling. 'What I find a bit of a farce is that Mrs Black accused Seb's mother of murdering him.'

Hannah's eyes danced. 'You are serious?'

Emma crossed her heart. 'Honest! You could say that Mrs Black taking off into the blue points to her having done it...but I keep asking myself why should she want him dead? He'd been coming to her for healing. Apparently they knew each other from years back. But you've met Mrs Black, so you'd know if she was capable of slipping something into his drink or food.'

Hannah's expression was thoughtful. 'Not without a good reason. Was there any mention of Mrs Black in Mr Waters' will?'

'Miss Waters said not but he did leave Mrs Bennett money.'

'Ahhh! Now she's the kind who might do...what do they call it in the newspapers?'

'A *crime passionelle?*'

'That's it,' said Hannah. 'Do we know what he died of?'

'The doctor put an apoplexy on the death certificate. Although, according to Miss Waters, he'd been suffering from stomach upsets for months.'

There was a short silence before Hannah said, 'It could be that one of them was putting something in his food but only enough to cause him discomfort. Perhaps syrup of figs to get him running.'

Emma smiled wryly. 'Mrs Bennett would have been more likely to do that I should think.'

'Having met her, I agree. Maybe at one time he was carrying on with both of them. You know what it says in the Bible...hell hath no fury like a woman scorned.' Hannah sat back, cradling her cup between her hands.

Emma nodded. 'I reckon Miss Waters only mentioned

the police to put the wind up Mrs Black. Now she's gone abroad, Miss Waters says it proves she was partly responsible for his death. Even so that didn't stop her getting rid of Mrs Bennett.'

Hannah started. 'Good God! I thought she'd be there until she was carried out in a box. I wonder what Seb will say? I suppose Kenny should write another letter and let him know.'

'That would be right and proper. Although, no doubt the solicitor might have done so. Miss Waters has no intentions of writing and telling Seb anything. She's so upset about it all that she doesn't want him and Alice back in the house. Mary, the maid, said she'll live to regret dismissing Mrs Bennett. Would you believe Mr Waters left her a thousand pounds in his will!'

'A thousand pounds! What couldn't I do with that!' cried Hannah. 'Of course she and Mr Waters were lovers. Could still have been until the day he died for all we know. What I do know is that he's Seb's father – Alice wrote and told us.'

Now it was Emma's turn to gasp. 'I didn't know! It explains a lot.'

Hannah nodded. 'I bet he's been left something in Mr Waters' will, too. The lucky thing,' she added with a sigh.

'You can bet your last penny that's why Miss Waters doesn't want him and Alice in the house,' said Emma.

They were both silent, each thinking of how lovely it would be to be left money and what they would buy with it. Needless to say both planned to spend some of it on their families. Emma was the first to stir and, draining her cocoa cup, looked at the clock.

'I'm going to have be going or Miss Victoria will have a face on her.'

'I should have gone by now,' said Hannah, reaching for her handbag and smiling. 'We didn't have very long but it was lovely meeting you.'

'Same here,' said Emma, returning her smile and getting to her feet.

They walked out of the cocoa house together, Emma promising to drop by Hannah's house as soon as she could, then they went their separate ways.

As Emma wended her way through the city centre towards the river, she wondered what Victoria Waters would have to say about Hannah's husband writing to Sebastian with the news of Mr Waters' death. Surely she would get in touch with him once she told her so. It was obvious to Emma in the short time she had been working for Victoria Waters that she wasn't fit to cope with running a household and helping with the business.

When Emma arrived back at the house, she was immediately called into the drawing room, where she found Victoria lying on the chaise longue, wearing a black serge skirt and a white blouse with a black silk tie. She was reading the *Chester Chronicle* and eating chocolates from a box on the occasional table nearby. 'So you're back, Emma. Good! Grandmamma's been banging on the floor upstairs, Mary's gone out on a message for me and the new cook refuses to see to her. Go up and see what's wrong.'

'Yes, miss,' said Emma, hesitating before adding, 'Won't you spoil your lunch by eating chocolates right now?'

Victoria stared at her in astonishment. 'Don't be impertinent. That decision is entirely mine. Now upstairs with you.'

A tight-lipped Emma turned on her heel and walked out and upstairs. She went to her own room in the attic first and took off her outdoor things and put on her apron before going to see the old woman. She discovered that she had not only fallen out of bed but also dirtied herself and was in a terrible stinking mess. Exasperated, Emma knew that she really needed another pair of hands to see to her but did the best she could, not wanting to leave her as she'd found her. By the time she had finished, there was a pain in the small of her back and, as she dumped the dirty linen and nightgown in the washroom downstairs, she was really angry. Having scrubbed her hands, she knocked on the drawing room door and was told to enter.

Victoria was still lying on the chaise longue. 'Oh, it's you again, Emma. How did you get on with Hannah Moran? Is she well?'

The question put Emma off her stride. It was as if Victoria had completely forgotten sending her up to see to Mrs Waters, but at least it gave Emma an opening to mention Seb and Alice. 'We got on very well. She was telling me that her husband had written to Sebastian Bennett and Alice about Mr Waters' death. Perhaps you could write to them. You could do with their help here.'

Victoria raised her eyebrows. Her hand shook as she reached for another chocolate. She did not put the sweetmeat straight in her mouth but licked the dark chocolate shell until the soft centre was revealed and only then did she pop it into her mouth.

Emma persisted. 'Perhaps I could write the letter for you. And while I'm at it I could dash off a note to put in the newspaper advertising that there's a vacancy for a nurse here.'

Victoria stared at her as if she had taken leave of her senses. 'A nurse? You mean to take care of Grandmamma? Surely you and Mary can manage between you?'

Emma did her best to stand up straight, her small head flung back. 'Mrs Waters needs proper nursing, she's just fallen out of bed and dirtied herself. Fortunately she doesn't appear to have broken anything but that could be because she took half the bedclothes with her.'

Victoria's eyes widened in dismay. 'Oh no! But surely it was just a one off?'

'If it happens again it'll prove it's no accident and that she needs professional help,' said Emma grimly. 'Besides, I didn't come here to be a housemaid or a nurse, Miss

Waters. You hired me to take over Alice's position, helping you to write letters and the like.'

Victoria licked her lips before saying, 'That's true, Emma, but Alice used to make my hats and you must admit that you have a shortcoming in that area. As for letter writing, the Cause must wait. I have other matters that require my attention.'

Emma said bluntly, 'If you were one of the working-class women whose rights you're so fond of spouting about, you'd just have to get on with things, miss.'

Victoria drew in her breath with a hiss. 'How dare you? Alice would never have spoken to me like that.'

Emma flushed but met her gaze squarely. 'Alice isn't here. Wouldn't you like her and Mr Bennett to be? They could help with Mrs Waters. Rumour has it that Mr Bennett is related to you and family are the best people to have around when you're in need,' she said glibly, instantly thinking that her own weren't of much help to her.

Victoria was silent so long that Emma thought she was working herself up to tell her she was dismissed but instead she said in a subdued weary tone, 'One shouldn't listen to rumours, Emma. No doubt you have a point, but I still don't want them here. I confess I miss Gabrielle. She had a way with macaroons that I loved and her mocha coffee was out of this world…but life is about more than food and drink.' Her hand reached for another chocolate. 'In the meantime you and Mary must manage as best you can if you want to keep your jobs here. Without a reference you'd have trouble getting another. It's not my intention to be awkward or mean but I have to be careful about what I spend. Mr Crane tells me that there isn't as much money in the bank as I had thought.'

'Yes, miss,' said Emma, gazing at the box of chocolates, before turning and walking away. Whether Victoria Waters liked it or not, Seb and Alice would be back in Chester at some point and they would want to know what had been going on here. Mrs Black, too, would be home one day and Emma wanted to be on hand when she did return. In the meantime, she had plenty to tell Hannah next time she saw her.

A week later, Hannah was thinking of Emma when Kenny came through the door with Tilly in tow. 'A postcard! We've had a postcard from Mrs Black,' she cried. 'She says that she went to see your father before going away. That he's well and she's told him about Bert. She's also sent a postcard for Emma care of this address.'

Kenny stared at her. 'Why should she mention Bert to my father?'

Hannah smiled. 'Don't ask me. But she's in Egypt and the picture's of a dhow on the Nile. At least it's different from the one Alice and Seb sent of the pyramids.'

Kenny shook his head in disbelief. 'That woman can always surprise. What else does she have to say?'

'Isn't that enough? But as it is she did write a PS. It says that one day our ship will come in.' Hannah pulled a face. 'How did she know how much we'd love to go there? I must say, her postcard's cheered me up.'

Kenny kissed the top of his wife's head. 'Well, that's good. I wonder if one of her reasons for sending it was the hope that it would stir me into visiting him.'

Hannah shook her head. 'I don't think so. She knows what you and your family suffered at his hands. Interesting that she's told him about Bert.'

Kenny shrugged. 'A fat lot of good that'll do with him in the asylum and Bert on the loose. No other post?'

'If you mean is there a reply to your letter to Alice and Seb or anything more from Bert then the answer's no.'

Kenny's expression was grim. 'Good about there being nothing from Bert but I'm disappointed we haven't heard from Alice and Seb. They must have reached India by now and the mail boat with my letter can't be far behind.'

Hannah agreed and, handing him the postcard, went to see to the supper.

A couple of days later Emma turned up on the doorstep. 'I was hoping I'd see you,' said Hannah, dragging her inside the house. 'We've had a postcard from Mrs Black and there's one for you.'

Emma looked pleased. 'I'm glad she hasn't forgotten me. You won't believe the nerve of her...she sent one to Victoria Waters and suggested that she take a holiday.' Hannah laughed. 'What about Seb and Alice, have they sent her one?'

Emma nodded. 'They wrote that they wished she could be there with them but that she wouldn't enjoy the heat. She was spitting mad at getting both cards.'

'I suppose I can understand that,' murmured Hannah.

'Part of me feels sorry for her but on the other hand, working for her is no doddle.' Emma grimaced. 'I'm only sticking it out in the hope that Mrs Black'll be back in a few months and take me on again. I told her what you said about your husband writing to Seb and Alice but it made no difference. She's still refusing to get in touch herself. And she's still determined not to have them living there. I can't wait to see what happens when they get back.'

'Seb's not going to take it lying down that she sacked his mother,' said Hannah decidedly.

'No.' Emma looked thoughtful but then smiled. 'Where's my postcard? I want to see what she has to say. Fancy her sending it here to you. It's probably because I asked for time off to meet you before she left.'

Hannah handed her the postcard and Emma read it swiftly and then sighed. 'Did you read it? She says she regrets not taking me with her but is sure I'll have lots to tell her when we see each other again.'

Hannah echoed her sigh. 'What an experience that would have been for you. Anyway, sit down. Have you anything else to tell me about Miss Victoria?'

Emma placed her postcard in her pocket and sat down near the fire. 'She's changed her mind about having no time for the Women's Suffrage Movement and has decided she's got to get out of the house. So the pair of us are to attend a meeting at the Newgate Assembly Room next Monday.'

'I read about that meeting. Isn't it being arranged by the Women's Freedom League?'

Emma nodded. 'I believe they have links with the socialist movement and although militant, they're anti-violence. Alderman Chunton will be chairing it. I can't remember the speakers' names offhand.'

Hannah's face brightened. 'Then perhaps I'll come along. Our Joy might, too, and Kenny. He can write it up for one of the newspapers. He's been doing bits like that this past year. I'll ask Granny Popo if she can sit with Tilly.'

Over a cup of tea, Emma asked Hannah whether she'd had any luck getting the photo of Bert. She shook her head. 'I have mentioned it to our Joy.'

'Did you tell her why I want it?'

Hannah nodded. 'You can trust Joy, she never could stand Bert. Hopefully she'll be able to come to the meeting, so you'll get to meet her. Now have you time for another cup of tea?'

Emma shook her head and, glancing out of the window, saw that it had started to rain. 'I have to go and see Mam. She'll probably still have a face on her because she's not pleased about Mrs Black's departure and the enormous drop in my wages.' She got to her feet.

Hannah saw her out and waved as she went down the street.

It was as Emma cut through an entry into Cornwall Street that she bumped into David. 'Long time no see,' she said, her heart skipping a beat.

'Oh, it's you Emma.' His voice was cool.

She frowned. 'You don't have to sound so glad to see me.'

He raised his eyebrows. 'I thought it was you that didn't want to see me.'

'What d'you mean by that?' she said indignantly. 'Not a word from you despite my being attacked by that swine on the bridge.'

His expression altered to one of puzzlement. 'I was in Crewe but I sent a letter to your family address, arranging a date to meet when I got back but you didn't turn up. I thought it might have got lost in the post, so I gave your dad another letter for you.'

Scarcely able to believe her ears, she clutched the front of his tweed jacket. 'I never got either. I asked after you but Dad said he hadn't seen you.'

David looked furious. 'I asked if he had an answer from you for me, he told me that you'd changed your job and were too busy to see me.'

'He's a liar! It's true I've changed my job and I'm earning buttons compared to when I worked for Mrs Black but...' She paused and her expression was wrathful. 'I bet that's it! Bloody money! I bet he's worried in case we get serious and they don't have my wages helping them out.'

'He should have said that if that's how he felt instead of lying to us both. So he'll have taken a cut of a shilling in his wages. All railwaymen have been told they're getting paid less. Us engine drivers have been told by the owners that it's our own fault for wanting to work less hours at a stretch, even though it's for safety's sake.'

'The mean things.'

'Aye! But never mind that now. It's your father I feel angry with...he really made me believe you didn't want to see me.'

'And that really mattered to you?' said Emma, holding her head on one side like a cocky little sparrow.

He nodded and put his arms round her. 'Perhaps you'll let me walk you to wherever you're going?'

She stayed still in his arms a moment, enjoying being held in his embrace. She breathed in the scent of him, shaving soap, smoke and damp tweed and, impulsively, kissed him on the chin before freeing herself. 'I was going to Mam's to give her some money but I don't think I'll bother now. You can walk me across the river and I'll show you the house where I'm working.'

He gazed down at her with an expression in his eyes that made her feel quite breathless. 'I'd like that. And in future any letters I write I'll address them there.' He took her hand and they began to walk back the way Emma had come. 'Why did you change your job? I thought you liked it at Mrs Black's.'

'Mrs Black's gone on an extended holiday and Alice Moran married her old flame and left with him for India. I've taken over her job.' Emma could not resist, watching his expression intently when she mentioned Alice marrying.

Meeting her gaze, he said mildly, 'I don't know why you can't accept that it's you I have a fancy for, Emma. I thought I'd made it plain. In fact I insist on you walking out with me. What do you say to us meeting the Sunday after next? I've got the day off and I thought we could take the ferry to Eccleston and have a picnic.'

Her eyes glowed. 'I'll see what I can do but I'll pay for my own ticket.'

'That you won't,' he said firmly.

'You've had a drop in your wages, so I'll have to say no if you don't agree,' she said, determinedly.

He frowned down at her. 'You've had a drop in your wages, too. I can afford two ferry tickets, believe me, lovey. You bring the picnic. Agreed?'

'OK! You've twisted my arm. Give me your address, so I can let you know if I can't make it.'

He told her where he lived and then they sauntered across town, catching up on the rest of each other's news, unaware that they were being followed as they crossed the bridge and walked up to Victoria Crescent.

Victoria gazed out of the window, watching Emma saying goodbye to the blond giant at the gate. He looked familiar but she could not place him and continued to watch as Emma dawdled up the path before vanishing from her sight round the side of the house.

She was about to move away from the window when she noticed another man leaning on the gate. He, too, was fair-haired and, although not as tall as the man who had escorted Emma home, he was definitely more handsome. Suddenly she realised his identity. He smiled, raised his right hand and saluted her, before walking away. She drew back from the window, her heartbeat rapid, and had to sit down in order to calm herself. After a few moments she went in search of Emma.

Victoria found her in the kitchen talking to cook and immediately interrupted them. 'You're back earlier than I thought you'd be, Emma. I noticed you didn't come alone, either.'

'That's David Davies,' said Emma, smiling. 'You've actually met him, miss. He helped you put up the hood of your motorcar that time it rained.'

Victoria remembered. 'So you didn't go home?'

'No, miss. I visited Hannah Moran, though.'

'And how is she?'

'You can see for yourself on Monday. She's hoping to get to the meeting.'

Victoria smiled. 'Good! The more the merrier.' She hesitated. 'Have they heard anything from Alice and Sebastian?'

Surprised, Emma replied, 'They've had a card but it must have been sent before they received Hannah's husband's letter. Could be that they've received it now, though. Maybe we…you…might like Mary and I to sort out a bedroom for them?'

Victoria bit on her lip. 'No. It could still be a while before they come home. Let's wait until I hear from them. Now if you could go upstairs and see if Grandmamma needs anything.'

'Yes, miss. Anything else you'd like me to do, miss?' said Emma politely, but not quite managing to conceal her irritation at being given that order.

'*Miss* doesn't like your tone. You'll be out on your ear if you don't watch yourself,' said Victoria, colouring.

Emma swept out of the kitchen with her head held high and a rebellious look in her eyes but when she reached the stairs, she climbed them as if there was all the time in the world, thinking that perhaps she should not have shown her annoyance. After all, if she wanted the following Sunday afternoon off to meet David she had better be good. But before then there was the women's suffrage meeting to attend.

The assembly room was decorated with garlands and banners of green, purple and white; the buzz of conversation was akin to a swarm of excited bees. Seated on the stage were members of the committee and their special guests, Miss Muriel Matters and Miss Margaret Milne Farquharson, MA.

Suddenly the chairman, Alderman Chunton, got to his feet and raised his hands, waving them slightly as if by doing this he would ensure silence. But it took a couple of good bangs with the gavel on the table to quieten the audience. 'Welcome, ladies…and the gentleman I can also see out there…to this meeting,' he said, smiling. 'A few days ago I was taken to task for attending this meeting. Others considered me courageous for my willingness to debate and be educated in the franchise of women.' There was a flurry of clapping and when it stopped, he continued, 'I believe that women should marry but I also accept they have a right to be involved in this country's public affairs. Some people worry because they believe women might overrule men simply by force of numbers, but I say we need women because of their marvellous perseverance...and as long as they are properly qualified for the tasks they take on, then they should have their say and be entitled to vote.'

A roar of approval swept through the hall and Miss Milne Farquharson MA, stood up and moved a motion that women should have the vote under the same conditions as men. 'We pay our taxes and so should have a voice in parliament,' she said loudly. 'It has been said that some women don't want the vote...that's because some don't see its value.' She shook her head and looked sad. 'They are foolish and ignorant and, in their place, some of the best men in the country want the vote for them. Had men never been under women? Look at Adam, Caesar, Solomon!' Laughter echoed around the room and she smiled. 'Every outstanding man in history has been under a woman. Austen Chamberlain says men are different from women, observant of him. But at least that's why he says his party wants women's votes.' She sat down and there was a thunderous clapping.

'She's so right. She's so right,' said Victoria in a breathless voice, her face ruddy. 'What – What a – a marvellous woman!'

Emma did not argue with her, but found herself wondering if there was a hidden meaning to the remarks about men being under women, but dared not say so to her employer, who might consider her vulgar.

Miss Muriel Matters stood up. 'It is not a proper democracy where only half the population have a say in running the country and where women are classed alongside paupers, lunatics, criminals and children,' she said in a slow deliberate voice. 'A plank in the opposite platform is that women cannot fight. Yet a man who has a wooden leg or one eye can still vote. Women bring life…men take it.' There was a roar of agreement.

Miss Muriel Matters held up her hand for silence. In the hush that followed a voice spoke up demanding an explanation for the recent violent tactics…stone throwing and window breaking…that the suffragettes had used in London.

'I expected someone to mention that,' she said with a sweet smile. 'We have tried all ways and means at our disposal to bring about change peacefully but we are tired of trusting the pledges of politicians which fail us. We have faith in the Cause and it is that which makes us go on fighting.'

There was a storm of clapping. The chairman and speakers were thanked. Victoria stood up and moved away.

Emma turned to Hannah and Joy. 'It's terrible us being classed with paupers, lunatics, criminals and children, isn't it? I never knew that.'

'It's like saying we're beyond the pale,' said Hannah indignantly.

'I never knew there were more women than men in the country,' said Joy, her brown eyes lively. 'You can see why they want to keep us down, all right.'

'There'll be even less if we don't get our way.' The three of them turned and, to her surprise, Emma recognised Mrs Stone.

'What do you mean?' Hannah was the first to speak.

'More women in the movement are choosing not to marry rather than live under a man's thumb, so there'll be less men being born.'

'That's all very well if you've plenty of money to support yourself,' said Joy. 'But working-class women can't be so choosy. If they don't marry then more often than not they're either dependant on a father or brother or they end up on the parish or in the workhouse.'

'There's nothing stopping several girls or women living together,' said Mrs Stone.

'And whose name goes on the rent book?' shot back Joy.

'The eldest I should think,' said Mrs Stone, smiling, before turning to Emma. 'I read about the attack on you. Are you all right now?'

Emma nodded. 'I'm working for Miss Waters. You might have read about her father's death in the *Chester Chronicle*.'

'I did indeed. I would have called on her if I hadn't been away myself. She must be terribly upset.'

'She's around here somewhere,' said Emma, gazing about the room and spotting Victoria talking to Miss Matters. 'There she is!'

Mrs Stone excused herself and walked away.

But before she could reach Victoria, her path was blocked by the shifting movement of women and by the time she reached the spot where last she had been seen, she had vanished.

Victoria was feeling drained by the heat, noise and excitement and would be glad when she reached home. Fortunately, the assembly room was only a short distance from the river and, as it was a fine evening, she and Emma had walked to the meeting. She supposed that she should have told her that she was leaving but the need to get out of the building and home had been overwhelming. She hurried across the footbridge and began the short ascent to Victoria Crescent. She was gasping for breath by the time she reached the house.

Taking her key from her handbag, she opened the door and was just about to step inside when a pleasant male voice said, 'Miss Waters, wasn't that a marvellous meeting? I'd really enjoy discussing it with you. May I come in?'

Chapter Thirteen

April, 1909

Victoria turned and instantly recognised the man. He was wearing a striped blazer, white shirt and bow tie with cream trousers. He removed his straw boater to reveal a head of slicked down fair hair. She could smell bay rum hair lotion and peppermint. Close up she could see that his eyes were blue and he had a cleft chin. He was still probably the handsomest man she had ever seen. 'Mr Temple, isn't it?' she gasped.

He smiled. 'You remembered. I'm flattered.'

The flush in her cheeks deepened. 'I saw you at the gate a short while ago.'

'I was visiting a house in the neighbourhood and caught sight of you at the window. I wondered then if you would be at the meeting. Miss Matters, what a marvellous woman!'

Victoria nodded. 'I do…so agree.' She put a hand to her breast. 'You…must excuse me. I need to…sit down.'

He brought his face so close to hers that she could feel his breath on her cheek. 'Are you unwell?'

'I just…need to rest.'

He replaced his hat. 'Please, let me help you.'

'Thank you.'

He moved her hand from the door and closed it behind him. 'Lean on me.' He slid an arm round her waist. 'Just tell me which room? The first door on the left or the one on the right?'

'Left.' She was feeling quite faint but was shocked and thrilled when he swept her off her feet and carried her into the drawing room. He placed her on the sofa, deftly took the pins from her hat and, removing it, fanned her face. 'Is there anything I can fetch you? A glass of water perhaps.'

If you…press the bell…over by the fireplace…Mary will come,' she said unevenly.

Bert did what she said and then returned to the sofa. He gazed down at her; she was definitely not as pretty as Alice but his mother had told him that she had married and was out of the country. The news had infuriated him but then he had seen the Griffiths girl enter this house and realised that she must work for Miss Waters. He heard a discreet knock and turned his head to smile at the young maid as she entered. 'You must be Mary. Miss Waters is unwell. Could you bring a glass of water?'

She stared at him in astonishment before glancing at her mistress. 'Has she had one of her turns?'

'It seems so. The glass of water if you please?' said Bert firmly.

Mary's cheeks pinked. 'Yes, sir! But she'll probably need to take one of her heart tablets. She must have forgotten them when she went to the meeting.' She glanced about her. 'Where's Emma?'

'I do not know, Miss Waters was alone when I met her. Please be so good as to fetch Miss Waters' tablets while I stay with her.' Mary hesitated. Bert's blond eyebrows drew together in a frown. 'What are you waiting for, girl? I'm not going to make off with the family silver.'

Mary's colour deepened and she hurried out of the room.

Bert thrust his hands into his trouser pockets and hummed as he gazed about him, trying to put a value on the furniture, ornaments and pictures. Then he looked at Victoria and thought that bitch Emma's absence could serve him a good turn; although he still meant to have his revenge on her for hurting him where she had. He roamed the room, picking up ornaments and inspecting them, only to jump when Victoria spoke. 'You don't have to stay. Mary will see to me now,' she murmured.

He replaced the Wedgwood vase gently and turning,

smiled at her. 'I don't mind staying. This is a nice room. Quiet and peaceful.'

She stared at him from beneath drooping eyelids. 'That's why I needed to get away from the meeting. It was dreadfully noisy.'

Mary entered the room carrying a glass of water and a pill box. 'Your tablets, Miss Victoria. And perhaps I should prepare your bed so you can rest properly.'

'If you would, Mary.' Victoria stretched out a hand for the pill box and glass.

'And I'll see the...gentleman out, shall I?' asked the maid.

Victoria nodded. 'Yes, please.' She turned her attention to Bert. 'It was kind of you to help me, Mr Temple. I'm sorry I haven't sent you any copies of *Votes For Women* for a while, but Papa died suddenly and I had so much to do.'

'There's no need to apologise. I'm sorry to hear about your father. I hope you'll feel better soon,' he said, taking one of her hands and raising it to his lips. 'Perhaps I could call again?'

She blushed as he kissed her fingers. 'Perhaps. And thank you again.'

'My pleasure. Good evening to you.' He raised his boater and left, satisfied he had made another good impression.

Once outside, he sauntered down the path and paused in the gateway to look back at the house. He imagined living in such a place with Miss Waters as his wife. The only serpent in his Eden was the Griffiths girl, Emma, but as she had no idea what he looked like, he could worm his way into her mistress's good graces without her being any the wiser. He frowned, considering he'd been fortunate in not being seen by his sisters at the meeting. Then he grinned, imagining their astonishment if they had spotted him. Still, best that they knew nothing of his interest in the Women's Suffrage Movement and the reason behind it.

He let his imagination take flight, picturing himself married to Miss Waters and lording it over Emma. She'd regret the day she had ever dared cross him.

'I shouldn't have let you go home on your own,' said Emma, placing a cup of tea on the bedside table. She was concerned for Victoria and extremely curious about the man Mary had mentioned being in the drawing room.

'It was my own decision and I'm feeling much better now,' said Victoria, nestling into the lace trimmed pillows before stretching out a hand for the tea. 'Tell me if anything interesting happened after I left the meeting.'

'I spoke to Mrs Stone. She was sorry to her about Mr Waters' death and spoke of coming to visit you.'

'That would be nice.'

Emma hesitated before saying, 'Mary said there was a man here.'

The colour rose in Victoria's cheeks. 'Yes. I felt faint and Mr Temple helped me into the house. You won't know about Mr Temple. We met in the Grosvenor Hotel and he's interested in the Cause. So there is no need for you to worry, Emma.'

'Yes, miss. Is there anything else you need before I go and check on Mrs Waters?'

'No, that'll be all. I'll see you in the morning.'

Emma left the bedroom, feeling slightly uneasy, despite her employer's reassurance about the man. She wouldn't be the first woman to voice anti-male sentiments and then to fall hook, line and sinker for one. Despite her book learning and education, Emma was pretty certain she was completely inexperienced when it came to handling the opposite sex and, without her father, uncle, or Seb, around to watch out for her, she just might be heading for a fall. Hopefully she was worrying unnecessarily and no more would be heard from him.

But a couple of days later, Emma was crossing the lobby

when the knocker sounded. Immediately she veered in that direction and opened the door. On the step stood a woman holding a small basket with an arrangement of gypsy grass and pink and white carnations. 'Miss Victoria Waters' residence?'

'Yes.'

The woman held out the basket. 'These are for her.'

Emma thanked her and closed the door before swiftly searching for a card. When she found it she read *To Miss Waters. I hope you are feeling better and that these flowers will cheer you up. From Arthur Temple.*

As the sweet, spicy fragrance of the carnations filled her nostrils Emma felt even more uneasy than she had the other evening. At this time of year, the flowers must have been grown in a hothouse or come from the Channel Isles, so must have cost a few bob. What was Mr Temple's game? Did he know that Mr Waters had died and believed that her employer had come into loads of money?

She heard the clearing of a throat and glanced in the direction of the drawing room. Victoria stood in the doorway. 'Who are those flowers for?' she asked.

'They're for you...from Mr Temple.'

Victoria's face turned pink with pleasure. 'Honestly?'

Emma swallowed a sigh and, not wanting to be a wet blanket by expressing her own thoughts, forced a smile and handed the basket to her.

Victoria read the note and then buried her nose in the carnations. When she lifted her head there was a sheen of tears in her eyes. 'No one has ever sent me flowers before.'

'Enjoy them then, miss. Where are you going to put them?'

'In the drawing room, I think. On the piano,' murmured Victoria, carrying the basket into the drawing room. 'Maybe he'll come and visit me again.'

Emma hoped he would so she could get a look at him.

The next day a bunch of late spring flowers was

delivered. This time the accompanying card not only asked after Victoria's health but requested permission to visit that coming Sunday afternoon. In the corner of the card written in tiny letters was an address and the words, *just in case you have forgotten it*. 'He's not backwards in coming forwards, is he?' murmured Emma, handing the flowers to her employer, remembering she had asked for time off to meet David that day.

Victoria stared at her as she took the flowers. 'Did you read the message?' Her voice was sharp.

Emma said woodenly, 'Couldn't help it, miss. It was staring me in the face.'

Victoria frowned. 'Even so. You should have resisted. It was for my eyes only. Get the blue vase and fill it with water and bring it into the drawing room.'

Emma did so and, when she took it into the drawing room, Victoria was sitting at the writing bureau, busily writing. As Emma placed the vase on an occasional table, her employer said, 'That will be all, Emma.'

'You don't have anything for me to post, miss?' she said, straightening her aching back.

Victoria shook her head. 'I'm quite capable of posting this myself. The walk will do me good. You can pop upstairs and see if there's anything my grandmother needs. And you can have this Sunday afternoon off to meet Mr Davies. You don't have to be back until six.'

'That's generous of you, miss,' said Emma politely, convinced she was being got out of the way. Of course, she wanted to be with David but she also wanted to get a gander at Mr Temple and guessed the only way she was going to be able to do that was to make sure she was back here well before six o'clock on Sunday.

'It's a charming garden,' said Bert, holding out a hand to Victoria to help her down the terrace steps and onto the lawn, thinking again that he might have been brought up in the working-class area of Newtown but could ape the middle classes perfectly.

'It's somewhat overgrown,' said Victoria, her hand trembling in his grasp. 'The gardener's getting too old to cope with all that needs doing.'

Bert led her over to a garden seat situated beneath a trestle archway of rambling roses and a tangle of honeysuckle that were showing tiny buds. She sat down, leaving enough space for him to sit next to her if he so wished. 'So you live here alone now your father's dead?' he asked.

Victoria gave a tinkling laugh. 'Hardly! There are the maids, Mary and Emma, as well as Cook...and of course, Grandmamma. She's good for nothing...old age, Mr Temple, is terrible...especially when the mind and body stop functioning properly.'

He would have liked to ask for more information about Emma but instead enquired whether she had any other relatives.

'I have an uncle who farms at Delamere.' She gazed up at him and patted the seat next to her. 'Tell me what is your profession?'

He sat beside her. 'I'm in engineering.'

Her face shone. 'How exciting! Do you build bridges?'

'No. I'm in shipping.' He slid his arm along the back of the bench and for ten minutes or so glibly told her a pack of lies about his status and his work before smiling and finishing with the words, 'But we've talked enough about me. I'm sure your life has been much more interesting. Tell me about yourself...have you always lived here?'

'No. I was brought up in Liverpool. My father was involved in the cotton trade. He would have liked me to marry but I felt I had work to do that was just as important as that of my married sisters – by sisters I don't mean blood relatives but those women united with me in the Cause.'

Bert thought her words didn't bode well for his plans. 'I'm sure you would make a wonderful wife and mother.' His hand touched her shoulder.

She flinched slightly but did not move away. 'You think so? I – I always believed I would die a spinster.'

'Perhaps you only believe that because you've never met the right man. Surely if you did, then you wouldn't refuse him?' He took hold of her hand.

She swallowed. 'I – I don't know. I would have to think about it.' Abruptly she pulled her hand free and rose to her feet. 'Shall we go inside and have tea?'

Bert followed her into the house. He decided that she was shy of men and knew that he would have to go carefully. Perhaps if he kept his hands to himself and showed even more interest in her stupid Cause that would do the trick. As he ate cake and drank tea served by the maid Mary, he found himself wondering, again, where Emma Griffiths was right now.

Emma was sitting on the grassy bank overlooking the river Dee at Eccleston. 'What wouldn't you give to have been the person who found those Roman coins?' said Emma, tossing a pebble into the water. The coins in question had brought Eccleston some fame, having been found in the grounds of its parish church.

'There's some who believe there's more to be found,' said David, who was lying on his back with his head resting on his knapsack and his eyes closed against the sun. 'We could go back up to the church if you like and see what we can find.'

'I'm too full to walk up there again,' murmured Emma. 'Besides you can bet your last penny, if I found anything, Dad would be there like a shot trying to get his grubby hands on it.'

'I didn't want to sully your ears by mentioning your dad,' said David, opening his eyes. 'But now you've done so, I can tell you that I had words with him.'

There was an arrested expression on her heart-shaped face. 'What kind of words?'

'Naughty ones. He tried to bluster his way out of trouble but when he realised I wasn't having any of his lies he turned nasty.'

'What did he say?' She broke off a grass stem and put it in her mouth without taking her gaze from David's face.

'He came the heavy father and forbid me to have anything to do with *his* daughter,' said David softly.

'He's got a cheek! I'm only his daughter when he wants something from me.' Her eyes glinted. 'I haven't been home since you told me what he'd done, he must realise why if you've had it out with him. I wonder what he's told Mam…if anything. I suppose I should go and see her. I don't want her and the kids suffering for his shortcomings. I must admit, I've half been expecting her to turn up at the Waters' kitchen door with her hand out for my wages before now. I'll just have to make sure he's not there when I go.'

'You're right there, lovey. But if he lays a finger on you he'll have me to answer to.' David's grey eyes were stony.

Emma threw away the blade of grass. 'My knight in shining armour. But you don't have to worry about Dad using his fists, it's words he hits us kids with.' She smiled. 'Even so, I appreciate what you've just said.'

He returned her smile and then suddenly reached up and seizing her by the shoulders, drew her down on top of him. She did not resist as his mouth searched for hers and found it. It was extremely pleasant so she allowed herself to be cajoled into sharing a second and third kiss. The last one seemed to go on for ever and, suddenly, she became aware of his arousal, which gave her a kind of thrill but also told her that in order to breathe and for him to calm down she'd best end the embrace.

She rolled off him and lay at his side, her bosom rising

and falling rapidly. He reached out and touched her breast with a gentle finger. Even through the fabric of her blouse she liked the sensation roused by that slightest of caresses. Still she knew that now was not the right time to encourage him to go further. It would have been nice to stay here a little longer but she knew by the position of the sun that it was time to get moving if she wanted to get a decko at Mr Temple. So she took his hand and moved it to his chest.

She knelt up and bending over, brushed his lips with hers. 'If we're to catch the next ferry, we'd best get a move on.'

He shook his head at her and said mournfully, 'I don't think you realise what you do to me, Emma lovey.'

'Oh yes, I do!' She smiled as she got to her feet and brushed grass and tiny bits of twig from her brown skirts. 'But I'm suspicious of this bloke sending Miss Victoria flowers twice in so many days.'

He pushed himself up from the ground. 'I agree it is an extravagant gesture. I'd have made do with some of these.' He plucked several dandelions and handed them to her.

Her response was a throaty chuckle. 'Now that's what I call a bunch of flowers. Shall we get going or we'll be late?'

He smiled, picked up his knapsack and swung it over his shoulder. Then, seizing her free hand, he ran with her to the jetty.

They arrived in Chester in plenty of time and were just saying goodbye at the footbridge when a man wearing a navy blue pin-striped suit hurried off the bridge and collided into her.

'Watch where you're going, mate!' said David.

The man glanced at them and then he grinned. 'Shouldn't it be Miss Griffiths who needs to watch where she's going?'

Before she could ask how he knew her name, he had walked off. 'Did you recognise him?' asked Emma.

David was staring after him, his brows knitted. 'I think I do. Wasn't he the bloke we saw in Brook Street that time?'

Emma nodded, wondering if that was the reason his voice sounded familiar or was there another reason. 'A handsome devil,' she muttered.

'Bad-mannered with it,' said David, looking down at her. 'Are you sure now you don't want me walking you back to Miss Waters' house?'

Emma shook her head and they said their goodbyes all over again. She was just about to step onto the footbridge when she bumped into Mrs Stone. Emma apologised and would have hurried off if the older woman had not grabbed her arm.

'Emma, just the person I want to see. I had intended calling on Miss Waters the other day but things happened and I never managed to get up to the house.'

'How can I help you?' asked Emma, inching her way onto the footbridge.

Mrs Stone smiled. 'Give her a message from me. Tell her if it's fine with her, I'll visit next Sunday afternoon after lunch? If that's not convenient perhaps you can let me know.'

'Of course,' said Emma.

'Thank you, Emma.' She walked away.

Emma raced across the bridge but unfortunately when she arrived at the house it was to discover that she was too late. She told Victoria about her meeting with Mrs Stone and had to repeat it.

'Mrs Stone is coming next Sunday afternoon, you say?' Victoria's voice was vague and she toyed with her fingers.

'Yes, miss.' Emma refrained from telling her that she'd already said that once. Something was obviously on her employer's mind. 'Did your visit from Mr Temple go off well, miss?'

Victoria did not answer but sat at the piano and opened

the lid. Then she took a sheet of music from the top of the instrument and opened it. 'He's going to come to the next Suffrage meeting.'

Emma raised her eyebrows. 'There's a surprise. Do you know when that is?'

'Not yet.' Victoria ran her fingers over the keys and a ripple of sound filled the room.

'Mr Temple...what does he look like, miss?'

Victoria frowned. 'You ask too many questions about him.'

'Sorry, miss.' If Victoria did not want to talk about him she felt certain Mary would, and if she told her what she was beginning to suspect then she would slip out of the house whilst Victoria was entertaining Mrs Stone and visit Hannah.

'Miss Waters, may I express my condolences on your sad loss.'

Victoria did not get up from her chair but held up a hand. 'Thank you. It's good to see you again. Please do sit down.'

Josephine Stone seated herself in the armchair near the open french window and glanced out over the garden. 'It's a lovely day.'

'Yes. Unseasonably warm.' Victoria sighed. 'This kind of weather saps my strength.'

'It's sensible not to overdo things.'

Victoria nodded. 'I do try to be sensible but what with Grandmamma's indisposition, it makes it difficult for me.'

There was a lull in the conversation. Josephine reached for her handbag. 'Do you mind if I smoke?'

Victoria stared at her in surprise. 'You smoke?'

'I started as one single act of defiance. My husband hates me doing so...said it was not womanly. Yet he smokes, drinks like a fish and carries on with the maids. Emma wouldn't put up with his disgusting behaviour and that's why she left my employment.' Josephine took a match from a silver embossed box, struck it and lit her cigarette.

'May I tell you something in confidence, Mrs Stone?'

Twin plumes of smoke issued from her nostrils. 'Of course! But call me Josephine.'

Victoria leaned towards her. 'I don't know if you heard that our housekeeper left our employment. She had been with Grandmamma as long as I can remember but only after Papa died did I discover that he and Gabrielle were lovers.'

'It happens, my dear.' Josephine's expression was sympathetic. 'The double standards of men! Imagine the outcry if we were to sleep with the servants.'

'But that is not all,' said Victoria hastily. 'Because I'm a woman, Papa didn't think I had the brains to run his business and instead allowed his bastard son to be his right-hand man. But on top of that he left Gabrielle a thousand pounds and Sebastian half the business. He married Alice and they're abroad at the moment.'

Josephine almost dropped her cigarette. 'I see! You poor dear.'

Victoria's mouth quivered. 'Please, don't feel sorry for me. I feel sorry enough for myself.'

'But surely your father left you well provided for?'

'Annoyingly, there isn't as much money as I thought there'd be. And this house belongs to Grandmamma. I know she's left it to me in her will but God only knows how long she'll take to die. I'm going to be stuck here until then unless I marry.'

Josephine almost choked on her cigarette. 'Marry? I – I didn't know…'

Victoria lowered her eyes and toyed with her fingers. 'Oh yes! There is a man interested in me. He's an engineer…in shipping. I don't know him very well yet, but he shares my beliefs…so I'm thinking about marrying him. Yes, I really am. I can't wait to see Sebastian and

Alice's faces when they walk through the front door and I tell them I'm getting married.'

Josephine said bluntly, 'Isn't this all rather sudden?'

'That's how love is, isn't it? He sent me flowers and no one has ever done that,' she said with a hint of breathlessness and placed a hand on her breast.

Josephine said with concern. 'You mustn't rush into things. Think hard, my dear, one of the aims of the movement is freedom from men's oppression and we're a long way from obtaining that in the bonds of marriage.'

Victoria shook her head and said defiantly, 'We would be equals. I believe that when he comes home, Sebastian won't let me have a say in the business because I'm a woman. He'll be like Papa, over-protective and make all the decisions. But if I had a husband he'd have to listen to us.'

Josephine looked incredulous. 'So you'd hand your share of the business over to a man you barely know just because he sent you a few flowers?'

Victoria's colour rose. 'I'm not that foolish. I won't rush into marriage. An engagement first.' She paused. 'Time for a cup of tea, I think.' She rang the bell.

Mary came in. 'Yes, miss?'

'Tea and cakes. And fetch Emma for me.'

Mary looked uncomfortable. 'I'll see if I can find her, miss.'

Victoria fixed her with a stare. 'You don't have to bother. I know that look. She's slipped out, hasn't she?'

Mary shifted from one foot to the other. 'Yes, miss. Something to do with that bloke who attacked her.'

'I see. Well, when she comes in, tell her I want to see her right away. I'll not have her taking time off that she's not entitled to.'

Chapter Fourteen

April, 1909

Emma and Hannah stopped outside the Kirks' house in
Francis Street. 'What if your mam's in?' asked Emma,
tense with excitement. If Joy'd had any luck in finding a
photograph then soon she would know if Bert was the
same man she had seen on Brook Street the day she had
nearly been trampled by the runaway horse and again by
the bridge last Sunday.

'She won't be in,' said Hannah firmly. 'Dad decided to
take her and Freddie out today...and what with the days
drawing out they won't be back until this evening.' She
slid her hand through the letterbox for the key on the
string, only to discover it was not there. With a shrug she
rapped on the door several times.

Almost immediately a voice called, 'Who's there?'

'Joy, it's Hanny and I've Emma with me.'

They heard bolts being drawn and raised their eyebrows
at each other. The door opened and Joy stood there,
smiling. 'I know what you're thinking but I'm not taking
any chances of his lordship turning up here and finding me
alone in the house.'

'Wise girl,' said Hannah, stepping over the threshold.
'Have you had any luck finding a photograph of him yet?
Emma has a feeling she might have bumped into him?'

'Wow! Where?' asked Joy, her brown eyes gleaming.

'Near the Queen's Park footbridge,' said Emma,
following Hannah into the house. 'Fair-haired and really
good-looking...and he had the nerve to call me Miss
Griffiths...just as Bert did when he attacked me.' She
smiled faintly, remembering how he had squealed when
she had fought back.

Joy sighed. 'Still no luck, I'm afraid. God only knows

what Mother's done with the one that was in a frame on the sideboard. She's been in a strange mood lately. We almost had an argument over my staying behind today.'

'How about her box of memories in their bedroom?' suggested Hannah, putting on the kettle.

'I've looked there. But I've an idea,' said Joy.

'What's that?' asked her sister, glancing in her direction.

'Why don't you get Kenny to draw Bert's likeness? He's good at that kind of thing.'

Hannah's face lit up. 'You're right! I don't know why I haven't thought of it earlier. I'll speak to him as soon as I get home.'

'When will I get a look at the drawing?' asked Emma.

'Depends on how long it takes,' said Hannah. 'I'll get it to you as soon as I can.'

'Bring it to Miss Waters' house, that'll be best.'

'I could always take it if you're busy, Hanny,' said Joy. 'It would be a nice little outing for me.'

'Go round to the back of the house,' said Emma. 'If I'm out, give it to Mary. I'll mention it to her and she'll see that it gets to me.' She told Joy the address and then they changed the subject to talk about the fair that would take place at the beginning of May. Tickets were like gold dust, so it was unlikely they'd get the chance to see the cinematograph show from America with people dancing the Great Flip Flap and the Yankee Cakewalk.

When Emma arrived back at the Waters' house, she was immediately told by Mary she was in trouble with their employer. 'She's in the drawing room and said you were to go and see her straight away.'

'Is Mrs Stone still with her?'

Mary shook her head. 'She left half an hour ago but I don't think what she had to say has improved Miss Victoria's temper.'

Damn! thought Emma, but took no time in reporting to her employer. Victoria was lying on the chaise longue and without preamble, said, 'How dare you go out without my permission! I won't give you any more warnings, Emma. Do this again and you'll be dismissed without a reference. There'll be no time off for you for a month now.'

'Yes, miss. Sorry, miss. I didn't think you needed me. It won't happen again,' said Emma with false meekness.

'No, it won't.' Victoria stared at her for several moments and then, said, 'What's this about the man who attacked you?'

'I've an idea who he might be.'

'I thought we knew who he was…Bert Kirk, wasn't it?' Victoria's lips were compressed together as she rustled the copy of the *Chester Chronicle*, open at the Ladies' Page. She had been reading the final episode of the serial *The Secret of the Iron Box* and its ending with a poor girl discovering she was the daughter of a millionaire, had not pleased her. 'I suppose the truth of the matter is that you were seeing that young man of yours.'

'No, miss. He's working. I told you the truth. We might know it was Bert who attacked me but he was masked, so I don't know what he looks like. Now I've an idea I might have seen him without his balaclava but I need to know if I'm right in my guess.'

'And how will you do that?'

'Hanny's husband is going to do a drawing of him. If he's as good as Hanny thinks, then I'll know whether I'm right or not.'

Victoria's expression thawed slightly. 'I'd like to see it when you get it.'

Emma smiled. 'Right, miss. Is there anything else I can do for you?'

'Yes! You can go and see how Grandmamma is. Perhaps she'll need changing.'

'Yes, miss,' said Emma woodenly. She made for the door, thinking *Mrs Black, please, come home soon!*

* * *

'Thine be the Glory risen conquering Son,' sang Bert, polishing his best shoes. It was the beginning of May and he was off to Chester, hoping to see something of his mother, Miss Victoria Waters and, later, to attend the fair. He had managed to get a ticket and was looking forward to seeing the cinematograph show that evening.

He glanced towards the fire grate at the charred remains of the latest copy of *Votes For Women* Miss Waters had sent him. A scowl darkened his face. Some of the antics the suffragettes were getting up to proved to him that they needed firmly keeping in their place.

He gave his toecaps a final burnish and pushed his feet into the brown brogues. In his imagination, he could clearly see himself standing at the altar beside Victoria Waters and her saying *I will!* Then he would say his bit and within minutes the vicar would pronounce them man and wife. Then, he would be in control of that household and, in no time at all, she would know who was boss. He would be able to lord it over Miss Emma Griffiths, too. She, who had dared to interfere with his plans. He frowned, thinking he shouldn't have given in to temptation and addressed her by name down by the bridge a few Sundays ago, but he had been unable to resist taking her by surprise. Still, it was done now and, as she didn't know he was Bert Kirk, what was the harm?

He washed his hands and then shrugged on his jacket, making sure he had money, door key, handkerchief, mints, a quarter of a pound of pear drops and a box of chocolates. He went downstairs and said a smiling good morning to his landlady before leaving the house. It was a lovely day and he expected it to get better.

Joy looked down at the pencil sketch of Bert with admiration. Kenny certainly had talent. He had caught her brother's smarmy expression and that arrogant tilt to the head perfectly. 'It's as good as a photograph,' she said.

Hannah smiled. 'That's what I thought. If you've got nothing better to do, perhaps you wouldn't mind taking it along to Emma for me? Afterwards you could come back here for tea if you like.'

Joy nodded. 'I will. Dah managed to get a couple of tickets for the fair and is taking Mother. I got the impression she wasn't that keen but he insisted. I can't understand her, I'd have been there like a shot.'

Hannah nodded. 'I've noticed she's not round here as much as she used to be and I have to admit that I'm glad about that. She was beginning to get on my nerves and that made me feel guilty.'

'Neither of us have any need to feel guilty when it comes to Mother,' said Joy, watching her sister slip the drawing into an envelope. 'I'll be able to avoid the crowds down by the river because they'll all be up at the other end at the Roodee for the fair. I hope I can get a look inside Miss Waters' house. I remember Alice saying there are some lovely ornaments and things.'

Hannah laughed. 'You're to go round the back to the kitchen, remember? And if Emma isn't in, then you give it to Mary.'

When Joy reached the Dee, she paused for a moment on the bridge. The sun was reflecting off the surface of the water and she watched a couple of young men, shirt sleeves rolled up, rowing a boat across the river. She wolf whistled and grinned as they looked up at the bridge. They waved to her and suggested she come and join them. She blushed, laughed and said another time perhaps and went on her way, daydreaming of being allowed to go out into the world one day and meet the man who would see her as an equal and yet also love and cherish her.

Joy found the Waters' house without any difficulty. With pleasure she gazed at the flowering trees and shrubs as she made her way round the back of the house. She knocked on what she took to be the kitchen door and it was opened by a pleasantly plump, middle-aged woman.

'Could I speak to Miss Emma Griffiths, please?' asked Joy.

'She's had to go on a message. Who shall I say called?'

'My name's Joy Kirk. I was to give this to Mary if Emma wasn't in.' She held out the envelope.

A girl's face appeared at the woman's shoulder. 'I'm Mary. What is it you've got there?'

Joy smiled. 'It's a drawing of Emma's attacker.'

'Ohhh!' exclaimed Mary, staring at the envelope so hard it was as if she was trying to bore a hole in it. Then she plucked it from Joy's fingers and turned it over between her hands. 'Have you come far with it?'

'Newtown.'

Mary smiled. 'You'll be thirsty, I bet. Come in and have a cuppa! Cook'll see to you while I take this up and put it in Emma's room.'

She hurried out but didn't even get as far as the stairs before her curiosity got the better of her and, as the envelope was not sealed, she gave in to temptation and took out the sheet of paper inside. Instantly she recognised Mr Temple. For a moment she was in a dither about what to do and then she knew she just had to show it to her mistress. She made for the drawing room and knocked on the door before entering.

'Miss, miss, I think you should see this,' she said, rushing forward with the envelope in her outstretched hand. 'A girl's just brought it for Emma but she's gone to the dressmaker's to pick up your new skirt. It's a picture, miss, and I think you'll recognise the person.'

Victoria placed the bill she had been scanning on an occasional table and took the envelope from her. Mary watched as her mistress's eyes widened. 'But – but this is Mr Arthur Temple,' she cried.

'Yes, miss! But he's also Emma's attacker,' babbled Mary. 'Is there anything you'd like me to do? Fetch a bobby?'

'Shhh!' silenced Victoria, unable to take her eyes off the drawing. 'Who brought this?' she whispered.

'A Miss Joy Kirk.'

'I see. She was at the Suffrage meeting with her sister and Emma. Is she still here?'

'Yes, miss.'

'Fetch her.'

'What about the police, miss? Should we inform them?'

Victoria put a hand to her head. 'Don't rush me! First I must speak to Miss Kirk.'

Mary left the drawing room. She returned with Joy, who glanced about her with interest before bringing her gaze to rest on Victoria's strained face. She was sitting at her writing desk with the drawing in front of her. She dismissed Mary before facing Joy.

'Miss Kirk. This drawing...is of your brother Bert?' asked Victoria through quivering lips.

'Yes, Miss Waters,' answered Joy, looking at her with concern.

'Your brother has been to this house, Miss Kirk.'

'What!' Joy's eyes rounded in shock.

'He said his name was Arthur Temple.' Victoria placed a hand to her breast as if to steady her heartbeat. 'He sent me flowers and behaved as if – if he shared my beliefs.'

'I'm so sorry, Miss Waters. But he's not a man to be trusted.'

Victoria swallowed and was silent for several moments, thinking how she had considered marrying him. Well, that wasn't going to happen now but she would have her revenge on Bert Kirk. 'I have his address here. You can give it to Hannah and she can do with it what she sees fit.'

Joy took the slip of paper and exclaimed, 'He's living in Ellesmere Port! So close. We believed him to be in Liverpool.'

Victoria nodded and with a wave of her hand, indicated that she leave. Joy looked at her stricken face with pity and cursed her brother. 'Are you sure you'll be all right on your own? Should I fetch Mary?'

She shook her head and indicated that she wanted to be left alone and, reluctantly, Joy left.

Victoria did not know how long she stayed sitting in front of the writing bureau with her hand on that likeness of the man who had deceived her. She had pains in her chest and knew she should have agreed for Mary to come to her but had not wanted her looking at her as if to say *He fooled you all right*. At that moment she was too weak to move and knew she should not dwell on why he had set out to deceive her. No doubt he had some kind of revenge in mind. She closed her eyes a moment and tried to relax before summoning up the strength to go over to the fireplace and press the bell.

Then she heard footsteps outside the french windows and, turning her head, she saw Bert Kirk standing in the doorway. He smiled with great charm and held out a box of chocolates. 'I hope you don't mind my turning up so unexpectedly but I wanted to see you.'

Victoria was unable to speak. How dare he come to her house and make up to her, flattering her with false words, lowering her defences with flowers…and now chocolates! She wanted to hit him but knew herself incapable of lifting a finger.

'Are you all right? You don't look well.' He sounded genuinely concerned as he started across the floor towards her.

Remembering the sketch in front of her, she attempted to slip it beneath the blotter, but she was in pain and her hands were shaking so much she only managed to conceal part of it. Somehow she stumbled to her feet and leaned against the desk, facing him. 'I – I was writing.'

'Writing? It must be something interesting. I thought to find you in the garden on such a fine day.'

'No! It's too warm.' Her voice was just a thread of

sound. 'P – Perhaps you'd like a cup of tea. I'll ring for Mary.' She did not know where she found the strength to talk and move. Hoping he would not give the desk a second glance, she managed to reach the fireplace. Her finger hovered over the bell and she was about to press the button when her wrist was seized and she was dragged away from the fireplace.

'Where did you get this from?' Bert's expression was ugly. 'It'll be that bitch Emma.' Enraged, he threw the paper into the fireplace and then shook Victoria like a rag doll. 'Where is she?'

'She – She's not here! Ge – Get out – of – my house,' gasped Victoria, as a vicious pain stabbed her in the chest and began to spread.

He stared down at her and then his expression changed and he smiled. 'In that case you'll have to do.' Before she realised what he was about he lifted her off her feet and carried her over to the chaise longue. He flung her down, knocking most of the breath out of her. The pain in her chest increased in intensity as he dragged up her skirts. She tried to scream but couldn't breathe. He removed her drawers and she could not put up any defence. Unable to believe this was happening to her she watched him unfasten his flies and then all pain ceased.

Bert pushed himself off Victoria and took a handkerchief from his pocket. 'I've finished. You can stop pretending now, Miss Hoity Toity Waters, and move yourself. I like a woman who puts up a fight. You were too easy.'

When there was no response, he glanced down at her. Her eyes were wide open and the expression in them made him feel uncomfortable. He became aware of a foul smell and he gagged. Putting a hand to his mouth, he mumbled, 'Come on, woman! I couldn't have hurt you that much. Not a squeak out of you.' He bent over and pulled down her skirts. Still no response. He shook her shoulder. 'If you get pregnant I'll marry you.'

Her arm flopped over the edge of the chaise longue. Bert stared closely into her face and a chill of fear charged down his spine. He fumbled for her pulse but couldn't find it. He took a deep breath to steady his nerves. Damn! Damn! And bloody damn! It bloody wasn't fair. He hadn't meant this to happen. He had to get out of here! Thank God he'd come in from the garden and none of the servants had seen him.

He buttoned his flies with trembling fingers and put on his boater, which had fallen off while he had been busy satisfying himself. He was about to leave the same way he had come in when he remembered the chocolates and the drawing. He hurried over to the fireplace and took the screwed up ball of paper from the empty grate and picked up the chocolates from the bureau. Then, with an angry regretful look in Victoria's direction, he left through the french windows.

Bert looked neither left nor right, thinking it best that no one had the opportunity of getting a good look at his face. Tipping his boater forward so that its brim cast a shadow over his face, he passed through the garden gate and made his way towards the footbridge. There was only one person he needed at that moment and so he ran across the bridge, scarcely aware of the distant sound of voices and laughter coming from the direction of the Roodee as he headed for Grosvenor Park. He began to relax a little. No one had seen him…he had got away with it.

A few moments later Bert changed his mind about that. Emma knew about the drawing, so he was not out of the woods yet. She would wonder what had happened to it…but he couldn't have left it there, could he? Damn! He could have. They'd have thought Victoria Waters had scrunched it up and flung it in the fireplace. Who the hell had known him well enough to make such a good likeness of him? Hannah and Joy weren't that talented. Then he realised the only possible person was that dummy Kenny. The swine who had taken his sister from him and then beaten him up. He'd get him somehow for this. His blue eyes warmed just thinking about it. Then he remembered the woman he had left dead and a shudder ran through him.

Why did she bloody have to die? He hadn't been that rough with her. Suddenly he remembered what she had said the first time he had seen her...something about having a bad heart. And hadn't the maid brought her some pills? He relaxed slightly. So it wasn't his fault that she'd died after all. Natural causes! She'd had heart failure. Even so he was frightened and he wanted his mother.

Over the last few weeks Bert had been very careful to disguise himself when he met her outside. He had figured that most people would think he'd had a tooth drawn when they saw the muffler across the bottom half of his face. But today he'd been feeling confident and ready to face his dah if need be; after all he was his bloody son so he should be a bit more forgiving as he'd never done him any harm. Besides his dah had sinned and fallen short of the glory of God. Ha! So he could keep his mouth shut.

To Bert's disappointment and fury, when he arrived at the house on Francis Street he could not get an answer and there was no key on the string to use to let himself in. He hammered his fist on the door in rage.

'They've gone out,' said a reedy voice. He spun round and immediately pinned a smile on his handsome face when he saw one of the neighbours. 'Good afternoon, Mrs Jones. How nice to see you.'

The old woman's eyes almost popped out of her head. 'Bert Kirk! Well, I never. We haven't seen you around here for a while.'

'That's because I've been away.' He thought quickly. 'America!'

'Goodness me! I thought the only water you'd crossed was the Mersey.'

Bert had forgotten that his mother had told him the neighbours believed him to be working in Liverpool. 'I was there for a while but then decided I needed to see more of the world.'

'Well, you're looking very well on it,' she said, her wrinkled face alight with admiration. 'Lovely blazer. Although your trousers could do with an iron.'

He frowned and glanced down at them. 'You're right.' Instantly the memory of how he had creased them so badly struck him like a blow and he felt sick.

'No need to look like you've broken the ten commandments,' said Mrs Jones cheerfully. 'I've got your mam's spare key if you want to go in and put a match to the fire and make yourself a cup of tea. You could always heat up the iron and press them yourself. I remember how you always liked to look smart.'

His frown vanished. 'Thank you, Mrs Jones. I'll take you up on your offer. Clothes get so easily creased when travelling,' he said smoothly. 'I've left my luggage at the station. Didn't want to carry it with me and then find no one was in.' He watched her toddle off to fetch the key and thought there was no way anyone could connect him to what happened this afternoon. And if he were to need an alibi then the old biddy could provide him with one. He'd always been able to charm the old ladies in the street in the past, unlike that bloody Emma. Where was she?

If only he had known it, Emma was not far away. She had been up to her mother's with some money. On the return journey she met David on his way to the General Station. She told him of her suspicions about her attacker and the man in Brook Street being one and the same, adding excitedly, 'Hanny's husband is doing a drawing of him. When I see it I'll know if I'm right; then we've got him!'

'So what I felt about him was right,' said David, seizing her by the shoulders and drawing her to one side. His expression was concerned. 'You've got to be careful, lovey. If he were to suspect what you were up to…'

Emma placed a finger against his lips. 'Shhh! It's lovely that you care what happens to me, but you mustn't worry. I'll keep my wits about me.'

He kissed her finger. 'If I get my hands on him, I'll deal with him for you, lovey.'

'I'd like that,' she said wistfully, thinking there was lot to be said for having a man feel protective towards her. 'When will I see you again?'

'I haven't got a Sunday afternoon off for a while.'

'What about an evening or the Whit bank holiday?'

He smiled. 'I'll see what I can do. I'll send you a letter.'

'I'll look forward to that,' she said softly.

He kissed her quickly and hurried off.

Emma watched him for a moment and then went on her way.

Mary tapped on the door of the drawing room but there was no response so she knocked again and called 'Miss Victoria, are you there? Would you like me to serve tea now?'

Still no answer.

Mary turned the door handle and went inside. When she saw her mistress lying on the chaise longue, her first thought was that she was asleep. Then she realised her eyes were wide open and there was a smell in the room that caused her to put a hand over her mouth and nose. It wasn't the first time that Mary had suffered a close encounter with death – she had been at the deathbeds of her granny, brother and sister – but there was another smell in the room that made her nose twitch cautiously like a rabbit sniffing a predator in the air. She could almost feel the blood rushing through her veins as her heart beat rapidly in her scrawny chest.

She gazed down into her mistress's face. Her lips

appeared blue and the expression in her eyes caused Mary's stomach to tie itself into knots. Gently the maid drew the eyelids over. That was better. Now Miss Victoria looked like she was sleeping. Mary had known she might die suddenly but hadn't imagined it would be so soon. Why hadn't she rung the bell for her to fetch her tablets? Could it have been the drawing that had brought on the attack? Life just wasn't fair, she thought sorrowfully, thinking of the old woman upstairs still going. She left the drawing room to go and tell Cook but as she walked towards the green baize door, it opened and Emma appeared. 'She's dead!' blurted out Mary.

Emma did not hear at first because she was still thinking of David.

Mary repeated what she had said and immediately Emma said, 'Thank God for that. No more having to clean her up and having to wash smelly sheets, answer that blinking bell and…'

'No, not her! I only wish it were.' Mary clutched Emma's arm. 'It's Miss Victoria.'

Emma's face blanched and she gripped the maid's hand. 'How did it happen? Where is she? Have you sent for the doctor?'

'I've only just found her. It could have been the shock of finding out that Mr Temple and the bloke who attacked you are one and the same.'

Emma swore. 'I knew there was something not right about him. Cook said something about an envelope being delivered for me with a picture in it. Where is it?'

'I opened it,' gulped Mary. 'And when I recognised the bloke in the drawing as Mr Temple I showed it to Miss Victoria. She went a dreadful colour. I suggested going for the bobby but she dismissed me and told me to fetch the girl who brought the picture. Joy somebody. It's my fault,' wailed Mary. 'I shouldn't have been so nosy and opened the envelope – but it wasn't sealed. I'm so sorry.'

Emma dismissed her words with a shake of the head. 'It doesn't matter now. Where is she?' she repeated.

'On the chaise longue in the drawing room. We're going to have to give it a good scrub.'

Emma baulked on entering the drawing room but reminded herself that she'd had to cope often enough with similar smells with the old lady. She walked to the chaise longue and gazed down at Victoria, thinking how annoyed she had been with her the other week. Reaching out a hand she caressed her cheek. 'It's a blinking shame,' she murmured.

Mary was wandering round the room. 'I can't see it. I wonder where she put it.'

'What?' asked Emma, turning and staring at her.

'The drawing.'

'I'll have a look for it. You tell Cook what's happened and then go round to the doctor's. Let's hope that Sebastian Bennett gets here soon.'

Mary left the room and Emma went over to the french windows and flung them open. She stood on the terrace breathing in the scents of the garden. An idea suddenly struck her and she went back inside and over to the chaise longue. Getting down on her hands and knees she peered underneath it, hoping to see the sheet of drawing paper. Instead her eyes lighted on something else and, reaching out a hand, she brought out a pair of flesh coloured silk drawers.

To say Emma was surprised was an understatement. She was completely mystified as to why they should be there and was still kneeling on the floor thinking about it when Mary entered the room. 'The doctor will be here in about ten minutes. Should we have tidied her up and moved her somewhere else?' she asked anxiously. 'You know how fussy she was about being just so for people.'

'She's past that now,' said Emma slowly. 'Besides I don't think we should move her. I found her drawers under the chaise longue and I've had this terrible thought.' She took a deep breath and lifted her dead employer's skirts. They both stared at the blood and mucus on the inside of her thighs.

'She must have been having her monthlies,' said Mary. 'Poor thing.'

'You're thick!' snapped Emma, a stony glint in her eye. 'She's minus her drawers and there's no bindings. He's had her.'

Mary's mouth gaped open. 'Wh – What d'you mean?'

'Hasn't your mother told you anything? That thing men keep in their trousers they use to wee with…it also helps make babies. He forced it in her and she probably died of fright.'

'Oh, Jesus, Mary and Joseph!' Mary's chest heaved and she put a hand over her mouth and ran out into the garden.

Carefully, Emma pulled down the skirts of Victoria's afternoon gown and followed her outside. As if drugged, she walked to the bench beneath the archway of twining honeysuckle and rambling roses and sat down. Her hands clenched and unclenched of their own volition. If she'd had Bert in front of her she'd have gone for his throat. How dare he think he could dip his wick wherever and whenever he had the urge and get away with it! She wanted to take a knife and slash his handsome face and cut off that thing he got such pleasure from.

'What are we going to do?' asked Mary in a shaky voice as she wiped her mouth with the back of her hand. Her face was pinched and drained of colour.

Emma glanced up at her and said in a low, fierce voice, 'We were all aware that she could die at anytime. The doctor knows that and despite it being a sudden death won't be looking for anything suspicious. At the moment we can't prove it was Bert Kirk, alias Mr Temple, who raped her. You say you offered to fetch a bobby but she refused. Perhaps she decided to deal with him in another way. I need to speak to Joy. Maybe she knows something that we don't.'

Chapter Fifteen

May, 1909

Bert settled himself comfortably in his father's chair and stretched his legs towards the fire he had lit. He felt so cold despite the warm weather. He crunched on a thick slice of buttered toast and, with his free hand, he picked up the black leather-backed Bible from the shelf in the alcove next to the fireplace. Reading the scriptures always made him feel better. Particularly the epistles of St Paul – as long as he confessed his sin and was sorry then he'd be forgiven and accepted into Heaven. And he was sorry that Victoria Waters had died the way she had. He'd had such plans. If it hadn't been for that soddin' Emma Griffiths' interference everything would have been fine. He should have been quicker than that bloody boyfriend of hers and pushed her in front of the horse and cart...but he'd do for her one day.

He glowered as he put down the Bible and reached for his mug of tea and gulped a large mouthful. Right now he wished his mother would come home. His insides hadn't stopped churning and he was annoyed with her for being out when he needed her. He supposed Freddie and Joy were with her and their dah.

For a moment he concentrated his thoughts on his younger sister, dark like their mother and brown-eyed, she was just like Hannah in that she was stubborn and had no time for him and would never have tried to please him like their youngest sister, Grace.

Grace! She had been so eager to spend time in his company, that was how they'd come to be on the bicycle but he'd never had the chance to do anything with her. Silly bitch! If she hadn't messed about but done as he'd told her then he could have shown her how to please him and she would have still been alive. Instead she'd had to drag on his arm, causing him to lose control of the bicycle so they'd ended up in the canal. He'd tried to save her but his leg had got tangled up in the wheel. God, his mother had been in a right state when he'd told her what happened.

He broke out in a sweat just thinking how she had beaten him over the head with her handbag and it was ages before she would speak to him. As for Joy, Hanny and Freddie, they had never forgiven him. Pity! Joy had been developing into an attractive young woman when he'd been forced to disappear. She'd had a real shapely figure, much more meat on her than Miss Victoria Waters. Just thinking of the dead woman caused his hand to shake and tea spilt onto his trouser leg. He swore and scrubbed at the spot with his sleeve. Then he glanced at the mantelpiece and realised that it was six o'clock and swore again. He hadn't realised it was so late. He should be on his way. The trains were going to be packed with trippers and he wouldn't be able to get a seat. Seeing his mother would have to wait until another time.

He finished the toast and tea in double quick time, shrugged on his blazer and tilted his boater at a jaunty angle. He had the door open and was just about to step out onto the street when he spotted Joy out of the corner of his eye. She was alone and, immediately, he stepped back inside the house and closed the door. He grinned as he returned to the kitchen and hid behind the door, thinking that the day had picked up again, just when he'd almost given up on it.

'We're soldiers of the queen, m'lads, the queen, m'lads,' sang Joy as she stepped over the threshold. She pushed open the kitchen door and saw the fire burning in the black-leaded range but the room appeared empty. She stepped further inside and closed the door. 'Mother,

Dad, Freddie!' she called.

Suddenly a pair of arms went round her from behind and lifted her off her feet. She caught the smell of peppermint and hair oil and screamed. Kicking backwards she had the satisfaction of knowing the heel of her shoe had caught her brother on the shins. 'Put me down,' she demanded, attempting to prise his hands apart. 'What are you playing at, and what the hell are you doing here?'

He thrust his knee between her legs. 'That's not a nice way to speak to your brother,' he hissed in her ear.

'You're not a nice brother,' she threw back at him, digging her finger-nails into the back of his hands.

Bert dropped her. 'You bloody bitch!' He stared at his hand as blood began to ooze through the broken skin. He looked down at her sprawled on the floor and kicked her.

'Swine,' she yelled, scrabbling away from him. 'Just carry on the way you are and Dah'll catch you. Then you'll be sorry.'

He laughed. 'You think I'm scared of Dah? Not these days, little sister. I could take him on with one arm tied behind my back and beat him.' He bent over and grabbed her by the front of her blouse and hoisted her to her feet. Ramming her against him he kissed her hard, crushing her lips against her teeth. Furious and scared she brought up both hands and slapped the sides of his face. He swore and then laughed. 'You're just how I like a girl...plenty of fight in her.'

Joy remembered what he had done to Hannah and fear tightened her stomach. Even so she looked him straight in the eye. 'You mightn't be scared of Dah but Mother's not going to like it if you dare rape me.'

'Rape!' His eyes hardened. 'That's an ugly word, little sister.'

'Aye, isn't it? Mother's not going to like it either when I tell her what you've been up to...threatening Alice, Hannah and Emma and making up to Miss Victoria Waters.'

He dropped her. 'How d'you know about that?'

This time Joy managed to pick herself up and reached for the poker. She gripped it firmly and said boldly, 'That's shocked you, hasn't it? If I was you I'd make a run for it before you find yourself in real hot water.'

He stared at her and without saying another word, he walked out of the kitchen. Joy could scarcely believe it and it took her several minutes to pull herself together and rush after him. He had already vanished from sight and she could only rejoice that she had resisted the temptation to fling at him the knowledge that they knew where he lived. Even now Kenny was on his way to the address she had given him. She experienced a momentary unease, thinking of what her brother had said about being able to beat their father with one hand tied behind his back. Perhaps Kenny should have waited for him, so there'd be two of them to face him, but her brother-in-law had been raring to have a go at Bert. She prayed that he had not taken on more than he could handle. He might have beaten Bert once but could he do it again?

A black and white cat dozed on the whitened doorstep in the early evening sun as Kenny pushed his cap to the back of his head and gazed at the terraced house with its brightly painted green door and small front garden. Floral curtains fluttered in the breeze that blew through the half-open sash window and he could see a woman glancing through the glass at him as she watered an aspidistra in the downstairs front room. For a moment, he wondered if Bert had found himself a live-in tart, but as he crossed the street he realised that the woman was elderly with white hair pinned up in a bun. As he watched she vanished, only to reappear when she opened the front door. She picked up the cat and held it to the bosom of her frilled cream blouse.

'D'you want something?' she asked.

Kenny removed his cap, revealing a mop of light brown hair. 'It's a fine evening.'

'It is indeed. Can I help you?'

His sensitive mouth eased into a smile and his hazel eyes creased at the corners. 'I hope so. I'm looking for Mr Temple. I've been informed he lives here.'

Her face lit up. 'You're the first visitor I've known him to have. He keeps himself to himself…not that he isn't polite and friendly,' she hastened to add.

'Is he in?' asked Kenny, reaching out and tickling the cat's head and stroking its back. It stretched and purred.

'You like cats?' He nodded. 'I don't think he does,' she said with a sigh. 'Threw it out when it got into his room once.'

'He's not in then?'

She shook her head. 'Went out about twelve. No doubt he'll be back soon. Supper's at seven.'

'I'll wait here then if you don't mind?' He raised a questioning eyebrow.

She shook her head. 'Although, you're welcome to wait inside. Have you come far, Mr…?'

'Chester,' said Kenny, leaning against the wall. The bricks were warm and he held his face up to the sun. There was a silence and he thought she'd gone inside and then suddenly she said, 'Perhaps you'd like a cup of tea. You must be thirsty? It's been a warm day.'

Kenny opened his eyes, thanked her and followed her inside the house. One obstacle over with, he thought, wondering what the woman would think if she knew what he planned for Mr Temple.

She showed him into the parlour and left him alone. On the way here he'd only been able to think about blackening both Bert's eyes and breaking his arms so he'd think twice before writing another threatening letter or attacking a woman, but now, sitting in this peaceful parlour with its occasional table, large leatherette three piece suite and piano, he came to the conclusion that he could hardly do that here.

He was wondering how best to leave without upsetting the woman when she reappeared, carrying a tray. He realised it was going to be impossible to leave without drinking a cup of tea and eating at least one drop scone.

She was obviously lonely because as she fussed over him her tongue wagged ceaselessly. She was a widow with two sons of whom she saw little. 'Do you have any children?' she asked.

Pain crossed Kenny's face. It didn't go unnoticed and she patted his hand but did not comment. He gained control of himself and having swallowed several mouthfuls of tea, said, 'I have a six-year-old half-sister who lives with us. My stepmother died in childbirth,' he added by way of explanation.

'Sad,' she murmured. 'I presume Mr Temple has never been married?'

Kenny shook his head, wondering again what she would think if he said Bert had almost married his other half-sister and had beaten her when she discovered that he'd raped his own sister, *Kenny's wife!* Anger and frustration twisted his gut and his finger tightened on the cup handle. It snapped and tea and crockery spilt on his lap. He grabbed hold of the cup and shot to his feet, apologising to the woman.

'You mustn't worry. I know there was a cup with a hairline crack but I can't always see it. I'm only sorry you're all wet.' She blinked at him. 'I'll get you a cloth and you can wipe yourself down.'

'No! Thank you...you mustn't bother yourself. I appreciate your kind hospitality but perhaps I'd better go.'

She looked up at him in surprise. 'But Mr Temple should be in soon.'

'I'll come again,' said Kenny, taking a handkerchief from his pocket and dabbing at his trousers.

She smiled. 'It'll be nice to see you. One thing's for

sure…you'll soon dry in the warm air.'

Kenny agreed. He took his cap from his pocket and pulled it on and then buttoned up his jacket, glad that it was long enough to hide the damp patch. He was half way along the road when he realised a train must be in as people were spilling out of the railway station. He began to run, excusing himself as he forced his way through the crowds. For a brief moment he thought he saw Bert then he disappeared. Kenny hesitated, thinking to go after him but then changed his mind. Here in the open with witnesses was not how he wanted to deal with Bert. He had been too hasty rushing here. The confrontation with Bert needed more consideration.

He showed his ticket at the barrier and then headed for the wrought iron stairway leading up to the walkway over the railway track to the platform on the other side.

He was at the top of the steps when he felt a blow in the centre of his back. He staggered, recovered his balance and then felt another blow. He made a grab for the handrail and hung on to it, but then a hand came down and chopped his fingers with a viciousness that caused him to lose his grip. Another push and he lost his footing and went sliding down the steps on his back at speed. He thrust out a leg to slow himself down and his foot hit the side of the stairway. The shock jarred right up his leg and through his body with shattering pain. He managed to grab hold of one of the rails and swung himself to a halt.

Thoroughly shaken he drew in his leg and sat down on one of the steps. The pain was so excruciating he felt sick and dizzy. He rested his head on his forearm and gulped air. Part of his mind was aware of running footsteps and voices and, within minutes, he felt a hand on his shoulder whilst several feet ran past him.

'Are you OK, pal? I could scarcely believe my eyes. You were deliberately pushed!' The man's voice rose in indignation.

Slowly Kenny lifted his head and stared into the concerned face of a middle-aged station master with a walrus moustache. 'Did...?' began Kenny weakly, only to have to pause to take another breath and steady his voice. 'Did you see who it was?'

'Fair haired, wearing a stripped blazer and white trousers,' said the porter. 'The engine driver saw it happen and has gone after him. He and his fireman were just topping up with water from our tank. He took off like a rocket.'

Bert! thought Kenny furious with himself for not being on his guard. He swore under his breath.

'You've gone a terrible colour. D'you want me to help you up? You can rest in the waiting room.' Before Kenny could answer, there was the shush-hiss-shush-hiss-shush of brakes being applied as a train steamed into the other platform and the man said hastily, 'I'll have to go but I'll be back.'

Kenny saw that his train was still waiting, its tank being filled with water. 'Help me up now! I need to get the Chester train.' The station master looked doubtful but he didn't argue with him and aided him in getting to his feet. Kenny gritted his teeth against the throbbing pain in his foot and ankle. The porter took one look at his face and asked for assistance from the youth now hurrying down the steps.

'Alf, give us a hand here. This gentleman wants the Chester train. I take it you didn't catch his assailant?'

'No, sir.' Alf removed his cap revealing ginger hair and wiped his brow. 'Mr Davies hasn't given up, though. For a bloke his size, he can't half leg it. Apparently he recognised the man...and I've seen him before, too.' The station master seemed about to ask another question when he remembered the train waiting at the other platform and hurried away.

Alf gazed into Kenny's tight-lipped face. 'Yer look a bit rough, sir.'

'I feel bloody lousy.' He rested his head against the rails. 'I was going to ask you to help me to get to the Chester train but I'll rest here and wait for your Mr Davies. You carry on with your work.'

The lad hesitated and then hurried down the steps.

David caught up with Bert in the act of opening the front door to his lodgings. He grabbed him by the collar of his blazer and pulled him backwards. Bert managed to stop himself from falling against him by jerking forwards and dragging himself out of it. David staggered back, clutching the empty blazer and Bert shot into the house. He made to slam the door but David thrust his foot in the gap and forced it open again. Bert made a hasty retreat into the parlour where he picked up the shovel from the coal scuttle. David got as far as the doorway when a quavering voice said, 'Who are you? What's going on here?'

He glanced down from his great height at the white haired old woman and said soothingly, 'Nothing for you to worry about, lovey. Just go into your kitchen and leave this to me. This swine has just pushed a man down the steps at the station.'

Her faded blue eyes showed astonishment. 'Mr Temple? Never!'

'That's right, Mrs Payne. Don't you believe him,' shouted Bert, from inside the parlour. 'He's a thieving debt collector and he's bleeding me dry.'

'You liar!' said David, a pained expression in his face. 'Do I look like a debt collector, lovey?'

'It's a disguise, Mrs Payne! You know how crafty these debt collectors are,' yelled Bert.

David wasted no more time going in after him.

Bert swung the shovel at his head but David brought up an arm and grabbed it. He tugged it out of Bert's grasp with one hand and then slammed his fist into the other man's face with the other. Bert moaned and staggered back, clutching his nose. He fell over the occasional table and was only prevented from landing on the floor by grabbing hold of the piano stool.

With a great deal of satisfaction David looked at Bert's bleeding nose, which was definitely a peculiar shape. He watched the other man shake his head as if to clear it. There was a venomous expression in his eyes as he grabbed the piano stool and with a string of foul sounding words attacked David with it. The Welshman only just managed to step aside in time but the leg of the stool whacked his arm and a hiss of pain sounded through his clenched teeth. The shovel he had wrenched from Bert slipped from his grasp. Bert went for him again with the piano stool. This time David managed to get a grip on two of the legs and he pushed with all his strength. Suddenly he released it and Bert fell back onto the sofa. Grim-faced, David bent over him and seized him by the throat. He was just about to heave Bert to his feet when something hit him over the head. He saw stars and there was a rushing in his ears as he lost consciousness.

When David came to it was to find himself stretched out on the sofa with a policeman and Alf sitting a few feet away, drinking tea. Hovering just behind them was the white-haired old woman. The relief on her face when he sat up was such that he felt he had to reassure her that he was OK.

'I did it,' she said in a trembling voice, clasping her hands in front of her bosom. 'I didn't realise Mr Temple was such a bad man. I believed what he said.'

'Where is he?' asked David, touching the back of his head gingerly.

'Scarpered,' said Alf. 'When the train was ready to go and you were still not back we had to get another driver. Mr Moran, the bloke who was pushed down the stairs, gave us this address and I was sent to fetch a bobby and here we are.'

David swore under his breath. 'How is he?'

'Someone took him home. He refused to go to the hospital.'

The policeman handed his cup to the woman. 'Perhaps you'd like to give us a statement, Mr Davies, on the way to the station. Then we'll get a search launched for Mr Kirk, alias Temple.'

David agreed, hoping he was not going to lose his job over this. Mucking up the company's timetable was not going to go down well with the owners, especially when he was known to belong to the union. But what else could he have done? He only hoped Emma would be pleased that he had at least caused some damage to the swine. But what of the bloke who'd been pushed down the stairs? He could only pray that his foot hadn't been completely smashed.

'You were a fool to go alone,' scolded Hannah, her expression strained as she eased off Kenny's shoe, aware of his indrawn hiss of pain as she performed this service. She removed his sock with gentle fingers, trying to conceal her dismay as she stared at his swollen ankle and foot that seemed to be fixed at a peculiar angle. 'I'll fetch a bowl of cold water.'

There came the rat-tat-tat of the knocker on the front door.

'Tilly, you get that,' said Hannah, wondering who it could be.

Tilly hurried to the front door and opened it. On the step stood Joy and Emma. 'Has Kenny arrived home yet?' asked Joy, her eyes sombre.

Tilly opened the door wide. 'You'd best come in. His foot's all swollen.' Her voice quivered. 'Uncle Bert pushed him down the steps. How could he be so wicked?'

Joy and Emma exchanged worried glances and hurriedly followed her inside. They gasped when they saw Kenny's foot.

'Oh, Kenny!' cried Joy, going over to him and putting an arm about his shoulders.

'I acted bloody daft,' he said in bitter tones. 'I'd forgotten what a crafty swine he was.'

'Stop blaming yourself,' chided Hannah, placing the bowl of cold water on the floor. She lifted his foot and he gritted his teeth as she placed it in the water.

'You're going to need a doctor for that,' said Emma, getting down on her knees and inspecting his injury. 'Cold water won't cure it. I worked in a doctor's house and I'd say it's broken. These days they can X-ray it for you so they know exactly how bad the break is. He'll have to go to Chester Infirmary.'

'But that would mean calling out the horse ambulance and that'll cost money,' said Hannah in dismay.

'You want him to get the best of care, don't you?' asked Emma. 'You be grateful he's still alive, Hanny. Poor Victoria Waters is dead.'

Hannah and Kenny stared at her. 'What d'you mean, dead?' they chorused.

She glanced at Tilly and then whispered, 'What I've to say isn't for her ears.'

Immediately Hannah asked Tilly to go upstairs and fetch a clean pair of Kenny's socks from the chest of drawers. No sooner was she out of the room than Emma commenced to tell them what had happened at the Waters' house.

Hannah and Kenny could not conceal their shocked horror. 'He must be out of his mind. I never thought he'd go that far,' said Hannah in a shaken voice.

'And he must have realised that I knew where he lived and panicked when he saw me,' rasped Kenny. 'I only hope to God that Mr Davies managed to get his hands on him before the police did.'

Emma stared at him in amazement. 'Mr Davies? Was he a big fella with fair hair?'

Kenny grimaced. 'Engine driver! I was on the ground, so I only saw his legs passing by. But apparently he saw what happened and went after him. The lad said he recognised him.'

Emma's expression was gleeful. 'I saw him today and I told him about my suspicions about Bert and about your drawing. No wonder he recognised him and went after him.' She clasped her hands together as if in prayer. 'Dear God, let David have beaten him into pulp.'

Hannah smiled. But Joy said, 'Kenny, you mentioned a bobby.'

'That's right.' He reached out and took his wife's hand. 'We both know what you're going to say, Joy…that your Mother won't be able to cope with Bert being arrested and hearing what he's been up to…but you know as well as we do that he's got to be stopped.'

Joy nodded. 'I agree. He was hiding in the house when I arrived home and attacked me. I fought back and said a few well chosen words and he left.' The two women gasped and Kenny swore. 'I'll tell you more later. I don't want to be caught talking about it when Tilly comes down. I just wish there was another way to punish Bert, his going to prison could kill Mother.'

Hannah frowned. 'We've tried to protect her in the past – and where's it got us?'

Emma got to her feet. 'I was all for leaving the police out of this. I wanted to deal with him ourselves but it's too late now. I told the doctor what I suspected and half-expected him to tell me to wash my mouth out with soap.' She hesitated. 'Give him his due, he said that he would inspect the body closely and, if it was as I believed, he would report it to the police. Although, without witnesses they might have trouble proving it was him that raped her, causing heart failure.' She sighed. 'I'm prepared to stand in the witness box and swear it was him who attacked me. I'd like to see him hang, meself, but I'll probably have to settle for a good stiff sentence with hard labour.'

The others agreed.

Soon after Emma and Joy left. They parted outside the Kirks' house, promising to get in touch when they had news. Emma would have liked to have called at David's house but knew it would be unfair to leave Mary and Cook alone any longer to cope with the aftermath of their mistress's death. She guessed it was going to be left to her to get in touch with Mr Crane, the solicitor, and Victoria's Uncle Martin to arrange the funeral.

In a church pew of St Mary-without-the-Walls, sat Emma and David, who had been suspended from his job while an enquiry was pending. Hannah and Joy were also there, as was Mary. Poor Kenny had wanted to attend the funeral but it would have been too much for him. His ankle was broken and the impact had also shattered a bone in his foot. It was possible he might never be completely free from pain and be left with a permanent limp. Cook had stayed behind to keep an eye on old Mrs Waters and to see to the funeral meal.

In the row in front of them were ranged several members of the Women's Suffrage Movement, including Josephine Stone. On the other side of the aisle sat Mr Martin Waters, Mr Crane, the solicitor, and the doctor. Other pews were occupied by neighbours and friends and business acquaintances of Mr Waters from Liverpool.

There had been no news from Sebastian and Alice or from Gabrielle Bennett. As for Bert, so far he had managed to escape capture and his mother was denying that he had done any of the things her daughters and Emma had accused him of doing.

The vicar announced the final hymn and the organist began to play 'Crimond'. The congregation stood up and started to sing 'The Lord is My Shepherd'. The hymn came to an end and the final words of the service were said. The bearers lifted the pale oak coffin, with its wreath of red and yellow roses, on to their shoulders and led the way down the aisle and outside.

Mary sniffed back tears and Emma dabbed her own eyes as Victoria was laid to rest beside her father. Again, Emma thought how unfair it was that she should have gone to meet her maker before her grandmother.

Hannah, Joy and David left Emma outside the Waters' gate. David had whispered in her ear that he would call round tomorrow and see her.

Later, as she helped serve drinks and hand round plates of food, she overheard Martin Waters echoing her sentiments as to the unfairness of his niece dying before his mother. Only after the other guests had left, did he ask Mr Crane about the contents of his niece's will. He must have forgotten Emma was there because he did not lower his voice, nor did the solicitor. Apparently Victoria Waters had not made a will. This news obviously did not please her uncle one little bit. He demanded to know what would happen to her shares in the company. Emma continued to empty ash trays and tidy up in general, her ears pricked for what came next.

'The shares in the business go to your brother's son, Sebastian Bennett. It is clearly stated in a codicil attached to his will,' said Mr Crane in a dry as dust voice.

Martin's face fell. 'I didn't know that.'

Mr Crane stared at him over his half-moon spectacles. 'As you didn't inherit shares in your brother's other businesses you didn't need to know, Mr Waters. He probably thought your involvement with the farm was enough to keep you fully occupied.'

'What about this house?' asked Martin, nursing the cut glass tumbler of whisky between his hands. 'Can I move Mama out and sell it? At the moment I rent the farm and an opportunity has risen for me to buy.'

The solicitor pursed his lips. 'That would be difficult.

Mrs Waters is very much alive, even though she is non compos mentis. Her will clearly states that the house and its possessions were to go to her granddaughter. As she was in her care she and I shared power of attorney. Now Miss Waters is dead, I suggest that you talk to your mother's doctor. It should be easy enough for the power she wielded to be made over to you if you wish. As for the inheritance that would have come to Miss Waters…when your mother dies then it will be divided between you and Mr Bennett, despite his illegitimacy.'

'But that isn't fair,' burst out Martin. 'I'm Mother's legal son. Surely I should have first claim on her property?'

Mr Crane said sternly, 'Fair or not, Mr Waters, that is the law. Your brother clearly accepted Mr Bennett as his son. I suggest we drop this matter for now…and may I add that it would be sensible if the servants remained here to look after your mother until Mr and Mrs Bennett's arrival from India. That is unless you want the responsibility of caring for her yourself?'

Martin sighed. 'My days are full enough with looking after the farm. I had thought of a good nursing home but, if I can't sell the house, it's out of the question. I'll speak to Sebastian when he returns home.' He drained his glass. 'What about the motorcar? Can I have that? It would be useful.'

'The motorcar belongs to the business so I'm sorry, Mr Waters, but again I must say no.'

Martin looked aggrieved. 'I'd best get back to the farm then. I presume I can leave it to you to see that the servants' wages are paid.'

Mr Crane nodded and both men drifted out of the room.

Emma was relieved to hear they were to stay on at the house until Seb and Alice returned. She opened the french windows to let in some fresh air and went and stood on the terrace for a few moments, wondering when that might be. They surely knew by now that Mr Waters was dead. His daughter's death was going to come as a terrible shock to them both. But once they had recovered and were ready to take stock of the change in their circumstances, what would they do? It could be that Emma might yet be out of a job before Mrs Black came home.

Chapter Sixteen

June, 1909

Seb dropped the suitcases and turned to his wife. With an encouraging smile, he swept her up into his arms and, nudging the door further open with his knee, he carried her over the threshold. Both allowed their eyes to sweep around the familiar hall before looking into the other's face. Alice nodded affirmation and he kissed her before setting her on her feet. Instantly she reached out a hand to him and he held it firmly. 'It's going to be all right,' he assured her. 'We can do this together.'

She hoped so and thought back to earlier that morning when the ship had docked in Liverpool and they had been given the news that Victoria was dead and the request that Mr Bennett call on Mr Crane that afternoon at two thirty. They presumed he had been checking the shipping arrivals and departures in the *Liverpool Echo*. Naturally the news had come as a terrible shock but both had known that her heart condition would shorten her life. Their concern was that the loss of her father and the news that Seb was her half-brother might have been partially to blame for her death and both had expressed guilt at not being there when she needed them.

'It's going to be strange her not being here,' said Alice, a tremor in her voice. 'I'll never forget how helpful she was to me when I was getting over that terrible time with Bert. I'll miss her.'

'Me too. I'd known her all my life and she was always there…bossing me around more often than not,' he added with a grim smile. 'Same with Ma.'

Suddenly the green baize door opened and Emma appeared in the doorway. She started and then the three of them spoke at once before stopping abruptly. Both women looked at Seb and he said easily, 'Sorry for startling you, Emma, but the door was on the latch so we came right in.'

'Welcome home, sir,' she said, smiling up into his suntanned face. 'You look well...if you don't mind my saying so.'

'Of course not, Emma.' He grinned. 'It seems odd being called sir by you. I'll just fetch the suitcases and if you could tell Alice which bedroom you've prepared for us.'

'Yes, sir.' She turned to Alice and experienced a twinge of envy. 'You look lovely, Mrs Bennett...or should I call you Mrs Waters?' Her brow puckered.

'Thank you, Emma!' Alice was gratified and her cheeks were rosy as she gazed down at the matching skirt and jacket in turquoise shot silk with a *crêpe-de-chine* lemon blouse. 'You think I'll pass muster with the others in the Crescent?'

'I don't see why not. They're only middle class and not the blinkin' aristocracy. I love your hat. Did you make it yourself?'

'Yes!' Alice removed the felt of palest green, trimmed with white tulle and imitation yellow roses, and shook out her auburn curls. 'Obviously you know about Seb,' she said, placing the hat on the hall table.

Emma nodded. 'Hannah mentioned it first and then...'

'So the pair of you did get to meet,' interrupted Alice. 'Have you been seeing much of her?'

'Yes! And Joy and Kenny...but perhaps I should leave it to them to tell you what's been going on.' Emma hesitated. 'Now, perhaps you'd like a nice cup of tea and a slice of Cook's seedcake? I'll bring it to the drawing room, shall I?'

'It feels odd you asking me that and calling Seb sir...but I'd love a cup of tea and I'm sure he will, too. Although we're both hungry and were hoping for some lunch.'

'Oh, Cook's prepared lunch for you. I just wasn't sure if you were ready for it yet.'

'A cup of tea first, skip the cake. We'll get changed after lunch,' murmured Alice, easing off yellow kid gloves. 'You wouldn't know, I suppose, how she compares with Seb's mother?'

'Miss Waters didn't rate her as good but then it was her own fault for sacking Gabrielle. Right, I'll go and tell Cook and bring some tea.'

Emma made for the green baize door but paused with her hand on it when Alice called, 'How's Mrs Waters?'

Emma turned and said in a droll voice, 'Still a blinking nuisance! Although, I probably shouldn't be saying that seeing as how she's Seb's granny. She won't recognise either of you.' Those last words were directed at Seb as he came through the door with the suitcases.

He frowned. 'Mr Crane hinted that she was past the post…although, those weren't his exact words. I reckon it's best for us that she's the way she is. Mightn't have wanted us in the house if she was in her right mind…she was a right stickler for people knowing their place.'

'You mean she'd think me a jumped up nobody,' said Alice in a rush. 'She mightn't have minded you so much because her blood runs in your veins.'

Seb shrugged. 'It doesn't matter now. She's not going to be telling us never to darken her doors again.'

Emma's gaze went from one to another. 'She's not easy to look after. You should be thinking perhaps of hiring a nurse. I've given you Mr Waters' old room, by the way. It's a nice size, as you know, and looks over the river.'

Seb thanked her and with a whisk of grey skirts Emma hurried through the baize door. He looked at Alice. 'Shall we go up now?'

'After tea. Emma's serving it in the drawing room.'

'OK! I'll take the suitcases up and join you in a few minutes.'

Alice nodded, thinking that perhaps he needed a little time alone in that bedroom, which would have memories of his father for him. She went into the drawing room, thinking now of the old woman, not only being Seb's grandmother, but also the great-grandmother of the baby Alice was almost certain she was carrying. Seb was over the moon about the possibility of being a father but it was something she wasn't looking forward to telling Hannah and Kenny. As far as she knew, Hannah hadn't had any luck conceiving but at least they had Tilly to brighten their lives. Alice wanted her younger sister to live with her and Seb, but would it be fair to remove her from Kenny and Hannah's care straight away? Perhaps she should discuss it with them first. After lunch she would go up and see Hannah. Seb had to call in at Mr Crane's office, so they could walk that far together.

She went over to the french windows and gazed out at the garden and noticed the roses were in bloom. Her husband joined her a few minutes later and immediately drew her into his arms and kissed her.

She stroked his cheek and murmured, 'Does it feel as strange to you as it does to me being here, waiting for Emma to bring us tea?'

He lifted his head. 'You don't mind her being here, do you?'

'I didn't say that. It's just that I'm not sure how to behave towards her.'

Seb's dark eyes were thoughtful. 'It could be awkward but she did call me sir and you Mrs Bennett...and I wouldn't like sacking her.'

'No!' Alice sighed.

Seb hugged her. 'As long as you don't treat her like the old woman treated you. After all, you and Emma are sisters in the Cause.'

Alice pursed her lips. 'You know, I've hardly thought of women's rights while we've been away. I never was as keen as Miss Victoria about it...and when we arrived back in England and I read in the newspaper that the suffragettes had marched on Parliament and smashed windows, and Mrs Pankhurst had struck a policeman in order to get arrested, I didn't want to be part of them. I hate violence.'

'Naturally you do. But what about the suffragists, who believe in peaceful protests?'

She nodded. 'I do believe spinsters and widows need to be treated equally with men when it comes to earning a decent wage but I was never sure just how useful having the vote would be for working-class women.'

'So you won't be taking over where Victoria left off?'

Alice shifted restlessly in his arms. 'I don't think I could do what she did. Besides I have the baby to think about. I wonder if Hanny's been to any meetings. Emma said she's been seeing her. That'll be to do with Bert. I wonder if he's still sending her letters? Emma said a lot's been happening.'

'Perhaps the swine's met his comeuppance at last,' said Seb, releasing her and gazing out over the garden.

'I think Emma would have told me,' murmured Alice, going over to the chaise longue. 'Have you noticed this has been re-upholstered. Nice material,' she added, stroking the red and cream damask fabric.

'Perhaps Victoria felt like a change,' he said, coming over to her.

Alice did not answer. In her mind's eye she could see Victoria lying on the chaise longue. They had spent such a lot of time in here together, writing letters in support of those who were suffering for the Cause. Her former employer's voice echoed in her head, dictating exactly what she wanted to say to those who needed her support. She had been so determined to change women's lives for the better and had so much wanted to achieve votes for women before she died. A deep sadness swept over Alice and, despite it being summer, she felt cold.

There was a knock on the door and Seb crossed the room and opened the door. Taking the tray from Emma, he said, 'Come and have a cup of tea with us. We need some answers.'

She hesitated and glanced in Alice's direction. 'I'm not sure if…'

'Sit down, Emma,' said Alice, feeling her colour rising. 'We might as well be comfortable. I don't want to get a crick in my neck staring up at you.'

Emma thanked her and followed Seb across the room. He placed the tray on a low table in front of the sofa and indicated that Emma sit down.

'Will I pour?' she asked.

He glanced at Alice, who nodded and said in a low voice. 'I suppose there's been no more macaroons in this house since Gabrielle left?'

Emma glanced at Seb. 'Nobody knows where she is. Miss Waters was furious with her, especially as your father left her a thousand pounds.'

'Payment for services rendered,' Seb said grimly.

'She could buy her own house for that,' said Alice.

'I bet she has but she'd have to spend money furnishing it and save some to live on,' said Seb in a dispassionate voice.

'She could take in lodgers,'said Emma. 'It's the kind of thing widows and spinsters with a bit of money do…that or open a little shop.'

'You're right.' Alice smiled. 'And the work wouldn't be different from what she did here if she cooked for them, as well.'

'Will you try and find her?' asked Emma, pouring tea and passing a cup to Alice.

She glanced at her husband, knowing he was still hurt by his mother's deception. 'I wouldn't know where to look,' he said, and changed the subject, asking Emma how she came to work for Victoria.

Emma decided to say as little as possible about that. 'Mrs Black went on an extended holiday and Miss Waters gave me a job. Your mother had gone by then.'

'How did Miss Victoria die? Where was she when it happened?' asked Alice, looking expectantly at Emma.

She hesitated but knew they had to know the truth. 'In this room...on the chaise longue...and she was as good as murdered.'

Alice started and spilled tea into her saucer. Seb placed an arm about her shoulders. 'Murdered? Mr Crane didn't mention murder. So why the melodrama? You're not working for Mrs Black now, you know,' he said tersely.

Emma's eyes flashed. 'Can I sit down, sir?'

'I told you to before.'

She fetched the straight-backed chair Victoria had used for sitting at the writing bureau and placed it the opposite side of the small table that held the tray. She gulped a mouthful of tea and then, nursing the cup between her hands, said, 'Bert found his way here.'

Alice gasped and Seb's arm tightened about her. 'Go on,' he ordered.

'He gave a false name and tried to butter up Miss Waters, sending her flowers and taking tea with her. I never saw him but Kenny did a drawing of him and Joy brought it here for me. I was out at the time but Mary recognised him and showed the picture to Miss Waters. Instead of sending for the police straight away she gave Joy his address to give to Kenny.'

'Joy! Joy's involved in this as well?' blurted out Alice.

Emma nodded, feeling her heart thumping, just remembering that day.

'Don't stop now!' Seb's eyes bored into hers.

She sipped more of her tea and then told them everything that had happened. 'It's terrible,' said Alice. 'If only I'd known earlier that Mr Temple and Bert were one and the same. She gave me an address so I could send him copies of *Votes for Women*.'

'How bad is Kenny's ankle?' asked Seb.

'He's in constant pain. They say he'll be left with a permanent limp.'

'And Bert?' Alice's voice was raw.

'He got away. David Davies, my young man…you've met him, Mrs Bennett…reckons he broke his nose and spoilt his handsome face but where he is we've no idea.'

Silence. Seb stood up. 'Is there any brandy or whisky in the drinks cupboard?'

Emma nodded. 'We bought some in for the funeral and the old lady still enjoys a glass of sherry every evening.'

He went over to the sideboard and took out a bottle of whisky that was almost half full, and opening the glass door of another cupboard he removed three glasses. He poured out decent measures for them all and handed a glass to Alice and Emma and remained standing. 'Forgive me, Emma, for accusing you of being melodramatic.' He tossed off the whisky, poured himself another and rested an elbow on the mantelshelf.

'It can't have been easy for you, Emma,' said Alice in a subdued voice. 'Who's been in charge here since Miss Victoria's death?'

'We've just muddled through between us. Mr Crane brings our wages and the housekeeping money.' Emma took a cautious sip of the whisky.

'What about Victoria's uncle, has he visited at all?' asked Seb.

'Barring the funeral, no,' said Emma, 'but there was a fire at Delemere a couple of weeks ago and acres of trees and land were destroyed. It was in the *Chronicle*. I don't know if he was affected by it but that could be why he hasn't been.'

'He hardly ever visited his mother,' said Seb, frowning. 'I'll speak to Mr Crane and see what he's got to say.'

There was another silence. Emma considered telling them that Martin Waters wanted to put the old woman in a nursing home and sell the house, but she decided to leave it to Mr Crane to give Seb that news. She took a larger sip of the whisky, could feel it warming her. 'Is there anything else you want to know? Or for me to do for that matter?'

'The bed's made up I presume?' said Alice.

Emma nodded.

Alice thanked her. 'We'll probably need to decorate the bedroom,' she murmured.

'Presuming we'll be living here,' said Seb. 'It's not guaranteed. But we should know where we stand by the end of the day.'

Two hours later Alice parted from Seb in Northgate Street. She stood a moment, watching him walk away with that loose-limbed stride of his until he disappeared amongst the crowds thronging the pavement. Only then did she turn and go inside the cathedral, feeling in need of religious comfort. She sat in a pew, watching sightseers wander through the cathedral's interior. The last time she had been in here was after she had broken her engagement to Bert and was recovering from the beating he had given her. She clenched her fists, her fingernails digging into the palms of her hands, and wished the bobbies had caught him.

She forced herself to relax, thinking of Seb and how she had gone to the Waters' house to apologise to him, only to be told by Victoria that he was in America. She had been devastated but Victoria had given her a job and encouraged her to hope. The tears trickled down Alice's cheeks. If Miss Victoria had not done so, then most likely she would still be alive today. Alice's heart felt heavy with guilt.

She pulled out a hassock and sank on to her knees. Resting her elbows on the ledge in front of her, she laced her hands together and prayed for forgiveness. She thanked God for giving Seb back to her and the happiness they had shared in their marriage so far. She also prayed that the baby growing inside her would be kept safe. Thinking of the baby reminded her of Tilly and Kenny. She

mustn't linger here long, but first she would pray that
Kenny's ankle would be healed and that God would
provide for his needs. She knew that Bert needed prayer if
he was to be saved and go to Heaven, but somehow the
words stuck in her throat. She didn't want him saved,
would much rather he went to Hell. Her expression
darkened and she scrambled to her feet; perhaps she could
try another time. For the moment, hopefully God would
forgive her where Bert and her father were concerned. She
wanted them to suffer for the pain they had caused others.

She quit the pew, intending to leave the cathedral by a
different door. Her heels tip-tapped on the tiled floor but
she was brought up short by a muted voice speaking her
name. She looked about her and, to her surprise and
delight, spotted Kenny sitting near the end of a back pew.
His foot jutted out into the aisle and she could see the
rubber stopper on the end of a walking stick. That fiercely
protective love she had felt towards this elder half-brother
came to the fore and she hurried over to him. 'Emma told
us what happened. What are you doing here?'

Her voice was louder than she intended and he shushed
her. 'People are praying,' he said softly, smiling up at her.
'It's good to see you.'

He took a firm grip on his stick and she would have
helped him get up if he had not shaken his head. Gripping
the pew, he pushed himself upright and a spasm of pain
dragged at the muscles of his face. Then it was gone and he
was smiling as he looked down at her. 'Did you have a
good time?' he whispered.

Her green eyes glowed and she stood on tiptoe and
kissed his cheek. 'It was wonderful! I said to Seb several
times how much you and Hanny with your love of history
would have enjoyed seeing the pyramids.'

'Don't!' he said abruptly, and began to walk, dragging
his damaged foot.

To see him so crippled tore at her heart and she

understood why she must say no more about the wonderful time she and Seb had enjoyed. Instead, she asked after Tilly and Hanny.

His face softened. 'She's grown in the five months you've been away. As for Hanny, she's angry, worried, frustrated and fussing over me like a mother hen, although she pretends she's none of those things. She chatters away to me as if my being crippled was the last thing she's worried about.'

Pity overwhelmed Alice but she knew Kenny would not want her pity, so she only asked how they were managing as they made their way to the exit.

'It's early days yet. I still do Mr Bushell's books and I'm able to do some writing and cartoons. I've sold an article on the X-ray machine "from a patient's point of view" to the *Liverpool Echo*, but I can't get out and about to events, like I used to.'

'Have you thought of advertising in the *Chester Chronicle* for more work as a bookkeeper?'

He nodded, easing his shoulders and stretching his arms as they came out into Abbey Square. 'So far nothing. But even if I can't get any more bookkeeping work, I'll not have Hanny working at Bannister's Bakery again.'

Alice said in surprise, 'She's suggested it?'

'No. Mr Bannister did,' he said tersely. 'Mrs Kirk told him I was crippled and that she didn't want to see her daughter go without.'

'Does Mrs Kirk know how you came to be crippled?' Alice's voice shook with anger.

His eyes glinted. 'Of course she does. The police interviewed her to see if she knew anything about Bert's whereabouts, but they had to give up because she got into such a state. She told Hanny and Joy, though, that it couldn't have been Bert who pushed me down the steps because he was out of the country.'

Alice looked at him in astonishment. 'How does she

work that out when his landlady told the police that he'd been living with her for the last two years?'

He shook his head more in sadness than anger. 'He told a neighbour in Francis Street that he'd just got back from America. He was lying, of course.'

'She's crazy. And I'm so sorry, Kenny, about what's happened to you. I feel it's all my fault.' She reached out and squeezed his arm.

He covered her hand with his own. 'Place the blame where it really belongs – with Bert.' Alice's eyes shone with tears and she lowered her head so he wouldn't see them. 'He attacked Joy but she struck back and he slunk off.'

'What did Mrs Kirk say about that?'

'She told Joy that she probably misunderstood his intentions.'

Alice drew in her breath with a hiss. 'I know I should feel sorry for her because she was good to us when we were young and a true friend to Mam but she's so blinkered when it comes to Bert. What reason had she come up with your fall if she won't admit it was him?'

'She's telling the neighbours it was my own careless fault and that I've always been clumsy. I'm sure she'd have been happy if I'd been killed,' he said bitterly. 'There's something wrong with the kind of mother's love that completely blinds a parent to the truth about their child. I'm worried about what she'll say and do next. The whole of Chester has read about him being accused of being the balaclava attacker but she, and some of the neighbours, just won't have it. They think we've got it in for him.'

Alice threw up her hands in disbelief. 'What do Hanny and Mr Kirk say about all this?'

'I told you, she's putting a brave face on things, but if they don't improve I might take up my cousin's offer and move to Scotland to make a fresh start,' he said seriously.

Alice opened her mouth to protest but then closed it

again. She would say no more until she had seen Hanny and explained the situation to Seb. 'And Mr Kirk?' she asked.

Kenny sighed and shook his head. 'He's slipped Hanny the odd florin but money's not what she really wants from him. She wants him to kill the rumours her mother's spreading but he just says give it time and that if she doesn't hear from him then it'll all die down.'

Alice shook her head in disbelief and Kenny murmured, 'That's how I felt. I want out of Newtown even if Hanny decides she doesn't want to go to Scotland.'

'I don't blame you,' she said.

Kenny changed the subject and asked whether the trip had been successful businesswise. She told him that Seb had been of the opinion that the increased production of cheap cotton goods in India meant they'd lost a market and that Britain would rue the day it had exported sewing machines over there. 'So what will he do now he's inherited the business?' asked Kenny.

She smiled. 'That's something he's going to discuss with Mr Crane, the solicitor. We also need to find out where we stand with living in the house.'

'I'm sure you'd like to carry on living there,' said Kenny with a smile.

Alice nodded.

They arrived at Kenny and Hanny's home to find not only the front door ajar but Mrs Kirk in the kitchen. Her grey hair hung like ribbons of dried seaweed over her shoulders and down her back; her brown eyes were wide and wild in her tear-stained, wrinkled face. She was holding Tilly but in such a way that the girl seemed in danger of falling on her head.

'Put my sister down!' cried Alice, not wanting to snatch Tilly out of her grasp in case she dropped her.

'Alice, you're back,' said her sister, a smile lighting up her pretty face.

'What are you doing with Tilly, Mrs Kirk? She's too heavy for you to be handling her like that,' said Kenny. 'Do as Alice says and put her down at once.'

Susannah Kirk made no move to do what either of them said. Alice's throat went dry. Such a scene was the last thing she had expected on entering this house. 'Where's Hanny?' she croaked.

'Joy's down the yard and Hanny's gone on a message,' answered Tilly, gazing at them from upside down.

The older woman, who had been staring at Alice as if she had seen a ghost, staggered and almost dropped the girl. Alice made a grab for her sister but Mrs Kirk swung her out of her reach. 'Give her to me,' demanded Alice.

'I shan't. You'll not get her,' said Mrs Kirk.

'Again!' said Tilly, her eyes sparkling. 'I like this game.'

'This is not a game,' cried Alice, lunging at her.

But Mrs Kirk whirled round, hoisting Tilly higher. 'It's all your fault, Alice,' she said with loathing. 'If you'd been half the woman your mother was then you'd have forgiven Bert and married him. Now he's gone and I'll never see him again.'

Alice flinched at the mention of her mother but knew that she must not let the distraught woman's words distract her from getting her sister from her. 'Mrs Kirk, put Tilly down before you hurt her. She hasn't done you any harm. You have to accept Bert for what he is, not what you and I once believed him to be. We were both deceived by him,' she said sadly.

'He was a good boy! It was you girls who led him astray.' Susannah Kirk wiped her wet eyes on Tilly's red-gold hair, and looked towards the photograph of her eldest daughter on her wedding day. Instantly Alice swooped and wrenched her sister free.

Susannah howled and tried to retrieve her but Alice held Tilly tightly, kissing her hair and whispering soothing words.

Suddenly Joy and Hannah entered from different doors.

'What's the noise?' asked Joy.

'Alice, you're back!' exclaimed Hannah, smiling at her old friend.

Susannah Kirk sank into her chair and gazed up at her daughter with the tears running down her cheeks. 'Go on, be nice to her. I didn't tell you before but Bert's gone...gone to the other side of the world. He bought a one way six pound ticket to Australia through the Emigration Society and he won't be coming back.'

They all stared at her in disbelief. Then as she continued to weep, Joy and Hannah went over to her and put their arms round her. 'If it's true, Mother, then it's for the best. He can start his life over again and hopefully so can we,' said Joy.

Chapter Seventeen

June, 1909

Emma glanced up as the door opened and Alice breezed into the dining room. She was singing 'Praise my soul the king of Heaven', but stopped when she saw Emma.

'Guess what!' exclaimed Alice, her face alight with joy.

'Kenny's found some more work? Or is it that his foot's better?'

Some of the sparkle dimmed in Alice's eyes and she heaved a sigh. 'It would take a miracle for his foot to be healed...and no, he hasn't got more work. But I do have good news...Bert's gone to Australia.'

Emma dropped a fork. 'You're serious?'

'His mother told us...she's in a right state. He's taken a one way ticket so we won't be seeing him again.' She swayed as if to an invisible orchestra and sang, 'He's gone, gone, gone and I hope...he'll...be bitten by a snake and...die a...horrible, horrible death.'

'Damn and bloody damn him!' swore Emma under her breath. She bent to pick up the fork and rubbed it vigorously with a napkin.

'What did you say, Emma?' asked Alice, pulling out a chair and sitting down. She placed an elbow on the lace edged tablecloth and rested her chin in her hand. 'I thought you'd be over the moon at the news.'

'I can see why you're pleased and perhaps I should be dancing with delight, as well, but I can't help being hopping mad because it seems to me he's never going to pay for what he's done,' said Emma without drawing breath. 'What I'd like to know is how he managed it? I would have thought the police would have alerted the port authorities in Liverpool and Birkenhead.'

'Perhaps he sailed from Southampton or Greenock.'

'I suppose you're right,' said Emma.

Alice was momentarily deflated but then she said seriously, 'My mam used to say that no one goes on forever escaping punishment. If they don't get it in this world then they'll get it in the next.'

'I'd like him to be doubly punished,' uttered Emma in a low passionate voice, placing the fork on the table. 'Not only for what he did to my sister and the rest of you but, also, because David might lose his job. It could be that no other company will take him on due to his involvement with the union. If it wasn't impossible, I'd go to Australia and find Bert. Then I'd bash him over the head when he was least expecting it, and as there's plenty of desert out there...or so I've heard, anyway...I'd bury him up to his neck in sand and leave him to die in the hot sun.'

Alice did not know whether to be shocked or amused but she couldn't hold back a nervous giggle. 'Honestly, Emma, I never realised you were so bloodthirsty.'

Emma smiled. 'You're one to talk. What about wanting him bitten by a snake and suffering a horrible death? Anyway, I'm sure Hannah and Kenny are pleased he's out of their lives for good.'

Alice nodded. 'Hopefully Kenny'll think no more about going to Scotland.' She was about to explain when she heard the front door open and slam and, certain it was Seb, got to her feet and skipped out of the room.

'Hello, luv! You look happy,' he said.

'I've a good reason to be happy.' She slipped her arms around his waist. 'Aren't I married to the handsomest man in Chester!' She held up her face for a kiss.

'I'm disappointed. I was hoping you thought I was the handsomest man in the whole world.' He kissed her in a leisurely fashion.

Emma had followed Alice and now stood in the doorway. 'What will the servants think of you two canoodling in the hall?' she said with a smile.

'Do we care?' asked Seb, gazing down at Alice, who shook her head. 'There's your answer, Emma.' He grinned at her. 'I need to ask you whether you're prepared to stay on here until the old lady dies?' When she hesitated he added, 'I'll give you an extra two shillings a week for helping with her and there'll be other perks.'

'In that case I won't say no,' she said, thinking there was no need to tell them that if Mrs Black came home and still wanted her, she'd go like a shot. Pushing open the baize door, she went through it, letting it swing shut behind her.

Alice gazed up at her husband. 'So we'll be staying here at least until her upstairs passes away?'

'You happy about that? Mr Crane is of the opinion my uncle will have to agree to it. He's going to get in touch with him, anyway, and put it to him. Once she's gone, then will be the time to think of moving. So what's made you so happy?'

She smiled. 'Bert's left the country. He's bought a one way ticket to Australia.'

He stared at her. 'How did you find that out?'

She told him, adding, 'His mother's really upset.'

'Not surprising. Long way to go for a visit.' Seb hugged her. 'Let's hope he has a lousy time of it. I've heard there's very few women out there compared to men...and those there are dead tough.'

'Good,' said Alice with that a sparkle in her eyes again. 'If a snake doesn't bite him then I hope he finds a wife who'll lead him a dog's life. Now let's get ready for dinner and you can tell me what else you discussed with Mr Crane.'

As they started up the stairs, Seb said, 'I've taken the plunge and done what you wanted me to do years ago. I've told Mr Crane I want out of cotton and into automobiles, buying, selling, repairing, hiring out. It means a lot of work but, he agreed with me, there's a future in it. Especially after I told him how the motorcar has taken off in America with Mr Ford's model T.' He grinned. 'I'm not sure he believed me when I told him its top speed was forty to forty-five miles an hour.'

Alice caught his excitement and squeezed his arm. 'When do you start?'

He laughed. 'Give us a chance, woman! We've only just got home. There's loads to arrange. Really I've got to look into things before I'm in business. I need to find a yard for doing the repairs, as well as a showroom and an office.' As they reached the top of the stairs he gazed down into her rapt face. 'At least it means I won't be flitting off to Liverpool and America. I'll be here with you when the baby comes. Talking of which, did you tell Hanny that you could be expecting?'

Alice shook her head. 'In all the excitement of finding out about Bert, I forgot. I'll do it once I've seen the doctor and it's been confirmed.' She sighed. 'Honestly, love, if it weren't for Miss Victoria's death and Kenny being crippled I could be completely happy. I really wish we could do something for him and Hanny. It just doesn't seem fair what's happened to them. I was in two minds to say that we'd have Tilly here while I was at the house. I don't want Mrs Kirk having anything to do with her but I'm sure it would have upset them both if I had.'

'Perhaps once we're settled, we can have them here and discuss the matter,' said Seb. 'We have to do something to help them.'

'Mind your foot!' Hannah frowned down at Kenny, who was writing a letter. Without lifting his eyes from the sheet of paper, Kenny drew up his leg so she could sweep the floor more easily. Hannah muttered under her breath, but once she had finished brushing the floor and had shovelled the results of her labour into the bin in the yard, she sat down opposite him. Stretching out a hand she placed it on the bottom of the page. 'Please, love, think again. I don't want to go to Scotland. With Bert on his way to Australia there's no need for us to worry about him anymore. Let me take that part-time job at the bakery until you find more work as a bookkeeper and sell more articles and cartoons. Why stop at newspapers? What about magazines? I bet you could even write a book.'

Kenny removed her hand from the paper. 'Now you are fantasising. I'm not good enough. As for work as a bookkeeper, I can't afford to advertise any more.'

She clamped her mouth shut on the angry words that sprang to her lips and counted to ten before saying, 'What about Tilly? She loves that school and it's not fair to take her away. You must realise how difficult it'll be for her to move away from everyone she knows.'

'We don't have to take her,' said Kenny, turning over the page and commencing to write on the other side. 'Alice and Seb have that big house, there's surely room for one little girl in it. In fact I'm surprised she hasn't suggested it.'

Hannah gasped. 'Tilly's like a daughter to me. I can't leave her behind.'

He gazed up at her and his expression was angry. 'It's the only solution to that problem. Besides, Alice always planned to have Tilly living with her once she had a proper home.'

Hannah clasped her hands together to stop them from shaking. 'I know that's true but she hasn't mentioned it yet and they've been home a fortnight. Besides, there's nothing stopping her and Seb having children of their own.'

Kenny froze. 'There's nothing stopping us except your stubbornness,' he said harshly.

She could scarcely believe he had said those words. 'Stubbornness?' she cried. 'What d'you mean stubbor-ness?'

He sighed and for a moment he rested his forehead

against his hand. 'I'm sorry. Forget I said it.'

'I can't forget it. I heard it loud and clear,' she said in a seething voice. 'You know exactly why trying to make a baby is difficult for me.'

'I know!' He did not look at her. 'But I sometimes wonder why you can't blank Bert out of your mind even for just ten minutes. You could fill it instead with pictures of us enjoying ourselves. Even imagine music playing. Then we might get somewhere. It's what I have to live on now...dreams of you and I dancing, walking the Wall...talking history.'

She was dumbstruck.

Kenny said sharply, 'There's no need to look like that. But I did think now Bert's gone that perhaps we could...I've been reading this book...'

She interrupted him, 'I'd like to make you happy but...'

He put down his pen and folded his arms. 'I know all there is to know about being scared and I'd be the last person to deny that's how you feel. I just think it's a blinking shame for both of us if we don't have a go of overcoming your fear now Bert's left the country. If you don't want to try, then you're still letting his spirit rule you.'

Outraged, she made a swipe at him across the table and cried, 'How dare you! It's not true!'

He drew back and struggled to his feet, wincing as he did so. 'Don't raise your hand to me,' he said fiercely. 'I won't tolerate physical violence in this house. I would have thought you felt the same.'

'I do!' Her face crumpled. Tears filled her eyes and she put a hand to her trembling mouth. 'What's happening to us? We should be happy now Bert's gone.'

The anger ebbed from his face and, limping round the table, he placed an arm about her shoulders. 'But he's left us with a legacy, hasn't he, love? Perhaps I should go to Scotland on my own...see how it goes before dragging you up there.'

Hannah was about to tell him not to be so stupid, that she was his wife and her place was by his side, when a little voice in her head said that maybe it wasn't such a bad idea. Worrying and being together most of the time was the cause of them arguing now. A break might do them good and she would be able to keep Tilly with her. 'How long would you give it?' she whispered.

He did not answer her immediately and she knew instantly that he had expected her to reject his suggestion. She was torn by guilt, yet something kept her from retracting her words. Several moments passed and then he said, 'I suppose it depends on how long my cousin and the family are prepared to put up with me.'

'Don't you mean *put you up*?'

'No. I meant what I said.' He limped back to his chair and sat down. Ripping the page from the notepad, he started again.

Hannah watched him for several minutes and then, with a heavy heart, stood up. Feeling like she was doing everything in slow motion, she took her almost empty purse from a drawer in the sideboard, shrugged on a jacket and pulled on her old felt hat because there was a cool breeze outside. Picking up her shopping basket, she left the house and went to her mother's.

There she found Joy peeling potatoes. 'Where's Mother?' asked Hannah.

'Granny Popo called round saying she needed her help.' Joy's tone was so casual that Hannah shot a second glance at her sister.

'You didn't ask her to come round, did you?'

Joy smiled. 'Of course I did, but don't let that slip in front of Mother. She's got to stop dwelling on Bert and what better way than her being needed by someone else. I've another idea, too. What do you think of Mother letting out a couple of rooms to lodgers again? I could help her and it would bring in some money.'

Hannah nodded, seated herself in her father's armchair and gazed into the empty fireplace. Several minutes ticked by without a word being exchanged between them. Then Joy said, 'Want to tell me about it?' She dropped a potato into a pan of salted water.

Hannah sighed. 'Kenny suggested going to Scotland on his own to see how things go and I didn't say I thought it was a lousy idea.'

Joy said lightly, 'What made him suggest it? You not wanting to go?'

'Aye!' Hannah fiddled with a button on her jacket. 'We had a row.'

Joy dried her hands and seated herself on the chair opposite her sister. 'You make that sound as if this is your first row since you got married.'

'Kenny isn't one for arguing. He's loving and kind, patient and understanding...normally.'

'Well, he's gone through a tough time recently, and if he's been all those things until now, I don't see what you've got to complain about,' stated Joy.

'I'm not complaining,' snapped Hannah, getting to her feet and going over to the table where there was a loaf and a pat of butter. She cut herself a slice of bread and buttered it. 'I thought you'd understand because of Bert.' She tore at the bread and butter with her teeth.

'So you're still letting that swine rule your life. You surprise me, Hanny,' she said crossly.

'I can't help it,' muttered Hannah.

'Then get someone else to help you to put him out of your mind,' said Joy firmly.

Mrs Black, thought Hannah wistfully, wondering when she would be back in Chester.

Joy continued, 'Do that and then you go to Scotland with Kenny, if he still wants to go.'

'That's not really the problem. It's Tilly. I thought it wasn't right to take her away from school and up to

Scotland, so Kenny suggested that we hand her over to Alice.' She bit savagely into the slice of bread.

'Sounds sensible to me. You and Kenny have done your share of looking after her. You're hard up and in lodgings whilst Alice and Seb are in the money and have that lovely house.'

Hannah's cheeks burned. 'Do you have to rub it in? You don't understand, do you? I love Tilly like my own.'

Joy said firmly, 'But she isn't your own, is she? We all love Tilly but she's Alice's sister, so she should take her turn at looking after her. You and Kenny have had little time on your own since you married and perhaps that's half your trouble. Why don't you visit Alice and see what she has to say? And, as there's no time like the present, why don't I go with you? The walk will do us both good.'

Hannah tried to come up with an excuse but she was all out of them.'OK!'

Joy smiled. 'We could take in the Cheese Fair on the way. I believe there's a giant cheese, weighing three hundred pounds, on exhibition. Imagine eating that much cheese?'

'I heard that it wasn't even made in Cheshire but Yorkshire of all places,' said Hannah, getting up. 'Perhaps I'll buy a quarter and make macaroni cheese for supper.'

Alice was curled up in an armchair in front of the fire in the room that had once been the dining room. She had decided to make a change because the old drawing room gave her creepy feelings. Every time she went in there, she could not help thinking of Bert and Victoria and had started to feel haunted. This was not as nice a room but it was better than being unable to relax. Now she was attempting to cope with the intricacies of a knitting pattern for a baby's matinée coat, whilst at the same time reading the women's serial in an old edition of the *Chester Chronicle* called 'The Secrets of the Iron Box'. It was not easy and she was about to put down the knitting because the serial had reached an exciting part when she heard the knocker sound.

She forced herself to stay where she was, knowing it was up to Emma or Mary to answer the door. Being a lady of leisure was taking some getting used to but it definitely beat being a dogsbody. The room was cosy and warm and she was comfortable. A few minutes later, she heard the murmur of voices in the hall and then a knock on the door. 'Come in!' she called.

Emma popped her head round the door. 'It's Mrs Hannah Moran and Miss Joy Kirk to see you, Mrs Bennett,' she said in the proper manner.

Alice's eyes lit up. The serial could wait. She would enjoy some company and it really was time she told Hannah about the baby and that Seb was going into the motorcar business. 'Tell them to come in...could we have a pot of tea...and are there any fresh scones, Emma?'

'There's shop bought muffins.'

Alice's mouth watered. 'They'll do and bring the toasting fork and butter. We'll toast them by the fire in here.'

Emma was no sooner out of the room than Hannah and Joy entered. 'It's lovely to see you both,' said Alice. 'Come and sit down. I've something to tell you. Although, I suppose I should tell Kenny before you two...but you can pass the message on, Hanny.'

'I think I can guess,' said Hannah, her gaze lighting on the white knitting as she sat down by the fire.

'You're having a baby,' cried Joy, perching on the arm of her sister's chair and smiling.

Alice stretched like a lazy cat and beamed at them. 'Clever you two! It's due next February and I can't wait to be a mother. I'm going to have the best perambulator money can buy and wheel him out into town.'

'You're sure it's a boy then,' said Hannah, determined to show pleasure.

Alice nodded. 'At the moment I feel everything is going my way and I want a boy, so one day Seb can paint over the door of the yard S Bennett & Son.'

'What yard?' asked Joy, swinging her leg and frowning at the scuffed toe of her shoe.

'Yes, what yard?' asked Hannah.

Alice leaned forward. 'He's done what I suggested ages ago and is going into the motorcar business…buying, selling, hiring and repairing.'

Joy's dark head shot up. 'If he's starting up another business then he'll be taking men on. He'll need a bookkeeper. Kenny!'

Alice's eyes danced. 'You are bright today. It's early days yet but when the time's right, I'm sure Seb'll give Kenny a job.'

Joy turned to her sister. 'There you are. Wasn't it right to come here? No need for Kenny to go to Scotland on his own after all.'

Alice looked at Hannah in astonishment. 'What's this? You weren't going to let Kenny go up there on his own, were you?'

'It was his idea,' said Hannah on the defensive.

'Like it was his idea that you have Tilly living here with you, Alice,' said Joy.

Hannah glared at her sister 'There was no need for you say that. It doesn't matter now.'

Alice's gaze went from one to the other. 'I get it. Kenny wanted me to have Tilly but you didn't. Is that why he was planning on going up to Scotland on his own so you could stay in Chester with her? Surely he should come first, Hanny?'

'What's the point in discussing it now?' said Hannah, toying with her fingers. 'If Seb offers Kenny a job he won't be going anywhere, so we'll be together and I can carry on taking care of Tilly. After all, with you having a baby it'll be too much for you.'

'But I've been thinking I should have her…or at least share the care of her,' she added hastily when she saw the expression on Hanny's face, 'and if Kenny is thinking the same thing, then…' Alice didn't finish what she was saying because there was a tap on the door.

Joy slid off the arm of the chair and opened it for Emma. She set the tray down on the low table and, straightening, stared at their set faces. 'What's up? Although, I suppose I shouldn't be asking.'

'No, you shouldn't Emma. But thanks all the same,' said Alice. 'You can pour.'

'I'll toast the muffins,' said Joy, picking up the toasting fork from the tray. 'I love muffins.'

Hannah was silent, watching Emma pour out the tea and wondering how she felt working for Alice and Seb. She had seen hardly anything of her since Alice had come home. In a way she and Emma were in the same boat, with both the men in their lives suffering because of Bert. It would be good if Seb could do something for David, as well. Perhaps if she got the chance she would suggest it to him. Her mind wandered and she asked herself what the neighbours made of the change in Seb's and Alice's circumstances? Did they know that Seb was Mr Waters' illegitimate son and did they consider him a touch below them because of that? But perhaps they accepted him because he had been left the business and was taking care of his grandmother. What would Mrs Black and Mal Moran make of Alice if they could have seen her hosting this little gathering in this house? Life suddenly seemed very unfair to Hannah, and she sighed as she accepted a cup of tea from Emma, hoping Alice would think no more about what Joy had said.

But Alice was not prepared to let the matter go. 'Seb and I have already spoken about Tilly,' she said, accepting a buttered muffin from Joy. 'And he'll want to see Kenny once I speak to him this evening about giving him a job.'

She frowned. 'It's a pity I don't drive. I could have picked him up in the car and brought him here without any effort.' Her brow cleared. 'I know! This Sunday Seb could fetch the three of you in the car and you can have Sunday dinner with us and we'll discuss Tilly's future.'

Hannah knew she had to agree and felt certain Kenny would fall in with his sister's plans for Tilly whatever they were. She dreaded going home because, for the first time in her life, she felt unable to take his love for granted after their quarrel.

When Hannah arrived home, it was a relief to discover Kenny not alone but sitting at the table with Mr Bushell, Tilly and Freddie. It had taken Hannah longer than she had allowed time for to walk from Alice's to the school. She presumed rightly that Freddie had spotted Tilly waiting outside the school gates and had brought her home. She thanked her younger brother and told him he'd best nip home or Mother would be worrying about him.

'She doesn't worry about me,' said Freddie without rancour. 'And Joy knows I can look after myself. I'll take Tilly back to school and bring her home at four, if you like,' he said cheerfully.

Kenny accepted his offer and at the same time handed the boy a stamped addressed envelope. Instantly Hannah said, 'There's no need to post that if it's going to Scotland.' Freddie looked at Kenny who told him firmly to post it. 'But, Kenny…' she said.

'Later!' He smiled at Freddie and thanked him for looking after Tilly.

Hannah was hurt and dismayed that Kenny had not been prepared to listen to her and, after washing the plates and cups, she brushed and scrubbed the backyard before walking into town without saying where she was going. It began to rain, so she took shelter in the covered walkways of the Rows. She mooched along, gazing into the clothes shops and taking a fancy to a swirly skirt with buttons down the front in blue serge, which cost five shillings and nine pence. She sighed, she couldn't even afford the nine pence. If only Kenny hadn't been so stubborn, she could have worked at Bannister's and been bringing some money into the house.

When she arrived back home, Kenny was working on the receipts and bills that Mr Bushell had brought to him, entering them in a ledger. She made the macaroni cheese and they barely exchanged a word with each other. She went up to bed without having told him her news. What had one of the teachers said in Sunday School when she was a girl? *Don't let the sun go down on your wrath.*

As soon as he came to bed she said, 'I went to see Alice. She's having a baby. They've invited us to Sunday dinner and Seb's coming for us and Tilly in the motorcar.'

He flinched, then without speaking, pushed back the bedcovers and eased his damaged foot onto the bed before lifting up the other one. He rested his head on the pillow and closed his eyes. As she gazed at him she felt a helplessness that was new to her. Never had she had to cope with such behaviour from him before. She whispered, 'Did you hear me?'

A muscle in his jaw clenched and then he nodded. She waited for him to say something but he just lay there without moving or speaking. She wanted him to hold her, to weep against his shoulder. Instead she switched off the gas lamp and turned her back on him. Only as she was about to drift off to sleep did she remember that she had not mentioned that there was a hope that Seb would give him a job.

'Hello, Ken! Hanny, Tilly!' Seb squashed the impulse to jump out of the driving seat and rush to help his brother-in-law as he limped across the pavement, followed by his wife and half-sister. They were all smiling and he should have been pleased they seemed glad to see him, but he felt that the adults' smiles were false. When Alice had broached the subject of his giving her half-brother a job to prevent his going to Scotland, he had immediately agreed. He considered himself lucky and wanted to pass on some of that good fortune. He felt sorry for Kenny and Hannah, whose clothes were shabby and well worn. He thought of all Alice's new clothes and determined to do something for Hannah, as well. He knew it would sting their pride if he were to offer them money but really good Christmas presents…surely they couldn't refuse those. As for Tilly, although, she was better dressed than Hannah, Alice would enjoy making her new clothes when she came to live with them. She was a pretty, outgoing little girl and he reckoned she would cheer the place up and take Alice's mind off what had happened to Victoria in the old drawing room.

'It's good of you to come and pick us up,' said Kenny, opening the rear door for Hannah and Tilly to climb into the back of the car.

'No skin off my nose,' said Seb, leaning over and opening the frontdoor for him. 'I thought we could have a look at the yard on the way.'

'What yard?' asked Kenny, as he sat in the front passenger seat.

Seb glanced over his shoulder at Hannah, who reddened and shrugged. 'I didn't expect you to work so fast.'

Kenny glanced at his wife and said lightly, 'Have you been keeping secrets from me?'

Hannah replied with a calmness she was far from feeling, 'You'd written the letter to your cousin and posted it, that's why I didn't say anything. Obviously you'd made up your mind to go to Scotland, so I thought it best not to mention Seb would most likely offer you a job when he starts his new business.'

With a mixture of hope and embarrassment in his eyes, Kenny gazed at Seb's profile as the motorcar started.

Without taking his eyes off the road, Seb said, 'I'm getting out of cotton and I'm going into the motorcar business. It'll probably be slow getting off the ground but I'm going to need someone to look after the paperwork and I thought you might be interested...but if you're going to Scotland, I'll have to find someone else.'

'I'm not going to Scotland. I'd like the job,' said Kenny calmly.

Hannah gasped, staring at the smooth brown hair shaped like a V in the nape of her husband's neck, and she poked him in the back. 'But you gave Freddie the letter to post.'

Kenny glanced over his shoulder. 'I gave him a letter to post to my cousin and grandmother but I didn't say anything about going up there to stay.'

'Why didn't you tell me?' she cried.

'Perhaps we can talk about my reasons later. Right now I want to hear what Seb's got to say about his new business.'

So Seb sketched in the bones of his plans for the business and just what he expected from Kenny. 'I thought you could look into different companies for me, write letters, as well as do the books. The automobile business is growing and I don't see how we can lose. We're in at the birth of a new industry so there's few skilled men around who know all there is to know about the automobile combustion engine.'

'What about Emma's David?' said Hannah. 'He knows something about engines.'

'The wrong kind of engines,' said Seb. 'I need a man who knows what he's doing. I plan on running the showroom, buying and selling.'

'Surely you'll need more than one man,' said Hannah, determined to try and do something for Emma. 'Emma saved Alice from Bert and it looks like David could lose his job for going after him. He's still suspended from work.'

'OK!' said Seb, his hands tightening on the steering wheel. 'I'll think about it.'

'Good,' said Hannah, leaning back against the leather squabs, knowing she could now enjoy the ride.

'I'm sure when you're buying cars, Mr Ford and the makers of the Rover and the Riley could provide you with plans of the workings of the different motors.' Kenny's face was shining with enthusiasm.

'The fact that you know those names shows that you're already interested in the motorcar,' said Seb.

'I read the newspapers in the library and, as I said to Hanny earlier this week, I can dream.'

'That's it, Kenny. Don't you give up on your dreams, mate,' said Seb, his face alight. 'I never believed I'd be in the position I'm in now.'

'Where is this yard?' asked Kenny.

'It backs on to the canal and used to be a stables. The owner died recently and, having no son to take over the business, his widow sold the horses and put the lease for the buildings and the yard on the market. We're almost there now.'

A few minutes later he stopped the car in front of a pair of large double doors and climbed out. He took a bundle of keys from his pocket, opened a Judas gate in one of the doors and indicated that Kenny should accompany him. The two men stood in the cobbled yard, enclosed on two sides by stabling, which Seb said could easily be converted into a workshop. On the third side was a house. 'I thought you and Hanny might like to move in there,' said Seb. 'It would be good to have someone living on the premises as a sort of caretaker.'

Kenny's eyes were suspiciously bright as he stared at his brother-in-law, and it was several moments before he had enough control over his voice to say, 'I'll work hard for you, Seb. I'm sure you know what this means to me. When I married Hanny and we took on Tilly, my aim was to look after them and see no harm came to them. When I broke this bloody foot I felt I'd let them both down.' He swallowed and his voice was husky when he added, 'Not only because I wasn't earning enough money to support the three of us in a modicum of comfort but I also kept asking myself if Bert were to turn up again, would I be able to protect them?'

'I can imagine how you feel,' said Seb, feeling quite emotional himself. 'But you don't have to worry about Bert now...and if you want to carry on having Tilly living with you and Hanny, Alice and I will understand. The other option is that we share her, so the four of us benefit from her company.'

'That sounds a good idea to me,' said Kenny, wiping his eyes with the back of his hand.

'What made you change your mind about going to Scotland before you even knew about this place and the job?'

Kenny smiled faintly and shoved his hands in his pockets. 'I realised worry had stopped me from thinking straight. With Tilly living with you and me up in Scotland, I thought Hanny might go and live with her parents. I didn't like that idea. Mrs Kirk doesn't like me. I could imagine her going on and on at Hanny and saying that I was selfish and took after my dad. There was also the possibility of Hanny going back to work for Bannister's Bakery and he'd tried it on with her in the past. I knew then I had to stay put, no running away. I ran once before when I should have stayed.'

'And lastly?' asked Seb softly.

'Lastly?' Kenny dropped his gaze. 'Lastly I have to carry on loving her and trying to make her forget what Bert did to her. I'm so sick of the thought of him, I want to bury her memory of him forever. I can only do that by being with her.'

Chapter Eighteen

August, 1909

Hannah stood in the kitchen, gazing through the window that overlooked a tiny garden and, beyond the wooden fence at the bottom, the canal. She found it hard to believe that she and Kenny were beginning a new life in this house. Her husband had explained why he had changed his mind about going to Scotland, and even though it was a fortnight ago, she still found herself struggling with emotions that threatened to choke her. She felt that she didn't deserve to be loved in such a patient way. She guessed that most married women just put up with their husband's sexual demands. If only she could talk to Alice about it but she knew that she was too ashamed to admit that she and Kenny hadn't had a child because she wouldn't allow it.

'So which room will we start first?' asked Emma, interrupting Hannah's reverie. 'This one or the master bedroom? You need both thoroughly cleaned before moving in. The mess they're in I think the woman must have been a bit of a slattern.'

'Perhaps she lost heart after her husband died,' murmured Hannah. 'It won't take us long once we get going and Joy said she might join us later. Although, now Mother's taking in lodgers, she expects Joy to do even more in the house. I really appreciate you giving up your afternoon off to help me, Emma.'

'Mr Bennett is paying me...but I would have done it anyhow, especially after him telling me that you'd suggested he offer David a job in his new business. Although, it's not necessary now he's been reinstated because they decided he acted properly after all. We can't have people performing violent acts on railway property.'

Emma smiled as she fastened a sack apron round her waist. 'So where do I start? Black-leading the range, sweeping the floor, cleaning the sink or washing the shelves?'

'Black-leading, I think. Might as well get that job done and then we'll be able to light a fire and heat up some water. Kenny's seen to sweeping the chimney, so we shouldn't have any trouble with soot coming down and making a mess,' she said happily.

Emma took a tin of Zebo and strips of torn up old sheeting out of the shopping bag and got down on her knees in front of the range.

'At least Kenny'll have his own office here and won't be under my feet when he's doing Seb's and Mr Bushell's books,' said Hannah, climbing on to a stool to remove curling lining paper from the shelves where she would place the crockery. 'He was a great friend of Alice's mother, you know, and knew Granny Popo when she was a girl.'

'I heard her granddaughter was expecting and the soldier husband's starting to look at Granny askance. He's stationed at the castle.'

'She told Mother that she thinks he wants her out.'

'Wouldn't it be nice if she and Mr Bushell could make a match of it? She'd have somewhere else to live and he'd have company.' Emma chuckled. 'They say there's no love like first love but I bet last love is just as good if you're lonely. At least Granny's still got her marbles, not like old Mrs Waters. She doesn't half stink...poor woman. We have to put nappies on her now.' She applied more blackening.

'Do you think she'll live much longer?' asked Hannah, lifting more paper from shelves.

'Hard to say. She's not eating enough to keep a sparrow alive but the doctor said she's got a heart as strong as a horse. I can't see her lasting into nineteen ten.'

'Alice's baby is due then,' murmured Hannah. 'Seems strange doesn't it, when you think of Mr Water and his daughter dying so young and she's still going.'

'Mrs Black…' began Emma, only to stop.

'Mrs Black what?' asked Hannah, glancing at her where she was applying blacking.

Emma hesitated and decided not to say what she had almost blurted out. Instead she changed tack. 'Mrs Bennett never has a good word to say about her but Mrs Black was fond of you and Kenny. If she'd been here when you were going through your bad patch, she'd have found a way to help you.'

Hannah's heart seemed to jerk in her breast. 'What bad patch?' Surely it wasn't that obvious that everything wasn't as satisfactory as it should be between her and Kenny?

'The trouble with his foot, of course, and his not being able to get full time work. It shows how good you're feeling that you've forgotten it already.'

Hannah felt the colour rush to her cheeks. How could she forget how bad things had been only a few weeks ago? Perhaps if Mrs Black had been here then she could have helped her to put her fears behind her. If she came home, Hannah determined she would go and see her.

November 1909

Eudora Black gazed up at her house and experienced a rush of happiness. She had seen some beautiful places on her travels but there was nowhere quite like home, and, now that the lodgers to whom she had rented her apartment had departed, she could move back and resume her work. It had been so hot out East and she was enjoying the feel of a cool wind on her face. Even though summer was over, everywhere looked so colourful compared to the arid landscape of the Holy Land, Egypt and the Far East. She was looking forward to sitting in front of a roaring fire and partaking of Emma's baking.

She had popped in to the Servants' Registry Office just

to see if Emma was on Mr Jones' books but unfortunately she wasn't. Even so she had her first client: Mrs Jones had made an appointment for healing. She must get Emma back. In a few weeks' time it would be Christmas and Emma made such delicious mince pies, as well as being helpful in so many other ways. But first she needed a bath and something to eat before catching up on the gossip from her lodgers downstairs; hopefully they would be able to tell her where Emma was because she had every intention of persuading her to come back and work for her.

A few hours later, Eudora was being regaled with all the goings on in the neighbourhood. The music teachers were extremely informative about the exciting, and occasionally disturbing, events that had taken place during her absence. But Eudora was really longing to hear Emma's version of events but knew that she would have to wait until the next day.

The following morning Eudora set out to do some shopping. On her return, she walked slowly past Mrs Waters' house, looking up at the windows, hoping to see Emma, but there was no sign of her. Eudora knew that it was most unlikely she would be made welcome if she called at the house, so decided that she needed an alternative strategy if she was going to make contact with her former housemaid.

A couple of hours later Eudora was out on the pavement, snipping off sprigs of privet. Earlier she had spotted Emma through the upstairs window but there had not been enough time to get downstairs and out into the Crescent to catch her. Goodness knows what her part time gardener would make of her doing his job, but she did not plan on doing much in the way of work.

There she is! Eudora watched Emma approaching and knew the exact moment when the young woman recognised her. It did her heart good when Emma smiled and waved. 'Good morning, Emma!' she called.

Emma hurried towards her. 'You're home!'

'You're smart.'

Emma chuckled. 'I know I was stating the obvious. Did you have a wonderful time? You look well.'

'I'm very well.' Eudora's dark eyes gleamed and she dropped the cutters and clapped her hands together and held them against her breast. 'The sights I've seen! I really should have taken you with me. You'd have had a wonderful time, too. But then you wouldn't have been here witnessing all the happenings that my lodgers have been telling me about.'

Emma's expression sobered. 'They probably don't know the half of it. Victoria Waters wouldn't have died if I'd have been there. It was *him*.'

Eudora stared at her. 'Him?'

'Hannah's brother, Bert,' said Emma in a low voice. 'But I've no concrete proof of it.'

Eudora was enthralled. 'Have you any time off today? We must discuss this and I'm asking you right now to come back and work for me. I'll give you an extra shilling on what I paid you before.'

Emma hesitated. She did not want to let Seb and Alice down, especially when the baby was due in February, and there was also that niggling worry that Mrs Black could have dosed Mr Waters with something unpleasant. On the other hand, she was fed up to the back teeth with having to care for old Mrs Waters. Sometimes she felt no better than a skivvy. She could also do with the extra money if she was to save up and still give her mother something. Her brother Alf had told David that money was really tight at home and Dad was hardly ever there. 'I'll come back but I'll have to stay until they find someone else,' she said firmly.

Eudora smiled. 'Just as you say, Emma dear,' she said mildly.

* * *

Alice stared at Emma as if she could not believe what she was hearing but when Seb spoke, it was obvious to both of them that he accepted what she had said and did not blame her for giving in her notice. 'I appreciate your sticking it out so long, Emma. It really isn't fair on you or Mary doing a job that really belongs to someone used to caring for the elderly.'

'I suppose, as she's your grandmother, I should look after Mrs Waters,' said Alice with a sigh.

Seb looked at her swollen figure and shook his head. 'Don't be daft, love. You can't be lifting her.'

'Perhaps you should put her in a nursing home like Mr Martin Waters suggested,' said Emma.

Immediately Alice's face brightened. 'I never knew he'd suggested that.'

Seb frowned. 'Mr Crane did mention it to me...but we've got to remember that if she wasn't here, my uncle might insist on us moving out and selling the house. He lost out by that fire at Delemere and is short of money.'

'But surely he wouldn't be able to get his hands on it until she's dead, anyway,' said Alice.

Emma thought this was a discussion that could go on for some time and so intervened. 'I'd like to leave as soon as possible. Mrs Black has a client coming and she needs me there, Mr Bennett.'

Alice frowned. 'I know she must be going to pay you more than we can but honestly, Emma, I hope you don't rue the day you go back to work for her.'

Emma tilted her chin. 'I'm sure I shan't and I bet if you advertised in the newspapers, you'd soon get someone to take my place. Although...have you thought of trying to find your mother, Mr Bennett?' Alice and Seb stiffened but Emma forced herself to continue. 'She was very fond of the old lady and might be prepared to nurse her if you asked her to come back.' Neither spoke, so Emma changed the subject and said, 'You'll be wanting your supper. Will I go now? And will you let me know as soon as you get someone?'

'Just work out your week's notice, Emma. That'll do,' said Seb.

Emma thanked him and left the room.

Knowing it would be unlikely that she would have any free time for a while, Emma decided she would have to tell her mother about her change in circumstances, saying she would see her all right once she was back with Mrs Black. She knew that news would cheer her mam, especially with Christmas in a few weeks' time. She presumed that Alice would tell Hannah she was going to work for Mrs Black and remembered talking about her when they had cleaned the house. She thought how wonderful it would be if Mrs Black could heal Kenny's foot...but that would need a miracle and Mrs Black did not deal in those.

'Isn't this cosy, Emma?' said Eudora.

Emma, who had just entered the sitting room carrying the tea tray, had to admit that it was. The thick velvet curtains shut out the cold dark November evening and the glow of the fire reflected on polished wood, cut glass and shining brass.

'So tell me everything, Emma,' said Eudora, taking a fairy cake from the plate.

'So much has happened since you've been away, that I'm not sure where to start.'

'Sit down! Have a cup of tea and a cake with me and start with after I left.'

Emma did just that, eating, drinking, telling Eudora about how she had been taken on by Victoria after she had sacked Gabrielle. 'I think it would be a good thing for her to come back to help nurse Mrs Waters but I feel Mr Bennett and Alice will be in two minds about that.'

'So what d'you think the Bennetts will do?'

Emma said, 'Hanny told me that Alice suggested that

Joy Kirk might like the job but her mother said she needed her at home as she's taken on a couple of lodgers. Now there's talk of them employing a middle-aged spinster who nursed her mother.'

'That sounds sensible. Alice wouldn't want Gabrielle back. She's a very bossy woman and would be bound to try and force Alice to do things her way when the baby's born. But that's enough of them. Tell me how Victoria Waters died?'

So Alice spoke of how upset Victoria had been when she discovered that Seb had been left half of their father's business and how she had planned never to let him and Alice set foot inside her grandmother's house again. 'She'd have been much better off getting in touch and asking them to come home. She'd probably still be alive if she had, because there was no one there to frighten off Bert.'

'My dear Emma, you're sure it was Bert?'

'I know it was Bert,' said Emma positively. 'He must have seen me and Miss Waters together in town. Either that or he'd seen her with Alice at some time and followed her home.'

'So how did you know it was him? How did you recognise him?'

Emma told her the rest of the story up to the moment they had discovered Bert had gone to Australia.

'You're sure of that?'

Emma bit into another scone without taking her eyes from her employer's face. She chewed slowly and swallowed. 'His mother believes it. She blamed everybody but him for what happened.'

'I see.' Her eyes narrowed thoughtfully.

Emma relaxed. 'Mrs Kirk was in a right state. I don't think she was putting it on to deceive us.'

Eudora nodded thoughtfully. 'So he was definitely responsible for Kenny's fall but you still don't have definite proof he killed Victoria Waters. Where did she pass over, exactly?'

'In the old drawing room. The Bennetts use it for a dining room now – Alice couldn't relax because Miss Waters had died…passed over there.'

Eudora leaned forward, her eyes shining. 'Does she feel a presence in the old drawing room?' Emma almost said *Don't start that!* 'A violent passing,' continued her employer, 'it is expected that some impression would remain in the room. Don't forget that Victoria Waters is a living soul – she might try to make contact. She will want justice.'

Emma wondered if her vivid reconstructions of what had happened in the drawing room had been due to that impression Mrs Black talked about – or was it all nonsense? As she pondered on Mr Waters' sudden death, she came to the conclusion that Mrs Black couldn't have had a hand in it. Surely with her beliefs, she'd have been frightened of his coming back to haunt her? But Mrs Black was definitely not a frightened woman, so she must be innocent of that charge.

'It would be interesting to have a séance in that room,' murmured Eudora, leaning back in her chair and closing her eyes.

'Alice would never allow it,' said Emma firmly.

'I fear you're right, dear. I suspect she is aware of a presence but doesn't want to say too much, probably so as not to frighten the little girl.'

'You know about Tilly then?'

'Yes.' Eudora moistened her lips. 'I was told she was Alice's sister.'

Emma nodded. 'She lived with Kenny and Hanny, until Alice and Seb returned home. Now they share her.'

'I see.' Eudora beamed at her. 'What a lucky child to have so much attention. But let's get back to what you said earlier about Victoria Waters being angry. That anger could be causing bad vibrations.'

Emma was astonished. 'I suppose they could always have the vicar round to exorcise the house if Alice started worrying about the place being haunted.'

Eudora wagged a finger at her. 'You're being provocative. Maybe an exorcism might be needed but it wouldn't tell us what happened there. If I could only get into that room... It reminds me, Emma, of your sister, Aggie. If you'd only allowed me to try and make contact. If you'd taken me to the spot where your sister was found we could have...'

The colour drained from Emma's face. 'I don't want to talk about Aggie right now. Please stop! I feel like I've let her down, what with Bert getting away scot-free.'

Eudora sighed. 'Just as you wish. Now tell me more about Kenny's injuries. I'm fond of that young man.'

Emma was happy to talk about Kenny, hoping Mrs Black could help him. When she finished telling her as much as she knew, the older woman said, 'Perhaps before Christmas you could visit them and extend an invitation to drop in for sherry and mince pies early evening on Boxing Day. I'd be interested to hear from their own lips how they are getting on since Bert vanished from their lives.'

'Will you want me here?' asked Emma.

'No, dear. As long as you make the mince pies, you can go off and see that young man of yours and visit your family. Although, I will want you here on Christmas Day, as I've invited a few friends around. You won't lose by it, dear...and you can make enough mince pies to take home with you.'

Emma thanked her.

'In the meantime, I see there's an exhibition on at the town hall about Palestine this coming week. Most likely it's part of the preparations for the festive season. You and that young man of yours might like to see it...give you a taste of the Holy Land...who knows, I might visit there again one day and I'd enjoy company,' murmured Eudora, smiling.

'I'd like to,' said Emma, delighted. 'I'll slip a note through David's letterbox and let him know it's on and he can let me know if he can make it any time.'

'Real enough for yer?' said Emma, twinkling up at David as they walked arm in arm between the mock whitewashed walls painted with doors and window openings. There were also stalls piled high with almonds, figs and dates, earthenware pots, carpets, jewellery and leather goods...and people dressed as Arabs called out their wares.

'This is supposed to be Jerusalem, so I'd like a bit more sun,' said David, holding his face up and closing his eyes.

She chuckled. 'Who wouldn't when it's chucking it down outside? Our Chris would know if it's true to life. He's out there now.'

David opened his eyes and gazed down at her. 'Lucky him. Seriously, though, is this a place, lovey, you'd like to go on your honeymoon?'

Her heart seemed to flip over and she thought keep it light. 'Chance would be a fine thing. You got the cash?'

'No!'

'Then why ask?'

'Because if we were to get married one day, I'd like to know how much I'll have to save up. A honeymoon in Llandudno would run much cheaper than Jerusalem.' His grey eyes creased at the corners. 'Don't look like that, lovey! Much as I'd like to marry you tomorrow, I know you'd say no right now.'

'Dad would never give his permission and you know how I'm situated.'

'I know, but my Dad's marrying the housekeeper and I've a feeling they'd like me out of there. You've never seen two lovey doves like it.'

She smiled. 'Oh, yes I have. Seb and Alice Bennett. Now change the subject.'

'Can I ask you again when you come of age? If you say yes, then I'll shut up and we'll go and see the five hundred Biblical objects in the next room.'

'Gosh, yer really know how to get round a girl,' she said, laughing. 'OK! Ask me next May when I'm twenty-one.'

David stole a quick kiss and promised he would keep her to her word and they went off to look at the exhibits.

It was a fortnight later that Emma made her way to the yard by the canal and, finding the gates open, she walked inside. Male voices and metallic clinking sounds could be heard coming from one of the converted stables but, as neither voice talking about a Daimler's four cylinder engine belonged to Kenny, she crossed the cobbles towards the house. Before she could knock, the door opened and Hannah reached out and dragged her inside.

'It's been ages. Why haven't you been to see me?' she demanded.

'I haven't been to see me family for ages, either. Didn't Alice or Seb tell you I'd left them because Mrs Black came back?' said Emma, surprised by her reaction.

'Aye, but I thought you'd have made time to come and see me. I've missed you,' she said, smiling. 'And don't you think it's strange her coming home after us talking about her last time you were here?'

'No!' said Emma, freeing herself and wiping her feet on the coconut matting. 'She has been away a long time and I thought she'd come home sooner or later.'

Hannah looked deflated. 'You're right. Anyhow you're here now. So tell me all the news. Has she asked about Tilly yet?' Hannah helped Emma off with her coat.

A puzzled Emma wrinkled her nose. 'Should she have?'

'Well, she does know Tilly's dad and she looks a bit like him, strange as that might seem. For all his wicked ways, he was a good-looking man, except for the red hair.'

Hannah led the way into the kitchen, knocking on a door as she passed and calling to Kenny that Emma was here and she was going to make a cup of tea.

'She already knows she exists but shows more interest in you and Kenny,' said Emma, sitting down at the well scrubbed table in the kitchen. She watched Hannah remove a bubbling pan from the fire and place it on the hob. 'I know it's a few weeks off but she sent me round to invite the pair of you to sherry and mince pies on Boxing Day…about five o'clock.'

Hannah paused in the act of removing the kettle from the hob and there was an excited gleam in her eyes. 'Fancy that! We'll say yes, of course. Never turn down free food and drink. Although, no doubt she's after something.'

'I told her about Bert and she's concerned about you both. Simple!'

Hannah's face fell. 'Nothing is ever simple where that woman's concerned and you and I both know it. Now, tell me what else she had to say.'

'She thinks Mrs Waters' drawing room is haunted.'

'Don't say that to Alice,' said Kenny from behind her. 'She'll end up seeing ghosts whether they're there or not.'

Emma glanced up into his pleasant face and said solemnly, 'All it takes is a little bit of imagination.'

He limped over to the chair opposite her and sat down. 'Am I to take it you're an unbeliever? What would Mrs Black think?' There was a twinkle in his eyes.

'Probably that it's more important I make decent pastry and bring her breakfast in bed every morning, me good man,' she replied, her lips twitching.

'I can see the truth in that…but don't you at least have to believe a little bit in what she's doing to be of use to her?' asked Kenny curiously.

'I believe she wants to help people and she pays well, and that's good enough for me,' said Emma, glancing at Hannah as she came to stand at her husband's shoulder. 'It means I can stop Mam going up the wall. One of the twins said Dad's seldom home and money's short.'

'Well, you have to help your family best you can,' agreed Kenny.

Hannah nodded, 'Mrs Black's invited us to sherry and mince pies on Boxing Day evening, love. I think we should go.'

He glanced up at her. 'OK.'

Emma smiled at them both. 'She serves a decent sherry and I'll make the mince pies. She might tell you about her travels if you ask her.'

'Will you be there?' asked Kenny.

She shook her head. 'I've been given the time off. So I've decided I'll go and visit the family and take them a few things.'

Chapter Nineteen

December, 1909

'So you've arrived at last, have yer!' said Olive, looking up from her place by the fire. 'Shut that door before yer let the heat out.'

'Yeah, Mam, and I love you, too. As you can see I haven't come empty-handed, so how about a decent welcome.' Emma lifted the two shopping bags in the air and smiled round at the younger members of her family.

'What have yer got in there?' asked little Johnny, leaving the wooden railway engine Alf had made him for Christmas and scurrying over. He tugged on her skirt and looked up at her eagerly.

'Food and drink and a few little presents.' She bent down and kissed his tangled hair. 'Someone make room on the table and I'll empty them out.'

Patsy, the eldest of her younger sisters, hurried to comply, moving the bread, jam tin, teapot and crockery out of the way. Emma placed the bags on the table and children surrounded her as she emptied out the contents.

'A rubber ball for Johnny.' She held it out to him and he grabbed it and clasped it to his chest, thanking her before backing away and beginning to bounce it on the linoleum. 'Skipping ropes with bells in the handles for the girls.' Her delighted sisters took them and turning to their mother asked could they go out and play in the street.

Olive nodded, telling them to take Johnny out, too. 'Where did you get it all?' She picked up a bottle of sherry from the table and read the label. 'This is good stuff,' she said in amazement. 'I've seen the price in the shop window.'

'The Rubber Shop had a grand Xmas Bazaar! But the sherry didn't come from there. Mrs Black sent that for you. It's the one she drinks.' Emma was warmed by her mother's reaction. 'I've socks for the twins and a couple of pairs of drawers for you. Mrs Black bought new and gave those to me. I thought you'd like them. They're made of a real good mixture of wool and silk.'

'Thanks, luv!' There was the sheen of tears in Olive's eyes.

Emma was really enjoying herself. 'She also gave me some leftover ham and allowed me to bake extra mince pies. I bought a pound of mixed sweets, some nuts and oranges,' she tapped each item as she named it, 'as well as a couple of bottles of ginger beer.' She glanced around. 'Where's Dad and the twins?'

'Haven't seen yer dad for days. I'd be thanking God for it, if it weren't that I needed his money. Alf's gone to play football with some of the other railway workers. Probably be yack-yacking about pay and conditions. Don't ask me where Pete is. I hope he's not getting interested in girls already. I want some real money out of him before he goes courting and getting himself wed at twenty-one.'

Emma wondered what her mother would think if she knew David was going to ask her to marry him when she was twenty-one, not that she intended mentioning that. She watched as her mother reached for two chipped cups.

'Right now, let's forget about the whole soddin' male race,' said Olive. 'How about you and me having a drink of this sherry and making a toast.' She rinsed out the cups while Emma opened the bottle. 'Be generous with it, Em, I really need this,' said her mother.

Emma filled the cups almost to the brim and, taking one, Olive said, 'To us, Mrs Black and our Chris. May God bring him home soon.'

Emma echoed her words, adding David's name silently. He was working today, so she would not be seeing him.

Olive took a mouthful, letting the taste of the sherry wash over her taste buds before swallowing. 'Ambrosia!' she said.

Emma smiled. 'Good God, Mam. Where did you learn a word like that?'

'Our Patsy mentioned it…said it was food for the gods. The things they learn yer at school. The quicker she's working the better.'

'Give her a chance, Mam. Let her have some fun before she has to buckle down. I'll make sure you don't end up in the workhouse,' she said with a sigh.

Olive smiled. 'You're a good girl. Now let's make another toast. We mustn't forget those women fighting for better conditions for the rest of us. I did hear they've been getting force-fed in prison. They stick tubes up their noses and down into their stomachs. Imagine that, Em, enough to make yer sick, isn't it?'

Emma nodded and both of them toasted the suffragettes and took another big swallow of sherry. After several more swallows, Olive said that she was beginning to feel mellow and suggested a couple of slices of ham on bread. Emma agreed-she was starting to feel a little light-headed herself, so they'd best have something to eat. She topped up their cups and remembered the last women's rights meeting she had attended. So much had happened. Poor Victoria Waters! Was it possible that her spirit still haunted her last home as Mrs Black believed? And what about Mrs Stone? Was she still putting up with that weak, selfish fool of a husband? She should have been the doctor, not him, no wonder she was a fighter for the Cause.

But what was she doing thinking about all this now? It must be the drink going to her head. Best have those ham sandwiches and a chat with her mam before she toddled back to Mrs Black's. She wondered how Hannah and Kenny were enjoying her hospitality. Was she just being generous or was there an ulterior motive behind her invitation?

* * *

'This is a lovely room,' said Hannah, her gaze roaming the walls painted with scenes of blue skies and meadows sprinkled with flowers. For a moment her gaze fell on the chaise longue and then shifted to the harp in a corner near the window. She glanced at Mrs Black. 'D'you play?'

Eudora smiled. 'I have a Welsh friend who comes from the spiritual church. Malcolm loved her playing.' She turned to Kenny. 'Sit down, dear. Your foot...'

'I doubt you can help.' He was slightly unnerved by her mention of his father but did as she said and sat down.

'You've had the laying on of hands in your church?' asked Eudora.

'And prayer. I can walk, I've work. Hanny and I have a home of our own.' He glanced at his wife and said seriously, 'Perhaps this happened for a reason.'

Hannah almost exploded. 'For what purpose? Why should God punish you? You've done no wrong. Unless he's punishing me?'

'I didn't say it was a punishment, Hanny,' said Kenny firmly. 'Often we can't see why things happen but later they seem to work into a pattern and things come right.'

'I don't see how.' Hannah's chin wobbled and she bit hard on her lower lip.

'Hush, Hanny.' Eudora's voice was gentle and briefly she rested a hand on the younger woman's shoulder. 'I sense a darkness in your spirit that needs dealing with.'

'Of course you do,' said Hannah, folding her arms across her breasts and forcing a smile. 'You know what there is to know.'

Eudora gazed at her piercingly and Hannah lowered her eyes. 'That's not true, dear, you're hiding something.'

'Fear,' said Kenny, staring at his wife. 'Despite Bert having left the country she can't forget, so it's with her all the time. Perhaps you can hypnotise her into forgetting, Mrs Black, because she won't ask for prayer.'

'I can't forgive so how can I expect God to answer my

prayers? Isn't that how it works?' asked Hannah bitterly, perching on the chaise longue.

Eudora did not comment but went over to Kenny and asked him what the doctor had said about his foot. He told her one of the little bones had been shattered and added with a wry smile, 'I need a new bone. You don't deal in them, do you, Mrs Black?'

'No, Kenny, I don't,' she said with a hint of sadness. 'I can't help you there.'

'At least you're not raising false hopes,' said Hannah with a catch in her voice. 'But perhaps you can hypnotise me into forgetting Bert ever existed, and we can be happy again?'

Eudora turned to her. 'I can help you to forget Bert but that might be dangerous. What if he were to return and find you alone and you didn't know who he was?'

A cold shiver shuddered down Hannah's spine. Kenny demanded, 'Why should he return? He'd be a fool to do that! Besides it would cost a lot of money and...why should he return?' he repeated angrily.

Eudora did not answer him. Instead she said, 'Perhaps Hannah should come and see me another time. We can discuss what it is that frightens her then.' She smiled and clapped her hands. 'Shall we go into the sitting room and have another sherry and more of Emma's delicious mince pies. Then perhaps you can tell me all about Tilly. Your younger half-sister, I believe, Kenny?'

Hannah darted a glance at her husband as if to say, *Now we're getting to it. This is why she invited us here.*

'You mustn't go in there,' cried Alice, seizing her sister by the arm and pulling her away from the old drawing room.

'Why?' asked Tilly, looking surprised. 'I want to play on the piano.'

'Because it's...'

'Alice!'

Alice almost jumped out of her skin and whirled round to see Seb standing in the front doorway. 'I didn't hear you come in,' she said, flushing uncomfortably.

He took off his cap and threw it on the chest in the hall. Then he walked over to the two sisters and, bending down, kissed Tilly's cheek and told her to go to the kitchen and stay there until Alice came for her.

'Why?' she asked, gazing up at him from wide hazel eyes.

He said firmly, 'Because I say so. I need to talk to Alice and it's grown-up talk.'

'When will I be grown-up enough to listen?'

He smiled faintly. 'A while yet…but you'll grow up quickly enough, I bet. Enjoy being a little girl while you can.' He turned her round and gave her a little push in the direction of the green baize door and watched her go through.

Alice cleared her throat and he whirled round and gazed into her pale strained face. 'You're going to tell me off, aren't you?' she said.

Exasperated, he said, 'You mustn't infect Tilly with your fear.'

'You think I'm imagining it. That it's a pregnant woman's fancy!' A single tear slid down her cheek.

Seb did not answer but turned the knob and pushed open the door into the old drawing room. He took out his silver matchbox and lit the gas before beckoning her inside

Alice remained rooted to the spot. She had not entered the room for months, since she had seen Victoria's ghost and sensed Bert's evil presence. She had taken to having breakfast in the bedroom and lunching in the nursery. She had explained this behaviour as merely economical – a way to save coal. Now they had their evening meal on a tray on their knees in the new drawing room.

Seb reached out, took her by the shoulders and propelled her into the old drawing room. Her pulse beat rapidly and she kept her eyes downcast, placing a hand over her swollen belly as if to protect her unborn child. As she did so, it moved beneath her hand and she prayed that God would keep her son, for she was certain it was a boy, safe from evil. She found herself also asking her mother to be close to her. She was shocked by her weakness; it seemed tantamount to getting in touch with spirits!

'Look around you, Alice! There's no ghost here,' said Seb.

She lifted her head slowly and stared at the spot where the chaise longue had stood. It had gone and in its place was a new sofa of brown moquette. A cry escaped her. 'Where did that come from?'

He kissed her hair. 'I had it delivered today while you were at the yard. I told Mary and the new woman to keep quiet about it so I could surprise you. Also, I've been thinking that it's time the piano was used and seeing as how Tilly has shown interest in banging on the instrument, perhaps she should start lessons. I'm sure one of Mrs Black's lodgers would be willing to come here and teach her.' He drew Alice against him and burrowed his face against her neck. 'Doesn't it say somewhere that *music calms the savage beast*?' he said in a muffled voice.

She whispered, 'I wouldn't know. Kenny and Hanny are the readers.'

'I could have it wrong but you know what I'm getting at?'

'I think so. But I'm not sure if it'll calm ghosts. And I don't want my sister taking lessons in this room from someone who lodges with *that woman*. Who's to say they haven't been affected by what she does?'

Seb lifted his head. 'From what I've heard, you couldn't have three more respectable music teachers. You mustn't let your prejudice against Mrs Black affect your sense of fairness…unless you've heard something about them that I haven't?'

Immediately Alice was ashamed of herself. 'No.'

'Then ask one of them what day they can come.'

'Me? Go to that woman's house?'

She felt his chest move as he drew in his breath and, before she could say anything else, he released her. 'I'll go then...and I'll go now.' His expression was stern.

She looked at him in dismay. 'Now? What about dinner?'

'I won't be long.' He left the room, and immediately, she lumbered after him.

'How long?'

'Ten minutes?' Seb opened the front door, pulling it to behind him. He turned up his topcoat collar against the chilly January evening and went down the path between shrubs, stunted by frost, and out of the gate.

Moonlight glistened on the frosty pavement, so that it appeared to be studded with hundreds of tiny diamonds. He took a deep lungful of air that was tinged with smoke from the chimneys and damp vegetation. It was a relief to have got through the first part of his plan without Alice bursting into tears. He did not want to upset her but she could not go on the way she was, avoiding the old drawing room and flinching at shadows.

He came to Mrs Black's gate, unlatched it and strode up the path. A lighted oil lamp hung on the wall next to the front door. That's new, he thought as he banged the knocker and heard the sound echoing along the hall and up the stairs. Then came the patter of hurrying footsteps and he moved backwards off the doorstep. The door opened and Emma stood in the doorway, looking down at him in obvious surprise.

'Hello, stranger! What are you doing here?' she asked.

'Is that how you're supposed to greet callers?' he responded and grinned.

She smiled. 'Naw! What can I do for you...sir?'

'I want Tilly to have piano lessons.'

'Oooh eh! They're out tonight...gone to the Liberal meeting at the Music Hall, what with the elections coming up. Even though they can't vote, they feel they've got to show their support for the new candidate and express how they feel about the rumours about the government taxing tea and bread. D'you want me to pass on the message?'

'If you would.'

There was a silence and then she said, 'Everything all right with you and Alice and the old lady?'

'Mrs Waters is going further down the nick...and as for Alice she's fancying things.' He hesitated, aware of an urge to unburden himself. Never before in his life had he had to handle such a situation.

Emma said softly, 'She'll probably be fine once the baby's born. Women do get strange fancies when they're in that condition.'

'She thinks the old drawing room is haunted,' he muttered.

Emma's face stiffened. 'Felt a presence, has she?'

He raked his dark curls with an impatient hand. 'It's all in her imagination.'

'None the less real for that.' Emma rested her shoulder against the doorjamb and folded her arms. 'Have you thought of asking someone to exorcise the room?'

Seb frowned, nudging the step with the toe of his boot. 'That would be like admitting there was something there.'

'What harm would it do?' asked Emma in a low voice. 'More likely to do good if it eases Alice's mind. She's a churchgoer, so must believe in good spirits as well as bad if she's read her Bible. Remind her that St Paul spoke of a host of heavenly witnesses cheering us on to the finish. Which means she's not alone when she feels haunted.'

'I didn't know you knew the Bible so well, Emma,' said Seb, encouraged despite his scepticism.

'We had Scripture lessons in school, you know! I mightn't go to church often but I'm not ignorant,' she said sharply with a toss of her head. 'Now get back to your wife and do what I said.'

'Yes, Emma,' he said meekly, and kissed her cheek. 'You're a good friend.'

'Gerraway with yer! What would me fella say if he saw yer now?' she said in a mocking voice.

He moved away then stopped, 'Talking about that fella of yours…if he ever gets fed up with the railway, tell him to come and see me. I'm not saying I've much work on at the moment but I'd enjoy a talk with him.'

'I'll mention it to him,' she said, gratified.

They wished each other goodnight and Emma closed the door.

'Who was that?' She jumped at the sound of Mrs Black's voice and turned to see her standing at the foot of the stairs.

'Someone wanting piano lessons,' she said glibly. 'I told him I'd pass the message on.'

'He seemed to be here a long time.'

'He wanted some advice, so I gave it to him,' she said chirpily. 'Shall I come and tidy the room now and then cook supper?'

Her employer nodded and went back upstairs.

Emma took a deep breath, knowing Mrs Black wouldn't have liked it one little bit if she knew of the advice she'd given to Seb. She'd lost count of the times her employer had expressed how she'd like to get into the room where Victoria Waters had passed over. Well, it wasn't going to happen, so she might as well give up, thought Emma, hoping that Seb would do as she suggested before Alice went completely to pieces. A lot of good she'd be looking after a baby then.

'You say your wife has seen a ghost?' The man in the dog collar with a large crucifix on his chest rested his elbows on his desk and tapped the tips of his fingers together, gazing over his tortoiseshell rimmed spectacles at Seb and Kenny.

'No. I said she *said* she'd seen a ghost.' Seb was wishing himself anywhere but in this man's study. With Alice attending the Methodist chapel and himself having been brought up a Catholic, he had sought out Kenny, who preferred the local C of E parish church. Seb had not attended his own church since his return from India, knowing that his marriage would not be regarded as binding by the priest. Kenny had spoken to his vicar, who had been in touch with the diocesan exorcist.

'Don't forget she felt a presence of evil,' put in Kenny.

'Ahhh!' The man's eyes blazed. 'And this emanated from the ghostly figure?'

'No. They're separate,' said Kenny, leaning towards him. 'The man responsible for the death of Miss Waters, who died in the room, is an evil man. He's left the country but just knowing he had been in the room is causing my sister distress. He was violent to her in the past and over a period of time was sending her and my wife threatening letters.'

'I see.' He frowned. 'So she's not scared of this ghost but of the memory of this man?'

Kenny and Seb exchanged glances. 'I'd say she'd be glad to get rid of the ghost, too,' muttered Seb, and then realised what he'd said. Damn! He didn't believe in ghosts and he'd never felt a presence. Why the bloody hell had he listened to Emma and come here?

Almost immediately he had his answer. 'My sister's having her first child, Reverend,' said Kenny. 'You would be doing her a kindness if you eased her mind. The baby is due in a few weeks.'

The vicar met his eyes and, after the barest of hesitations, suggested that perhaps a full blown exorcism was not the right procedure in this case. The best course would be for him to pray and simply lay hands on Mrs

Bennett and banish these thoughts and feelings that were troubling her.

Kenny and Seb exchanged looks and both nodded. An appointment was made for the following week. 'You think she'll agree to a vicar laying hands on her?' asked Seb, as he watched Kenny climb into the passenger seat of the Ford model T, which he'd had imported from America along with several others for the customers he'd already secured. 'We never talk about religion but I would have thought she'd rather have her own minister.'

With a surety that Seb almost envied, Kenny said, 'She won't want her church knowing she believes in any other ghosts except the Holy One. If you don't want to be there, what about Hanny keeping Alice company?'

Seb agreed with relief, adding that women were so much better at the emotional and spiritual stuff than men.

Hannah shaded her eyes to cut out the reflection of the sun on the glass, whilst taking care that the latest *Votes for Women* magazine did not slip from beneath her arm. Now she could see the piano clearly. The last time she had been in the drawing room, she really hadn't taken notice of the instrument. But there was talk of Tilly taking lessons and Hannah could not help wishing that she and Kenny could have provided her with a piano at their house. When she had expressed that thought to Kenny, he had replied with some heat that material objects weren't everything. They gave her their love and time...and didn't she appear happy when she came and stayed with them? Hannah could not argue with that but even so, she wished they had more money so they could give her more of this world's goods. Her gaze took in as much of the room as possible in the gap between the curtains, now looking for a sign of a ghost. Unlike Seb she had an open mind when it came to the supernatural...or so she liked to believe.

She moved away from the window and banged on the

knocker again but there was no response, so she decided to go round to the back of the house, just in case Alice was in the kitchen. Opening the door she saw her sister-in-law seated in a cushioned wheel-backed chair, toasting a crumpet on the red embers of the fire. Her cheeks were flushed prettily and her auburn curls seemed to glow in the reflected warmth of the hot coals. Her pregnant state was well advanced now and Hannah wondered, not for the first time, whether the child would be a boy as Alice had predicted. She was alone in the room.

'So you've arrived,' said Alice, removing the crumpet and tossing it onto the table before balancing the toasting fork on the highly polished brass fender. 'D'you want a crumpet? There's a bag of them on the table.'

Hannah nodded and placed the magazine down. 'You feeling all right? I brought you the latest *Votes for Women.*'

'I'm nervous.' Alice pushed herself up from the chair and went over to the table. She buttered the crumpet and sank her teeth into it before picking up the magazine, but she only glanced at the front cover before putting it down. 'D'you think I'm going mad like my dad?' she said in a rush.

Hannah did not hesitate, 'Of course not! Where are the servants by the way?'

'Cook's gone to the market and I've given Mary a couple of hours off…Sybil, who I still think of as the new one, is upstairs reading to Mrs Waters…not that she understands a word as far as I can tell. I read the Bible to her sometimes but I don't get a flicker.'

'I hope you read the nice parts not the bloodthirsty ones.'

'No! I'm a bloody nervous wreck as it is without reading the Old Testament,' said Alice, a catch in her voice. 'I shouldn't be swearing,' she muttered.

'Who cares? You're upset,' said Hannah soothingly. 'But you'll soon be fine. I wonder if he'll bring oil and anoint you.'

'They only did that to the sick in the Bible or when they were being anointed as God's servants,' murmured Alice, absently stroking her bump. 'I think they did it to the King at his coronation, too.' She looked at Hannah. 'Did you read in the newspaper that he hasn't been well?'

Hannah nodded. 'He's getting on, isn't he? And he's been a bit of a lad. Never gone short, has he? The best of everything. Women, wine, cigars and good food. I forget how many pheasants they said he shot when he came and stayed at Eaton Hall last. Anyway, let's change the subject. Has Tilly had a piano lesson yet?'

Alice shook her head. 'Tomorrow. I wanted to get this out of the way first.'

'Makes sense. Then you can put it all behind you and look forward to the birth of the baby.' Hannah removed the crumpet and went over to the table. 'As soon as I've eaten this, we'd best go to the front of the house. We don't want to miss the Reverend when he comes calling, do we?'

Eudora stood on her balcony, overlooking the Dee, letting the cold air cool her heated face. She did not want to believe she had seen what she had just seen but surely her eyes had not deceived her. She might be past her fiftieth birthday but there wasn't anything wrong with her sight. The figure in the flowing black cloak had clearly been someone she had clashed swords with before. A man of the cloth, he strode up the path to the Bennetts' house as if he knew exactly where he was going. They must have called him in to exorcise that room.

She swore under her breath, knowing it would be pointless getting in there now. Earlier, she had seen Hannah crossing the bridge and had hoped she was coming to call on her, but it was obvious that she must have come to visit Alice. What a pity Hannah had not seen fit to take up her offer of help. 'Still, it was never too late,' she murmured, now noticing Emma crossing the bridge in her direction. Knowing she did not have a moment to waste, Eudora hurried into the drawing room.

'So how do you feel now?' asked Hannah, perching on the piano stool and gazing at Alice. Despite the time of day they were sipping sherry.

'Better,' said Alice, smiling as she put the photograph taken of Seb and herself in a studio on Liverpool's Church Street after their wedding on the top of the piano. 'I definitely felt something happen when he placed his hands on my head. The fear's gone. I feel all peaceful inside. It makes me wonder perhaps if my father had been prepared to accept such help, instead of going to Mrs Black, we'd have had a different kind of life; Mam might have still been alive for a start.' She paused and then said softly, 'Although, in a way I suppose she's always with me.'

'You probably wouldn't have met Seb and be living here if it wasn't for your dad consulting Mrs Black,' said Hannah, lifting the piano lid and pressing a couple of keys.

Alice said thoughtfully, 'That's true. But think how different your life might have been. Bert might never have…'

'It's no use us thinking like that,' said Hannah firmly. 'The past is the past and no amount of hoping and wishing will change it. He's gone, thank God, so let's not think about him.' She closed the piano lid and stood up. 'What next?'

Alice started. 'In what way?'

'This room. Are you going to redecorate? Put yours and Seb's stamp on it? Make it a real family room to relax in?'

Alice drained her sherry glass and took Hannah's place on the piano stool. 'I'll see what Seb says. He'll probably agree because he likes this room. It's such a nice shape and gets the sun most of the day.' She hesitated and then blurted out, 'You've never said how you really feel about me having the baby! So how do you? Truthfully!'

Hannah was taken aback by the suddenness of the question. 'I thought I had. I can't wait for him to be born and see whether he has your red hair or Seb's black curls.'

'Honest?'

Hannah smiled. 'Haven't I just said so? And Kenny feels the same.' As soon as the words were out she knew that she was lying. Her husband had never spoken to her about how he felt about his expected niece or nephew. Yet there was no doubt in her mind, he would ache with longing when he held the child in his arms. How could she be so mean as to withhold from him that which he so wanted? She tossed off the remaining sherry and said, 'I'd best be going. You'll be all right on your own?'

Alice looked relieved. 'Mary and Cook will be back soon. And thanks for coming.' She kissed Hannah's cheek and saw her out.

Feeling depressed because she had not only lied to Alice but was filled with guilt about her treatment of her husband, Hannah walked down the path, past the open gate and then hesitated before turning in the direction of Mrs Black's house. She banged the knocker and almost immediately the door was opened by Emma in her outdoor clothes.

'There's a coincidence,' said the younger woman. 'I was just about to pop along to the Bennetts' and see if you were there. Mrs Black spotted you on the bridge and wanted me to ask if you'd like to call on her. She's been expecting you to do so since Boxing Day.'

'I don't know why. I didn't say I'd come,' said Hannah, her tone slightly aggressive.

'You're here now.'

Hannah shrugged and fiddled with a strand of her hair. 'Guilt! Although, my coming here probably won't do me any good.'

Emma smiled. 'I hope it does. You and Kenny could do with a break.'

Hannah gave her a measuring look. 'You like Kenny, don't you?'

'Of course, I do. Why ask? He's a good man.'

'But you love David?'

Emma looked amused. 'The questions you ask! I think I love him…at least I fancy him like mad. So are you coming in or not?'

Hannah stepped over the threshold and followed Emma upstairs, wondering, if Mrs Black had spotted her on the bridge, whether she had also seen the Reverend? Emma saw her to the drawing room, announced her and then went to her room.

Eudora told Hannah to sit by the fire and poured out two glasses of sherry. Having handed her visitor a glass, Eudora sat down and asked Hannah straight out what the Reverend had been doing at the house.

'Bringing peace,' said Hannah, a tiny smile playing round her mouth.

'A positive result then?' Eudora could not help but sound a little disappointed.

'Definitely. Alice is no longer frightened, the lucky duck!'

Eudora's expression changed and she stared at her thoughtfully. 'You are, though. So why did you not ask for prayer and the laying on of hands?'

Hannah said ruefully, 'I knew it wouldn't work for me. Mine isn't a spiritual matter. I'm just a coward.' She took a sip of the sherry. 'I'm dishonest, too.'

'I'm sure that's not true, dear,' said Eudora, sounding surprised.

'Oh, it is!' Hannah's voice was low. 'Kenny believes I don't want to make babies because of what Bert did…and that used to be the truth. But if I'm honest, there's always been part of me that doesn't want to have children. I'm terrified of childbirth.'

Eudora stared into Hannah's miserable face. 'You

surprise me, Hannah,' she said crossly. 'You're no different from thousands of women. No, probably millions! It's natural to fear suffering and possible death.'

'Alice isn't scared!'

'Has she told you that?'

'No. She never mentions it.'

'But her mother died in childbirth, so surely she can't have forgotten it?' said Eudora firmly.

'I haven't forgotten it!' Hannah prodded her chest with a finger. 'How could I? Her death changed my life forever.'

Eudora clicked her tongue against her teeth and said impatiently, 'It changed several lives, dear, including mine. But your mother...she has given birth how many times?'

'Five, no more than that...I think she lost two children.'

'There you are then. Your mother gave birth seven times and she survived. There's no reason why you shouldn't either.'

'I've thought of that and I'm still scared.' Hannah gulped down the rest of the sherry.

'And you'll carry on being so...even if you never have children...and there's no guarantee you will have. So isn't it better to accept that we all have our fears and have to live with them.' Eudora's dark eyes were compassionate. 'What we mustn't do is allow them to cripple our spirit and spoil the happiness that could be ours. I'm sure Alice has just put aside her fear of childbirth until she has to face up to it...which she will because she knows there is no getting out of it.'

'I'm sure you're right,' said Hannah, a flush on her cheeks, 'but...'

'No buts, dear! Action!' Eudora hit the arm of her chair with her fist and leaned towards her. 'Spit in the eye of that demon fear and make your husband and yourself happy. You love him and you'll carry on being miserable if you don't do what you know in your heart is best for you both.'

Hannah felt uplifted, as if she had been given marching orders and had to obey them. 'I'll do that.'

'Of course you will, dear...you're a sensible young woman.'

'Is there anything I can do for you?'

'You already have, dear.' Eudora beamed at her.

Hannah couldn't help wondering just what she had done that had been of help to Mrs Black. But there was no time to think about that now, she had to get home. She was halfway down the stairs when Emma's voice stopped her. She turned her head and saw her leaning over the banister rail with a copy of *Votes for Women* in her hand. 'Is everything OK?' asked Emma.

'Yes. I'm going home.'

'Have you seen the latest issue of *Votes for Women*?'

Hannah nodded, and carried on downstairs.

Emma followed her. 'Did you read about Lady Constance Lytton being arrested disguised as a common woman and ending up being given hard labour and force-fed in Liverpool's Walton prison?'

'I didn't read it all.' Hannah did not want to talk about it now. She wanted to get home to Kenny, hoping this lunch time they would have the house to themselves as Seb was bound to go home to see how Alice had got on with the Reverend.

'So you never read that not only Mrs Stone was imprisoned but so was Seb's mother!'

Hannah gasped. 'You're joking!'

Emma shook her head. 'Don't ask me how she got involved in the Cause. I never knew she was interested.'

'As far as I know she isn't.'

'Interestingly they gave their addresses.'

Hannah paused in the act of opening the front door. 'I left my copy with Alice. I wonder if she'll notice.'

Emma nodded. 'I wonder.'

'Anyway, I must go,' said Hannah in a vague voice. 'I'll

talk to you again.' She hurried down the path.

Hannah let herself into the house, bolted the door and checked that the room at the front, which served as an office, was empty. Unbuttoning her coat on the move, she hurried into the kitchen. Kenny was standing in front of the fireplace, stirring the pan of ham bone and lentil soup she had left ready for lunch on the hob.

He glanced at her and immediately said, 'You've got a sparkle in your eye. Things must have gone OK.'

Hannah had to think for a moment about what he meant because her mind was so concentrated on what she was planning to do. 'Yes. Alice is no longer frightened and is talking about redecorating the drawing room.' She dropped her coat on the back of a chair and went over to him. 'Leave that. Let's go to bed,' she said, placing a hand on his arm.

The ladle slipped from his fingers into the pan, splattering his skin with hot liquid. Swiftly she lifted his hand and licked off the soup before reaching up and drawing down his head towards hers. She kissed him. His lips were warm but hers were still chilled from being in the fresh air despite having licked the soup from his fingers. She held the kiss until she was breathless and had to break off to gulp in air.

'What was that for?' he asked, his chest rising and falling rapidly.

'Let's go upstairs now,' she said, taking hold of his hand.

'What's got into you?' demanded Kenny, allowing himself to be drawn towards the staircase.

'Don't ask questions. This is the time for action.'

He opened his mouth and then shut it again, deciding he was not going to waste time insisting on the reason for why she was doing this. After all, they might get to the bedroom and it would be the same old story. She would allow him so far and no further.

Because she was in such a rush, he was almost treading

on her heels as they climbed the stairs. It was difficult to ignore the pain in his foot but the swell of her bottom brushing tantalisingly against him aroused him. For a fraction of a second she paused and to his surprise, giggled, but then she carried on upstairs as if nothing had happened. For a moment he wondered if she and Alice had been at the sherry bottle. There had certainly been a sweetness on her breath.

She opened the bedroom door and drew him inside and then she seemed to lose her impetus because she moved no further. 'Hannah, please, don't change your mind now,' he pleaded.

She lifted her head and her smile almost dazzled him. 'I should have thought about it being cold in this room…so definitely not here!' Releasing his hand she went over to the bed and dragged off the cotton bedcover. 'Sorry, love, for dragging you up here, only to make you go down again.' She bundled the bedcover under her arm and, brushing past him, left the room.

He followed her downstairs as if in a daze and watched her fling open the bedcover and throw it over the rag rug. Then she drew the curtains and turned towards him. 'It'll be different here,' she said in a low voice as she began to undo the buttons on the bodice of her woollen dress.

Kenny could only stare at her as she dragged the dress down over her hips and watched it fall in a swirl of navy blue on the linoleum. She stood in her camisole and the cotton underskirt she had worn beneath her wedding gown. She raised her eyebrows. 'We haven't got all day,' she said briskly.

Kenny shook his head as if to clear it and began to unbutton his waistcoat, then his shirt. He hung them over the back of a chair as Hannah removed her undergarments. Fascinated by the gleam of the firelight on her soft white skin, he could not take his eyes off her. Suddenly he was aware that she was humming beneath her breath. For an instant he couldn't work out the tune, then he realised it was 'Onward Christian Soldiers'. He did not know what to make of that as he drank in the vision of his wife in the firelight. She stopped humming as he moved towards her, and she took several paces forward to meet him. Then they were in each other's arms and kissing hungrily, and this time there was no stopping him as they made passionate love. Afterwards, saturated with pleasure, Hannah wondered why no one had ever told her making babies could be so good.

Chapter Twenty

February, 1910

'Have you read this?'

'Read what?' asked Alice, lifting her head and glancing across the fireplace at Seb, who was sprawled in the other armchair.

'This copy of *Votes for Women*. I found it under the cushion.'

She shook her head as she bit off the thread and decided to embroider blue flowers on the yoke of the baby-sized cream flannelette nightgown in her lap. 'It must be the one Hanny brought a while ago.'

'There's an article by Lady Constance Lytton. She was released from Walton jail after being force-fed whilst pretending to be a commoner. They sentenced her to hard labour, not realising who she was and that she had a heart condition.'

'It's a wonder it didn't kill her,' murmured Alice, reaching for her sewing box on the floor. 'I suppose the heart condition reminded you of Victoria.'

He nodded. 'It's what's in the rest of the article that really caught my eye. It mentions a Mrs Gabrielle Bennett being imprisoned and it gives an address in Liverpool.'

Alice's head jerked up, her green eyes startled. 'Are you sure they haven't made a mistake? How did she get involved with the Suffragette movement?'

He shook his head. 'Don't ask me! But it's here in black and white. And how many Gabrielle Bennetts could there be in this part of the world?'

'You're not thinking what I think you're thinking?'

'Of course I am!' He stared moodily into the fire. 'I've had time to get over the upset now. I miss Ma...and what with us having the baby, I know she'll be over the moon.

If she came back here, she'll be a help to you when the baby arrives.'

Alice's heart sank. 'I can understand how you feel, Seb, but…' She paused, struggling to find the right words to express how she felt without sounding as if she was completely against having his mother living here.

He didn't let her finish. 'I know you and Ma didn't always see eye to eye,' he said, getting up and coming over to sit on the arm of her chair. He put his arm round her.

Alice tried not to pull a face. 'We got on OK at times but she's such a strong personality and I can see me either turning into a dormouse or us clashing.'

'I'll tell her that you're the mistress here now and your word goes.' He dropped a kiss on her hair and hugged her. 'I'll write asking her to call on us. Don't want to give her too much of a shock by arriving unexpectedly on her doorstep.'

She flashed him a smile but, inwardly, she was dismayed and could only pray that her mother-in-law would turn down Seb's offer to come home. Then again, who was to say that Gabrielle hadn't been praying for this moment for a long time?

Emma was cleaning the upstairs front window, thinking about David and him having to cancel the meeting arranged with Seb in a couple of days, when she noticed two women pause outside Mrs Waters' gate. She pressed her nose against the glass to get a closer look at them. Suddenly the dark, flamboyantly dressed woman carrying a carpet bag, opened the gate and slipped through the gap. She made to close the gate on the other woman but she was too quick for her. 'Don't be childish, Gabrielle,' she said, sounding exasperated.

Emma recognised that voice and was glad that Mrs Black had said she would be out for the afternoon. Throwing down the chamois leather she raced downstairs. By the time she reached the gate where they had stood, arguing, they were out of sight. She hesitated a moment and then hurried up the path and round the back of the house. She could hear raised voices and, when she knocked on the door, there was no response. She opened the door and peeked inside.

As if frozen, Gabrielle and Josephine Stone stood either side of the table, the former was glaring at the other, who looked outraged. Alice sat at the head of the table with her chin cupped in her hands, her eyes closed and her lips moving silently as if in prayer. Mary was putting on the kettle. Tilly was sitting on a stool with the toasting fork in her hand but her gaze was fixed on Gabrielle as if she had never seen anyone quite like her before. Emma stepped inside the kitchen and slammed the door.

Alice's eyes opened and she sighed. 'Emma, how good to see you. Perhaps you can give me a hand up. We'll go into the drawing room and Mary can serve tea there.'

Gabrielle turned and gazed disdainfully at Emma. 'What is she doing here? I recognise this young woman. She works for Mrs Black, who is a murderess.'

'Rubbish! If you're not careful, Mrs Bennett, you'll be had up for slander,' said Emma, scowling at her.

'That's what I've been telling her,' said Josephine, her hands curling tightly on the back of a chair as she gazed at her previous maid. 'I'm glad to see you, Emma.'

Gabrielle's dark eyes glinted. 'How can you say that? She's a spy and in league with her mistress, that evil whore.'

'That's slanderous, too,' groaned Josephine. 'I don't know why you asked me to accompany you here when you don't listen to a word I say.'

Alice beckoned Emma and she hurried over to her. 'Would you believe these two have been carrying on like this since they set foot in my kitchen,' she whispered. 'I had no idea Seb's mother was living with Mrs Stone. The people at the address in Liverpool must have forwarded Seb's letter to the Stones' house.'

'I heard them arguing in the crescent, that's what brought me here.'

Josephine heard them and had the grace to blush and apologise. 'It was not my intention to upset you, Mrs Bennett. If I'd known Gabrielle would start ranting about Mrs Black as soon as we arrived, I would have come another time. My intention was to be of moral support to her as she said she was nervous. Hard to believe I know. But I also wanted to ask for your help. I thought you might be willing to take poor Victoria Waters' place in planning a rally to drum up more support for women's rights here in Chester.'

'I'm hardly in a condition to get involved in the Cause right now, Mrs Stone,' said Alice, grasping Emma's arm and pulling herself to her feet.

Josephine gaped. 'I'm sorry. I didn't realise you were so far gone in your pregnancy. Of course I wouldn't expect you to help us in your condition.'

'The baby's due any day now.'

Gabrielle tossed her head. 'I could have told you that it would be a waste of your time, Mrs Stone. You might as well leave.'

Alice was annoyed. 'Mrs Stone doesn't have to leave. She's come all this way, so deserves a cup of tea and a cake.'

'You would go against me?' Gabrielle's chin jutted and she folded her arms beneath her bosom and hoisted it up. 'Do not forget, Alice, I knew you when you were in a lowly position.'

Alice blurted out, 'At least I wasn't warming Mr Waters' bed when I worked here.'

The blood rushed to Gabrielle's face and she raised her hand as if about to strike her daughter-in-law.

'Don't you dare!' said Emma, her arm going round the trembling Alice. 'You've no right to upset her. We all know what Alice says is true. Otherwise your son wouldn't be doing so well for himself…and that's not slander.'

Gabrielle looked about ready to turn her wrath on Emma but Josephine seized her arm and said firmly, 'Calm down, Gabrielle. We are both guests in this house and you are behaving abominably. I understand it can't be easy for you coming back here and facing your shameful past but it was you who wanted to come, so control your feelings. Perhaps we should both leave young Mrs Bennett to recover.'

Alice thanked her. 'But please don't go yet. Join me in the drawing room once Mary's made the tea.' She turned to Emma and slipped her hand through her arm. 'Let's go.'

Emma left the kitchen with Alice. 'What a nice woman that Mrs Stone is,' said the latter, as they made their way to the drawing room. 'What on earth made her take in Seb's mother?'

'Probably desperation if Dr Stone's still up to his old tricks and they've lost another servant. Remember the reason I left was because he was too ready to touch me all over. He got one of the maids pregnant.'

'Not much different from Mr Waters then,' said Alice, and then put a hand to her mouth. 'I shouldn't have said that. And I shouldn't have lost my temper back there.'

'I'd have wanted to say the same,' said Emma, smiling. 'I think Seb's mad wanting her back here.'

Alice groaned. 'I know! But it's his mother and he thinks she'll be of help to me after the baby's born. I reckon Granny Popo would be better than her. I was hoping the baby would arrive before Gabrielle did.'

'So what are you going to do?' asked Emma.

Alice sighed. 'I suppose I'll have to give it a try for Seb's sake. She is his mother.'

Emma opened the drawing room door and settled Alice comfortably in front of the fire. 'Shall I go and see how things are in the kitchen?'

Alice nodded. 'Thanks. And you'll have a cup of tea with us, won't you?'

Emma smiled. 'If you want me to...but I can't stay long.'

Alice returned her smile. 'I wouldn't have asked if I didn't want your support.'

Emma nodded and hurried back to the kitchen. Mrs Stone looked relieved to see her. 'How is Mrs Bennett?'

'She'll be fine as long as nobody goes upsetting her. She's had enough to cope with over the last few months. But, please, go and join her in the drawing room.'

Gabrielle did not say a word but her eyes spoke volumes as she stalked out of the kitchen in Josephine's wake. If looks could kill, thought Emma, wondering if that was because Mrs Stone knew the reason why Gabrielle had gone to prison. She went to help Mary with the tea tray.

As Emma carried the tea and cakes into the drawing room, she could feel the atmosphere. She placed the tray on a low table in front of the sofa where Alice and Josephine Stone were sitting discussing the rally. Emma heard Alice say that, although she couldn't help her, Hannah might be willing to do so. Gabrielle was several feet away, perched on the straight-backed chair that Victoria had used when writing letters at her bureau. She looked straight through Emma, who turned her back on her and poured the tea. Gabrielle turned her attention to the cakes on offer, looking at them with disdain.

Alice said, 'You were in prison with Lady Constance Lytton...tell us what it was like?'

Josephine shuddered. 'Very unpleasant and not something I want to do again. I won't say any more. I believe Lady Constance plans to write a book about her experiences, so I'll not steal her thunder.'

There was silence as they sipped their tea. Alice decided she must make the effort and try and be friendly to her mother-in-law, so turned to her. 'I was surprised to see your name in *Votes for Women*. How did you get involved?' Hot colour stained Gabrielle's cheeks, and without speaking, she put down her cup and saucer and hurried out of the room. 'What did I say wrong?' whispered Alice, her own face flushing as she gazed after her.

Josephine hesitated. 'I think it's best if I say as little as possible. Suffice to say that there was a mix-up. She isn't one of us but was picked up by the same Black Maria that took me and Lady Constance and a couple of others to the police station and then prison.'

'I see,' said Alice, who didn't. She exchanged glances with Emma and just knew she was longing to know as much as she was why Gabrielle had ended up in jail.

'So have you thought of any names for the baby yet?' asked Josephine, smiling.

Alice was not averse to talking on such a topic. Emma slipped away without them noticing, imagining what her mother would have said if she'd heard them extolling the joys of motherhood. She returned to Mrs Black's, impatient to tell her of Gabrielle Bennett's return.

Eudora was scarcely through the door when Emma broke the news to her. Her reaction was different from what Emma had expected. Only by the narrowing of her eyes and the barest tightening of her lips did she show that she had heard her. Then, with the order to have supper on the table in ten minutes, she went to her bedroom. Later, when she sat in front of the fire, making short work of the ham and cheese omelette that Emma had whipped up, she asked how Alice had reacted to her mother-in-law's arrival.

'She's none too happy. But if Seb Bennett's asked her back, Alice can scarcely tell his mother to pack her bags again and go...that's for sure.'

Eudora frowned. 'That woman is trouble and I feel sorry for poor little Alice. Did she have anything to say about me?'

'When she saw me, you bet she did,' said Emma, pulling a face.

Eudora said crossly, 'Don't do that, Emma, if the wind changes you just might stick like that.'

'That's an old wives' tale.'

'Never mind that. What did she say?'

Irritated, Emma thought that if she wanted the truth then she could have it. 'She called me your spy...and said that you were a whore.'

'Slanderous! And she can talk,' said Eudora with a sniff. 'She's been paid for lying on her back for years. Fetch me the sherry bottle and a glass if you would, Emma.'

Emma fetched the best cream sherry, unsure whether to mention the accusation of murder.

Eudora took tiny sips of the sherry and was silent for so long that Emma had cleared her plate and cutlery and departed to the kitchen, where she made custard to accompany the treacle tart she had baked earlier. As she placed the dessert on the table, her mistress said, 'There's something else, isn't there? Has she made wild accusations about me being a murderess again?'

'You've guessed it in one,' said Emma, thinking she might have known Mrs Black would have worked that out.

'She would hardly accuse you of being my spy if it was solely because she'd called me a whore. Unless she thinks I use this house as a bordello amongst other things,' said Eudora, her dark eyes alight with amusement all of a sudden. She picked up her spoon. 'I'm going to have to give careful thought to her future. We'd be doing Alice a favour if we could get rid of her, wouldn't we?'

Emma's stomach flipped over like a pancake on Shrove Tuesday. 'How?' she squeaked, hoping that Gabrielle's accusation of murder was untrue.

Eudora's eyes widened. 'Emma, dear, I do believe you still have your doubts about me.' She raised a spoonful of sponge and custard to her mouth.

'No, I don't, Mrs Black,' lied Emma. 'Although, I could have murdered her myself the way she looked at me...like I was a bedbug or a bluebottle.'

'That's the spirit, dear. What I will do is have my solicitor send a warning letter to her, saying I will sue if she continues to slander me.' She changed the subject. 'Now, do you know where I went this afternoon? You don't have to answer, I'll tell you. To see Alice's father in the asylum. He's been on my conscience because I haven't visited him since my return from my travels.'

'Is he any better?'

'It's difficult to tell.' Eudora pursed her lips. 'Of course he could be putting it on. I told him I'd seen his other daughter, Tilly, and what a beauty she is and there was definitely a reaction. I also informed him that Alice is having a baby – although it seems to be keeping the prospective parents waiting so I heard on the grapevine. I even mentioned your sister to him...'

'Did you tell him what we suspect Bert of doing to Miss Waters?'

'He didn't know her, so what would be the point? What's most important is that he doesn't forget Bert was responsible for his being caught and placed in the asylum.'

'You told him Bert's gone to Australia?'

Eudora said smoothly, 'No, dear, because I'm not convinced he has and if he were ever to get out of that place, he's the man to deal with Bert. Now coffee, dear.'

Emma whipped the pudding bowl away and left the room, thinking if Mrs Black was right about Bert then it was worrying. Perhaps she should have a word with Hanny and see what she had to say.

'Emma!' Hannah stood in the doorway, smiling. 'Come in!'

Emma wiped her feet on the coconut mat and followed her friend into the kitchen. 'I'm on my way to me mam's, so I can't stay long.'

'Sit down! You won't mind if I carry on with the dinner?'

'Of course not.'

Emma sat by the fire, watching Hannah slice carrots into a blackened pot, wondering how to broach the subject of Bert. Hannah had blossomed in the last few weeks. How could she spoil things for her by mentioning Mrs Black's conviction that he hadn't gone to Australia?

'Mrs Stone's been here,' said Hannah. 'She brought *them*.' She pointed to the parcel on the table. 'I'm supposed to go putting them through as many doors as I can or hand them out in the centre of town. Joy's going to help me but it's still going to be a bit of job.'

'Leaflets are they?' asked Emma, glad to have her mind taken off Bert.

'Have a look. I've cut the string.'

Emma went over and opened the brown paper. She took out the top sheet of paper. The writing was big, black and bold and beneath the date in March, as well as the time and place was printed:

WOMEN OF CHESTER, DO YOU EARN A PITTANCE WORKING THE SAME HOURS AS MEN? WOMEN OF CHESTER, ARE YOU ALONE IN HAVING TO SUPPORT YOURSELF OR A FAMILY ON THAT PITTANCE BECAUSE YOU'RE WIDOWED OR YOUR HUSBAND HAS SUFFERED AN INJURY AND CAN'T GET WORK? WOULD YOU LIKE A BETTER EDUCATION FOR YOUR DAUGHTERS? WOULD YOU LIKE THE SAME WAGES AS MEN? COME AND HEAR HOW YOU CAN BRING ABOUT CHANGES IN THE LAW SO YOU CAN TAKE YOUR SHARE IN KEEPING BRITAIN GREAT. WOMEN MUST HAVE THE VOTE. JOIN THE FIGHT!

Emma nodded slowly. 'It's good. If only they could bring it off but it's true that they've got a fight on their hands, just like the working men have to get better wages.'

'You say *they*. Don't you feel you're one of us any more? I'd really appreciate your help, Emma.'

She hesitated. 'I really haven't got time to get involved but perhaps I can take a few and put them through the doors in Mam's street.'

'What about Victoria Crescent?'

Emma smiled. 'Now you're asking something. I could have the dogs set on me...but then what's that compared to those who've been put in prison and suffered? The question is what class of women do they want at the meeting? Can us working-class women change things? They're not after the vote for us, are they?'

Hannah put down the vegetable knife and tucked a loose strand of hair behind her ear. 'The vote for women householders aged thirty and over is just the first step. Besides, you should know by now this is about more than women getting the vote. We need to change attitudes about a woman's place in the scheme of things. We've got more brains than most men are prepared to give us credit for. Anyway, as I said to Alice, we should carry on Miss Victoria's work. It's exactly what she would have wanted.'

'What did she say to that?'

'She'd like to help but she can't think of anything else but the baby right now – it should have arrived by now – it's the first of March tomorrow. But she did give me some money to help with expenses.'

'Have you found out anything more about Seb's mother and why she was in prison?'

Hannah's face darkened. 'No, I haven't. I wish you hadn't mentioned her. I'm disappointed in her. She's driving Alice mad, saying she's no better than her because Alice isn't legally married as she wasn't wed in a Catholic church. Also she criticises the decisions she makes in running the household.'

'What does Seb say?'

Hannah snorted. 'She doesn't say it when he's around. Just babbles on about the baby and what a wonderful father he'll make.'

'Why doesn't Alice tell him what his mother's saying?'

'She doesn't want to upset him. She thinks he's got enough on his plate getting the business on its feet. Besides, she's as sweet as honey to Alice when Seb's there.'

Emma said slowly, 'Alice should stand up to her.'

Hannah nodded. 'She says she couldn't cope with a row at the moment. Besides, she's grateful to Gabrielle for looking after Mrs Waters, so they were able to dispense with one of the servants, which is a help financially.'

Emma wondered what Seb's mother had to gain by it. 'What about Tilly? How does she get on with her?'

Hannah's mouth tightened. 'As you know, Tilly's got a lovely nature and most people take to her...but not Mrs Bennett. According to Alice, Tilly only has to open her mouth and Mrs Bennett shuts her up, saying little girls should be seen and not heard. She complains about her practising the piano or singing about the place. At the moment, she's staying with us until after the baby's born and Alice is up and about again. We're glad to have her company. She's a little love.'

'The woman's jealous. If it weren't for Alice, she'd be ruling the roost. She resents Tilly because she's Alice's sister and Seb is fond of her.'

'I think it's a great shame she can't be nicer and accept that she can't have things all her own way. Anyway, how about a cuppa?'

Emma glanced at the clock on the mantelpiece and decided now wasn't the time to bring up the subject of Bert. 'I better hadn't if I'm going to put some of those leaflets through doors and see Mam.' She picked up a wad of them. Hannah thanked her and saw her out.

The smell of petrol hung in the air and, as Emma crossed the yard, Seb came out from one of the old stable buildings, wiping his oily hands on a rag. He smiled when he saw her. 'Hello, Emma. How are things with you?'

She returned his smile. 'Fine! I'm just on my way to see me mam.'

'It looks like Hannah's roped you in to help.' He nodded towards the leaflets in her hand.

She said ruefully, 'I couldn't say no. Although, I'm not convinced they'll do any good. I know me dad would hit the roof if he was home long enough to read one of them. He thinks if there's any money going spare from the government, it should be used to up his wages not those for women. A woman's place is in the home and not in competition with men for jobs.' She mimicked his voice.

His eyes twinkled. 'You should have said no if you think it's a waste of time. You're too soft-hearted.'

'I wouldn't say that. Besides, I do believe in their aims. Mrs Black pays me well and that means our Johnny doesn't have to damage his feet wearing tatty cast-off boots but can have a brand new pair once a year.'

'I'm sorry I couldn't keep you on by paying you more, Emma,' he said sincerely. 'But you know how things are and it'll be some time before I start making a decent profit.'

'I understand. Anyway, at least you're working for yourself.'

'I know I'm lucky. I feel sorry for the likes of David. How is he, by the way? He still hasn't been to see me.'

She shrugged. 'He's fine as far as I know. We don't really get the chance to see much of each other with us both working long hours and him still involved with the union.'

'Alice thought there was something serious between the pair of you.'

Emma smiled. 'Possibly. I'd best be going. See you around.'

'Tarrah!'

She left the yard, wondering if she should have said something to him about Bert. Seb would have been able to take it in his stride without worrying Alice. For a moment, she thought of going back but if she did that then she was going to have even less time at her mam's.

When Emma reached the street, she realised that it wasn't going to be easy slipping the leaflets through letterboxes unseen. The weather was unusually warm for February and several housewives were either scrubbing their doorsteps or gossiping; her mam was one of them. Ah well, nothing ventured, nothing gained, thought Emma, deciding to hand out leaflets to those taking the air, too. It would be useful to hear their opinions and then she could pass them on to Hannah, who could give them to Mrs Stone. She pushed leaflets through several doors and a childhood friend, now married and with a baby, asked what she was doing. Emma told her.

'Bloody 'ell, Em! Haven't yer got anything better to do? Yer should find yerself a husband and he'd keep yer too busy for that malarkey. They should know better the lot of them, throwing stones and smashing windows. They're not going to get people supporting them doing that sort of thing.'

'They're not all like that,' said Emma defensively. 'And when the government say they'll do one thing and then does another or doesn't do anything at all it gets yer dander up. Anyway, if you don't want to come you don't have to.'

'I won't.'

'It's your loss.'

Emma walked on, handing out leaflets to several women. One of whom looked at it and turned it over. 'Nice clean back to it. Thanks, Emma. It'll do for one of the kids to pencil on.'

'You do what you want with it, Mrs Evans, I'm just

doing my bit for the advancement of women,' said Emma, not surprised.

The woman smiled. 'Good luck to you, luv. We need someone speaking up for us.'

Emma thanked her for the encouragement but did not bother posting any more leaflets. Instead, she quickened her pace until she reached her parents' house. As soon as Olive spotted her daughter, she broke off from talking and delved into the pocket of her apron. 'A letter, Em, from our Chris. Alf's read it to me and it says he's coming home.'

Emma's spirits soared. 'Does he say when?'

'Doesn't give a date but it shouldn't be long.' Olive's eyes were shining. 'When he comes, he might be home for good. He's finished his time and says he's in no hurry to sign on again. He's going to wait and see what's going on here. Isn't that the gear? He'll sort yer dad out for me.'

Emma was over the moon. She couldn't wait to get back to Mrs Black and tell her the good news.

But Emma had no sooner reached the crescent, when she spotted Mary coming out of Mrs Waters' gate. When she saw Emma, she hurried towards her. 'Guess what?'

'Alice's baby's started.'

Mary smiled. 'It's arrived! Dead quick for a first despite it having kept them waiting the last week or so. It's a lovely bouncing boy!'

Emma was delighted. 'Is Alice all right?'

'Tired but happy! I'm going up to the yard to tell Mr Bennett right now. See you!' Mary hurried away in the direction of the footbridge.

Half an hour later Emma saw Seb and Mary chugging along the crescent in the Ford automobile. He parked at the kerb and was out of the motorcar in seconds and running up the path to the house, his face alight with happiness. She gazed after him, remembering the conversation she had overheard the day of Victoria Waters' funeral between the solicitor and Mr Martin Waters. She wondered what he would think of a great-grandchild being born to Mrs Waters, to share her estate with when she died.

But such thoughts did not enter the new parents' minds as they gazed down at their first-born, nestling in his father's arms. 'He's so tiny,' marvelled Seb.

'He's a good weight,' assured Alice, her eyes alight with love.

'He's got your perfect nose.' Seb kissed the baby's tiny button and then Alice's mouth. 'You clever girl.'

'Aren't I just?' she said smugly.

Seb chuckled. 'He has my hair, though.'

'I'm glad about that. I didn't want him to have my father's carrot top...but have you ever seen such a mop of black curly hair on a baby?'

'I've never taken much interest in babies before...but my hair was probably just the same...you'll have to ask Ma.'

Alice sighed. 'She's going to get at me...I just know it.'

Seb had no need to ask her what she meant. 'Leave her to me. Now names – we don't want a fancy name.' The baby whimpered and Seb rocked him awkwardly.

Alice smiled mischievously and held out her arms for her son. 'We've already discussed this; you don't want him named after you.'

'Correct, Mrs Bennett. I like sensible names.'

'James! He was one of Jesus' disciples, one of the Sons of Thunder.'

Seb nodded. 'Our son doesn't look like he's going to be hot-tempered.'

'It would be good if he grew up able to stand up for himself, though.'

'Yes. And for a middle name – Thomas after my father. Only because it's due to him I was able to set up in the automobile business.'

'He wasn't a bad man,' murmured Alice. 'I can think of worse fathers.'

'I'm aiming to be the best dad in the world,' said Seb, a doting expression on his face as he watched her cradle James Thomas.

'And I want to be the perfect mum,' said Alice firmly.

That seemed to bring the discussion on names to an end, which was fortunate because at that moment the nurse entered. 'New mothers need lots of rest,' she said, and shooed Seb from the room.

Chapter Twenty-One

March, 1910

Hannah cooed over the baby, rocking him in her arms.

'You're a natural,' said Emma, polishing the brass door knocker with vigour.

Hannah smiled. 'Someone's got to look after James Thomas when his mother's having a rest now the nurse has gone.'

'I see Mr Martin Waters has remembered he has a mother.' Emma glanced in the direction of the man talking to Gabrielle a couple of gardens up.

Hannah lowered her voice. 'Alice told me that he must have left the farm as soon as he received the news about the baby and was off to see the solicitor. He's desperate to pay off the loan he borrowed because of the fire damage last year, but he's still going to have to wait for his inheritance until the old woman dies...which can't be much longer. When that happens Seb might have to sell up and move somewhere smaller.'

'I wonder how Alice feels about that. Although, it could be for the best. No fear of Bert finding her then,' said Emma without thinking.

Hannah blinked. 'Come again? Bert's in Australia. Mother said she's had letters...not that she's ever shown them to me.'

Emma flushed. 'Sorry. I don't know why I said that. How did Seb's mother take the news about the house having to be sold when the old woman dies? She didn't offer to help them out with the money she was left by Mr Waters?'

Hannah smiled mirthlessly. 'She's not speaking to Alice because she's dug in her heels and refused to have this little man here...' Hannah kissed the baby's black curls, 'baptised into the Catholic church. Seb told his mother that the decision was Alice's and that's the end of it.'

'I'm glad he's supporting Alice. What do you think she'll do when they move? She can't have gone through all her inheritance, surely?'

'I've no idea.' Hannah frowned. 'Kenny's wondering whether we should offer to move out of the house in the yard and find somewhere else, so Seb and Alice and the baby can move in there.'

Emma looked surprised. 'Surely Seb wouldn't put the pair of you and Tilly out. Besides, would Alice think it was good enough for her? I'm not saying you haven't got the house nice,' she added hastily.

'You didn't have to say that,' said Hannah dryly. 'I know exactly what you mean. What concerns me is if my dah suggests us living with them. One of the lodgers has moved out and Mother's looking for someone else. It would never work, not with the way she feels about Kenny.' She changed the subject. 'So what's this I hear about your brother coming home?'

'April! I can't wait to see him. Although, it's going to be strange after all this time.'

Chris Griffiths marched up the street with his kitbag on his shoulder and a cheery hello for everyone he passed. He was a couple of inches short of six foot, with broad shoulders and a finely shaped head. His blue-green eyes appeared lighter than they truly were in contrast with his sunburnt face, and his jaw was strong and firm. He whistled a marching song, which took him back for a moment to the heat and dust of Palestine, and he thought how bloody glad he was to be in England at the beginning of Spring with the Chester races to look forward to and the processions and events in May...and, if he was not mistaken, it was Emma's twenty-first birthday that month, too. He must buy her a real nice present, as it was unlikely she'd get anything decent from their parents. For a moment his eyes darkened, thinking about what she had said in her last letter about their father. Then he became aware that several women, young and old, couldn't take their eyes off him and he put his father out of his mind. He was not so modest that it didn't please him to know that the opposite sex found him attractive but he made no sign of having noticed them. Even so, he was grinning when he came to his parents' house.

The door was open and on the front step sat a small boy eating a slice of bread spread with jam; a small amount of the conserve was smeared on his chin and nose. His mouth fell open as he gazed up at Chris. 'You must be young Johnny!' said the man.

The boy nodded and pointed a finger at him. 'Soldier!'

Chris slid the rucksack from his shoulder to the pavement and got down on his haunches and ruffled the boy's hair. 'I'm your big brother Chris. How are you doing, little fella?' He had an attractive baritone voice and the sound of it was enough to bring his mother to the door.

As Olive let out a shriek, he stood up. She flung herself at him. He caught her and, lifting her up, danced around the pavement with her clinging to him. She laughed until the tears rolled down her thin, sallow cheeks and then he set her down. Taking a large handkerchief from his trouser pocket, he wiped her damp face and kissed her cheek.

By then several of the neighbours had gathered round, patting him on the back or touching his arm and saying how good it was to see him home. He thanked them, asking after sons and daughters that he had known in his youth. Although Emma had been quite thorough in keeping him up to date with their neighbours' news, he still considered it good manners to ask these questions and listen to what they were up to now.

'Enough, enough,' said Olive, putting out an arm as if to

ward the women off. 'My boy will be wanting a cup of tea and a bite to eat. So leave him alone now and let's get inside.'

The neighbours dispersed with only a second prompting and Chris followed his mother indoors, tailed by little Johnny. The kitchen seemed so much smaller than he remembered and he wondered how his mother stood it, day in, day out, existing in the same four walls, never going away on holiday but having to bring up the kids on very little money in such a small space. He knew there were thousands like her but he wasn't particularly concerned about them. She was his mother and it saddened him that she looked ten years older than her age. He wanted to make life easier for her but knew he could only ease her troubles temporarily. From his pocket he took a wallet and removed a white banknote. 'Here you are, Mam, do whatever you want with that.'

Olive stared at the money as if it might vanish into thin air and then she snatched the five pound note from his hand and kissed it. Her eyes were bright with unshed tears. 'I've never had one of these before. I heard soldiers only earned about a bob a day, so I won't ask where yer got it from.'

He grinned and tiny lines formed at the corners of his eyes. 'Good, because I wouldn't like lying to you...not that I've done anything dishonest.'

She placed it in her apron pocket. 'Don't mention it to yer dad.'

'You don't have to say that, Mam. Yer know I've no time for him. Especially after what happened to our Aggie.'

A shadow crossed Olive's face. 'Don't remind me...and don't go talking about it to our Em when yer see her. She still hasn't got over it.'

He made no promise but asked after his sister. Olive poured milk into two chipped cups. 'Thank God she's still working for that Mrs Black. I'd be round at the pawnshop more often if it weren't for that and what you send me. I don't know if she's mentioned yer dad and me not seeing eye to eye and that he's away from this house more than he's here. If I didn't believe he was too tight to spend his money on another woman, I'd think he'd found someone else.'

'You're well rid of him, Ma. And while I'm around, I'll see that you don't go short. But our Em…her I'd like to see. So when's her next afternoon off?'

'Now yer asking me something.' She pursed her lips. 'I know she was thinking of going along to some rally down in the town to do with women's rights if she could get away. I've a feeling it was today, but whether she made it or not, I can't say. It all depends on what Mrs Black's got on.'

He nodded thoughtfully. 'I think I might take a walk over there and give her a surprise.'

Olive started. 'I don't know if yer should do that. Mrs Black mightn't like Em having callers.'

Chris grinned. 'I can always pretend to be a client. Our Em's told me a fair bit about her. She makes a good story of the happenings that go on in that house.'

Olive sniffed. 'She never tells me anything much. When I ask she says where some things are concerned she's sworn to secrecy.'

'I was thousands of miles away, Mam, so it didn't matter me knowing.'

'That's true…but now yer here,' she said, frowning as she handed him a steaming cup. 'I don't know where yer going to sleep, son. I'm really glad to see yer back but…'

He smiled. 'Don't worry, Mam, I'll find somewhere. But I'll leave my kit here for now if yer don't mind.'

'No trouble, son. Here's to you.' She raised her teacup and clinked it with his and then began to tell him more about the trouble she'd been having with his dad and the kids.

Emma opened the front door and ushered out a middle-aged man and two chattering women who had come for a sitting. From listening to their whisperings as she led them downstairs, she knew he wasn't convinced that the message received from his wife's sister's husband was genuine...but the sister seemed happy enough with what she had seen and heard. Another satisfied customer, she thought, watching the three figures go down the path.

It was a pity about the rally but she felt that she'd done her bit for the Cause by at least delivering some leaflets. Besides which, she had other things to think about. Something really spooky had happened as she'd taken in the tea and cake after the sitting today. Aggie had been in her thoughts, which was not that unusual at such times, but then she could have sworn she heard her sister speak to her right inside her head. She had put it down to tiredness, having shifted furniture and been on her feet since she had got up. Now she couldn't get the words out of her head. Guilt, sadness and frustration clouded her spirits and instead of going back inside the house she walked down the path, pausing to sniff a daffodil.

'Hello, Em!'

She almost jumped out of her skin, could feel warm breath on the back of her neck as a hand touched her shoulder. She turned and her face lit up. 'Bloody hell, it's you!' she exclaimed, collapsing against her brother's chest. 'You didn't half give me a fright.'

'You thought me a ghost...be honest!' said Chris, his eyes teasing her.

'A living soul, Chris,' she responded in a mocking voice. 'It's lovely to see you.'

'You, too.' He hugged her. 'Mam said she didn't know when you next had time off, so I thought I'd come and look yer up...take yer out for a drink and a bite to eat.'

Emma gnawed on her lip. 'I'd love that. But I'm not sure Mrs Black'll let me have time off right now. I've the furniture to move and then her supper to prepare.'

He frowned. 'You shouldn't be moving furniture about, Em. There's not much of you and you could put your back out.'

She smiled. 'Now you mention it…' She put a hand to the small of the back and hobbled up the path like an old woman.

'Exactly,' said Chris. 'I'm sure she won't mind if I give you a hand. I'd like to meet her anyway.'

'She'll probably be interested to meet you, too. I've told her all about you.' Emma led him inside and up the carpeted stairs. He touched the embossed wallpaper lightly, 'Nice place she's got here.'

'Wait until you see the drawing room, she's got some really nice stuff in there,' whispered Emma.

'Is that where she does her *getting in touch with the other side*?'

'No. She has a special room for that and another for her healing sessions. That's really peaceful that one.'

'She must do well out of it.'

Emma gave him a severe stare. 'She doesn't do it for the money. Didn't I tell you in one of my letters that her husband left her plenty of money and property in Liverpool.'

His eyes danced. 'I do remember you saying she had no kids. Are there any relatives?'

'Not that I've ever seen,' she said in a low voice and hushed him as they reached the landing, for both the door to the drawing room and the 'sittings' room were ajar.

'Have you someone with you, Emma?' called Eudora.

'Yes, Mrs Black. It's me brother, Chris. I thought you might like to meet him and he said he'd help me move the furniture…if that's OK?'

'Bring him in here.'

Emma winked at Chris and led the way into the drawing room.

Mrs Black was standing over by the door that led out on to the balcony with a glass of sherry in her hand. She stared at Chris without speaking and he returned her stare boldly. Slowly she smiled and beckoned him over. 'I suppose Emma's told you, I'd given up on your being of help to us.'

'No, missus. What help would that be then?' asked Chris, exchanging a swift questioning glance with his sister as he crossed the room.

'Ridding this earth of the man responsible for your sister's death before he can hurt anyone else.' Emma drew in her breath and Chris raised his eyebrows but remained silent. 'I hope I haven't shocked you, Mr Griffiths?' added Eudora. 'You're a soldier, so I'm sure it wouldn't be too difficult for you to capture this despicable man?'

Chris stared at her woodenly. 'Capture him? It wasn't in your mind then that I creep up on him in a dark alley and slit his throat?'

Mrs Black's smile deepened. 'You have a sense of humour, I like that.'

'I could say the same about you, missus. A soldier of the British Army doesn't take the law into his own hands even if the man involved is a violent no good bloody murdering rapist…if you'll excuse my language.'

'Well said! But you've served your time according to Emma. So officially you're no longer in the army. Am I right? Unless you've made the decision already to sign on again?'

Chris shook his head and resisted glancing at his sister again. 'We are talking about Bert; who last I heard had gone to Australia.'

'Mrs Black doesn't believe he has,' said Emma.

Chris could not conceal his surprise. 'You have proof of that, missus?'

'Only my experience of dealing with people. It would be enough for him to write to his poor deluded mother and convince her to fool those out for his blood.' She pursed her lips. 'I've given much thought to his character and I think he'd certainly deceive his own mother if it suited his purposes. I believe his intention is to lull those he's tormented into a false sense of security and then strike when they're least expecting it.'

Chris stared at her from narrowed eyes. 'None of this is proof that he's still here.'

'That, young man, is where you come in. Now, having seen you, I've decided to entrust you with that task. You have the time and I'll see that you're not out of pocket.'

He smiled. 'That's generous of you, missus, although, I did have a few things in mind that I wanted to do now I'm back home.'

'Naturally! But surely a bit more money in your pocket would help you enjoy yourself even more.' He did not deny that and Mrs Black turned to Emma. 'Pour your brother a glass of whisky, dear! Sit down, Mr Griffiths, and I'll explain.' She waved him to a chair. 'I thought you might start in Liverpool. It shouldn't be too difficult to check the records of passengers travelling to Australia around the time Bert sent that letter telling his mother he was emigrating.'

'If it's that simple, it makes me wonder why you didn't pay someone to do it before now,' said Chris.

'I had thought of it but then I decided I'd rather keep this between as few people as possible. Those who really want to see Bert punished. I'm sure I can number you amongst them.'

He nodded and, without looking up, murmured his thanks to Emma as she handed him a cut glass tumbler. He took a mouthful of the whisky and let it lie on his tongue a moment before swallowing. 'Good stuff,' he said, then, leaning towards Mrs Black, 'When I do get my hands on him, what are your plans for him?'

She smiled. 'I'm sure we can come up with something

that will make him see the error of his ways.'

He stared at her fixedly. 'Sure. Why not? Give me a couple of days to get me bearings and find somewhere to stay.'

'Certainly. Shall we agree to your returning here next Monday when I'll give you some money for expenses, and then see how you go on from there.'

'That's fine with me.' He raised his glass. 'To your good health, Mrs Black, and a successful conclusion to our venture.' He swallowed the whisky straight down, stood up, and handed the glass to Emma. 'Now perhaps you'd like to show me where this furniture is you want moving and, if you could spare my sister for a couple of hours, Mrs Black, I'd appreciate that.'

She agreed. 'I'm sure you've plenty to say to each other. Make sure you have her back here no later than seven o'clock.'

He nodded and left the room with Emma.

Half an hour later Emma, with her arm linked through that of her brother, was crossing the footbridge. 'So what do you think of her?' she asked.

'She seems very sure of herself...but maybe having plenty of money does that for you,' said Chris, pausing in the middle of the bridge to gaze down at the water.

'I think it's also having the power to change people's lives as well,' said Emma. 'What d'you make of her plan to find Bert?'

'It's OK as far as it goes, although, I have a simpler plan of my own.'

'What's that?'

He smiled. 'I'll explain over a bite to eat. You recommend a place and I'll treat you to a slap up meal. In the meantime, maybe you can give some thought to where I can stay.'

Emma suggested a café on Eastgate Street to eat and, on the way there, they talked about his travels and the family.

It was not until they were settled at a table that Emma remembered what Hannah had said when last she spoke to her. 'There is somewhere you could try for a room and it's not that far from Mam's.'

He lowered the menu. 'Where's that?'

Her eyes gleamed with mischief. 'Bert's mother's. Last time I saw Hanny she told me one of her mother's lodgers had just left.'

A slow smile lighted Chris's face. 'Funny you should say that. It struck me while I was crossing the bridge that there was something missing in what Mrs Black had to say.'

'And what was that?'

'The absence of letters. Bert wrote to his mother saying he was going to Australia. Has he written to her since then?'

'Supposedly. Hanny told me that her mother says she's had letters from him but Hanny's never seen them. There could be letters without them coming all the way from Australia.'

'And in that case, it'd be easier to find out where they do come from without searching through the shipping booking records in Liverpool.'

Emma frowned. 'If Mrs Black's right, Joy can't have seen the envelopes. Otherwise she'd have her suspicions because of the stamp and postmark. Anyway, I'll take you to Hanny's after we've eaten. We can speak to her and Kenny about this...see what they have to say.'

Chris agreed and turned back to the menu. Over a plate of lamb chops, potatoes and mashed carrot and turnip, they talked about their father's absence from the family home and whether it was due to the unrest in the railway industry and his involvement with the union, just like David, or whether their mother was wrong and he had another woman.

'Who'd have him?' said Emma with an expressive shrug.

'People are different with different people,' said Chris.

'Anyway, tell me how you're getting on with David.'

Emma sighed. 'We see little of each other, but perhaps that's for the best. I really am fond of him but what with Mam needing my wages and my being under age and us both working long hours…' Her voice trailed off.

Chris said bluntly, 'Has he asked you to marry him? You'd see more of each other if you were wed. You're an attractive girl and you could easily be snapped up by someone else if he's not careful.'

She smiled faintly. 'Actually he said he was going to ask me to marry him when I'm twenty-one.'

Chris's eyes glinted. 'You say yes. Stop worrying about Mam and the kids. I'm here to keep my eye on them now.'

'How long will you be staying, though?' she murmured.

Chris shrugged. 'At least as long as it takes to catch the swine that did for Aggie.'

She was pleased to hear that and part of her hoped it would take some time, whilst at the same time wanting Bert caught as soon as possible. In the meantime, her brother had made her mind up for her about David. Perhaps she could slip a note through his father's letterbox. But, before then, she had to take Chris to meet Hanny and Kenny.

'So you're Emma's big brother.' Hannah smiled and held out a hand to Chris. 'We've been dying to meet you.'

'Now you have, I hope I pass muster.' He grinned as he shook her hand.

'You certainly do,' she answered instantly. 'Come in and have a cup of tea. You must meet Kenny. We're both fond of Emma.'

'How did the Rally go?' whispered Emma as they followed her into the kitchen where Tilly sat at the table, practising writing. She glanced up at them, smiled, and then lowered her head again.

'There was trouble! Isn't there always when it's an

outdoor one?' said Hanny, rolling her eyes. 'Eggs were thrown! Waste of good food, I thought.'

'I presume Mrs Stone was there. Was anyone arrested?'

'The police were there in force. There was quite a crowd so I couldn't see everything that was going on. I didn't even get to speak to Mrs Stone.'

A pot of tea was made. Kenny was called in from the office and introduced to Chris. They made small talk for a few minutes while they drank tea but then Chris said bluntly, 'I don't want to waste time, so I'll get to the point of why I'm here.' He placed his empty cup and saucer down on the hearth. 'It's about your brother, Bert.'

Tilly lifted her head and glanced in their direction.

'What about him?' asked Kenny, looking disturbed.

'I want to find him,' said Chris.

Hannah stared at him. 'Surely Emma's told you that he's in Australia?'

Chris nodded. 'But is he? I know this is distressing for you both but Mrs Black believes he's not there.'

'Why?' asked Hannah in a startled voice, 'Has she seen him?'

'She wouldn't know him if she saw him,' said Emma.

'Neither would I,' said Chris, turning to Kenny. 'So it would be handy, pal, if you could do a drawing of him for me. Mrs Black thinks he's fooling you all…that Bert's just biding his time over here somewhere, waiting to get his revenge.'

Hannah shook her head. 'I don't believe it. I don't want to believe it!' Her face had lost its colour.

Kenny put his arm round her. 'It's OK, love.'

'I'm sorry to upset you both,' said Chris, planting both hands on his knees. 'But pussy-footing around the subject won't help us. We need to know if the letters Bert sent to your mother really did come from Australia.'

Hannah sighed. 'Joy might be able to find out. I should imagine Mother would have kept all his letters.'

Chris leaned forward. 'Em was saying that your mother takes in lodgers. D'you think you could put a word in for me with your mother?'

Hannah was taken aback. 'Why?'

Chris smiled. 'I need somewhere to stay. Don't worry, I won't go as myself. Bert knows the name Griffiths. I'll think up a new identity.'

'Joy would need to know the truth,' said Hannah.

'Sure! As long as she can keep her mouth shut and doesn't blow my cover,' said Chris.

'I'd best not repeat that to my sister,' said Hannah.

'Good,' said Chris absently, his brow puckered. 'There's always the possibility that Bert arranged for your mother to pick up the letters at the post office. In that case your sister wouldn't have seen them.'

Hannah frowned. 'You could be right. Thinking about it, I can't say I see any need for you to stay there.'

'Trust Chris. He didn't work his way up to sergeant without having a reason for everything he does,' said Emma, pride in her voice. 'He has something in mind, I'm sure.'

'Sure I have,' said Chris, who only had the vaguest idea what he was going to do but he was not about to disillusion his sister.

Hannah glanced at Kenny, who nodded. 'All right!' she said. 'Do you want to go now?'

'Sure. And on the way I'll think up something to explain why you're recommending me.'

'Probably best you stick with your Christian name,' said Emma. 'You might find yourself not answering straight away to another and that would rouse suspicion.'

They all stood up and Emma said, 'I'm going to have to go back to Mrs Black's. I suppose you don't want me saying anything to her yet about what you're doing, Chris?'

He nodded. 'I'll be seeing her on Monday, I'll make the decision then what to tell her.'

Chapter Twenty-Two

April, 1910

The young woman lifted her skirts and booted the ball down the street in the lad's direction. Chris caught a glimpse of shapely calves before she dropped her skirts.

Hannah called, 'Joy!'

She turned and came hurrying towards them. Several wisps of dark hair had come loose from their pins and she tucked a curl behind an ear as she approached them. Her figure was small but nicely rounded and, immediately, Chris wanted her. He gazed into her flushed, oval shaped face with its small nose, dimpled chin and full lips, and found himself being studied just as intently. Her lively, curious eyes were the purplish-brown of ripe figs he recalled eating in Palestine.

Wiping perspiration from her brow, Joy said, 'Who's this, Hanny?'

'Hopefully Mother's new lodger,' said Hannah easily. 'Is the room still vacant?'

Joy nodded. 'What's his name? Where's he from? He looks like he's been in the sun.'

'That's because I have been in the sun,' said Chris, smiling and holding out his hand. 'I'm Emma's brother, but keep that under your hat.'

'What's he doing here?' asked Joy, ignoring the proffered hand and glancing at her sister. 'And what's he mean, *Keep it under your hat*?'

Hannah said, 'You've to forget what he's just said. We tell Mother his name is Chris Williams and he's been a clerk for the British government in India. Now he's home on leave and needs somewhere to stay for a couple of months as he's writing a book of his travels. He met Kenny in the library and they got talking and Kenny suggested I spoke to Mother about him.'

Joy raised thick dark eyebrows. 'Why the story? I thought he was in the army.'

'Bert might remember Aggie had a brother in the army,' said Chris.

Joy fixed him with a stare. 'What's Bert got to do with this?'

'Just listen,' said Chris. 'Mrs Black has this feeling that Bert never went to Australia. That he lied to fool you all into thinking he was out of the way.'

Joy's face registered disbelief and she glanced at her sister. 'You go along with this?'

Hannah said wryly, 'I'm here with him, aren't I?'

Smiling grimly, Chris said, 'From what I've heard about your brother, he's a conniving, murdering, filthy swine, whom I'd like to wipe from the face of the earth. He'd enjoy deceiving the lot of you just to get his own back.'

Joy stared at him in fascination. 'You don't pull your punches, do you? But I think you're mad. Mother's had letters from him.'

'You've seen them, have you?'

She frowned. 'No, but she's mentioned them to me and was genuinely upset when she got the first one saying he was emigrating.'

'He knew he would have to convince her that he was going that first time so you'd believe her. But afterwards he'd tell her the truth,' said Chris. 'From what I've heard she seems to be the only person he genuinely cares about.'

Joy was silent, her eyes downcast as the other two watched her, waiting. Finally, she said, 'Why haven't I thought before about never having seen one of his letters on the doormat? I'm an idiot!'

'You didn't want to think about him,' said Hannah. 'We just wanted him out of our lives.'

'Too right,' muttered Joy. 'But I should have been suspicious. He must have sent her another letter, though, to explain what he was up to...that's if it's true and he's not in Australia. After that he could arrange a meeting every now and again to keep her quiet and happy.'

'That's after he convinced her that all the stuff in the newspaper about him was lies and that it's us who are the liars,' said Hannah. 'She needs to believe he's innocent as much as we need to prove he's guilty.'

'You're smart the pair of you,' said Chris quietly. 'They're probably still meeting if he is over here.'

Joy turned her lovely eyes on him. 'You plan to watch and follow Mother and hope she leads you to him? I could do that. I'm not allowed a job outside the house, so I'm nearly always around.'

Chris shook his head. 'Even if she didn't spot you, which she easily might...what would you do if Bert were to see you? No! I want to get my hands on him and I intend to do just that.'

'He's no weakling, you know? You'd have a real fight on your hands.' Then her expression changed and she chuckled. 'We're talking as if Mrs Black's right. She could be completely wrong and Bert's in Australia. He might never have sent Mother any letters but she's lied about it, wanting to convince us that he still cares about her.'

Chris rasped his unshaven chin with a fingernail. 'If that's the truth, then we've got to prove it.'

'How are you going to do that...go all the way to Australia?' said Joy tartly.

'No. Liverpool, to check the departure records of the shipping lines to Australia...but first I'd like to meet your mother and we'll take it from there.'

Joy sighed and, without another word, walked in the direction of her parents' home. Chris raised an eyebrow and looked at Hannah, who smiled. 'She'll go along with whatever you want. She hates Bert as much as the rest of us. Come on, let's catch her up.'

* * *

'I'll want a month's rent in advance, Mr Williams,' said Susannah Kirk, gazing at him through wire-rimmed spectacles, which made her eyes appear much larger than they really were.

'That's no problem, Mrs Kirk. But does the price you quoted include meals…and will I have a room to myself?' asked Chris.

'Certainly!' She drew herself up to her full height of five feet, one inch and clasped her hands against her bosom. 'It's on the second floor and the only other person up there is my other lodger, Mr James. A very quiet gentleman, who works in the ticket office at the theatre. As for meals, I provide breakfast and an evening meal and a roast dinner fortnightly. Every other Sunday I visit a relative.'

'Fair enough,' said Chris cheerfully, his ears pricking up at the mention of the word *relative*. He reached into his pocket, taking out his wallet and removing a couple of bank notes, which he handed over to her.

Susannah thanked him and turned to Joy, 'Show Mr Williams to his room but no lingering,' she said firmly.

Joy turned a speaking look on her sister as if to say *You know what she's thinking*.

'I'll leave you to it then,' said Hannah hastily. 'I'll tell my husband you're safely settled, Mr Williams. I'm sure you'll be comfortable here. Bye for now, Mother.' She brushed Susannah's cheek with her lips and hurried out of the house, having found it difficult to look her mother straight in the eye.

'This way, Mr Williams,' said Joy in a cool voice as she led Chris towards the staircase.

He followed her, unable to take his gaze from her swaying hips. On close inspection her clothes were much more worn than Hannah's or Emma's and he guessed she didn't see anything in the way of wages for helping out at home with the paying guests. He wondered if she had any kind of life outside. If she didn't, then it was unlikely there was a boyfriend in the offing. He'd like to see her dressed in a silken sari just like the women in India. Instantly, he asked himself why the hell he was thinking such thoughts. He had a job to do and had to keep his mind on it.

He cleared his throat. 'I'll need to go out again to fetch my things.'

'Fine. There's a cup of cocoa and a biscuit at nine o'clock. You can either have it with us or on a tray in your room.' Her voice was pleasant to the ear with a hint of huskiness.

'I'll eat with the family. I'd like to get to know your mother. Make her feel at ease with me…that way she might just forget to be on her guard and slip up when talking.'

They had reached the first landing and Joy stopped and gave him a startled look. 'Surely you're not going to mention Bert to her?'

'Do you take me for a fool?' His eyes locked with hers and he smiled.

She did not look away but colour stained her cheeks. 'I don't know you, but Hanny seems to think we can trust you, so I'll try and do the same.'

'That's real good of you. I'll try and not disappoint,' he said dryly.

'I hope so.' Joy turned away and started up the next flight of stairs.

Chris kept his distance, so it was easier to watch that seductive sway of her hips. 'Your mother said that she visits a relative. Who's that?'

'Her cousin who lives in Moreton. She's getting on. Every fortnight she goes to see her.'

'Are you sure about that?'

She paused. 'I was until you put doubt in my mind.'

'You don't ever go with her?'

'The odd time if asked. I prefer having some time to

myself. I'd like a job outside the house but Mother's nerves are bad and she needs me at home.'

'What if you were to marry?'

She had reached the top landing and stood waiting for him. 'I don't see what that's got to do with you,' she said firmly.

'I'm just curious. You're real nice looking...have lovely eyes.'

She moistened her lips and then, with a toss of her head, said abruptly, 'I'll have none of that talk.'

'You don't like compliments?'

'It's what's behind the compliment that bothers me. You've probably had loads of girls falling over themselves to please you.'

'Not loads,' he said, a smile in his voice. 'I've been in the army abroad, luv, didn't get to mix with many decent lasses. That's why I appreciate meeting someone like you.'

She said crossly, 'You're doing it again.'

He tried to look innocent. 'Doing what? Being nice to you? Why are you so suspicious of me? Is your mother to blame or is it having a brother like Bert that's put you off men?'

Her eyes flashed. 'I know there are lots of men who are decent. I just don't want you turning on the charm, thinking I'm desperate for a man.' She walked over to a door on their left, turned the key that was in the lock and pushed open the door.

Sunlight flooded out, momentarily blinding her. She stepped backwards and bumped into Chris, who grabbed her by the shoulders. For an instant she remained still in his hold and he could not resist lowering his head and kissing the nape of her neck. She gasped and tore herself out of his grasp, turned and glared at him. 'You've got a nerve after what I said. Touch me again and you'll know about it.' She left him and hurried down the stairs.

Chris swore beneath his breath but did not go after her.

It looked like he really couldn't rush things with Joy or her mother.

He went into his room and inspected it swiftly; single bed, chest-of-drawers, washbasin in a stand with a jug beneath, hanging space in an alcove one side of the fireplace, shelves the other, as well as a text *Till He Comes* on the wall behind the made up bed. There was an easy chair and a small table. He glanced under the bed and saw a po. It looked like Mrs Kirk had thought of most things. He left the room, locking the door after him and pocketing the key. Then he ran downstairs and quit the house to go and collect his things from his mother's.

Joy heard the front door close and hurried into the parlour. She lifted the net curtain and gazed after him. She liked a tall man...and those shoulders. A sigh escaped her. She had never thought Emma's brother would be so attractive. When he had touched her, it had started a chain reaction that had not only turned her limbs to jelly but set her heart fluttering like a caged canary. But she'd had to put a stop to his advances. If her mother was to get a hint that he had caught her fancy, she'd have him out of the house like a shot. And what hope would there be of finding out where Bert was then? She had to keep her wayward body and emotions under control and her mind on why he was here at all times.

'More potatoes, Mr Williams?' Joy offered the tureen to Chris.

It was the evening of the following day.

'Thank you, Miss Kirk.' As he took the dish, his fingers brushed hers. They quivered and he shot a glance at her face but she gazed back at him woodenly. He forked out a potato and asked if anyone else wanted the last one.

'You go ahead, lad,' said Jock. 'I've had sufficient.'

'Mrs Kirk?' offered Chris.

She smiled and waved him away. He offered the dish to

the other lodger, who shook his fair head, and then to young Master Kirk. Freddie nodded and speared the remaining potato and put it straight into his mouth.

'He's a growing boy,' excused Joy hastily for this show of bad table manners.

Susannah was frowning at her youngest son. 'It's a pity your brother isn't here. He had perfect table manners.'

Joy could not resist saying, 'Perhaps Bert shouldn't have gone to Australia but stayed here to be the perfect example to Freddie.'

Chris could scarcely believe what he heard her say and decided not to let the opportunity slip. 'You have a son in Australia, Mrs Kirk?' he asked.

Her answer was short and to the point. 'Yes.'

'What part of Australia? I have a couple of cousins who work for a telegraph company out there,' he lied glibly.

Susannah hesitated. 'He's an engineer like his father and works at something to do with shipping. I can never remember the name of the place. At my age, Mr Williams, the memory starts to go.' Her smile was that of a sweet, forgetful, old lady.

'I think yer told me it was Perth, Sue,' said Jock.

'Did I? Then it must be there.' Her eyes showed relief and she turned to Chris. 'Are your cousins anywhere nearby?'

Chris had his answer ready. 'They travel about connecting telegraph lines as well as doing repairs. I never know where to get in touch with them. It's a vast country, Mrs Kirk, as I'm sure your son's told you.'

She nodded vaguely and then asked her daughter to clear the dishes away and fetch the pudding. Joy hurried to comply with her orders, determined to get the meal over with, the dishes washed and put away. Then she would go to her room and finish her library book, hopefully it would help her to put the last half hour out of her mind. Yet she could not help but admire Emma's brother for his seizing of the moment. She wondered if he really did have cousins in Australia. If not, it proved just what a smooth talker he was. As for what her mother had said...was she as forgetful as she had made out? Surely if Bert was writing to her then he would have written descriptions of the place where he lived and worked. Joy would much rather her elder brother was in Perth, than somewhere at large in the North West of England.

'Miss Kirk, can I talk to you?' Chris caught up with Joy as she strode down Egerton Street with a shopping basket on her arm several days later.

Joy barely glanced at him. 'I thought the idea was that you persuade my mother to divulge secrets, not me.'

He looked incredulous. 'On a Monday morning? She's doing the washing and I don't think she'd appreciate my bothering her. If washing day in your house is anything like it was in ours, then she's going to be at it all day. Besides, I've an appointment with Mrs Black...and I want to call in on your sister and her husband on the way. I'm hoping he has that drawing of Bert for me.'

Joy hesitated only a moment before saying, 'I was going to call in on them, too, and ask Hannah if she wants to go shopping with me.'

'Perhaps I can walk with you then.'

She said dryly, 'If I say no you'll probably follow me, anyhow. So perhaps it's better if I have you under my eye, rather than behind my back.'

He smiled. 'I suppose you'd like me to say sorry for the other day?'

'Are you sorry?'

'No. You have a lovely neck.'

She rolled her eyes. 'Then what's the point of saying sorry? Perhaps we'd better change the subject.'

Chris adopted a mournful expression. 'It was only a little kiss.'

'Little or large…we'd only just met.'

'Then perhaps when we know each other better I could try again?' There was a gleam in his eye that made her feel hot. She gave him a withering glance and changed the subject.

'Will you tell Mrs Black that you're lodging at our house and what you've found out so far?'

'I can't see any point in not telling her. Our aim is the same…to see that your brother can't hurt anyone else and that he gets his just desserts.'

Joy looked thoughtful. 'I can't help wondering why she cares so much. Unless she's just one of those people who can't help interfering in other people's lives.'

'You could be partly right.'

'Hanny seems to think well of her, despite what she does.'

There was a note in Joy's voice that caused Chris to grin. 'You think it's all codswallop?'

She raised her eyes to the heavens. 'What do you think?'

'When I was in India and Palestine I saw things that I'd have said were impossible. Strange things happen in life. Why is it that you can feel something for a person the first time you meet them that makes you think this is the one?'

Joy's step faltered and she glanced at him. 'Are you talking in general, Mr Williams?'

'No, Miss Kirk,' said Chris solemnly. 'But perhaps we should change the subject before you swipe me one. Tell me what you do with yourself when you're not helping your mother or visiting your sister?'

'I read, I walk…I've been along to several Women's Suffrage meetings.'

'You're one of them, too.'

She stiffened. 'You make it sound as if there's something funny about us. The law needs to change so women on their own can support themselves.'

'If they can do that, then maybe they won't want to get married,' said Chris.

'And who can blame them? I don't want to be under a man's thumb. Although, at the moment it's Mother who orders me around,' she said ruefully.

'At least if you marry, you'll have a home of your own.'

'True. But if I marry, I want to have an equal say in everything,' she said robustly.

He frowned. 'There's nothing wrong with having your say but in the end if a couple can't agree, someone has to make the final decision and that should be the man.'

'Why?' She didn't give him a chance to answer. 'I suppose you're one of those men who thinks women's brains aren't as good as a man's?'

'Well, my sister did make the big mistake of going out with your brother and ending up dead,' he said, exasperated.

His words shocked Joy into silence and, for several moments, she could not answer him. Then she found her voice. 'She wasn't the first person to be fooled by Bert. She must have really fallen for him and love makes fools of both women and men from what I've heard.'

'Then you've never been in love?'

She stared at him and felt the colour rush to her cheeks. Mad at him for making her feel the way she did, she made no answer but hurried away.

Chris caught up with her just before she reached the gates to the yard. 'There was no need to run away,' he said.

'No! But I feel better for it.'

'You certainly look it. Your cheeks are all rosy and your eyes are sparkling.'

Joy stamped her foot. 'Don't start paying me compliments again. It won't wash.'

'You're really hard to please,' he said mildly. 'But have it your way, I'll keep my thoughts to myself in future.' He walked through the open gates and across the yard, leaving her to follow him this time.

Kenny had a sketch of Bert ready, having etched him in

coloured chalks on blue sugar paper. Chris gazed down at the face of the man believed responsible for his sister's death and understood, for the first time, why Aggie had fallen for him. 'Handsome devil, isn't he?'

'Devil is the right word,' said Kenny grimly. 'You know what it says in the Bible about the devil? That he looks like an angel of light.'

'It was the way Bert used to say things that got me going,' said Hannah. 'The words could sound so innocent when he said them to Mother but I knew he meant something else entirely.'

'Mother always took him at face value,' said Joy, turning away. 'I don't want to look at him anymore. Are you coming, Hanny?'

Hannah took her purse out of the dresser drawer, picked up her shopping bag and shrugged on her coat. With a 'See you later!' the sisters left.

Kenny placed the drawing in a large envelope and handed it to Chris. 'It's up to you now. My foot has put me out of the reckoning. I hope next time I see you that you've found out where he is.'

Chris nodded. 'Me too.'

It did not take Chris long to reach Mrs Black's house. He arrived there as Emma was on her way out. She was wearing a russet coloured costume with a mandarin collared cream blouse underneath. On her hair she wore a brown beribboned straw hat.

'You look nice. Where are you going?' said her brother, smiling.

She bobbed him a curtsey. 'Thank yer kindly sir! I've got a couple of hours off, so I'm nipping along to David's house and popping a note through the letterbox, asking him to meet me. Hopefully he can find the time to do so.'

'He'll be a fool if he lets you go, Em.'

She gave a faint smile. 'Fingers crossed. But before I go, tell me whether you've learnt anything so far, staying at the Kirks'?' Chris told her about the exchange between himself and Mrs Kirk at the table and he showed her the drawing of Bert. Her mouth tightened. 'That's him to a T.'

'Then you can leave him to me. Go and sort out your love life.' He squeezed her shoulder, stepped inside the house and headed on upstairs.

Emma hesitated at the foot of the step, thinking of the reasons why she was doing this. David was strong where her father was weak. She found him physically attractive and he held views similar to her own…and, although, he could be forgetful at times, he could also be extremely thoughtful. Most of all, though, she thought she loved him. Taking a deep breath, she went up the step and without hesitation, pushed the envelope through the letterbox.

She was almost at the bottom of the street when she heard running feet behind her and her name being called. She whirled round and saw David. His arm was in a sling and there was bruising on his face.

She hurried towards him. 'What's happened to yer?' she cried in distress, seizing the hand that held her letter and crushing it.

'I was attacked,' he said with a grim smile.

She gaped at him. 'Hell! Did yer see who attacked you?'

'No. He came from behind.'

'Have yer any idea who it was?'

He shook his head. 'It came out of the blue. I could understand it, if it had happened a year or so ago. I know I made enemies when we were striking for better working conditions and more money.'

'Where did it happen?'

'I was pushed down the station stairway and was no good for anything for a week. If I didn't know that swine, Bert, was in Australia, I'd have blamed him. Have you got time to come back to the house now? My stepmother's out and it feels ages since I've seen you.'

She gazed up into his face and reaching up a hand, gently caressed his cheek. 'I'll make the time,' she said unsteadily.

He kissed the fingers so close to his mouth and then with his undamaged arm about her shoulders, they walked back to the house.

They sat on the sofa in the parlour and she nestled within David's sound arm. Bringing down his face close to hers, she kissed him. In between kisses she told him that she was fed up of living without him and wanted to marry him as soon as she was twenty-one. He accepted her proposal and for a while after that there was little time for sensible thought or talk.

Later, over a cup of tea and a sandwich, Emma told him how Mrs Black was convinced Bert was not in Australia. 'If she's right, then it could have been him who pushed you down those steps, just as he did Kenny; an act of revenge for you punching him in the face.'

David glowered. 'If that's true then we've got to warn the others,' he said.

Emma nodded. 'We can go to the yard first and tell Hanny.'

'I'm coming with you. My arm might be broken but I'll get the walking stick that belonged to my old granny just in case we bump into Bert. I'm not going to let him get away this time.'

Chapter Twenty-Three

April, 1910

'So Mrs Black could be right,' said Hannah, gripping Kenny's hand.

'We don't know for sure,' he said hastily. 'But it seems too much of a coincidence both David and I being pushed from behind down steps at railway stations for it not to be Bert.'

'So what do we do about this?' said Emma.

'I'll speak to Joy,' said Hannah. 'See what she thinks is the best way to approach Mother. She must know where he is.'

'But will she tell you?' said Kenny. 'Without proof, she'll refuse to believe him guilty.'

'We've got to give her the chance to help us,' said Hannah fiercely.

'But if she refuses you'll have put her on her guard and there'll be no chance of her meeting Bert and Chris being able to follow her,' cried Emma, banging her fist on the table.

'She's right,' said David. 'Once she knows we suspect him of being around, then she'll stay away from him.'

'So what do we do?' said Hannah, exasperated. 'I for one am going to find it difficult acting like nothing has changed. I'll be looking over my shoulder all the time.'

'There's no need for that. He must have a job, so it's unlikely he'll be around weekdays,' said Kenny. 'If he's going to try anything it'll be evenings or Sunday. And they're the times you don't go out on your own.'

'I'd go further than that,' put in David. 'None of the women or Tilly should be out on their own until we catch him. He could be working shifts.'

They all looked at each other, aghast.

Emma rose from her chair, glancing at the clock on the mantelpiece. 'I'd best get back to Victoria Crescent. On the way, we could slip into the car showroom in Lower Bridge Street and let Seb know what's happened. He can tell Alice.'

'At least she's not alone in the house,' said Hannah rapidly.

David got to his feet and so did the other two.

Hannah looked at Kenny and shook her head. 'You don't really want to come to Mother's with me.'

'I know you'll be quicker without me, love, but I'd best go with you,' he said.

She did not argue with him.

As soon as David and Emma had spoken to Seb, he closed the showroom and went with them to Victoria Crescent. It came as something of a surprise to Seb and Emma to hear the sound of heated voices as they approached the two houses. 'That's Ma's voice,' said Seb, and put on a spurt. Emma realised the other voice belonged to Mrs Black and immediately guessed it was about the warning letter that Mrs Black's solicitor had sent to the older Mrs Bennett. So, it appeared, did Seb. 'I just hope Ma's not tearing her hair out,' he added.

No sooner were the words out of his mouth, than they saw the two women. They were on the pavement close to Mrs Black's gate. Alice was also there, nursing the baby. Several of the neighbours were peeping over their hedges or loitering just outside their gates. Seb marched up to his mother and said quietly, 'In the house, Ma!'

'Not until this woman says she's sorry for threatening me and insulting me,' shrieked Gabrielle.

'I told only the truth,' said Mrs Black, her dark eyes angry as she smoothed down her hair with a hand. 'Your mother needs putting in a cage, Mr Bennett. She has the manners of an alley cat...but that's not so surprising seeing as how that's where she came from.'

'You liar!' Gabrielle lifted a hand but Seb caught hold of her and pulled her back against him.

'Stop it, Ma! D'you want her to have you up for assault?'

Gabrielle's magnificent dark eyes flashed. 'She wouldn't dare! I could tell people things about her. How she came from the slums and worked her way up to where she is now.'

Mrs Black smiled. 'I'm not ashamed of where I came from. It's pride I feel, Gertie, for what I've achieved.'

'Gertie?' exclaimed Alice.

'That's her real name,' said Mrs Black. 'We came from the same street and there was nothing she enjoyed better then making up stories and pretending to be someone else. And who could blame her?'

'Is this true?' asked Alice, glancing at her mother-in-law.

'Lies! It's all lies,' said Gabrielle without conviction.

Mrs Black said, almost dreamily, 'She had a mother who liked the gin bottle too much and couldn't cope with eight children. Her husband was away at sea most of the time. A nice singing voice Gertie had when she was young.'

'That's true,' said Gabrielle.

Mrs Black smiled. 'She eventually made it to the stage. That's where we met up again. My mother used to read the teacups and told fortunes at fairs. I don't remember my father. I discovered I had a gift and was starting to make a name for myself. Gertie was glad to see a familiar face and when Thomas Waters was wracked with guilt, she introduced us and I fell for him…that was the end of any friendship between us. He insisted on me getting rid of my baby.' There was a tremor in her voice and she swallowed before continuing. 'But she refused because she was such a good Catholic girl despite being his mistress. Isn't that true, Gertie?'

Gabrielle nodded and her eyes were damp. 'I loved him and I wanted his child.' She sighed. 'I should never have come back here. I should have stayed in my little house in Liverpool and taken up good works at St Anthony's.

Instead I decided to try singing again, starting in a couple of pubs where I was once popular…but things did not happen as quickly as I wanted them to and I lost heart; I was drinking as much as I was singing. Eventually I was arrested for being drunk and disorderly. I hit a policeman and that's how I ended up in a Black Maria with Mrs Stone. I'll leave straight away.' Without glancing at her son, she walked up the path.

Seb stared at Mrs Black in amazement and understanding. 'Truth will out,' she said softly.

Emma couldn't take her eyes off her. 'You're full of surprises, aren't yer? I must say a few things make more sense now.'

Mrs Black smiled. 'You, Emma, not yer. But I'm glad you believe me…and that you've brought your young man to see me…for healing perhaps.'

'I think my arm can heal itself, Mrs Black,' said David, amused. 'But we're here because we think you could be right about Bert.'

'Then you'd both best come in and bring me up to date,' said Mrs Black with a satisfied gleam in her eye. 'We'll leave Mr and Mrs Bennett to sort out Gertie.'

Seb and Alice stood in the doorway of Gabrielle's bedroom, watching her pack her things into a suitcase. 'You don't have to go, Ma. I'm not ashamed of your upbringing. You did well to make it on to the stage in the first place,' said Seb.

'You think I don't know that,' she said, without looking up. 'Now get out of my room. I want to change into my best costume before I leave.'

Against her better judgement but feeling sorry for her mother-in-law, Alice said, 'Seb's right, Mrs Bennett. You don't have to go. James needs a grandmother.'

'It is kind of you to say so, Alice, but you'll do better without me.'

'What about the old lady, Ma?' asked Seb in a low voice. 'Are you going to desert her, as well?'

Gabrielle stilled and then she moved swiftly and closed the door in their faces.

Alice looked at Seb. 'What do we do?'

'Give her time to think,' he said quietly, 'Now I've another surprise for you.'

'Has it anything to do with Emma and David? Are they getting married?' asked Alice, a smile lighting her face.

Seb shrugged. 'I don't know anything about that. What I do know is that David was pushed down the steps at the General Station and they think it might have been Bert.'

Alice's smile faded. 'Bu – but it can't be! He's in Australia. He wrote to his mother telling her he was going.'

'I know. But think, Alice. If you wanted someone to stop looking for you, what would you do if you were Bert?' She did not speak and then blindly she reached out for him. He put his arms round her and she rested her head against his chest. 'You mustn't be scared,' he said. 'I'll look after you.'

'I'm not scared for myself.' Alice lifted her head. 'I'm not alone. Cook's here as well as Mary. She knows what he looks like. But perhaps you should tell the police about your suspicions.'

Seb smoothed back her auburn hair. 'They can't be everywhere. Besides, they'd want more proof than we've got. But apparently Emma's brother is home from the army and he's trying to find Bert. He's actually lodging with the Kirks so as to keep an eye on Mrs Kirk, hoping she'll lead him to him.'

Alice nodded. 'Then I'm not going to worry about Bert. If he's still over here, then she'll know where he is. I must stay calm for the baby's sake. I'll do what Hanny did...lock all the doors and windows and make sure he can't get in.'

'You won't forget?'

Alice said calmly, 'I'm a mother now.' For a moment she thought about Mrs Black and how she had sounded when she had spoken of having to get rid of her baby. For the first time ever, she felt some pity for the woman for never having had the pleasure of holding her child in her arms.

Eudora gazed out of the front window, watching David and Emma saying their goodbyes at the front gate. She wondered how much longer she would have the services of that young woman, guessing that wedding bells would soon be ringing out for the couple. She would miss Emma, but people had to move on and, perhaps after that public quarrel and declaration, it was time for her to consider living elsewhere, too.

She moved away from the window as Emma turned and began to make her way up the path. There was no rush. She would take her time searching for a suitable house. Perhaps with a sea view this time. But, before then, she would look forward to the next visit from Emma's resourceful brother. Fancy his coming up with the idea of lodging with the Kirks. The young man showed plenty of promise and would be useful to have around.

The following Sunday morning, Chris left the Kirks' house straight after breakfast, so as to get to Chester General Station before Mrs Kirk. She had mentioned last evening that she was visiting her cousin in Moreton but he doubted the truth of that since discovering what had happened to Emma's David. Armed with last evening's Wirral edition of the *Liverpool Echo*, he stood near the ticket windows, with his cap pulled forward, pretending to read the newspaper.

Here was Mrs Kirk now! She was wearing a black hat with what appeared to be a whole blackbird's wing as decoration. She carried a basket on her arm and seemed to be in a hurry. He strained his ears to hear her state her destination and a satisfied smile creased his sunburnt face. As soon as she was away from the window, he folded his newspaper and hurried to buy a ticket. Then he raced up the metallic steps and across the overhead bridge to the platform where the train to Liverpool would be leaving in five minutes, unaware that he was being watched.

On reaching the head of the steps going down to the platform where the train was waiting, he was in time to note which carriage Mrs Kirk entered. He chose the next one for himself to travel in. He was going to have to keep his eyes open when they reached Liverpool, as there were three stations where she might alight and he mustn't lose sight of her.

Fortunately he knew the port well. As a lad, he had run away from home and, before joining the army, had gone to Liverpool. Living on his wits, he'd run errands for those visiting the city by train or ship. Susannah Kirk did not alight at James Street or Exchange Station in Liverpool, so he was prepared when the train reached its destination at Central Station to give her a few minutes' headstart before climbing down from the carriage. Despite being a small woman who could easily be lost in a crowd, he was able to keep his eye on her as she made her way to the turnstile because of that black hat.

He was not far behind her as she left the station and turned into Ranelagh Street in the direction of Church Street. Any other day, the pavements would be packed with workers, shoppers and pickpockets, the roads jammed with horse drawn carts, motor vehicles, trams and bicycles. Today the streets were Sunday quiet with just a few window-shoppers and the occasional vehicle, tram or bicycle. He knew he was going to have to keep a reasonable distance behind her, so as to be certain that she would not spot him if she suddenly turned round.

She bobbed along, her black skirts brushing the ground, reminding him of a clockwork toy. She reached the gates of Liverpool's parish church of St Peter, situated opposite the twin-towered Compton Hotel, and entered the grounds.

Chris swore under his breath before going through the open gates. The soot-begrimed bulk of the church lay ahead of him but Mrs Kirk had already vanished from sight. She could have entered the church or hurried up the side to the gardens at the rear. There she would find benches for people to relax on and enjoy this green oasis in the heart of the town. He should have looked at the board displaying the times of services, but as he couldn't hear any hymn singing he presumed the morning service was over. Still it could be quiet because people were praying. He didn't dare go inside. From his experience of church, he knew that even if he was on tiptoe, someone would hear him and heads would turn. So he chose to stay out in the fresh air. Directing his gaze downwards so his face was partially hidden by his cap, he made his way to the gardens to the rear.

Almost immediately he spotted Mrs Kirk's hat. She was sitting on a bench the other side of a triangular flowerbed planted with tulips and wallflowers. Her back was towards him so she faced the sun. Next to her sat a man wearing a straw boater tipped forward so that Chris could clearly see the neatly cut fair hair in the nape of his neck. He had powerful shoulders and dwarfed the woman. If it came to a fight, he wouldn't be a pushover, that was for sure, thought Chris grimly, recalling what Joy had said.

Noticing an empty bench, facing the opposite direction to them, Chris strolled over to it. He wouldn't be able to watch but hopefully he could hear them talking and, when they got up to leave, he could follow. He sat down on the sun-warmed timber and, closing his eyes, held his face up to the sun.

'You make lovely sandwiches, Mother…and you've brought my favourite cake. You're a marvel.' There was affection in Bert's voice.

'I worry. I worry that widow you lodge with doesn't feed you properly,' said Susannah loudly. Chris guessed she was going deaf and because of that, did not pitch her voice at a normal level. 'I wish you could come home.'

'Look at me, Mother. Do I look half-starved?' teased Bert. 'She feeds me fine but her cooking's not a patch on yours...and Mrs O'Shaughnessy does have her good points. She changes the sheets regular and makes sure my room is kept spick and span.'

'So you've told me before.' Bert's mother sounded peeved.

'That's because I know those sort of things are important to you.'

There was a silence and Chris imagined them eating the lovely sandwiches. He was hungry after leaving the house early. A few minutes passed and he heard the muted sound of footsteps. They stopped nearby and he sensed someone had sat down the other end of his bench. He was tempted to open his eyes but then Mrs Kirk spoke and he pricked up his ears, not wanting to miss a word.

'I've got a new lodger,' she said.

'Oh ay! Woman or man?' asked Bert.

'A Mr Williams. He's been working for the government in India and is on leave. He's writing a book, so Hannah said.'

'A book? A pen pusher, is he?' His tone was disparaging. 'Young or middle-aged?'

'About your age or maybe a couple of years older. Sun ages the skin, so it's difficult to pinpoint his age exactly.' She sighed. 'He's nice looking, though.'

'I hope Dah's making sure he keeps his distance from our Joy,' growled Bert.

'I must admit that worries me. I can sense there's already something between the pair of them but they scarcely exchange two words. I've warned her, anyway. She knows where her duty lies. If anything were to happen to Jock, I couldn't live on my own and our Freddie's not going to hang around once he leaves school. He's only ten and is talking about going to sea as soon as he's old enough.'

'You need to keep a tight rein on our Joy. This women's suffrage thing is filling girls' heads with all kinds of nonsense, making them think they can be men's equals,' he sneered.

'I know! It's all wrong. God only knows where it'll lead if they were to get their way. Here, son, have a drink of this ginger beer. I made it specially for you.'

He thanked her and there was a break in the conversation while he drank. Then abruptly he said, 'You mentioned our Hannah telling you this lodger bloke is writing a book. How does she know that?'

Chris opened his eyes, blinked against the sun's brightness and closed them again.

'She brought him round. Apparently Kenny met him in the library. He said he was looking for digs and she remembered I had a vacancy. I wish she'd brought Tilly with her, I hardly see her now. I blame Alice. She was a good girl when her mother was alive but since that husband of hers came into money, she thinks she's somebody. She's got a baby now. A son, who should have been yours. He could have been my grandchild if she'd married you.'

'Are they still living in the same house?'

'As far as I know. Now remind me where is it in Australia you're supposed to be living? Jock said Perth. I had to agree because I couldn't remember what you'd written that first time.'

'It was Perth. I read about it in a book. They have black swans on the river. Remember that, Mother, if the subject should come up. Now how about a walk to the Pierhead? You can take the ferry to Birkenhead and catch the train home from there. It's such a lovely spring day and the sea breezes will be good for you. You can look in the shop windows on the way and see how they're getting on with the Royal Liver Building. They reckon it's not far off finished now.'

Damn, damn, damn, thought Chris, not moving and keeping his head down in case they happened to walk round his side of the flowerbed. A few minutes passed and he heard the person sitting on his bench get up and opened his eyes. He caught a swift glimpse of a neat pair of ankles in short buttoned boots and the swirl of a blue skirt and then they vanished from his sight. He stayed where he was but no one else passed him and, after several moments, he got up and strolled towards the open gates.

Once outside the gates he stood on the pavement, thinking. He had decided not to follow them to the Pierhead – Bert was his prey, not Mrs Kirk – so what was the point of such a long walk. On such a fine Sunday there would be quite a crowd on the landing stage and he could easily lose Bert in the crush. Then there would be the walk back up, following in his tracks. There must be an easier way to discover where he lived than doing that. Why meet here in the grounds of St Peter's church? Mrs Kirk could have got off the train in James Street to go to the Pierhead if Bert lived down that way. Could be that Bert's lodgings were within walking distance of Central Station, as well as Lime Street, which was only a few minutes away.

There were several streets in the area that boasted temperance hotels, guest houses and the like. Recalling Bert's mention of his landlady, the widow O'Shaughnessy, he decided that he could look her up in the *Kelly's Directory*, a copy of which he would probably find in the free library in William Brown Street. There was bound to be a number of people of that name with so many Irish living in the port, but he knew to look for a widow running a boarding house. He would have to come back tomorrow, but as Mrs Black was paying him generous expenses, that was no hardship. Right now he was hungry and thirsty, so decided to head for the nearest pub. With a bit of luck the pub might serve scouse pie or spare ribs and cabbage. He'd order one or the other and, afterwards, take the train back to Chester.

The train drew in to James Street station and Chris opened one eye and looked out of the window at the few passengers on the platform. Then he opened the other eye and sat up straight. *It couldn't be. What the hell was she doing here?* He watched Joy climb into the neighbouring compartment and was about to turn away when he saw a man, wearing a straw boater and striped blazer, come running along the platform and dive into the compartment after her, just in time because the train began to move.

Chris blinked. He had only seen the back of Bert but he was convinced it was him. Reaching into his inside pocket, he took out a folded sheet of paper and gazed down at the drawing. Despite the nose being crooked on the man he had just seen, he was convinced it was him. Cramming the sheet of paper back in his pocket, Chris got up. Joy could be alone with the swine and God only knew what he might do to her. He slid open the door and hurried along the swaying corridor until he came to the next compartment. Keeping his face hidden as much as he could, he glanced through the window and ran a quick eye over the four occupants.

Whatever terrible fate he had imagined happening to Joy proved false. It was true she looked tense. The muscles of her face were set rigid and her lips compressed. Her arms were folded defensively across her bosom and her gaze was focused on her tapping foot. A smiling Bert sat across from her. There was something about that smile that reminded Chris of a Commanding Sergeant Major who had tried to scare the living daylights out of him during his army training. He wanted to rush into the compartment and wipe the smile off his face. He imagined that smile being the last thing Aggie had seen before she had plunged into the canal. Anger and grief tightened his chest but he knew the wisest course at the moment was not to draw attention to himself. With two witnesses present, it was hardly the right time to confront Bert.

Chris returned to his seat, determined to keep a watch for anyone leaving Joy's compartment at the next station. As it happened it was Bert who left the train at Birkenhead's Hamilton Square. For a moment Chris thought of following him but even as he watched, Bert was swallowed up by the passengers on the busy platform. Instead, he decided to join Joy in the next compartment.

He made his way along the corridor and slid open the door. Joy glanced up, but except for a sudden widening of her brown eyes and two bright spots of colour on her cheeks, she showed little surprise at seeing him. He sat beside her and his shoulder brushed her arm.

She sniffed. 'You've been drinking,' she murmured.

'I was thirsty.'

'You've just missed Bert.'

'I saw him.'

'Then why didn't you go after him?' she whispered.

Chris said in a barely audible voice, 'When I take on your brother, I want to be perfectly sober when I wipe that smile off his face.'

'But he knows now that I know he's not in Australia. He could vanish again.'

'Why should he? You don't know where he lives, and I'd hazard a guess that your mother has never been to his lodgings. Perhaps he'll think of moving but I doubt he'll do it straight away.'

Joy leaned towards him. 'That doesn't help us to find him. You could have followed him, drunk or not.'

'I'm not drunk,' he said indignantly. 'I'm just drowsy after being up since the crack of dawn so as to get to the station before your mam.'

'And what good did that do you if we still don't know where he lives? Fine detective you are! You didn't even follow them when you had the chance.' She sounded cross.

How did she know that? Unless…had she been the girl who'd sat on the same bench and got up after Bert and his mother left? He opened his eyes and her face was only inches away. The urge to kiss her was irresistible. His lips barely touched hers but it was long enough for him to know he was going to have to do it again and at greater length.

She drew back as if bitten and hissed, 'How dare you kiss me with people watching.'

Chris glanced at the young couple sitting circumspectly across from each other, gazing out of the window obviously listening to every word they were saying but pretending otherwise. 'The gentleman would probably like to do the same but is more respectable than me,' he murmured.

'You're not respectable at all,' retorted Joy. 'Besides, how was it that I sat a few feet away from you and you didn't even know I was there?'

He said lazily, 'I noticed you had pretty ankles when you left to follow Bert and your mam. Pity you trailed them because it must have been then that he spotted you.'

She looked uncomfortable. 'I know. Could you have done any better?'

'He wasn't going home, so I didn't see the point. You'd have been much better off saying hello to me. I'd have taken you for a drink and a bowl of scouse. We could have discussed the best way to find out where Bert is living from their conversation and the meeting place.'

'So you've worked it out, have you?'

He smiled and closed his eyes. 'You heard what I heard. You believe you're my equal, so work it out for yourself. When you do, I'll believe your brain is as good as mine.'

Chapter Twenty-Four

April, 1910

'I'll show him,' muttered Joy, scrapping at egg yolk that had hardened on a breakfast plate. 'He thinks he's so clever. Well, I'll prove I'm just as smart as he is.'

'Did you say something?'

Joy almost jumped out of her skin at the sound of her mother's voice. 'Just talking to myself,' she said hastily.

Susannah pursed her lips and shook her head. 'Keep your eye on the whites while I nip to the shops. I'm out of washing soda. After that you can brush the lobby and wash the step. I don't want you wasting time talking to Mr Williams when he leaves his room.'

Joy did not answer but her chest swelled with indignation, recalling the conversation between her brother and mother yesterday. She had always known her mother cared for Bert more than the rest of her children. But how could she have kept his whereabouts a secret from them, turning a blind eye to his wickedness? It was wrong. So why was she working her fingers to the bone for her mother and remaining at her beck and call? She was nineteen, and, if she did what her mother wanted, she'd be too old to get a man by the time she was free. The women's rights movement might go on about men lording it over women but there must be thousands like herself, dictated to by their mothers with little chance of ever making a life for themselves, whilst encouraging their sons to believe that women were only fit to lick their boots. Well, this worm was about to turn. The lobby and step could wait...they only got dirty again, anyway. She would raid the tin of coppers in the cupboard and go and prove to Chris Griffiths, at least, that she was his equal.

During the night hours, when she had tried to forget

how his kiss had made her feel and instead think of a way of finding Bert's whereabouts, it had suddenly struck her that she could look up the name of his landlady in a street directory. She was not sure where to find one but bet a pound to a penny Hanny would know. She finished the dishes and changed into her Sunday best clothes.

'You want to know what?' asked Hannah.

'Where to find a street directory for Liverpool,' replied Joy.

'It's called a *Kelly's Directory* and I doubt you'll find one in Chester library. You'll have to go to the free library in William Brown Street in Liverpool.'

'Thanks!' Joy hugged her before heading for the front door.

'Hang on. What d'you want it for?'

'Tell you next time I see you.' She waved a hand and hurried out, hoping she would not bump into her mother on the way to the station.

Joy was in luck and was soon sitting next to the window in a third-class carriage. When she reached Liverpool, she asked a railway porter for directions to the free library. In no time at all, she was walking through St John's Gardens to the rear of St George's Hall and soon arrived at her destination. She voiced her request to the librarian at the counter, who told her exactly where to find the latest copy of *Kelly's Directory.*

Filled with a sense of triumph, she took it off the shelf and began to search its pages. To her dismay she discovered there was at least seventy people of the name O'Shaughnessy. Oh Lord! She should have remembered that Liverpool was snowing with Irish. Then her face brightened as she recalled that she was looking for a widow woman, so that would get rid of a fair number of them. She counted the women. Eight! She would need to write them down. She patted the pockets of her jacket, even as she realised that stupidly she hadn't thought to bring pencil and paper.

'Looking for these?' said a voice behind her.

Joy spun round and saw Chris holding out a pencil and paper. 'I'm impressed,' he said, smiling.

'So you should be,' she retorted, taking the pencil and paper from him. Her fingers shook as she began to write down the first name and address, conscious of him standing over her.

'There's no need to write down the whole lot.'

She looked up at him. 'All right. I'm not proud. Go on, tell me why not?'

'You might have noticed there's a part of the directory that has addresses in alphabetical order. We're looking for a lodging house. So along with Mrs O'Shaughnessy there'll be other people living at the same address, say a 2a or 6b…something like that.'

'You mean we could find Bert's name in here?'

'Depends on how long he's lived there and whether he's given a false name. Also, how well do you know Liverpool?'

She looked up at him. 'You're saying I need a street map.'

'I'm saying that these two addresses…' he put a finger on them, 'are the most likely places for Bert to be lodging. They're about a ten minute walk from Lime Street station and not much further from the grounds of St Peter's where your mam met him. They're in an area where there's a great number of lodging houses, small hotels and guest houses.' His eyes met hers. 'What say we go and look them over?'

Joy could see no reason to refuse and wrote down the two addresses. Chris closed the directory and placed it back on the shelf. Then he offered her his arm. She thought of what her mother had said about not wasting time with Mr Williams and decided not only to ignore it, but to encourage him. She slipped her hand through his arm and hugged it against her for a moment. He gave her such a smile that she had to admit to being completely bowled over by him as they left the library.

The first house had three storeys, as well as a basement, and was situated on Mount Pleasant. Luck was partially with them because there they met Mrs Bridget O'Shaughnessy. She was a big woman with shoulders like a wrestler and a bosom that you could rest a tray on. Her hair appeared unnaturally jet black and her lips and cheeks were rouged.

'We're looking for one of your lodgers,' said Chris.

'So the bleedin' hell, am I,' she retorted.

'It's my brother, Bert Kirk,' said Joy. 'Although, he might be going under the name of Arthur Temple. Fair haired, blue eyes, smooth talking…oh, and with a broken nose.'

Her face turned ugly. 'Name doesn't fit but the face does. He's done a bleedin' moonlight flit…and not only that he's bleedin' robbed me of me savings. After all I've bleedin' done for him,' raged Mrs O'Shaughnessy. 'I've been down to his works but he didn't turn up this morning. No need to work, I thought, because he has all me bleedin' money.'

Joy was dumbfounded and then wrathful. Turning on Chris, she cried, 'You were wrong! He's damn well got away again. You should have gone after him yesterday when you could.'

Stormy-faced, Chris grabbed her hand and almost dragged her out of the lodging house. 'So I misjudged him. But I bet you anything that he's headed for Chester.'

Joy paled. 'You think so?'

'Yes! At least they're on their guard.' As he was speaking, Chris was striding down Mount Pleasant so fast that Joy had to run to keep up with him.

'He could be at our house,' she cried.

'Well, he's not going to find you there, so that's OK, and

your sister'll be safe because Kenny's there. That leaves Emma and Seb's wife as possible prey.'

'You're forgetting Tilly.'

'Tilly?'

'Kenny and Alice's sister. Bert took her once before on Hanny's and Kenny's wedding day.' Joy's voice shook.

'How old is she?'

'She'll be seven in July.'

'So she'll be in school.'

'Yes! And they lock the gates so nobody can get in or out.'

'Who's he got most against?' asked Chris.

'Bert blames Alice for his life going wrong but, perhaps even more, he could have it in for Emma because she fought back, went to the police, and it was her boyfriend who broke his nose,' said Joy rapidly.

Chris's eyes met hers. 'Let's hope there's a train in.' Then they ran, both thinking that getting to Emma could be a matter of life and death.

As Emma polished the front door brass knocker she hummed to herself, happy because she and David had an appointment with the vicar of Christ Church to fix a date for their wedding in May. She hoped Chris would still be home because she had decided to ask him to give her away. What a phrase to use! It was as if she was a possession, but at least she did not mind that so much with her brother.

She bent to pick up the tin of brass cleaner and a blow hit her in the back, sending her sprawling into the lobby. She felt sick and lay gasping for breath. The door slammed behind her as she struggled to get to her feet, only to be seized by the back of her frock and dragged to her feet.

'Surprise, surprise, Miss Griffiths?' hissed a voice she had never forgotten. She tried to speak but the top button of her frock was digging into her windpipe. The breath gurgled in her throat as she reached behind her and clawed at Bert's hands. He swore as her fingernails drew blood and clouted her across the side of the head. The force of the blow caused her to fall against the newel post and she slid to the floor.

'Thought yourself smarter than me, did you? But I tricked the lot of you.' He yanked her to her feet and thrust her against the newel post, pressing against her so she could not move.

Emma rasped, 'You're not so clever. If you were smart, you would have gone to Australia. My brother's on your trail.'

'You mean one of those twins?' he sneered.

'No! My soldier brother and he's got it in for you for what happened to our Aggie. You'd better run. He knows how to fight…how to kill.'

'You're lying.' Bert's eyelids blinked rapidly. 'I hung around your mother's house for a while and saw no sign of an older brother.'

'He's staying at your mother's house that's why. He'll have followed her. He'll find you, never fear.'

'No!' Bert's expression was ugly as his grip on the bodice of her frock tightened. 'I don't believe you. It was Joy who followed Mother.'

'Have it your own way,' she wheezed, pulling on his arm. If only he wasn't so close she would have attempted to knee him in the groin. As it was, she knew she had to keep him talking, hoping someone would come before he raped and possibly killed her. If only she wasn't alone in the house, but Mrs Black had left earlier to see an old friend and she didn't know where the music teachers had gone. 'You shouldn't have pushed David down the steps,' she gasped. 'It was too like what you did to Kenny. Chris worked out that Australia could have been a trick…and we all know how much your mother loves you.'

Bert smiled. 'Mother knows what a good boy I can be.'

'She wouldn't be pleased that you're here instead of with her.'

He nodded and his grip slackened. 'You're right. I've decided to take her to America. My dah doesn't appreciate her. It's a big country, America, and I've plenty of money. She could cook for me and look after the house.'

'It sounds lovely. Why don't you go and tell her now?' urged Emma.

Bert fixed his eyes on her flushed face. 'You look like Agnes. Her face went red when she got angry. She threatened me, you know…said she'd tell Mother I'd given her a baby. She shouldn't have done that. I don't like being threatened.' He paused. 'But you're smarter than your sister, although, not as smart as me. If your brother really is at Mother's you'll want me to go there so I won't go.'

'He won't be there right now!' said Emma, her heart thumping. Oh, God! If only she had a weapon, but all she had was her voice. 'He could be on his way here, so you're best letting me go, Bert. Go collect your mother if you want to sail to America with her.'

This time he was silent for so long that Emma's hopes were raised but then he glanced upstairs and, before she could prevent it, had clapped a hand over her mouth and lifted her off her feet. She tried to kick him but he grabbed her ankles with his other hand and carried her upstairs. She prayed like she had never prayed before.

He had to remove his hand to open the door into the drawing room. She screamed and he smacked her across the head, setting her ears ringing, 'Don't do that again. You'll only make things worse for yourself, you stupid girl. Nice,' he said, glancing about him and heading for the open glass doors that led to the balcony. For a moment he hesitated before carrying her outside and going over to the rail. He gazed down towards the river. 'Some view…and it's a good way down to the ground.' He lifted her above his head and she almost wet herself with fear. 'How would you like it if I dropped you over right now? People would think it was an accident.' Sky, trees, river and bridge whizzed about her and then abruptly he brought her against his chest and took her back inside.

Emma forced her body to go limp, hoping he would believe she had fainted. He started to sing 'Come into the garden, Maud' as he walked across the landing to another door. This had a key in it and he turned it in the lock and pushed the door open. Emma guessed that he had no idea that this room was where Mrs Black carried out her sittings.

'This is a bloody funny bedroom with no bed,' he muttered, glancing at the polished table in the middle of the room and the chairs that stood against the walls. He was about to leave when a slithering noise and a crash caused him to spin round. 'What the hell was that?' he asked, his hand sliding from her mouth.

An idea came to Emma and she decided to come out of her faint. 'Just a picture falling off the wall. It does that sometimes without anybody touching it. This is where Mrs Black has her séances. This is where she calls up the dead.'

He glanced uneasily about him. 'Are you saying the woman you work for is a medium?'

'Yes!'

'But – but that's wrong! It says so in the Bible.'

Remembering the way he had looked at her on the bridge and run, Emma seized her opportunity as she felt a stir of hope and excitement. 'But spirits must exist if it says so in the Bible. Didn't Saul get the witch of Endor to call up Samuel's ghost?' she said. He made no answer so Emma continued, 'Mrs Black got in touch with our Aggie in here and Victoria Waters. Living spirits can hang around a place if they rest uneasily,' she said in a chatty voice. 'You wouldn't believe some of the things that can happen when they go into action.'

'You're having me on,' said Bert.

Emma shook her head. 'Honestly! Some spirits are mischievous and our Aggie had a good sense of humour. They draw attention to themselves by clashing pans, breaking glass or making pictures fall from walls like that one. I've got nothing to be scared of from our Aggie or Victoria Waters…but perhaps you have.'

'Are you saying their spirits spoke to you about me?' he said.

'No! They spoke to Mrs Black. Told her what had happened to them, just before they died. They said…' He clapped a trembling hand over her mouth.

Emma thrashed about in his arms. He staggered and almost dropped her and his hand slipped from her mouth again. 'Stop it, stop it, you bitch!' he yelled.

Emma managed to shout, 'Aggie, help me! Miss Victoria, come and be revenged.' She could feel him shaking and struggled even more. He dropped her and before he could stop her, she crawled under the table. She was banking on his coming after her and her hands shook as she searched for the wedges that kept the top firm. Thank you, God, she whispered, removing them.

Emma was just in time, because as she pulled the wedges out, Bert placed a hand on the table top and bent to drag her out. The table began to spin and tilt. His hand shot off the polished wood and he lost his balance and went crashing to the floor.

Emma scrambled from beneath the table on the other side and, on her hands and knees, hurried to the door. She was out of the doorway and on her feet, trying to stop her hands from shaking as she turned the key in the lock. Then she stepped back, expecting him to throw his weight against the door.

Nothing. She pocketed the key and, with her heart banging against her ribs, she went over to the door and pressed her ear against one of the wooden panels. Was that a groan? Perhaps he had hurt himself when he had fallen so heavily. She bloody hoped so.

Her knees trembled as she made her way to the drawing room. Going over to the drinks cupboard, she looked for the sherry but there was none. So she removed the whisky and a bottle of ginger ale and made herself a drink. Clutching the cut glass tumbler, she went and sat in one of the armchairs.

She did not know how long it was before she heard feet on the stairs but she had poured herself another drink and was feeling relaxed and pleased with herself when Chris and Joy entered the room.

They both stared at her. 'You're drinking!' accused Joy. 'We thought…'

'Thought you might find Bert here?' enquired Emma with a twisted smile.

Chris took the empty glass from her hand and peered into her face. 'He has been here,' he said hoarsely, touching Emma's cheek with a gentle hand. 'Where is he?'

Emma giggled. 'I've locked him in with Aggie and Miss Victoria.'

Joy knelt in front of her and gazed into her face with concern. 'Poor Emma. He's knocked her silly.'

'No, he hasn't,' said Emma, trying to sit up straight. 'I locked him in the room where Mrs Black has her sittings. I don't know what he's done to himself but I heard him groan and he hasn't managed to get out.'

Chris placed a hand on his sister's head and ruffled her tangled hair. 'Good for you, kid.' He left the room, followed by Joy.

'What are you going to do?' she asked.

He stopped in front of the locked door. 'Perhaps you should go back to Emma and leave this to me,' he said, flexing his fingers. She raised dark eyebrows and made no move to obey his order.

'Who's there?' demanded a querulous voice.

Chris and Joy exchanged glances. 'That you, Bert?' she

queried. 'You don't sound like yourself.'

'That's because I've broken my shoulder. I – I'm in agony.'

'Good! You've caused enough suffering to others in your time, I'm glad it's your turn now,' said Joy. 'I'm going to fetch the police.'

'I thought we were keeping the police out of this,' said Chris. 'He might just talk his way out of trouble and I want justice done for my sister.'

'What were you thinking of doing with him? Cutting his throat?' she asked. 'The only problem with that is where do we dump his body?'

'There's the Dee, the Mersey, or even the Irish Sea.'

Bert yelled, 'Let me out of here! When I get my hands on you, Joy, I'll kill you.'

'That's not the right thing to say, Bert,' snapped Chris. 'I'm definitely for getting rid of you for good.'

'You just try it,' snarled Bert. 'We'll see who comes off best in a fight.'

Before Chris could respond, there was the noise of the front door opening and a voice called Emma's name. 'It's Mrs Black,' he said.

A few moments later she appeared at the top of the stairs. Her dark eyes rested a moment on Joy. 'Who's this? Where's Emma? There's a tin of brass cleaner and a cloth downstairs.'

At the sound of her voice Emma called, 'A lot's been happening while you've been out.'

'Emma's caught Bert,' said Chris.

Eudora gaped at him and for several seconds was speechless. Then she smiled and removed her hat. 'I think this calls for a drink. Come into the drawing room and you can tell me all about it.'

She led the way only to stop suddenly when she saw Emma's face.

Emma smiled at her drowsily. 'After two whiskies, it

doesn't hurt as much. Besides, I'm happy I got him with the help of God, our Aggie and Miss Victoria. Who's to say they weren't there in spirit?'

Eudora patted her shoulder. 'Dear Emma. I am going to miss you when you marry that young man of yours.' She turned to Chris. 'Pour drinks for us all and then the three of you can tell me what happened.'

So it was that when they had come to the end of their story, Eudora beamed at the three of them. 'If he's spoiling for a fight with you, Christopher, he's lying about that shoulder.'

'That's what I thought,' said Chris. 'A ruse to make us believe he's not as dangerous as a man desperate to escape a long prison sentence would be. I'd still like to get my hands on him…'

'But…' interrupted Joy, resting a hand on his arm, 'perhaps we've had enough violence. I – I don't want you to get hurt.'

Chris raised his eyebrows and was about to stress the likelihood of Bert coming off the worst when Emma intervened, 'Joy's right. In the past I've thought of things I'd like done to Bert, but let's leave it to the bobbies. I'm prepared to go into the witness box and no doubt Alice will be, too.'

'Where Victoria Waters' death is concerned, it's unlikely he'll hang for murder,' said Eudora, 'but I wouldn't be surprised if there's enough circumstantial evidence for him to be sentenced for her manslaughter.'

'There's also Mrs O'Shaughnessy,' said Chris.

'Who's Mrs O'Shaughnessy?' asked Emma drowsily.

A smiling Joy said, 'His landlady.'

'Built like a wrestler, she's hopping mad with him because he stole her savings,' said Chris, taking her hand and squeezing it.

'He's a thief, too? Then, we've definitely got him,' said Emma triumphantly.

Chapter Twenty-Five

May, 1910

Emma gazed wildly about the untidy parlour, thinking she might have made a mistake giving in to her mother's plea to leave for church from the family home. But Alf had told Chris that he'd heard a rumour on the railway that his father had been seen coming out of a widow woman's house the other side of the railway, so she felt that she had to comply with her mother's request. Olive had received the news of her husband's unfaithfulness with characteristic language and emotion and then, to Emma's admiration, she pulled herself together and got herself a charring job.

'Where's my bouquet?' asked Emma. 'You haven't gone and hocked it, have you, Mam?'

'Very funny,' said Olive, looking smart in a navy-blue costume with white piping, which she'd bought second hand from the market. She turned to thirteen-year-old Patsy, who was a bridesmaid, 'You should have been keeping your eye on it,' she snapped.

'I am,' protested Patsy. 'I put the flowers in the kitchen sink to keep them fresh. I'll go and get them, shall I?'

Emma nodded and told herself to keep calm. She'd soon be out of here, never to sleep under this roof again. Although, it wasn't so bad now her father wasn't living there any more. Tonight, she'd be in Rhyl with David. When they returned to Chester it would be to a big Victorian house in Garden Lane, recently purchased by Mrs Black and split into several apartments. Emma and David's rooms were on the first floor and the coal merchant, Mr Bushell, was renting the ground floor flat and Granny Popo was his live-in housekeeper.

'Are you ready yet, our kid?' asked Chris, entering the room.

'You look smart,' said Emma, smiling at him.

'Can't let the side down.' He winked at her. 'You look pretty good yerself.'

Emma did a twirl.

Olive turned to Patsy. 'Get the others to come down here. Time me and the lads were on our way.'

'OK, Ma, give us a minute.' She handed the bouquet of white lilac, yellow irises and orange blossom to Emma. The colours of the flowers matched exactly those of the yellow figured silk wedding gown trimmed with lace, purchased from the generous wedding gift which Mrs Black had given to Emma. When it came to buying her wedding gown common sense had deserted Emma. 'After all,' she had said to Hannah, Alice and Joy, 'a girl only gets married once.'

Emma smiled, remembering the joyous expressions on Hannah's and Alice's faces when they had broken the news that Bert had been caught. They had all danced round Alice's drawing room. Half an hour later Alice had told them some other news; Gabrielle was getting a divorce from her long-absent husband and marrying Martin Waters. Of course, they all agreed that he was marrying Gabrielle for her money as old Mrs Waters still hadn't kicked the bucket.

As Emma left the house on Chris's arm, she thought back to another day, the one when she had caught that glimpse of Hannah and Kenny's wedding and had recognised Alice. She recalled being aware of someone standing behind her and the smell of peppermint – it could have only been Bert. Well, there was no chance of his being an unwelcome watcher at *her* wedding. He was in jail and it looked like he was going to be there for a very long time.

But now was not the time to think of Bert. This was her wedding day and David would be waiting for her.

Epilogue

May, 1910

'Hello, Malcolm dear! How are you today?' asked Eudora, sitting on the garden bench beside him in the grounds of the asylum.

'Better than I was,' he said slowly.

Her face lit up. 'I'm so glad.' She placed a hand on his resting on his thigh. 'I've news that will make you feel even better. Bert Kirk is in prison. I admit to being delighted. I'm sure you feel the same because of the threat he was to your children's happiness.'

Mal nodded jerkily. 'My children?'

Eudora moved her hand. 'Kenny is coping with his handicap bravely, so I'm planning a little treat for him and Hanny. A Mediterranean cruise! I'm sure it will do them both good, and who knows, she might have some happy news for us when they return. As for Alice, she is blooming and your grandson thriving. I have no doubt that your younger daughter Tilly will grow into a beautiful young woman, too. She is a delightful child.'

'Could yer get a likeness of Tilly for me…please?'

Eudora smiled. 'I'll see what I can do. Emma and her young man were married yesterday and there was a photographer there. I will miss Emma. But I've taken her brother and Joy Kirk into my employment. I've an idea how I may use their talents.'

'What of Mrs Kirk?'

Eudora showed surprise. 'Do you care what happens to her?'

'I'm curious.'

Eudora hesitated. 'She's had a complete breakdown and had to be taken away. Do you feel remorse for what you did to her?'

Mal appeared to struggle to get words out but managed at last to say, 'I suppose I am to blame...I punished my second wife for the death of my first when really it was my mother who needed punishing. Mrs Kirk was a good friend to my wife and encouraged her to stand up to me. I couldn't cope with that...she was far braver than I was...but at the same time I hated her for her religious convictions...so like Mother. When Mrs Kirk confronted me with what I'd done to my wife I lost my rag. I shouldn't have used violence on her...although, I still think she was an interfering awld besom.'

Eudora fixed him with a stare. 'Don't spoil the confession, Malcolm. They say it's good for the soul.'

He returned her stare, letting out a sigh. 'I overheard a nurse say that the King is dead. How stands his soul with his womanising, drinking and gambling?'

'That is between him and his maker,' murmured Eudora, remembering the crowds in front of the town hall after Edward VII had died. The mayor had stood on a balcony draped in purple and black velvet and made the loyal declaration. He had started by saying, 'The King is dead, long live the King.' George V now stood in his father's shoes. The Edwardian era had ended and a new one had dawned. She saw unrest and chaos ahead but would say nothing of that to her young friends. Let them enjoy their dreams while they may.

Other titles available from
ALLISON & BUSBY
by June Francis

- Step by Step   978-0-7490-8329-8   Pbk
- A Place to Call Home   978-0-7490-8324-3   Pbk
- Look for the Silver   978-0-7490-8109-6   Pbk
  Lining
- When the Clouds   978-0-7490-7947-5   Pbk
  Go Rolling By
- Tilly's Story   978-0-7490-0700-3   Pbk
- Sunshine and Showers   978-0-7490-0783-6   Hbk

All Allison & Busby titles are available to order
through our website: *www.allisonandbusby.com*

You can also order by calling us on 0207 580 1080.
Please have your credit/debit card ready.

Alternatively, send a cheque made out to
Allison and Busby Ltd to:
Allison & Busby
12 Fitzroy Mews
London, W1T 6DW

Postage and package is free of charge to addresses in the UK.

Please contact Allison & Busby for current prices.

*Allison & Busby reserves the right to show new
retail prices on covers which may differ from those
previously advertised in the text or elsewhere.*